To Jenifer, Adara, and Arthur, who are my past, present, and future

Fyushu

KITINI

TABICHI   KORITO

IWIKARU

TATSUMA

Yatamoro

SHITIMI   YUNIGIRI   OBANARI

CHIBIRI

SARUTO   HOCHIRO

BEZENKAI

MINIRI

NARIYARI

Higinasi

RIMBAKU

Scale   Miles

CAST OF CHARACTERS

Hibikitsu: the young emperor of Rimbaku. Descended from the First Emperor, Taido Segei.

The Rojiri (the emperor's royal counselors):

- Kagiri: A young man, older brother to Noniki. Gensaiba ("legendary warrior") and now Dogenriku, Lord General of the aiashe (the armies). Nicknamed Giri.
- Noniki: a young man, brother to Kagiri. The first new Matekai (wizard) of Rimbaku. Nicknamed Niki.
- Kishin Narai: a wealthy merchant, leader of the cabal that backed Kagiri.
- Chohu Eijiri: a wealthy merchant, minor noble, and the head of house Chohu, a merchant house specializing in gems.
- Fujitai Takami: A young nobleman, formerly the second son of House Kazutai, now head of House Fujitai and Dogen-kaishu, Lord Admiral of the aikaye (the navies).
- Heiayuki Futoba: A noblewoman, head of House Heiayuki. House crest: a silver crane.
- Misataki Shizumi: Taikoro (Lord Commander) of the Honjofu, the empire's elite warriors.
- Atukai Reizei: Newly appointed Taikoro of the Honteno, the emperor's household guard.
- Seikoku: a young woman and former thief, clever, graceful, and pretty. Now Buhiyo (mayor) of Sorainasei, the new "town" in Atsani.

Members of Sorainasei:

- Jitu Kanai: a potter from Ginsai
- Isoro: a young herbalist from Hochiro.
- Sanedi: a basketweaver

- Sukame and Minawa: an old married couple
- Ratal: a fisherman
- Amon: a netmender
- Otokai: a horsetrader
- Junko and Eiji: a couple who make clothes
- Kuma: a washer-woman from Shakomi
- Eisen: a "law clerk" and possible thug
- Ryoji: an older gentleman
- Ohiro: a gardener and caretaker, formerly for House Etsuya.
- Ibaru and Iraku: two brothers, formerly hands of Kaemusei.

Honjofu:

- Norio Shinjuru: the chuisu (lieutenant) responsible for training new recruits.
- Akino: a gunso (sergeant), one of Shizumi's most trusted.
- Geniji: The other gunso, Shizumi's self-appointed body-guard when in the field.
- Isano: a sharp-eyed archer
- Diritan
- Nioko
- Ganema
- Kori
- Sanjou
- Kenso
- Masai
- Reiko
- Nori
- Itami Kane
- Enomoto and Satake: two new Honjofu

Honteno:

- Itamon: a chuisu
- Manari:
- Dairamu: A new Honteno, formerly Honjofu and part of Shizumi's bantao
- Onomi: A new recruit
- Totsu, Kaya, and Date: new recruits
- Nao and Okito: new recruits

"Hello!" she called out as they drew closer, close enough for her to see his wild hair, long beard, and frayed clothes. "Do you need help, sir?"

The man stopped and turned to face her. "Help?" he replied, his voice deep and echoing. "We all need help. This whole land needs help. It is dying, decaying, in the final stages of ruin. It must be swept clean and planted afresh."

Something in his eyes made Sechimi pause. They were alight, the way she'd seen in only the very fervent—or the very crazed.

"By order of the Emperor, I am placing you under arrest!" she declared, swinging her naritaba around and down, its sharp edge halted inches from the man's throat. "Resist and we will be forced to attack!"

He laughed at her, despite the blade hovering near his neck. "Resist? Oh, yes, I believe I shall resist. And I acknowledge no emperor. Stand aside or perish." His words were measured, cold, with a trace of mockery, and Sechimi did not bother to respond.

Instead she tightened her grip and swung.

There was a crackle of heat, a flash. Her naritaba melted away before it could brush the stranger's skin. Whatever had caused that swept up the weapon and over her hands and arms. Sechimi screamed as her limbs disintegrated.

Her shotao attacked. There were screams and cries, arrows and spears and swords.

The man grinned, baring yellowed teeth—and a wind flung the entire platoon back. Horses were bowled off their feet, crushing their riders beneath them. Weapons spun away. Blades snapped.

The burning had spread to Sechimi's chest, and down to her legs.

Tamura charged—and burst into flame.

Crazy 8 Press is an imprint of Clockworks

© 2025 by Aaron Rosenberg

Design by Aaron Rosenberg
Cover art by Lilly Repine
ISBN: 978-1-892544-32-2

THE RELICANT CHRONICLES, BOOK 5

BONES PAST

AARON ROSENBERG

CRAZY 8 PRESS

Aiashe:
- Daishin Nishoji: a taisho (general)
- Masagi Matsu: another taisho
- Soma Yamani: a taisu (captain)
- Tsuneto: another taisu
- Fuko Miyosi: a shosu (junior lieutenant)
- Hurito Yakai: another taisu
- Mori Yukeno: another taisu
- Ichiro Tamori: a chusa (lieutenant colonel)
- Kiso Akinari: an issa (colonel) in charge of the fortifications along the southern border.
- Junjii Naohito: a shosu under Akinari, his clerk.
- Haga Emitsu: a shosa (major) serving under Akinari.
- Makino Tsunaka: a second shosa serving under Akinari.
- Sue Ishui: a taisu under Akinari, reporting to Emitsu.
- Sechimi: a chuisu under Akinari, reporting to Ishui.
- Tamura: a gunso under Akinari, reporting to Sechimi.
- Haru: an aiashe under Tamura
- Tori: another aiashe under Tamura.
- Yatsu: another aiashe under Tamura.
- Yoshitaro: an aiashe on guard at the docks outside Awaihinshi
- Tokutomi: a guard stationed at the gates between Motohiri and Sakiriti
- Akita: another guard stationed at the gates between Motohiri and Sakiriti
- Kahei: a gocho (corporal)
- Tomoko: an issa
- Morita: A chusa
- Atsumi Izo: a former taisho, now forcibly retired.
- Noboru Juniri: former taisho, now forcibly retired.

Aikaye:
- Kuyo Aoimoto: a kagono (admiral)
- Ugata Genichi: another kagono
- Nukimon Torazo: a kagusho (vice-admiral)
- Daijikaga Manhachi: another kagusho
- Enotaba Harukano: a daiso (captain)

- Juntari Sejiro: another daiso
- Genpai Iwakiri: another daiso
- Heiikiri Fusichi: another daiso
- Kouiji Nofasa: a kogashiri (lieutenant commander)
- Nakori Enyo: a chudai (lieutenant)
- Babeda Saimi: another chudai

Nihiro Omeshi: Fyushan emissary to Rimbaku.

Makono Takari: Fyushan dignitary, assistant to Nihiro Omeshi.

Hu Yongian: Chief Ambassador from Yatamoro to Rimbaku.

Shen Liang and Wei Bingwen: ambassadors from Yatamoro to Rimbaku.

Yakami Morinaga: Higinasan ambassador to Rimbaku

Yakami Tsuya: Ambassador Yakami's wife

Ogawa Tsuni: princess of Higinasi

Ogawa Kunetai: king of Higinasi

Watane Yatahei: a former Rojiri who was also Dogenkaishu. House crest: an emerald wave.

Sunao Iensen: A noble, son of the late Rojiri Sunao Tadazi. House crest: a black bear.

Ushi: a cook in Onokura, a small village in Bezenkai

Aki, Bin, and Miya: three women in Onokura

Tenbo, Gohei, and Seibu: three men in Onokura

Moto: Fujitai Takami's one servant

Kazutai Katani: Takami's older brother, a shugodiri (minor noble) in Awaihinshi. Family crest: orange leaves and white petals on crimson.

Kazutai Yojuin: Takami and Katani's mother

Ujihime and Yodogimi: Takami and Katani's younger sisters

Iri: otanui (head housekeeper) of House Kazutai

Kame: Kazutai Yojuin's personal maid

Furi: Ujihime and Yodogimi's maid/nanny/teacher

Uhei: a servant of House Kazutai

Toro: another servant of House Kazutai

Hana: Futoba's personal maid

Arima: head housekeeper of House Heiayuki

Natsu: housekeeper of House Heiayuki's estate in Awaihinshi

Koma: former head housekeeper of House Ieyuki

Maki: Koma's husband, former chitiju (majordomo, steward) to House Ieuyuki

Iefusa: Futoba's husband.

Inomi: Futoba's daughter, six

Kiyo: Futoba's son, two

Medeiko: a senkousa or Bone Reader in Mazihini.

Utami: another senkousa, based in Bejinuri.

Wani: another senkousa, based in Sakiriti.

Shizu Yokori: Narai's second in the cabal that backed Kajiri.

Jiro Masute: Another member of the cabal.

Eien Kawatai: Another member of the cabal, now deceased.

Fujiko Oritano: Final member of the cabal.

Hara Koriko: head housekeeper in Aihiri

Yamana Muiada: head chef in Aihiri

Hajime: a dessert-maker with a shop in Bejinuri

Jimouen Muhimoto: essa (doctor) to the Emperor and his staff.

Zhen Shu: a Yatamoran darakada and assassin, now deceased

Dai Yi: a Yataramoran darakada and assassin, Zhen Shu's partner

Wakiza Yukane: karo of Atsani. Seikoku's superior.

Iwaki Matsu: a merchant in Awaihinshi with a small warehouse and showroom in Sakiriti.

Makino Horeki: a young man in House Makino and a soldier in the aiashe.

Yosuke Fujita: the imperial groundskeeper

Shisino sukudo: "Speed of Thought," Hikibitsu's horse, a black stallion nicknamed Shisi.

Hasebe Towa: karo of Bejinuri, a baker

Akihiro Tatsuya: karo of Sakiriti

Obi Ren: a merchant whose house specializes in fish and fishing

Doiyu Soda: an imperial scribe in Aihiri

Chiya: a little girl in Awaihinshi and a regular customer of Hajime's

House Chohu:

- Master Ganyeki: a trader
- Yuni: a cleaning lady
- Ritaru: another cleaning lady

- Kaznori: a member
- Madam Ponsoi: the senior housekeeper
- Master Atunobu: a trader

Rilani: Empress of Fyushu, called "Mistress of All She Surveys."

Aganaka: an old ishtaya (tailor) with a shop in Bejinuri

Denaya: Aganaka's dead wife

The six Gensaiba matekan (wizards' warriors):

- Geido Shinen
- Shito Kibi
- Onyoku Jeizen
- Bushiki Kenin
- Komu Setsui
- Nikiyu Sinchu

The seven Matekai (wizards):

- Geido Isami
- Shito Daiko
- Onyoku Ebima
- Bushiki Honei
- Komu Juroji
- Nikiyu Bezaitin
- Taido Fukuru

Maniko Kohori: Former Taikoro of the Honteno, now deceased.

Yanitai Lai: Former Dogenriku of the Fyushan army. Deceased.

Kaemusei: the Silent Change, an inhuman being comprised of magic and hunger. Now dispersed.

PROLOGUE

Once, there was a beautiful tower.

It stood near the mouth of a river, with lofty cliffs behind and a frenetic waterfall beside, the wide sea spread out before it. Made of wood lacquered a bright, cheerful red and plaster kept a pristine white, the tower had four stories, the upper three with their own angled roof that curved up slightly at the corners, providing cover for their expansive balconies. The lowest level required no roof, as the second-floor balcony was large enough to provide ample shade below. At the tower's peak, a ringed spire made all of gold caught the sun's rays and cast a happy glow down upon the dwelling.

Lovely and serene, the tower could be seen for leagues, despite the cliffs—for it did not rest upon the ground. Instead, it floated beside the waterfall, hovering in mid-air, its grand front doors attainable only by the same magic that kept the structure aloft. Visitors would know whether their petition to enter had been accepted if a gleaming stair of translucent jade formed before their feet.

Stories told of those who were not welcome, for whom those stairs vanished midway to the safety of the wide courtyard before those doors.

Furotingawa, the place was called, "the floating tower," and while many admired its beauty, they did so from a distance, rather than tempt the wrath of its owner. For everyone knew mighty wizards were not to be trifled with, and the most powerful matekai of all dwelled there, with only his sworn servant for a companion.

For many years, Furotingawa was a fixture upon the landscape. Until it fell.

That was the day of the Cataclysm, when magic fled the kingdom. With its passing, the power that held Furotingawa aloft vanished like the morning mist, sending the elegant tower crashing onto the rocks below. Wood and plaster shattered, showering the nearby cliffs with splinters and shards, clouding the waterfall with dust and glitter. The four stories collapsed into each other, the golden spire crumbling into pieces amid the other rubble, until only a mound of broken bits remained.

Still no one dared go near it. Even demolished as it was, the place held a shadow of its former aura, when power hung about it like a halo. That power was now diminished, tarnished, yet enough traces remained to scare away any who might otherwise have sifted through the wreckage, seeking fallen treasure.

For many years, the remains of Furotingawa sat atop the cliff's edge, spray from the waterfall dampening its broken timbers until they began to rot away. Moss grew to cover much of the rubble, mud and dirt borne by wind filling in gaps here and there, until it resembled a small hillock more than a former palace.

Then a new wind arose from the east. A stark, harsh gale, reeking of change. And of power.

The ruins of Furotingawa trembled.

The wind passed by, sweeping north toward the kingdom's center, toward its gleaming white capital midway along the west coast. Toward Awaihinshi.

A short time later, a breath of fresh air washed back from that great city, clearing away the staleness and decay that wind had brought and left behind like a heavy blanket over the land. This cleansing breeze brightened the world, restoring its color and vibrancy, adding a spring to the step and a gleam to the eye.

And, deep within what had been Furotingawa, buried in a chamber at its center—a vast vaulted stone room that had maintained its shape against all calamity—something stirred within that hidden space.

For the first time in centuries, power once more washed over Furotingawa.

And the floating tower's remains rose from its grave, soaring up and out to scatter across the landscape, leaving only that stone chamber, now open to the brisk sea air.

The chamber—and its lone inhabitant, stumbling upright to shake off a generations-long slumber.

The matekai of Furotingawa was awake once more.

CHAPTER ONE

Hibikitsu, Echo of Victory and Emperor of all Rimbaku, drew in a deep breath. Straightening, he called upon his ancestors all the way back to Taido Segei, the legendary forebear who had founded their nation. He summoned all of his will, all of his training, all of his discipline.

And, even with all that, he suspected his smile was too tight-lipped, too narrow, too forced to be taken as much more than the polite fiction it was.

"Thank you, Ambassador Hu, for that fascinating explanation." His voice, at least, was clear and steady when he spoke, neither throbbing with fury nor dulled by boredom. Both of which he was feeling in abundance, after being forced to endure the Yatamoran emissary's stultifying lecture on societal demands for the past three hours.

For his part, Hu Yongian bowed, as unruffled as ever, the hem of his yellow satin robe brushing the floor, its high collar framing his long, narrow face and setting off the tight black braid that swayed behind him with the motion. "It has been my pleasure, your Majesty." Behind the man his two subordinates, Shen Liang and Wei Bingwen, also bowed, their motions perfectly matched and their appearances so similar Hibikitsu might have thought himself feverish and seeing triple if others had not confirmed the trio's presence. "It is my hope that this has helped clarify how our own nation is structured, and the duty that has been placed upon us."

Hibikitsu forced himself not to snarl, or to reach for Kosshiki's hilt at his side. "It does indeed," he managed instead. "You have given us much to think upon."

The ambassador at least recognized that for the dismissal it was, and, with a final bow, withdrew, his subordinates flanking him like doubled shadows made flesh. Hibikitsu remained upright and alert until the throne room doors had shut behind him, then slumped in his throne.

"By the first Emperor, the arrogance of it all!" he muttered, scrubbing one hand over his face as if that might clear away the torrent of words he had been subjected to—or the presumptions laced through them.

The nearest person to him, a sturdy woman standing at attention against one wall just beyond the lacquered railings surrounding the dais, frowned. "Sire?" Her crimson armor was gilded at the edges and bore his household symbol, the higeibara, stamped upon each plate. She stood in the traditional location just before the first of the handsomely carved pillars that lined the room's side walls, yet his eyes had automatically gone to a point a full handspan above her head, expecting to see an older, grayer visage there.

Except, of course, that Maniko Kohori was no more. She had been murdered in this very compound, slain by the assassin Chimehera at the tail end of the Saisaihyu. Reizei was Taikoro of his Honteno now and attended him as the captain of his household guard must. Nor had he found any reason to fault the younger woman, despite her still walking with a cane while her wounded leg healed.

It was only that she was not Kohori, not the woman who had known and guarded and often advised or even chided him since birth. Just another way in which his world had changed.

He waved those thoughts away. "It is nothing." He sighed, pushing himself to his feet to pace about the dais a moment, restoring circulation to his aching legs. "Is that all for the day?"

Reizei glanced toward the door and the two soldiers who stood guard there. Despite the size of the room, they had evidently heard or at least inferred his question, and the taller of them nodded, fist to chest in salute. "It is, your Imperial Majesty," the man called out, his voice easily carrying that distance. "No petitioners await without."

That was some relief, at least—he had half expected the Fyushan emissary to be begging an audience next, or, worse, the Higinasan delegation—though even here, with none but his loyal guards around, Hibikitsu was careful not to show just how welcome that news was. "Very well," he said instead, hopping the rail and landing lightly on the polished main floor beyond. "Let us adjourn for the day. Reizei, are any of my Rojiri in their chamber?"

She frowned. "I do not know, your Majesty," she admitted after a moment. "But I can find out."

Kohori would have known—she had known where everyone in Aihiri was at all times, as if the imperial compound was somehow an extension of her own body. She had especially kept track of his royal councillors, in part because they had the most authority in the realm after him and the most access to him, in part merely because she did not trust them—a suspicion that had been borne out many times, with near-disastrous consequences in the end. But Reizei had been Taikoro less than a week—it was unfair of him to compare her to her predecessor, and unkind as well.

"No matter," he told her now. "I will simply see for myself." Previously he had rarely visited his advisors in their council chamber, but this was a new assemblage, one he had hand-selected and felt far closer to. Another change, and one he believed was for the better. These Rojiri would not object to his visiting them, as those before them might have. Of course, his new advisors also had their own responsibilities and might not be lounging about the palace, but it was a simple enough matter to find out. And gave him an excuse to stroll the compound after a long day of sitting still.

He hoped in particular that he might find Master Eijiri there. The master merchant had come to him nearly in tears after the events of Saisaihyu and had surprised Hibikitsu by dropping to his knees and laying his head and palms upon the floor. "I am at your Imperial Majesty's mercy, and beg your forgiveness," the man had cried.

Not that he had not known the reason why, but Hibikitsu had been quick to reassure him, stepping down from his throne to raise the elderly gentleman with his own hand. "I bear you no ill will," he assured Eijiri. "You were taken in, as was I. As were we all." He had shaken his head. "She deceived even Amani Denbi, and that woman was no one's fool." Though life might have been easier if the canny old noblewoman had been less clever! Her sharp mind had not saved her in the end, though.

Eijiri had allowed himself to be restored to his feet, but had still insisted, "It is my fault, sire. I brought her to your court."

Which was true enough, as far as it went. But Hibikitsu had found it in himself to laugh. "I suspect, if you had not, she would have found another way." From what little he had seen of Chimehara, the beautiful but deadly woman had been nothing if not resourceful. She would have reached Aihiri in the end. It was just tragic that she had done so at the cost of Kohori's life.

That was all in the past, however, and Hibikitsu was doing his best to move beyond it. Like now, when he wished to ensure Master Eijiri still felt welcome, wanted, and appreciated.

Reizei saluted and took up her cane where it had rested unobtrusively against the wall behind her. "Of course, sire." When he moved to skirt the dais, taking the door that led from there into his private study, she was at his side, the cane's tip clacking against the polished floor with each step. The two guards set the heavy crossbeam across the room's main doors, barring it from further entry, before falling in behind them.

For an instant, Hibikitsu felt the urge to laugh or to rage. Was it really necessary for him to be so heavily guarded in his own palace, a part of him asked. Was he never to be free to move about on his own, even here? Yet he remembered the assassin who had invaded his study and attacked him there, and the one who had confronted him here in this very room with one of his traitorous former Rojiri by her side, plus a slew of other attempts. And had he not just had an audience with three Yatamorans, the very people who had sent another assassin to kill his citizens and take their places until he could strike at Hibikitsu, right there on the throne he had just vacated?

No, sadly, he was not so free, and perhaps never would be. Especially now, when he had finally begun enacting some much-needed reform to shake off the cobwebs and restore his kingdom to full vigor, despite ages-old traditions and more than a few people's objections. But if having loyal men and women at his side was the price he had to pay in order to guide and protect his nation and its people, Hibikitsu was willing to pay it.

And he would only rail against it on occasion, and only in the privacy of his own mind.

CHAPTER TWO

Heiayuki Futoba started when the chamber door opened and one of the Honteno entered, followed by a handsome man in elegant, jewel-encrusted silk robes, scabbarded sword swaying at his side with each step. Instantly she turned away from where she'd been chatting with Noniki by one hand-painted wall and dropped to her knees, stretching her arms over her head and leaning down to press palms and forehead flat to the floor, feeling the grain of the tatami mats against her skin. "Your Imperial Majesty," she intoned.

Above her, someone chuckled. Another echoed it, and perhaps a third—it was hard to tell from this position. "Please, Futoba, get up." That was the emperor, and so of course she obeyed, scrambling to her feet and surreptitiously brushing off her black robes as she did. She still was not used to the silver cranes embroidered along their length. Hibikitsu was smiling, though not meanly, and beside him Noniki had a similarly amused expression. The Honteno were keeping their expressions carefully blank and professional, of course.

"There is no need to stand on ceremony when it's just us," the emperor informed her, not for the first time. "And especially not when I'm invading your own council chambers."

Futoba frowned at that. "You may have granted us the use of this space, sire," she replied after a second's pause, tugging absently at the thin gold chain around her neck, "but it still belongs to you, as does all of Aihiri and indeed all of Rimbaku. Naturally, then, you are free to enter as you please."

Now Noniki did laugh. "I suppose it's good one of us knows proper etiquette and all that," the stocky young man commented, "since bones know Giri and I don't have a clue. Still, I think you can relax a little, Futoba."

She knew he meant well, but Futoba found the suggestion unsettling. This was the emperor himself! She was still reeling from the fact that he had appointed her one of his Rojiri. After all, she had come to the capital to beg mercy for her house after their parent house, the Ieuyuki, had been found guilty of treason. Now she was supposed to forego all formality and respect and, what, call the nation's supreme ruler by his first name? Nod and wave when he entered the room? It flew in the face of all she had been taught since her earliest days.

The room's other two occupants, at least, were looking on sympathetically. "Leave her alone, Niki," the pretty young woman seated at the long council table chided. "She's still finding her feet." The smile she sent Futoba's way was as warm as it was lovely, and despite the reprimand Noniki laughed and smiled back. That was another thing Futoba was having to adjust her thinking on. Seikoku was bright, warm, and thoughtful—but she was, near as Futoba could tell, a commoner who had been something of a nomad before reaching Awaihinshi. And perhaps had engaged in less than strictly legal activities, if some of the things she'd hinted at were true. Yet now she was not only a Rojiri but the first Buhiyo in Awaihinshi, issued a blanket pardon by the emperor for any prior offenses and in charge of the strange little town/community of Sorainasei, itself a new addition to the city's tier of Atsani.

And the man she'd corrected, the same unassuming, handsome young fellow Futoba herself had been conversing with, was not only a fellow Rojiri but Rimbaku's first—and, as far as she knew, only—matekai. Who would dare treat a wizard so cavalierly?

The two were clearly romantically involved, however, which no doubt gave Seikoku additional leeway.

The young man sitting beside the pretty mayor showed more understanding. But that was no surprise, as Fujitai Takami was himself a noble, his own house crest of an otter among waves patterning his silvered robes. "It is certainly not how I was taught to behave toward our emperor," the young sailor said now, leaning back in his chair. "But I am beginning to learn—and to appreciate—just how much is changing here, and for the better." He inclined his head toward Hibikitsu. "Sire."

The emperor nodded back. "Takami." Then his keen jade gaze returned to Futoba. "I am sorry to have made you uncomfortable," he said, "and assure you, such was not my intent. The others are correct, I prefer a more casual, collegial relationship among us, particularly when we are alone. But I also appreciate your attempts to follow protocol, and the respect evident in such actions." His smile was kind. "Believe me, I do not mock you. No one here does."

"Oh, absolutely not," their resident wizard quickly agreed. "I'm sorry if I seemed to." He was so earnest, so open about his thoughts and emotions, that Futoba would have found him impossible not to like even if he had been less considerate.

The emperor—Hibikitsu, she had to remind herself—was glancing about the room. "It is only the four of you at the moment?" he asked, then peered back over his shoulder at the red-armored warrior there. "Five, sorry."

Seikoku was the first to reply. "Yes, Kagiri is off handling some matters involving the aiashe, I believe, and Shizumi is doing the same with the Honjofu. Master Eijiri is back at House Chohu, and I would assume Master Narai is dealing with business as well. Was there something you needed in particular, sire?"

He frowned for a second, then chuckled, shaking his head. "I've no one to blame but myself, I suppose," he commented, taking a seat at the table. "If I select advisors with other responsibilities, how can I be upset when they must take time fulfilling them?" He sighed before leaning forward to accept the cup of tea Seikoku had just poured him. "There wasn't anything in particular, no. I merely wished to check in and see if there was anything we needed to discuss."

Futoba took a seat as well, as did Noniki, and it was him who nudged her to speak. "Actually, there is something significant, sire," she began, weighing her words carefully. "It has to do with the aishone." Hibikitsu waved for her to continue, yet she paused an instant before committing to the topic. "We all respect and agree with your plan to free our kingdom from its dependence upon the relic bones," she said slowly. "It is the only way for our nation to restore itself and move forward. But for centuries the aishone has been at the heart of our economy. If we are encouraging people to stop using those, and eventually even ordering them to cease such practices, what does that do to our nation, financially? What does it do to our people?"

To his credit, the emperor did not shout at her, or order her to silence, or any of the other things some might do upon hearing something they did not like. Instead, he sipped his tea, his eyes thoughtful. "Yes, I see what you mean," he commented at last, carefully setting the cup down atop the polished table. "So many people count their wealth in aishone, if we render those worthless all at once we could plunge the country into chaos. The rich will become poor overnight, while the poor will be at least equal to them, if not better off, given they had little in the way of such wealth to begin with."

"Which might not be entirely a bad thing," Noniki pointed out. "A lot of those rich do nothing but sit back and count their wealth. They don't produce anything, they don't contribute anything, so why shouldn't they fall and let people with true talent and skill rise in their place?" Which was spoken like one who'd been born poor and had to work for his own success, and he held up a hand to stop Futoba's inevitable reply. "Yes, I know, it's not as simple as all that," he assured her, then grinned. "At least, I do now that you've explained it to me."

Hibikitsu was nodding. "I would assume it has to do with power vacuums and the collapse of our existing societal structure," he said, tapping his chin with a forefinger. "We're better off replacing one piece at a time than ripping it all out wholesale and having nothing but chaos until we can install something new and better."

"Exactly so, sire," Takami agreed. "You've already started, of course, both by gathering us and then by holding that Saisaihyu. The question now is how to continue without throwing your people into more disarray than necessary?"

Futoba took up the thread. "The issue is with individuals more than houses or officials," she pointed out. "Most noble houses have some gold and jewels as reserves, or goods like silk or timber or rice. And towns and cities have the same, plus they can call upon the government for aid if need be. It's the people who will suffer most if we declare aishone to have no value."

"So we buy them first," Seikoku suggested, sitting forward. "Like the Senkousa do, we offer coin for bones. At a good rate, better than they'd get elsewhere. That way, people have actual money in hand already."

Noniki was nodding. "We could even enlist the Bone Readers themselves," he said. "Offer them a commission for whatever we buy back. People already know to go to them with aishone. We can set up our own buy-back sites, of course, but to start with, this would be quicker, easier, and more familiar."

Hibikitsu shook his head. "You know, when I first came to power and realized what was happening to Rimbaku because of the aishone, I vowed to remove the laws that allowed officials to seize control of those bones. I thought that, at least if people owned the bones of their own parents, spouses, and children, that would help." He chuckled, though to Futoba's ear it sounded self-deprecating and vaguely bitter. "My Dojo Kuge, with the help of my Rojiri, convinced me I was being foolish. I would destroy the throne's money reserves, they said, and bankrupt my government. I allowed myself to be persuaded, which I suppose is a good thing, since we still possess the largest store of aishone by far. Now we just need to collect the rest. But what would we do with the bones once we had them? Destroy them somehow?" Water would do the trick—aishone had to remain dry, lest mold and mildew and rot set in and render them useless. Or just lock them away for safe-keeping, since they still contain the collected knowledge of our ancestors, but no longer sell any back to the people?"

Takami had an answer for that. "We don't need to decide that just yet," he pointed out. "I'd say we keep them safe for a time, in case we need them somehow, then slowly start purging them. But we do need to collect them in the first place."

The emperor turned to the red-plated warrior-woman at his side. "What do you think, Reizei?" he asked. "You've been quiet thus far." The fact that he was asking his personal guard her opinion—that he'd made her one of his Rojiri—was another unheard-of act.

Then again, so had been his forgiving Futoba and her house for their past associations. Or any of the other kind and thoughtful acts she'd seen him perform since.

Reizei considered carefully. "I agree that we need to get the bones back out of people's hands before we declare them worthless," she said at last, her voice low and sharp. "And buying them back is the most honorable way to do that, and the least disruptive. Can we afford it, though?"

That was a fair question, and fortunately one Futoba had already considered. "I believe so," she answered now. "I've been consulting with your Dojo Kuge, Your Majesty." The imperial bureaucrats who handled the empire's day-to-day finances had been a treasure trove of information. "It is true that, not so long ago, the empire's coffers were at low ebb. That is no longer the case, however. The throne has seized the assets of those houses that revolted, many of whom it seems had been caching money for years. Between that and the generous gift you received recently from Yatamoro, and those from several of the merchant houses, we should have enough to buy back most of the aishone here in Awaihinshi and still have money set aside in case of any emergencies. We will need to draw upon the reserves in each province and region to do the same in those places, but we can start the program here and then expand outward once we are sure it will work."

Hibikitsu nodded again and favored her with a smile. "I like this plan," he stated firmly, rising to his feet. "Let us start putting the pieces in place and testing things out. Seikoku, Futoba, the two of you seem to have the clearest idea of the way forward. Can I entrust you with beginning this?"

Futoba had stood as well, and now bowed. "Of course, Your Imperial Majesty." Across the table from her, Seikoku echoed her assent.

"Excellent. Thank you." With that, the emperor swept from the room, his Honteno following and sliding the door shut again behind them. Once he'd left, Futoba allowed herself to slump, just a little.

"I know," Seikoku told her, grinning. "You always hear about people having a palpable presence, but he really does. It's like the way the air gets charged right before a storm." Moving quickly, she circled the table with an easy grace Futoba envied and put an arm around Noniki. "You and Kagiri are the same." And she kissed him quickly on the cheek.

"Thank you for salvaging my bruised ego," he replied, laughing and kissing her back. "I completely agree, though. Our emperor is a force to be reckoned with."

He was, and Futoba marveled again that she should be in the presence of such people. Not just that, but actively working with them, and being treated as an equal.

How much her life had changed since arriving in the capital! And she sensed those changes had only just begun.

It was almost dark by the time Futoba left Aihiri. She was not terribly concerned as she passed under the white marble arch, the Honteno on duty there nodding to her before parting the gates. Entering Atsani was much like stepping from a private estate into an exclusive enclave, the single avenue broad and clean, the lanterns spaced just far enough apart for their light to overlap along the edges, the illumination providing a pleasant counterpoint to the dusk beyond. There were only ten estates at this level, she knew—those of the ten oldest, most influential houses in all Rimbaku—and many of those gates were shuttered and dark now, but there were still guards patrolling the streets and a handful of workers hurrying toward their homes in the lower levels.

She followed them through the second set of gates, yellow walls rising at her back and a peach walkway spreading out before her, feeling some of her tension fade with each step. She was back in Motohiri now, and near her own home, such as it was for the moment.

This level had more estates, of course, and quite a few were lighting lanterns by their gates, either to guide their own residents' home more easily or just to warm the neighbourhood as a whole. Futoba saw a pair of ladies by one entryway and knew by the blue-gray hawk feather design on their kitoros that they belonged to House Ichiro. She had known a member of that house, Ichiro Tamori, many years ago, when they were both youths being instructed in the courtier's arts. Curious how he had fared, Futoba angled her steps toward the women.

"Good evening to you both," she called as she approached, lest she startle them. They turned, and two sets of dark eyes studied her, taking in her own clothing and the crest evident upon it. "I wonder if you might tell me—"

But her words faded like a tamped-out candle's light when the pair lifted their chins and turned, deliberately putting their backs to her.

Startled by such blatant rudeness, Futoba ceased moving and simply stared at them a moment. The snub was deliberate, and she could guess why. She might wear a crane motif now, but people remembered the blue and green swallows that had preceded them—and the golden swallows those had descended from.

Sure enough, as she turned away, she heard one of the women mutter, loud enough for her to hear but soft enough to claim ignorance of, "Traitor."

Futoba lengthened her stride, letting her long legs carry her swiftly from that place. The breeze generated by her brisk pace helped brush the tears from her eyes. Would no one let her forget what had happened? Was no one willing to look past the Ieuyuki's guilt and find the Heiayuki's innocence? The emperor himself had forgiven her!

Clearly, his people were not inclined to be as generous. Perhaps they might be, someday.

For now, however, it seemed not everything had changed.

CHAPTER THREE

"**N**o, no, no! Halt this instant!" The tiny woman's voice was high and shrill, each syllable cutting at Hajime's ears like so many knives, and he froze, wincing at the sharp-edged sounds. She stormed up, stamping her small feet, and glared up at him, though he was no giant himself.

"Where, exactly, do you think you are going, hm?" she demanded, hands on hips, eyes blazing with fury.

"I was taking these to the kitchens," he replied, his own voice softening as if to offset her caustic tirade. He indicated the broad, shallow bamboo tray he carried, its one cord slung around his waist and the other around his neck to support its weight and that of the items arrayed upon it. "I thought this would be the quickest route."

For an instant he thought she would slice him open where he stood. "Quickest? Yes, quite." Her words were sharp as any sword, inflicting blood with each utterance. "Through the Imperial dining room and straight into the kitchen." She bared her teeth. "If, of course, you were the Emperor himself, and thus had the freedom of the house. You, however, do not."

He could not lower himself, not without spilling his precious cargo, but Hajime dipped his head until his chin grazed his chest. "No, of course not. Please forgive me, milady."

That earned a short bark of a laugh. "I am no lady—I work for a living. And part of my job is keeping riffraff from sullying these halls. Now, out with you."

"I—" he began to protest, only for her to start pushing him away, nearly upsetting his tray in the process. "Please, madam, I—"

He was rescued by an eerie shriek from behind his current tormentor, as a large, red-faced man in flour-spattered clothes and apron burst into the room. "Ah, there you are, Hajime! I was beginning to worry that you'd been beset by thieves!" Yamana Muiada, head chef of Aihiri, wrung his hands. "But I see you are safe, and your wares intact. Excellent."

The diminutive woman between them spun about, and Hajime assumed by the way the chef flinched that she had unleashed upon him the same deadly glare he had just received. "You know this man, then, Muiada?"

"Oh, yes, of course," the chef replied quickly, a broad smile spreading across his face, if a trifle unsteadily. "Hajime is the finest sweetsmaker in all of Awaihinshi! It was his desserts that we featured at the reception following the noble Taikoro Manikoro's funeral." His eyes, large and pleading, met Hajime's over her head. "And I see that you have met Hara Kuriko, principal housekeeper here. The compound is her domain, much as the kitchens are mine."

Madam Hara sniffed. "Yet here I find your...guest in my realm, rather than yours. Why is that, Muiada?"

"I am sure he merely became turned about while trying to find me," the chef assured her, skirting her as carefully as one might a wild boar and wrapping an arm around Hajime's shoulders to steer him back across the room. "But come, Hajime. We must get your kabingo, nigasi, and ujiro on ice before they lose any of their subtle flavor and sublime texture. Good day to you, Kuriko."

She merely sniffed again, pivoting to follow them with her eyes as they fled the room, slipping through the plain door at the far corner, but Hajime was sure he could still feel her stare well past the point when she'd vanished from view.

"And now you have met, and survived, the Dragon Lady of Aihiri," Muiada told him, giggling nervously as he stepped away, his poise and confidence regained the moment they had left the little housekeeper's presence. "But let me welcome you instead to my tiny kingdom, my fiefdom, my demesne. The imperial kitchens!"

The space was large enough to seem low-ceilinged, Hajime noticed as he glanced about, even though the slim-looking beams running overhead were some twenty feet up and most likely as thick as his torso. The walls were all whitewashed, though those nearest the fires were blackened by soot, and the floor was a cheerful red tile. Long tables lined the walls and marched down the room's center as well, broken up here and there by large basins or wide ovens with sturdy chimneys. A half dozen men and women scurried about, all dressed in simple, sturdy clothes under well-worn aprons. The air was thick with the smell of cooking rice, roasting beans, grilling meat and fish and vegetables, and various spices.

Though he worked alone, and dealt only in sweets himself, Hajime instantly felt at home.

"Come, come, bring those over this way," Muiada instructed, leading him to one of the basins, which was filled with ice. "Set them there, that will allow them to keep until after dinner." Hajime did as he was told, carefully transferring his smaller trays into the basin—all except one, which he saved for last and then presented to the head chef himself.

"These are for you," he said, and the man's face creased into a delighted grin as he beheld the neat trio of ujiri there. "I know how much you like them."

"Ah, Hajime, you are a prince among men!" Muiada accepted the little tray eagerly, and deft fingers plucked forth one of the sweets, quickly popping it into his mouth. "Perfect!"

Hajime waited patiently while the other man delighted in the dessert, chewing and swallowing with obvious gusto. But at last Muiada straightened and, setting the tray to one side with a sigh, drew a surprisingly delicate iniro from under his apron.

"I ask yet again, are you sure I cannot hire you on full-time?" he asked, already fumbling with the cord that held the segmented box together. Loosening it enough to separate the sections, he extracted a quartet of gold coins from within. "I could offer you far more than this pittance."

The sweetsmaker laughed and took the coins, bowing over them. "As always, I appreciate the offer. But no, I am content where I am, in my shop. I am always happy to deliver an order such as this to you, however, whenever you desire." He winked at his friend. "As long as I don't have to cut through the Imperial dining room to do it!"

Muiada laughed with him, clapping him on the back. "No, please don't! I would hate to lose you to Kuriko's venomous tongue!" He shook his head. "Well, if I cannot sway you, I will not keep you. This time. But I will keep asking!"

"Please do," Hajime replied, bowing and backing toward the door the chef indicated for him to use. "Who knows, one of these days I might even say yes!"

Slipping out of the kitchen, the artisan known as Hajime underwent a subtle but profound transformation. Straightening, all hint of subservience or hesitation fell from him like water sliding off a duck's back. His face calmed and stilled, the shadows across it deepening even as his eyes brightened, becoming twin red fires amid a narrow gloom. His footfalls quieted and then vanished as he walked soundlessly across the room, his empty tray now slung across his back like a shield, his hands loose and free at his sides, every motion as graceful as a snake's—and as deadly.

For Hajime was no more, and the Yamoran sorcerer-assassin Dai Yi stood in his place.

He had felt, when he'd killed the sweetsmaker and taken his identity, that the disguise would prove useful. But how could he have guessed at just how much? Because here he was, freely entering the Imperial compound! And the more often he came up here with his sweets, the more the guards would come to know him, and to relax in his presence.

True, he could not roam freely. Not yet. But he had plans for that already.

There was no hurry, however. For now, he would merely lay the groundwork. That and keep his eyes and ears open. The right opportunity would present itself, and when it did he would be ready.

Then, and only then, would he strike.

Then, and only then, would the Relicant Emperor die.

CHAPTER FOUR

The young man stood easily, body relaxed but at the ready, nihono extended before him, its braided hilt held comfortably in both hands. His armor gleamed in the early morning light, each plate polished and perfect, and his menatu appeared gilded as its equally glossy surface caught the sun's rays. Behind the mask, his eyes were narrowed in concentration, and possibly rage.

"Hai!" he shouted, timing his lunge with the exhortation, a quick step launching him forward even as his arms snapped up and then back down, bringing his blade down in a sweeping silver arc toward the head of his foe.

That same opponent did not block the blow. Indeed, the tall, slim figure all in shades of green carried no blade, only a heavy wooden baton, currently clasped behind his back. But he twisted to one side, allowing the strike to slice the air before him and no more.

"Surely," the green-armored man said, his voice soft and deep, his tone thoughtful, "you can do better than that?"

The swordsman's face twisted in fury and he thrust his blade forward, hoping to skewer his adversary. But again the tall man shifted, the blow sliding harmlessly past him.

"No," he said with the hint of a sigh. "Perhaps not."

That was the final straw, and the gleaming man raised his sword high, his face purpling with rage. "Die!" he screamed, charging forward—only to stop dead as the other man's chasai lashed out once, twice, the metal-capped baton crashing against his jingaso and making it ring like a bell, with his head as the clapper caught within. Dropping his sword, the man cried out in agony, clutching at his head, and fell to his knees. After a second, the baton's tip pushed his helmet back, forcing his gaze up to meet that of his vanquisher.

"Mori Yukeno," the emerald-armored man declared. "Do you yield?"

Yukeno glared up at the man, but finally nodded. "I yield."

Nodding, Kagiri—Gensaiba, and Dogenriku of the aiashe— offered his free hand and hauled the young nobleman and officer to his feet. "You must not let your anger get the best of you," he warned. "When it does, all your skill deserts you."

The defeated warrior nodded, hand going to his chest in salute. But Kagiri could read the anger still present in the other man's eyes. This was not someone who could be trusted to oversee others, to preserve their lives. "Application denied," he stated, and Yukeno started to say something, then thought better of it and merely bowed instead.

Turning away from him, Kagiri studied the next applicant in line. This one was equally as polished as Yukeno had been, which was no surprise—though only a younger son, the new candidate still hailed from a house as old and highly placed and wealthy as the last. "Name?" he asked, though he already knew it, as he knew all four of those who had presented themselves thus far and were now here today, in the small practice yard just outside his private study.

"Chusa Ichiro Tamori, noble Dogenriku," the young man announced, tapping fist to chest in a salute that somehow managed to be dismissive even as it technically showed respect.

"Chusa Ichiro," Kagiri repeated, holding out a hand. Fuko Miyosi hurried over, the timid little scribe placing a scroll in his hand and then quickly withdrawing to the safety of the raised porch. Kagiri studied the document and frowned. "I required two recommendations," he reminded the applicant. "One from a superior or peer, one from a subordinate. You have here a letter from a shosa and another from a chuisu." Both ranks were below the candidate's own.

Tamori's thin lips twisted into a smirk—he was not a handsome man, and the expression did him no favors. "You will forgive me for saying so, Dogenriku, but I have difficulty locating any I would consider my peer, much less my superior. I was forced to make do."

Ignoring the man's overwhelming arrogance, Kagiri scanned the letters themselves. "These are...interesting recommendations," he commented at last, lowering the scroll to study the man instead. "They are flattering but vague, as if the writers were desperate to find anything complimentary to say." The officer's nostrils flared, but he said nothing, and Kagiri continued, "Do you know why I required a letter from a superior officer? Because you would be less able to threaten or bribe one into writing something you did not deserve. With subordinates, it is all too easy to pressure them."

The young man's spine was now so stiff it could have been used for a flagpole. "You insult my honor, sir, and the honor of my house. I must demand an apology, or else satisfaction."

Kagiri allowed himself a small, wolfish smile. "Oh, must you? Very well. You may try to wring an apology from me by force."

The skirmish took even less time to resolve than the previous bout, and saw the young noble sprawled out upon the ground, bleeding from a split lip and a smashed nose. He had been too cocky to even fasten his menatu in place. "Application denied," Kagiri told him, turning away. Tamori was sputtering in outrage as he clambered back to his feet, but at least he showed enough sense not to go after Kagiri with his back turned.

The third applicant was a woman, as tall as the two nobles who'd preceded her. Her tailored armor displayed a womanly form, yet her features were composed, her stance professional. When she banged her fist against her chest, Kagiri saw from the motion that she was strong, and had good reflexes. "Taisu Soma Yamani, at your service and that of the empire, Dogenriku!" Her words were strong and clear, but Kagiri thought he saw a flicker around her eyes. Fear? Doubt?

"Taisu." He looked over the report Miyosi had brought him. "Your peer, Hurito Yakai, speaks favorably of you. So does your gunso." He liked that she had gone to a sergeant rather than a junior officer. It showed that she knew the value of real soldiers. "I see you have been a taisu for seven years already." And, indeed, he could see faint lines around her eyes and mouth, suggesting she was at least a few years older than him, and possibly more. "Why is that?"

That flicker was back, only now he could make it out more clearly. It was disappointment, mixed with bitterness and some anger. Her voice was steady, nearly bland, however, as she replied, "No opportunities for promotion arose, sir."

He frowned. She was noble born, if from a minor house. Her armor showed real use, and he judged her to be capable, and certainly more experienced than many shosas or chusas. Yet she was still a captain. Which meant either she had angered someone well above her and they'd stifled her military career as revenge or she'd made a major mistake somewhere. Or it was simply that she was a woman. Many noblemen would be offended by the notion of her matching or exceeding them in rank.

Fortunately, Kagiri did not care about such things.

"Attack me," he instructed, rolling up the scroll but keeping it in one hand, his chasai in the other. She did so at once, without hesitation, and her attack was strong, confident, and skilled. Kagiri sparred with her a moment, then two, and was pleased. She was no match for him, of course, but that had never been in question, nor was it the point. She had both skill and experience. Furthermore, he liked what he saw in her, and felt for her at having been held back just become of some people's wounded pride.

"Congratulations, Taisho Soma," he told her, and for the first time her face showed expression as she broke into a surprised but delighted smile.

"Thank you, sir!" She fell to her knees, offering up her sword in both hands, forehead tapping the blade. "I pledge myself to you and to the empire!"

He smiled and offered her a hand up, which she accepted unselfconsciously. Another good sign, that she was not too proud to accept help. "Come see me in my office at dawn tomorrow," he instructed. "We will go over your new duties then."

She bowed, backing away, and he turned to the final applicant of the day. "Name?" he asked, considering this last man. Short, stocky, almost bow-legged, with a wide mouth and dark, clever eyes.

"Taisu Tsuneto, sir." The man offered his blade. "I live to serve the empire!" His voice was raspy, and as rough as his features.

"Indeed." No house name, which meant the man was a commoner—much like Kagiri himself. "Your letters are excellent," he noted, skimming them. "And you, like Taisho Soma, have served within the aiashe for many years, with many commendations but no advancement."

Tsuneto shook his head, lowering his blade and resheathing it at his side. "I have no family to buy me advancements, my lord," the man stated bluntly. "I have to earn each and every promotion. There are also many who look down on me, and do their best to keep me down, due to my birth."

Kagiri nodded. "Yes. I am familiar with such things myself. Very well. Attack me."

Like Soma Yamani, Tsuneto did so without delay, diving immediately into a quick, deadly flurry of blows. Kagiri liked that the man did not hold back. He had decent speed and plenty of power in those broad shoulders. There was no question that the man was a capable soldier. But according to the file, he had served as a scout more than once, which meant he was capable of independent thought, and of looking out for himself. He'd also overseen a chotao, so he did have some leadership experience.

Still, managing a single company was very different from handling an entire tyodao or sudao, and he had no desire to raise this man up if it just meant removing him again later.

On the other hand, the vacancies did need to be filled. And, like the woman before him, Tsuneto proved to be strong, quick, and fully proficient. After a moment or two, Kagiri reached a decision.

"Thank you, Taisho Tsuneto," he declared after turning aside one final lunge and taking a step back to indicate they should disengage. "Return here tomorrow at dawn to discuss your new duties."

"Sir!" the man saluted, head bowed—he did not smile, but there was both pride and joy in those dark eyes. "I pledge myself to you and to the empire. Thank you, sir!" A quick turn, and Kagiri's newest general was striding away, his walk quick and focused.

Along with Daishin Nishoji and Masagi Matsu, the only two previous taisho Kagiri had allowed to remain, that brought him to four generals. Out of the five his army needed to maintain itself properly.

Well, he would simply have to hope that one more good candidate presented him- or herself. In the meantime, he could work with what he had.

Fuko Miyosi had remained after the others left, both the rejected and the accepted, and Kagiri now turned to his clerk. "File the paperwork for Soma Yamani and Tsuneto's immediate advancement to taisho," he ordered. "And requisition the necessary armor and other signs of rank for them."

Miyosi nodded, saluting awkwardly. "Right away, sir."

At last Kagiri was left alone and removed his helmet, going over to the porch and setting that and the baton aside in favor of a pitcher waiting there. He poured some of the water directly into his mouth, then splashed more of it about his head and face. Ah, that was better! These examinations were tiring, but at least they were better than sitting at his desk all day, reading reports.

He wondered what Shizumi was doing right about now.

CHAPTER FIVE

Misataki Shizumi, Taikoro of the Honjofu and considered by many to be the finest warrior in all Rimbaku, was accustomed to fighting. As a soldier, she had spent many hours in combat, all across the kingdom.

She had even, in recent weeks, been forced to fight right here in Aihiri, a place that had long been considered too holy to ever suffer such indignities. But Shizumi knew better—she had battled would-be assassins in the throne room itself, and fought off traitors on the palace grounds, just inside the main gates.

What she had not expected was to face fighting in the halls of the Imperial compound set aside for her Honjofu or their counterparts the Honteno—or for that fighting to be between members of those two royal detachments.

Which was why she allowed herself a split second to stare in utter shock at the four young men tussling in the corridor, two of them clad all in red and the other two all in black. At least no blades had been drawn, but there were fists and kicks aplenty.

"Enough!" she shouted at last, shaking off her surprise and stomping toward the battling foursome. "Stop that right now!"

None of them paid any attention. And, though younger than her, all four had several inches on her in height. Possibly in muscle, too, though Shizumi was no slouch. Fortunately, what she lacked in size and brawn—and volume, evidently—she more than made up for in skill, focus, and sheer bullheadedness.

Which was why, when she was still a few feet from the quartet, she kicked out, letting her feet lift off the polished floorboards and landing on her hip to slide into their midst, bowling the quarreling soldiers off their feet. Shizumi had yanked her sword free of her sash on the way down, scabbard and all, and now laid about her with it, thwacking each of the men soundly in the temple, forehead, or neck and knocking them aside so that she was able to roll and spring to her feet, pivoting to face them while they were still sprawled about, grunting and groaning and clutching their heads.

"Now," she declared, sliding the weapon back into place before crossing her arms. "Let's try this again. Stand up. Now!" That last was said with the crack of a drill sergeant, and all four scrambled upright and stood at attention, eyes focused on some point past her. "Explain yourself." She moved to the first of the men—boys, really—and glared at him until he was forced to meet her eyes. "Enomoto. What is this disgraceful display all about?"

He reddened, but managed not to look away. "They started it, Taikoro," he muttered. "They had no right!"

The boy next to him, Satake, nodded. They were hers, clad in proper Honjofu black. The other two were among the handful she had granted to Kohori to fill out her badly depleted ranks, and wore the Honteno red. It was to the first of them, Nao, that Shizumi turned next. "Well?" she demanded.

He scowled, though he couldn't bring himself to look at her as he did. "I don't take orders from you," he muttered. "I'm not with the Honjofu anymore." The other boy, Okito, paled, most likely from seeing Shizumi's expression, and quickly raised his hands, taking a step back. She remembered the trial, when she'd challenged all the new recruits to defeat her. These two had worked together, but it had been Nao who'd led the attack. Evidently that pattern had not changed.

Shizumi reached out, grabbed the boy's chin, and dragged his face about until he was staring back at her. "I am not your commander," she agreed, her voice low and clear, each word sharp as a knife. "But I am *a* commander, a Taikoro, one of two in the nation. I answer directly to the emperor himself. Do you claim that I hold no authority here?" She tightened her grip until he winced. "Do you?"

"No," he managed through gritted teeth, then added, "no, Taikoro."

"Good." She released him and he reeled back a pace. "Forget it again and I will take you back out to the practice yard—just you, me, and live steel. And I will show you what happens to those who disrespect me. Now. What happened here?"

Nao rubbed at his chin. "Nothing. We bumped into each other in the hall. They took offense. That's it."

"You ordered us to stand aside for our betters!" the other new Honjofu, Satake, snapped. "We all trained together! You're no better than we are!"

That brought a nasty sneer to Nao's lips. "Except I am, aren't I?" he shot back. "Because I'm a gunso. All Honteno are. And you, you're not even a gocho. You're just a foot soldier."

Ah. So that's what this was about. Shizumi deliberately took a single step forward—and tried not to laugh as both Nao and Okito practically fell over attempting to backpedal out of her way. "Listen very carefully," she told them both. "The Honteno are an elite unit, yes. But so are the Honjofu. As you know, since up until recently you were desperate to be one of us. We are two sides of the same coin, both dedicated to protecting the emperor and the empire—us from without, you from within. That armor you wear gives you authority over aiashe, so that you may command them in times of need and know that you will be obeyed." She rapped a knuckle against Nao's crimson deo, eliciting a hollow thud. "But do not ever presume to order my warriors about. You have no authority over them. If you ever attempt it again, you will answer to me. And not even your own Taikoro will save you. Do I make myself clear?" Both boys nodded desperately, and she pivoted to the side. "Go."

As they hurried away, she turned to her own two. "Who threw the first punch?" she asked.

"I did, Taikoro," Enomoto admitted. "I'm sorry. Nao has always been mean-spirited and bossy, and he was lording it over us. Okito just backs him up. When we didn't move aside, he made to push me, and I hit him."

Shizumi shook her head. "Do not let them goad you again," she warned. "Any more trouble, bring it to me." She paused, but there was no one else around. "And next time you punch someone, make sure you put them down, hm?"

"Sir, yes, sir!" Both boys saluted, fists to chests, and she returned it, then shooed them away. Only once they'd gone did Shizumi lean against one wall, tipping her head back against its cool silk panels. Was this what she was reduced to now? Breaking up hallway brawls? She was a warrior, by the Bones! She lived for the thrill of battle, the joy of victory.

Where was the thrill in this?

With a sigh, she pushed away and started back down the corridor herself, heading toward her study. There were still reports to file, expenses to check over, rosters to fill out. Paperwork. Her hands were made for naritaba and nihono, not for quill and kogotano! But that was the work of a Taikoro, it seemed. Moments of battle might be few and far between from this point forward, with a great deal more bureaucracy, accounting, and even diplomacy in between.

None of which she was any good at. Or enjoyed. Or had ever wanted.

Even the fact that she now had an office was foreign to her. She was used to sleeping out under the stars, marching or riding the roads, eating in the saddle or around a fire. She had not been made for comfortable living quarters, cozy writing chambers, and soft beds.

But there was nothing to be done about all that. Her emperor had chosen her for this honor, and she would not disappoint or fail him. She served the empire, even if this was not what she had intended.

Perhaps the paperwork could wait a while, though, she decided, pausing as she reached the hall's end and the door there, which led into the stretch of offices that now included her own. Surely Geniji or Isano or Akino might be around and interested in playing at dice or cards. Or at sparring, though when she thought of matching blades the figure that immediately leapt to mind was none of her bantao but instead a young man, tall and slim and clad all in green.

Stop that, she told herself sternly. *Kagiri has his own duties, just as you do. You cannot simply drag him off to practice swordplay any time you wish.*

And was that all she wanted from him? Or were there other activities that also suggested themselves?

She shook her head, laughing at her own silliness. She was no moon-eyed girl, nor even a dewy-eyed maiden. She was a hardened warrior. Kagiri was a friend, a comrade, and a peer. Nothing more.

As if to punish herself for her thoughts, Shizumi made herself slide the door aside and enter the corridor beyond. She would tackle that paperwork. That was the job she had accepted.

But perhaps, after she'd finished enough of them, she'd look for her old squadmates.

Or see if Kagiri would like to join her for food and some exercise. By which she meant sparring, of course.

After she was done. Not before.

CHAPTER SIX

Ushi glanced up, surprised, when the stranger appeared. They did not get many visitors here in Onokura, beyond the occasional trader or merchant who'd followed the Rumiri all the way down, or who'd detoured too far when passing from Ginzai to Yudishu. Still, a customer was a customer, and so he set aside the cup he'd been wiping down and rounded the simple bar, approaching the man.

He was an odd-looking fellow, to be sure. Tall and thin, almost unhealthily so, the planes of his face sharp as knives beneath his pale skin, his hair long and shaggy and his beard equally so, Ushi might have thought him a beggar and a vagabond if not for his clothes. Those were faded but fine, rich silks embroidered with metallic thread and small gems. The man's boots, too, had once been fine leather, elegantly made, but now they were so brittle and cracked they shed bits with each step.

"Welcome, good sir!" Ushi said nonetheless, bowing. "Take a seat anywhere you like! What can I get for you?"

The stranger glanced around, eyeing the half dozen tables there under the uzumoya. Aki, Bin, and Miya were already clustered around one, their usual chatter paused as they watched the newcomer, though their hands continued their work of knitting and mending. Tenbo was ensconced at another, though his confederates Gohei and Seibu had not yet arrived. That left the other two corners and the two tables in the center, and the stranger chose the closer of the latter, seating himself with a flourish that told Ushi this was indeed a man of quality fallen on hard times.

"I have adai with fresh uridon," Ushi continued, "and I was

just about to make aragei and heioki. To drink I can offer you water, tea, and rice wine."

That last one drew a flicker of interest, and Ushi laughed. "Tsekuri it is." Returning to the bar, he collected a jug and a glass, bringing them over to the man's table and filling the earthenware cup. "There you are."

Ushi had worked in the town's little restaurant—the only one, really—since he was a child. Most of the villagers ate here a few times a week, and nearly all the adults gathered to drink each night after the work was done. Over the years, he had seen many of them savoring that first sip, cool and fresh after a long day of laboring at the nets or the traps or the paddies.

None of them had matched this man.

His eyes fluttered closed as he lifted the cup to his chapped lips, and he tilted it slowly, so slowly, the barest trickle of wine pouring forth to wet his dry skin. Yet the sigh that escaped him, the way his lips curled up—and how he smacked them, the tip of his tongue emerging to dab the flavor from them, one might have thought it was a torrent of the finest liquor imaginable.

A second sip followed, a little longer and fuller than the first, and the man swallowed, the sound of it audible on such a quiet day. He licked his lower lip more fully, gulped, then set the cup down with an unsteady hand.

"The chicken," he said, his voice hoarse and dry as dust but somehow deep, almost echoing. "And the octopus balls. With rice. Please."

Ushi bowed. "Of course, sir. Coming right up." He didn't worry much about the man paying, not with all the jewels displayed on his sleeves. So, hurrying back to the bar and then the little kitchen area curtained off behind it, he readied his ingredients. Chicken and octopus balls, rice flour, oil, and spice. All good, and the fire already hot, the pot of oil bubbling above it.

Reaching for the pouch around his neck, Ushi drew forth a pinch of his grandfather's bones and tossed them into his mouth.

The feeling of knowledge flowing into him, of skill coming to his limbs, of his fingers growing more deft, his glance more steady, his motions more precise, was second nature to him by now.

The scream that emerged from beyond the curtain, however, was new.

Next thing he knew, Ushi had been flung over and past the cookfire, to land hard on his back in the dirt past the pavilion's edge. He had to squint up at the figure floating into view, almost glowing against the sun—

But wait. The sun was behind Ushi. And he could see the stranger's feet as he drifted clear over the fire and settled to the ground with those shattered boots on either side of Ushi's torso.

"What magic is this?" the man hissed, crouching over him, his eyes glazed with a strange light and something that did not seem entirely rational. "Are you matekai, then, come to battle me while I am yet weak and disoriented?" Ushi could smell the man now, dusty and musty like old rags—or old bones. "You will not best me!" the man shouted down at him, his mouth fortunately still too dry for any spittle to fly.

"I don't know what you mean, sir!" Ushi protested, trying to shield his face with both hands. "I'm no wizard! I was just about to cook your meal!"

The man practically growled at him. "Do not lie to me!" he insisted. "I can feel the magic in you!" He frowned. "Yet it was not there when you served me. Some trick to hide it until you were ready?"

Now Ushi understood at least part of the man's ranting. "You mean my aitachi, sir?" He reached—slowly, carefully—for his pouch, holding it up for the stranger to see. "It's just my grandfather's aishone. He was the real cook. I'm just borrowing his skill. That's what we do." He wasn't sure how anyone could not know about the Relicant Touch, but perhaps the man was from farther away than he'd realized. Could he be from Higinasi? It was a long way to travel, and they'd never had anyone from the neighboring kingdom show up in Onokura before, but that was the only thing that made sense.

And, indeed, the man stepped back now, frowning in obvious confusion. "Aitachi?" he repeated. "You borrow your grandfather's skill...through his bones? What foul taint is this?"

Ushi levered himself up into a sitting position but didn't dare stand, in case the man attacked him again. "It's just the way things are," he answered. "People draw on the bones for skill and knowledge. All of Rimbaku's the same way."

"Rimbaku?" Now he knew the man had to be a foreigner! "Yes, it is, isn't it?" He turned and fixed Ushi with his too-bright gaze. "Where are the other matekai, then?"

"The other matekai? There aren't any, far as I know," Ushi answered. "Haven't been since the Schism."

The stranger was nodding. "So." He stroked his chin—which, given his long and unkempt hair, appeared oddly smooth and clean. "No other wizards. I see. And the whole land cursed to rely upon these bones?" Ushi saw him shudder. "Horrible. Absolutely horrible."

"It's what we have," Ushi told him, finally chancing it and standing up again. "It's all we have. Without the bones, we're nothing."

Suddenly the man was in his face, though Ushi hadn't seen him move. "No!" he shouted. "*With* them you are nothing! You are ghosts walking, memories playing at life, relics pretending to be people! This land was indeed cursed, and you are its carriers!" He pushed Ushi away, and though the man's hand was nearly skeletal and the touch light as a feather, it flung him across the street to slam hard into the wall of Seibu's hut beyond. He slid down it with a groan, his head spinning, chest tight, every inch of him aching.

"Please," Ushi whimpered as the man approached again, not walking but hovering just above the ground. "Please, don't hurt me. I didn't do anything wrong."

"It is not your actions," the man whispered, his eyes wide and his expression fevered, cheeks taut and lips pulled back. "It is your very nature that is wrong. All of this is wrong." He dropped to one knee beside Ushi and rested a hand against his cheek. "But do not worry. I will make it right again. I will restore things to the way they were, the way they should be."

His touch was warm, soothing. But the heat increased, growing from comforting to unpleasant to agonizing. Ushi flinched and cried out. The man had already pulled back, rising to his full height again and sliding back a pace, but the heat continued. Now it was spreading all through Ushi's head and neck and shoulders, traveling rapidly down and through his body, until every inch of him felt aflame.

It was only as his senses failed that he realized the bright light was coming from his own burning flesh.

CHAPTER SEVEN

Seikoku was doing her best not to fume openly as she entered the small but airy office given to the karo of Atsani. She suspected, however, that she was failing miserably at the attempt, and discovered that she did not particularly care as she marched across the well-appointed room, stopping only inches from the handsomely carved desk at the far side.

"Madame Buhiyo." Wakiza Yukane set down his teacup and folded his fleshy but beautifully manicured hands around it almost protectively, studying her from beneath his bushy eyebrows. His robes today were jade green, with his family's pink crab crest patterned around the hem, collar, and cuffs. "What can I do for you?"

"You can tell me the meaning of this," she replied, all but flinging a scroll down onto his desk.

Lifting the document, he scanned it quickly, then offered it back to her with a frown through his thick beard. "I believe it is straightforward enough. In order to gather funds for various repairs needed to our demesne as a whole, each resident is required to pay a small tax. Hardly onerous."

"That's easy to say when there are two of you, or four," Seikoku snapped, snatching the scroll from his hands. "We have over thirty in Sorainasei! And your so-called tax is two gold apiece! Most of my residents don't have that kind of money total, let alone to hand over for road repairs!"

The sectional governor regarded her carefully. "Perhaps, then, this is not the place for them," he suggested slowly, but she did not miss the gleam in his eye. "Other sectors may have lower costs and thus be more amenable. Here in Atsani, so close to the emperor himself, we are paying for our position."

She glared at him, but he did not flinch. "Was there anything else?" he asked, fingers curling around his cup.

"Yes, actually," she answered. "When was this new tax decided? It says 'as agreed by all residents present during deliberations.' I knew of no such gathering and certainly was not asked my opinion on any such proposal. And these…taxes are to be collected 'by the end of the next meeting.' What meeting is that?"

"No? Oh, dear, had I forgotten to mention? That is unfortunate. We meet once a week to discuss matters pertaining to all our residents," Lord Wakiza told her. "Every Dayabei at sunset. You are, of course, welcome to attend, as is everyone in Atsani."

"Tomorrow is Dayabei," she reminded him. "So you're saying this"—she rapped the scroll on the corner of his desk, making him flinch—"was decided almost a week ago, and we are just hearing about it now? When these monies are to be collected the next day?"

Their region's governor shrugged. "The details took time to finesse," he stated blandly. "And then to distribute. It was all handled as quickly and expeditiously as possible." She huffed at that, and he raised an eyebrow, clearly daring her to contradict him. When she did not, an oily smile sprang from his lips. "Now, if *that* is all…"

She scowled down at him. "For now. But this isn't over." And, turning on her heel, she stormed out. She waited until she was out of earshot before releasing a series of blistering curses that scorched the air. Was this why she had accepted the post? To be bullied and tricked and scorned by those around her? Better to abandon the place than have to put up with nonsense like this!

She'd barely returned to Sorainasei, passing through its beautiful sun-over-garden doors and following the vine-patterned mosaic toward the compound's central courtyard, when Seikoku found herself confronted by a large, heavyset man in rich red silks patterned in black bear paws. "You there," he stated, striding forward and blocking her path to glare down at her. "You are in charge here, are you not?" He made it sound like an insult, and her eyes narrowed, but she refused to be cowed by some bully, no matter how fine his clothing.

"I am the mayor, yes," she agreed. "And you are?"

He sniffed at her, though how he could smell anything through the haze of candied orange surrounding him was unclear. "Sunao Iensen. I am here with an offer, and a generous one." He let his gaze sweep the compound, skirting over the people hard at work in the courtyard and out on the grounds, taking in only the small lake and the gardens and the buildings. "I will give you twenty gold for the lot," he stated. "And you may have two days in which to gather your belongings and depart."

He was already reaching for his iniro, but stopped at her spurt of laughter, his face reddening. "You seem to be laboring under some misapprehension," Seikoku informed him archly. "Soraina-sei is not for sale, not even at a price far above your insulting one."

Lord Sunao—she had heard the family name before some-where, though she could not remember where—looked torn between a scowl and a blank stare. "You know you and your... residents cannot hope to pay the required tax," he stated bluntly. "You will have little choice but to depart. I am offering you a chance to do so with coin in your pocket, rather than running like some thief in the night. But so be it." He folded his arms over his thick chest. "You have brought it upon yourself."

Seikoku favored him with a brilliant smile—and a tone that was so sweet it made her own teeth ache. "Thank you so much for your neighborly concern," she told him. "Now, I would hate to take you from your other duties any longer, and I'm sure you wish to be well away from here, lest our common nature somehow rub off on you. Have a lovely rest of your day." She pushed past him, not bothering to go around as her shoulder bumped him aside, and stormed down the path, leaving the arrogant lord sputtering behind her. The nerve of him!

Minawa and Kanai were waiting for her on the broad steps leading up to the main building, having apparently watched the entire encounter. "I'm sorry," Kanai said when Seikoku reached them. "He marched right in, demanding to talk to someone, and I…I was afraid to face him." The stocky potter's face was twisted in shame and regret.

Seikoku patted his arm. "Don't be," she assured the fiercely loyal man who, with her, had been the first to follow Noniki down the long road that had ultimately led them all here. "It's my responsibility." She frowned, staring at the noble who was even now stomping away, then down at the scroll still crumpled in her hand. "He's not wrong about one thing, though. I don't know what we're going to do about this." She could ask the emperor for the money, certainly, but that was relying upon someone else to solve their problem, and would only delay the inevitable.

"It's just to get rid of us," Minawa pointed out, and the older woman was of course right. It was an obvious ploy. None of the nobles would bat an eye at the tax, but it would ruin everyone here. And Lord Sunao had clearly known all about it—no doubt he had been at that surreptitious meeting, and one of the "all residents present" who'd agreed to this farce.

That gave her an idea, however, and Seikoku found herself grinning suddenly. "Spread the word," she told her friends, hugging them both. "Tomorrow is Dayabei, and we have a gathering to attend."

The next day, Seikoku took some time to travel down through Motohiri to Sakiriti. She preferred this level to the ones above it, with its bustling activity and the storefronts and galleries and showrooms displaying various wares and crafts. It was one of those very places she sought out, and she smiled when she found it, momentarily setting her other troubles aside.

It was a fine day out, clear and sunny with just enough breeze to keep pleasantly cool and the showroom had its front walls slid back, creating a wide and inviting entrance. The space beyond that was well laid out, with windows high along the walls allowing a good deal of light even with the walls shut. Now, the space was nearly as bright as the world beyond it, and the wares displayed upon stands and tables there practically glowed.

A man was standing among the goods and smiled as she approached. "Madam Buhiyo!" he called out, bowing to her. "A good day to you!"

"And to you, Iwaki-san," Seikoku replied, for this was the showroom's owner. "But I've told you before, call me Seikoku." It still felt strange, inviting everyone to use her real name. When she'd been a thief back in Ginzai, she'd had a different name for each aspect of her life, and none of them the correct one.

The merchant she faced knew none of that, of course, but his face still creased in a broad, friendly smile. "And you must call me Matsu," he reminded her with a wink. "But come in, come in! Your friends' goods are selling well; they are all of excellent quality and in high demand." When some of Atsani's other residents had complained about Sorainasei's members selling their creations right there, Iwaki Matsu had offered a solution. He allowed Seikoku's friends to sell their items in his showroom, taking only a small commission for his trouble and the space he was giving up. That had satisfied everyone, and Seikoku suspected the various rugs and pots and scarves and tinctures sold better here where people were more accustomed to shopping. Up there they had only been a novelty, and one you had to cross two levels to reach.

"I am very glad to hear that, and wished to thank you yet again for your kindness and generosity," Seikoku told the man, who dipped his head, his cheeks turning red. "I do not know what we would have done without you."

"You would have found another willing to help," he answered. "Or some other way entirely. But I am glad to be of service."

They chatted a moment or two longer before a customer entered the showroom. Letting Matsu step forward to greet them, Seikoku took the opportunity to really scan the space. But this time, she used skills she'd spent much of her young life building up.

This time, she looked at it like a thief.

He had put her friend's wares in prominent positions, she saw at once. Exactly where you would place items of value, in clear line of sight from the main entrance and raised up enough to be spotted easily from a distance. Simple bases and stands and white, black, or gold backgrounds, depending upon the piece's colors, to make sure the items themselves were what stood out. The items caught the eye, presented as the most desirable things present.

All in all, it added up to one thing—Matsu was playing straight with her. He was genuinely looking to help.

That was all she'd needed to know. And knowing it restored at least some of her faith in humanity.

Now it was time to see about the rest.

That evening, she delighted in the look of shock on Wakiza Yukane's face as she and her friends filed into his office, filling it to overflowing. "What is the meaning of this?" the karo demanded. Seated in one of the chairs before his desk, Lord Sunao was rising to his feet, evidently alarmed at the flood of commoners encroaching upon his space. Another man, clad in blue and gray with an emerald wave embroidered upon his breast, also stood and stepped back to the safety of the desk.

"Good evening, my lord karo," Seikoku replied cheerfully. "And to you, gentlemen. We have come to attend this evening's meeting. I hope we are not late."

"You cannot be here!" Lord Sunao declared, his voice rising to near panic. "This is for residents only!"

"Yes, I know," she told him. "And we are. All of us." She tilted her head, tapping her lip in thought. "At least, that is what the new tax stated, is it not? It is two gold per resident, correct? And if my residents are being taxed thus, then surely they each count as one resident for all other matters pertaining to our neighborhood?" She smiled. "I know those fees are to be collected at meeting's end, but in the meantime I have a proposal to put forth. We have noticed that there is an overabundance of manure on our streets, and both the sound and stench of horseflesh in the air. We therefore propose that all horses be banned from Atsani, effective immediately. All in favor?" She'd raised her voice at the last bit, and her companions all responded with a resounding "Aye!" and a forest of raised hands.

"Now, see here..." Lord Wakiza started, but the third gentleman cut him off.

"Well played, madam," he stated, bowing to her. "Watane Yatahei, at your service. You are correct—either the tax does not apply to each of your residents individually or, if it does, each of them carries a full vote and thus your compound can dictate terms throughout all Atsani." He smiled. "I propose an addendum to the recent tax, clarifying that each *household* is to pay that amount, not each individual. And that a household is determined by shared address, meaning all of your friends would be recognized as a single unit for such purposes." He dipped his head at her. "What say you and yours?"

Seikoku nodded back politely. "We say aye, sir, and thank you for being so considerate." All her people nodded. "I would gather, then, that each household likewise has a single vote on matters?" She glanced at her friends. "I will represent Sorainasei, so the rest of you may go."

The others filed back out, though not without nods and waves and pats on the arm, leaving Seikoku alone with the three noblemen. That imbalance did not last long, however. Immediately after Ryoji shuffled out, a new arrival appeared: a young man in silver marked with an otter among the waves.

"Ah, I am just in time, it appears!" Takami said with a smile. "Buhiyo Seikoku mentioned the meeting to me and I wished to attend, now that I am a resident here as well. Fujitai Takami, at your service." He bowed to the gentlemen before moving to stand beside Seikoku, even as both Wakiza and Sunao sputtered. Clearly this meeting had been their little secret, and one they were not eager to share.

"I believe you will require a few more chairs in future, lord karo," Seikoku told her superior with a bright smile. "And perhaps some tea, so that people's throats do not grow parched as we discuss matters?" There was a wide, shallow table to one side of the door; she carefully removed the decorative vase placed atop it, then folded herself into a lotus position there instead. "Now, what is the first order of business?"

Sunao fumed, Wakiza muttered, but Lord Watane laughed, as did Takami.

Perhaps, Seikoku decided, being in charge of her little community would not be so awful after all.

CHAPTER EIGHT

Deep within the gardens of Sorainasei, a young man sat cross-legged upon the ground, bare feet brushing against soil and grass, face tilted up to feel the wind across his face and the last rays of the day's sunlight upon his eyelids.

Taking a deep breath, Noniki released it slowly and let himself drift out of his body along with it.

The first time had been involuntary. He'd been staying with the monks at the Ikibanichari, helping with basic chores while he recovered from losing his brother and the trauma that had followed, and had been struck down by a patient gone mad. His body broken beyond repair, Noniki had found his spirit detaching itself from that shattered husk and floating up into the sky.

He might have kept going, his body dying as his soul moved on, if he had not been attacked by the strange, chaotic cloud he'd later come to know as Kaemusei, the Silent Change. Instinctively fighting back, Noniki had won free, regained the will to live, and returned to his body, finding it miraculously restored. And, though he had not realized it at the time, filled with something strange and wondrous and new: magic. Not the Relicant Touch but true magic, the kind that had been lost to their kingdom since the Cataclysm.

Since then, he had been busy, of course, guiding his friends here to Awaihinshi, meeting the emperor, confronting and defeating Kaemusei, and everything since. He had learned some control over his magic, but most of that had been under duress, responding instinctively to danger and need.

But now, with no immediate crisis, he was taking the time to do something the monks had urged upon him before but he'd rarely found the patience for: meditate.

Though Noniki doubted even the Brothers of Many Spirits usually found themselves looking down upon their own still forms, and the world around them.

He felt a great wave of peace wash over him, soothing as a soft breeze or a warm bath. The aches of his body faded away, as did the urgency of his thoughts. Sitting like this, half in and half out of his own flesh, he could simply exist, enjoying the calmness that was the natural world. It did not care about any worries or concerns, any fears or qualms. It was not swayed by politics or war or love or greed or anything else. It simply was.

And, for the moment, Noniki was one with it.

From his partially detached perspective he could see all of Awaihinshi, in its concentric circles: Aihiri above, with its walls of pale, pure white marble; Atsani here, encircled by pale yellow; Motohori just below, surrounded by peach stone; and so on, all the way down to Mazihini, whose outer walls were tipped in pale blue resembling the water beyond them before shading down to nearly black.

But many of those walls were still crumbled in places. It had not been that long since the Silent Change had struck, with its wave of reanimated skeletons, and the city had yet to recover from the damage those creatures had caused, especially when the magic had vanished and the invasion's aerial members, lifeless once more, had plummeted from the sky. Hibikitsu had dispatched work crews to patch the walls where needed, of course, but there was still a great deal of work to be done.

Snapping back into himself, Noniki opened his eyes and smiled. What was the good of being the kingdom's only living matekai if he could not help with something like that?

Exiting their compound, Noniki briefly considered looking to see if there was any lingering damage here in Atsani but quickly decided against that. After all, this was the wealthiest level by far. Those who lived here could surely afford their own repairs. Instead he circled around to the gates leading down to Motohiri, then through there and around to the gates exiting that section as well. Below there was Sakiriti, then Bejinuri, and it was that lower level where Noniki heard the noise of men still laboring despite the twilight beginning to shadow the world.

Following the sounds, he soon came across a band of workers setting stones in a large gap of the section's outer wall. Perfect. "Help you?" one of the men called out, stepping away from the work to approach Noniki. He was a sturdy fellow, not much taller than Noniki but broader, with hair buzzed to stubble that matched his short, graying beard.

"I was hoping I might help you instead," Noniki answered. Slipping around the worker, he neared the damaged wall, finally laying a hand flat against it right near the start of the hole.

Then, closing his eyes, Noniki called upon the magic.

This was getting easier with time and practice. Particularly, he'd found, when he was asking it to do something that reinforced the natural order of things.

Like this did. Because a wall, after all, wanted to be whole.

Guiding the magic to the gap, Noniki felt it filling that space the way water poured into a cup, splashing up along the sides and quickly rising, spreading from side to side, thinly at first but thicker with each passing second. He heard gasps off to the side but continued on, allowing the magic to guide him rather than the other way round. Only when it seemed sated, when the need to restore ebbed, did he lower his hand and step back, blinking to see what he had wrought.

The wall was whole once more.

It was not, however, tidy. Where the damage had been, the pale violet stone was again intact, but rough, even jagged, like natural rock rather than dressed stone.

Still, that had to be an improvement. The wall could serve as an effective barrier between Bejinuri and Mazihini, for one thing. All they had to do was smooth that section out again for it to match the rest.

With a satisfied nod, Noniki walked away, leaving the workers to gape at his retreating back and at the wall he'd just rebuilt for them.

Returning home, he arrived just as a certain lovely young lady was approaching the front gates. "That's good timing," he said, going to greet her with a quick hug. "How did it go?"

Seikoku laughed, hugging him back. As they parted, she kissed him on the cheek, quick and tentative, and Noniki felt himself flush with pleasure. He wanted to return the gesture, but would that be acceptable? Or awkward? Was it too late now? Or could he still?

Fortunately, she was answering his question, sparing him the need to agonize over choices any further. For now. "It was good," she told him, sliding an arm around his waist as they walked toward the gates together. "They weren't too happy with me, of course, but there's not much they can do about that now. Having Takami there helped."

He could read the question in her eyes and sighed. "I know, and I wanted to attend as well, but think about it. What would've happened if I'd gone with you?"

"They would've fallen all over themselves trying to make you happy," she answered at once. Then paused, frowning.

"Exactly." He mirrored her pose, squeezing her to him just a little. "It would've been about me basically bossing them around. That wouldn't have helped you any. It'd just have made them more resentful."

She nodded. "Whereas now it had nothing to do with you. They've had to accept me into their little club on my terms, not theirs and not even yours." She tapped his nose with a forefinger. "All right, Niki, I forgive you."

"Thank you. I feel much better now." Though, truth be told, Noniki did. But then, he always did when she was around. He also liked that she'd started using the nickname Giri had given him when they were little. He could hear the affection in her tone when she said it, like a warm embrace.

"And what about you?" Seikoku asked as they crossed the courtyard and took the wide steps up to the main building. It housed only two bedchambers, one for Noniki and one for Kagiri, but more importantly right now, it also held their little community's dining hall.

A hall that was already half full, with Jitu Kanai gesturing while he told Eisen and Ryoji some story, Otokai and Amon chatting quietly, Isoro and Minawa tending to the large stewpot over the central cookfire, and a few others gathering bowls and spoons. Everyone quieted when they entered, then resumed talking all at once, half shouts of hello to Noniki and Seikoku, the other half questions about this or that matter.

"Just in time," Minawa greeted them, and Noniki laughed, giving the fierce older woman a quick hug before hurrying with Seikoku to sit on a pair of cushions along the center of the middle table. A minute later, a young man was handing them each a bowl and a set of eating sticks.

A young man with strangely mottled skin and white-streaked black hair.

"Hello, Iraku," Noniki said as their server stepped back. "How is everyone treating you so far?"

Iraku nodded, not meeting his eyes. "Everyone's been very kind and welcoming, sir. Thank you." It had not been long since Iraku and his brother Ibaru had been servants of the Silent Change, determined to wreak havoc across the nation in their master's name. But Noniki had put the cloud's trapped spirits to rest, then purged its influence from the pair. Now they were Sorainasei's newest residents.

"Ibaru has been helping Ohiro and Sukame," Seikoku explained now as Iraku went back to fetch food for some of the other residents. "But that doesn't interest Iraku, and he doesn't have any other skills yet, so we've been putting him to work helping fetch and carry and deliver. Basic things, but it keeps him out of trouble."

Noniki smiled. "That's good. It may take him some time, but eventually he'll find his place." When the brothers had asked him for help, he'd seen them as almost having a hole in them, at least in their souls, where Kaemusei had stolen part of their lives and left nothing but hunger in its place. Much like the wall he'd repaired earlier. That thought made him smile, and Seikoku poked him in the side.

"What?" she asked. So he told her what he'd done. She smiled and nodded once he had, but Noniki found her response less enthusiastic than he'd hoped. He waited, however, rather than badgering her to explain, and after a moment she spoke. "It was a good thought," she assured him first, which warned that what followed would be far less complimentary. "But I'm not sure how much you really helped them, in the long run."

"I fixed the wall!" he protested. "It had a huge hole in it, and now it doesn't! They just have to smooth it all out and the job's done!"

The look she gave him was kind, and fond, but still she shook her head. "That kind of work," Seikoku explained, "it's for a skilled artisan, a master stonecutter. Whereas what they were doing before, that's just setting bricks. Anyone can do that."

He got what she wasn't saying outright and groaned. "So instead of helping them finish their job, I turned it into a job they've got to get someone else to finish for them—someone with more experience, and so more expensive. I just made things worse."

She covered his hand with her own. "Don't blame yourself, Niki. You didn't realize. Next time, you'll do it better. And at least the wall's already intact again, so that *is* something."

Noniki laughed, if a little bitterly. "Thanks for taking some of the sting out of it. Tomorrow I'll see if I can smooth the surface myself, so they don't have to hire an artisan. I will do better, though." He took a sip of tea and a bite of food, which was simple but filling fare, grilled fish and greens over rice. "I need to."

Beside him, Seikoku poked the back of his hand with her sticks. "Stop putting yourself down. You're the first matekai in generations. The first since the Schism. It's not like you have anyone to teach you how to do all this."

Perhaps not, he admitted. But, looking around, Noniki saw a thriving, active little community. No one had taught them how to live together like this, either, or taught Seikoku how to run it. Yet she was, and they were. So why should his own journey be any different? Should mastering his magic really be any harder than managing the first town within the capital, and the first community outside the monks to use no aishone at all?

He had to do better.

For now, however, he did his best to put aside his own guilt and doubts and listen as Seikoku recounted the tale of her meeting with the lords of Atsani for him and the others. As always, he marveled at her poise, her wit, her cleverness. And when she glanced his way and smiled, his heart sped up, his pulse pounding and his cheeks flushing.

She was a wonder. And he didn't deserve her.

But he was trying his best to correct that.

CHAPTER NINE

Atukai Reizei was in a foul mood when she stomped across the veranda and back into her office. She would have felt far better had she been able to participate in martial training with her Honteno, but her leg was still too injured for her to do much more than stand on the sidelines and watch.

Reizei hated being on the sidelines.

She moved around behind her desk but did not sit, knowing that once she did, she would have difficulty standing again. Curse this wound! Besides, the news she'd just received had her too agitated to focus on such things as rosters and inventories, even though she knew she should.

Instead, she circled the desk and limped to the door, tapping her cane alongside with each step. Sliding the door open, she stepped out into the hall, following that down to a juncture and another, wider door across it. Pushing that one open, Reizei startled slightly as a pair of figures came into view. One was tall and the other short, and both were clad in full armor but the former's was all in mottled green while the latter wore black trimmed in gold. It was the second Reizei focused on.

"Ah, Taikoro Misataki," she called out, clomping toward the pair, who broke off their conversation and turned to greet her. "I wondered if I might have a quick word? Lord Rojiri." That last was said with a bow to the tall young man, who nodded in return.

"Taikoro Atukai. Of course," Misataki Shizumi replied.

At her side, Kagiri smiled. "I'll leave you both to it."

Reizei started to nod but then had a thought. "Actually, you might wish to join us as well, my lord. It could be informative, and it will save me having to repeat myself." Turning, she retraced her steps, returning to her office and placing herself behind her desk, though she did not sit right away. Instead, she rested both hands on it and leaned forward, taking the weight off her damaged leg. Ah, bones, that felt better!

Her two guests paused before the desk, where two simple chairs were set, but after a second they chose to follow her example and remain standing. Reizei saw the emerald-armored warrior's eyes dart to the alcove behind her, and knew he was looking at the urn there, its matte finish all blue and black like the night sky. He and Shizumi had both been present when the emperor had entrusted the container—and its contents—to her. For that held the bones of Reizei's predecessor, the legendary Maniko Kohori.

Thinking about her former commander threatened to overwhelm Reizei, and so she focused on the present instead. "I've received some unsettling news," she began, focusing on the black-clad young woman before her. "Two of my Honteno reported that you bullied them in the halls earlier, ordering them about as if they were servants." Shizumi bristled and opened her mouth, but Reizei held up a hand, cutting her off. "I will have to ask you not to disrupt the chain of command by interfering with my guards. If you need something from them, you can bring it to me and I will decide whether to acquiesce to your demands."

Shizumi's narrowed eyes and flushed cheeks showed her displeasure. "Your Honteno were in fact bullying my Honjofu," she snapped. "My only orders to them, as you put it, were to show some respect for their fellow warriors and not attempt to boss *them* around!"

Reizei considered that. "That is not what they told me," she said slowly, "but then they would paint themselves in the best possible light for this. What exactly did you tell your soldiers to do?"

The other woman recounted the incident in full and Reizei wasn't sure whether to laugh, cry, or scream. Had she ever been that young? Or that arrogant? Probably. "Very well," she said finally. "You were correct to act, of course, as your own were involved. But in future I would ask you, again, to bring any concerns to me first. Aihiri is my domain, not yours."

"Excuse me?" Shizumi took a step forward, and Reizei's every instinct screamed at her to draw her blade, nock an arrow, or duck under the desk—either fight or take cover from the battle clearly about to engulf her. But the other woman got control of herself after a moment and stopped with a few inches still between her and the desk, though her hands were clenched and her neck taut as she spoke, nearly spitting the words in her fury.

"The Honteno are responsible for the security of Aihiri, and the safety of its occupants, particularly the emperor," she all but recited. "But the Honjofu are also quartered here. My offices are in the next corridor over. My bed is in the barracks beyond that. So while your duties may be here, this is as much my home as yours." Now she leaned on the desk, her face within inches of Reizei's own, dark eyes boring into hers. "So do not presume to tell me what to do, Taikoro Atukai. And do not *ever* attempt to give me orders. We are of equal rank, you and I. No more."

She stayed there an instant, glaring, before pushing off from the desk and spinning about, marching out of the room, and nearly tearing the door free as she slammed it shut behind her. Reizei felt the air pressure shift and lessen as if a storm had just passed through and found herself sagging slightly in relief.

"Well," her remaining guest commented. "That could have gone better, I think."

"Could it, now?" she shot back, her frayed nerves snapping. "How insightful of you. No wonder the emperor chose you for his Rojiri, with a keen eye like that."

He offered a slight smile, holding up spread hands. "No need to pick a fight with me," he said. "I'm not your enemy and I've no part in this little feud you've started with her."

His mild tone and calm demeanor only served to anger her further. "I didn't start this fight!" she declared, aware that her voice was rising but unable to force it back down. "She can't go around telling my people what to do! Outside Awaihinshi, the Honjofu may call the shots, but in here is Honteno territory and she'd do well to remember that!" She eyed him anew as another thought struck her. "For that matter, your soldiers don't belong here at all. Make sure you keep them out of my way."

Kagiri actually laughed at her. "I've hardly been parading them about," he pointed out. "My generals and a few of my other officers report to me here, certainly, but our training grounds and barracks are down in Mazihini. Not exactly an issue."

"Good." She sniffed and straightened, trying to regain her composure and her dignity. "Make sure you keep it that way or I'll be forced to take steps."

Shizumi's rage had been a bonfire, burning hot and bright and raising sweat on Reizei's brow. But now it was as if frost had descended upon them, the temperature of the room plummeting until she shivered. She could almost see her breath pluming out before her as Kagiri shifted, suddenly much, much closer. Gone was the genial smile, the relaxed posture. In the friendly young man's place now stood a demon in green, face as hard as a menatu, each motion as fluid and deadly as a quisuin.

"I command the armies of Rimbaku," he reminded her, his voice chillingly calm. "I am, as you so rightly recall, one of the emperor's Rojiri. But first and foremost, I am Gensaiba. Do not attempt to give me orders, little Taikoro. Or you will find yourself facing me, not across a desk but in the yard, with drawn blades." He smiled, the expression as pointed and deadly as a tiger's. "And you will be welcome to use whatever aishone you like. It will not make a bit of difference." His departure was quieter than Shizumi's had been, smooth and swift like an arrow, leaving his warning lingering in the air behind him.

It took two full breaths for Reizei to unlock her limbs and sink into the chair behind her.

"Bones." She rested her head in her hands. "That *really* could have gone better."

She had meant merely to discuss the incident her warriors had mentioned and to resolve any lingering tensions. Instead she'd attempted to bully, and had infuriated in return, both her fellow Taikoro and the Dogenriku. The two deadliest warriors in all Rimbaku. Both of whom now wanted to kill her.

"Because, let's face it, Reizei," she told herself. "You were an ass."

How had that gone so incredibly, horribly wrong? And what, if anything, could she do to fix it?

Reizei was a career soldier. She'd served in the Honteno for years. But she'd never had to be in charge of anything more than the occasional bantao before. What did she know about leadership? About command? Or about working with the leaders of other forces?

Clearly, not very much.

With a sigh she glanced behind her. Kohori would have known what to do. She never would have made such a mess of things. Reizei had always admired that about her commander, both her calm and her patience.

Patience was not one of Reizei's strong suits.

She frowned as a thought struck her, and turned to regard the urn more fully. All of Kohori's wisdom was contained within that ceramic shell. All her experience. All her knowledge. All right there, waiting to be used.

Of course, that was the Relicant Way. The old way. The way the emperor and his Rojiri were determined to change.

Yet they had not changed it yet.

"Only in the direst of circumstances," she'd promised. Only then would she use the aishone.

But wasn't this dire, having Shizumi and Kagiri furious with her? When could she be more in need of Kohori's guidance?

Shifting, she pulled herself forward enough to grab the urn and lift it from its alcove, swinging around to set it down on her desk instead.

Reizei stared at it for several long moments, then reached slowly for the lid. Surely, one time would not hurt anything.

CHAPTER TEN

Fujitai Takami was doing his best. He truly was.

But the way his eyelids were growing heavy and his body was drooping, he suspected he was losing this battle.

With an effort, he sat up straight, blinked rapidly several times, and, when even that failed to help, clenched his hands below the table, digging his nails into his palms.

That last one finally helped stave off the impending doze that kept threatening him while Master Eijiri and Master Narai droned on.

He was not being kind, he knew. His two fellow Rojiri were both well-educated, well-spoken men, both master merchants, with Eijiri the head of the great Chohu gem house and Narai a more diversified merchant and trader who dabbled in many industries. Hibikitsu had recruited them specifically because they knew the workings of the world and especially of business and trading and money, in ways no noble-born ever could. They brought a different perspective to the council, and that was immensely valuable.

If only it wasn't also so immensely boring!

"Surely two tan is reasonable," Eijiri was saying now, stroking his neat little beard as he often did, his jeweled rings winking in the lantern light. "If a family can sustain itself on half a tan, this is four times that amount, allowing them to sell the other three portions or trade them or stockpile them, as they see fit."

"But why limit it?" Narai replied, equally stylish as his fellow merchant if far less flashy, with no jewels in evidence and no gold or silver thread to his clothes, yet all of it sewn from the finest cloth. "Why not let each man, each woman, each family rise to the level of their own ability? If someone has the means and the wherewithal to claim three tan, or four, or six, why not allow it?"

They were arguing over rice. Rice! Takami groaned and rubbed at his cheek. What did it matter? It was rice, for the First Emperor's sake!

But of course it *did* matter. Particularly since no one outside the ten highest families could farm more than half a tan, meaning those ten houses controlled all the rice production in Rimbaku. They also controlled the cotton, silk, and iron, but for now Narai in particular was focused on the rice.

Seikoku shifted, as always reminding Takami of a cat with her quiet grace and agility. "I agree that we shouldn't prevent people from achieving as much as they can," she offered, her clear voice cutting through the argument for the moment as the two merchants gave her their attention. "But perhaps it makes sense to ease into this gradually, as we are doing in other areas? Allow up to two tan per household to start. Then, if successful, in a year or so increase that to four? I'd hate to see people overreach themselves and wind up unable to feed their families because they got greedy and grabbed for more than they could handle."

Across from her, Shizumi nodded. "I agree. Let people get used to the idea first. Going from half a tan to two is still a vast improvement." They were an interesting contrast, Takami thought, both young women and both graceful but in different ways. Seikoku had the sleekness of a cat, while Shizumi had the fluidity and speed of a warrior. Both impressive and both highly capable, though.

The third woman at the table stirred as if about to speak, but did not, only the rustling of her crimson armor shattering the quiet. He had noticed, when they'd gathered this morning, that she and Shizumi had bristled at each other like warring serpents, which was odd—he'd thought the Honteno and the Honjofu were allies, particularly here in Aihiri. But perhaps something had stirred up trouble between them.

Kagiri was the next to weigh in. "I think two is an excellent start," he said, as soft-spoken and serious as ever, though he then added with a small smile, "I cannot even imagine what our village would have done with such a bounty!"

His brother laughed. "They'd have thrown a feast and gotten sick off it!" he said, grinning. Noniki was often smiling or laughing, but in that way that made you want to join in. It was an admirable trait, and one Takami wished he shared. He felt he was more like Kagiri, however, somber and thoughtful. Also not bad traits, of course.

"I believe we are all in agreement, then?" Narai asked, seemingly forgetting his own opposition to the proposed new limit as he glanced around the table. Takami nodded, as did Futoba and Noniki. "Excellent. We should present this plan to the emperor. If he agrees, we can confer with him and the karos to determine when best to proclaim this reform." He favored the rest of them with a smile Takami still found a little oily, for all that it was also charming. "I would be happy to take the lead on writing this up."

The others all agreed—none of them seemed as inclined toward the task, so why argue about it?—and they all rose, stretching and yawning as they did. They had been in discussion for several hours, and the sun was already more than halfway past the midpoint. Soon it would be dusk once more.

Eijiri was the first to make his goodbyes. "I must attend to my house, though of course they manage well enough with most things in my absence," the master jeweler explained, bowing to each of them before exiting the council chamber. Narai was next, and Takami did not miss Kagiri's frown as the merchant left, favoring one side as he walked. He knew they had a shared history of some sort, and Kagiri had been the one to bring Narai to first speak with the emperor. At the same time, it seemed their Gensaiba did not fully trust the man.

That made Takami cautious, since he was learning to value the emerald warrior's opinion. Could Narai's passion for this question of rice have a more selfish component? He wondered if the man owned property beyond Awaihinshi—land suitable for rice paddies, for example—and how he might find out.

Still considering that question, Takami filed out with the others. Kagiri and Shizumi soon excused themselves to practice swordplay together—notably not inviting Reizei to join them, though her injury would have precluded participation anyway— while Noniki and Seikoku headed back to their own little community. Reizei clattered away to see to her troops, which left only Futoba and himself.

"What are your plans for the evening?" he asked his fellow noble, and she favored him with a small smile.

"I must tend to my house," she answered. "We are still settling in, and no doubt my housekeeper will be waiting by the door with a list of questions. Hopefully, she'll at least wait until I've eaten something before demanding answers." With a tip of her head and a small wave, Futoba departed as well.

Yes, Takami thought as he followed after. *I understand the "still settling in" part, at least.*

Part of that "settling in" involved his next stop, and the meeting he had arranged there. Takami had initially been surprised to learn that the Dogenkaishu's office was here in the imperial compound, rather than down by the docks. After all, this was the farthest point from the water in all of Awaihinshi! Still, the Lord Commander of the aikaye, the Royal Navy, was traditionally part of the Rojiiri, and from one of the ten major noble houses. Naturally, that meant no one could expect him to traipse all the way down to Mazihini, much less venture into Suranmui beyond!

Personally, Takami found that exceedingly foolish and short-sighted. But he was hardly surprised to encounter such among the nobility, even if by blood and training he was one of that number himself.

In future, he would consider relocating his offices. For now, however, he'd decided it was best to leave them where they were.

Likewise, he had invited—with that subtle hint that it was not the sort of invitation one refused—his ranking officers to attend him there this afternoon. He had heard of Kagiri's stunt with his taisho, of course—the Dogenriku had offered to battle any and all of the generals for leadership, then removed those who had accepted his challenge and lost—and heartily approved. Most of those men had been known to Takami personally, though he had been of a low enough house to not merit their attention directly, and had always struck him as blowhards and fools. But that had left the aiashe short on leadership, and while he knew his emerald counterpart was working on correcting that, Takami had decided upon a less drastic approach, at least to start.

How this meeting went would determine if he changed his mind about that.

He had already visited his official study the previous day, to familiarize himself with it, and had been pleased enough—it was of a decent size, with sufficient lighting, and had been elegantly furnished but left largely uncluttered. A map took up much of one wall, showing Rimbaku and its surroundings but focused on detailing the rivers, lakes, and oceans rather than the land. A handsome painting of a hozaiburi hung beside the entrance; the massive but sleek warship was depicted cresting a wave, warriors lining its railings, its sails billowed out by the wind driving them on and fluttering the pennants atop each mast. The heavy teak desk that dominated the floor looked as if it had been repurposed from an old hull, and Takami approved of both the symbolism and the idea of still getting use from a ship long after it was rendered unseaworthy. The room smelled faintly of the sea as well, of oiled wood and tar and brine, and he took a deep breath as he entered now, wishing he were aboard a boat instead.

But that would have to wait. Duty came first.

A stocky man with thick white hair pulled into a tidy taikam-age was the first to arrive. He walked with the aid of a cane, and Takami recognized the worn-smooth cedar and simple brass cap as belonging to an old tsao. A bit eccentric, but certainly appropriate for a naval officer!

"Sir!" The man saluted, fist to chest. "Kagusho Daijikaga Manhachi, at your service and the empire's!"

"Kagusho Daijikaga." Takami inclined his head in response. "The emperor appreciates that, and so do I."

Another man arrived as he was speaking, this one taller and slimmer and far less rough around the edges. "Dogenkaishu," he stated, saluting while also bowing. "Kagono Ugata Genichi, at your service and that of the empire."

The next two arrived together, the younger holding the door for the elder. These were Kuyo Aoimoto, the aikaye's other kagono, and Nukimon Torazo, its other kagusho. Takami knew the army required five taisho to function fully, but the navy was smaller, since a single boat crew could transport an entire platoon.

"Gentlemen," he began once Nukimon had shut the door and they were all gathered around his desk. "Thank you for coming. I am Fujitai Takami, appointed as Dogenkaishu by our emperor." He smiled at the four, all of whom were older than him. "I am a sailor, and love the sea, but I have never been in the aikaye and I am aware that there will be gaps in my education on how things normally work. I will trust in you to help me overcome those, just as I trust that we all wish the same thing—to keep our navy strong, active, and efficient, in order to best serve the empire. I will be meeting with each of you separately at some point, to get a better sense of your duties and to see how I might best support those. For now I simply wished to introduce myself, to assure you of my intentions, and to make sure that we are currently at a state of readiness, should we be needed."

His two admirals both visibly relaxed at this news that he was not planning to replace them here and now—no doubt word of the shake-up in the aiashe had left them concerned for a similar fate. Daijikaga simply nodded, seemingly unfazed. Nukimon, on the other hand, had straightened and was eyeing Takami with increased interest. He knew that look all too well. This was a man with ambition, who saw an opportunity to advance still further. Whether he merited such advancement, only time would tell.

"We are indeed in excellent readiness, Dogenkaishu," Kuyo replied with a dismissive sniff. "Genichi and I make sure that our sailors are all fit and ready, and our officers trained and responsive."

Beside him, Ugata nodded. "Yes, our ships are all in excellent shape," he added, "all sails and hulls and ropes checked and cleaned. The fleet will make the empire proud, sir."

"All the men know their duty, and we run frequent drills and training exercises," was Nukimon's contribution. "All ships and men are fully accounted for." His words were crisp, as if to deliberately counterpoint the lazier recitals of his superiors.

Daijikaga laughed. "Nobody cares about the spit and polish," he stated baldly. "But they're good ships, and good men. They won't let you down." Takami liked him right off.

"Thank you, gentlemen," he told them all. "As I said, I'll look forward to meeting with each of you individually in the coming days and receiving more detail. For now, I am satisfied, and I know the emperor will be happy to hear he can continue to rely upon his aikaye, as always."

The four took that for the dismissal it was, and filed out, only Nukimon lingering a moment. "If you need anything else, sir, anything at all, please let me know. I am happy to assist at any time," the vice-admiral promised. Takami had to work to keep a smile on his face in the light of such naked ambition.

When he was alone again, he settled into his desk chair, which he'd been happy to discover yesterday was not only elegant but comfortable, and took a moment to simply breathe. Then he selected the first paper off the pile waiting for him and began going through the reports and requests that had gathered during the interim since his predecessor's removal. He would be getting home late, it seemed.

"Moto!" Takami called as he finally stepped through the front gates, letting the heavy beamed doors slide shut behind him. "Are you here? Please tell me you've scrounged together something to eat!"

His words echoed across the expansive courtyard. The estate had belonged to the Fujibuki, one of the ten great families, but their last member had died—been murdered, in point of fact, as part of a plot to kill the emperor himself—a few weeks ago. With no heirs left, not even distant cousins, the house was now extinct. Hibikitsu had granted Takami the lands and titles when he became a Rojiri, and so now this grand home was his, with all its gardens and courtyards and ponds and bridges and towers. It was an impressive place, and easily capable of supporting a large family in lavish style.

Takami just wished he had the family to go with it.

Crossing the courtyard and then the small bridge over the little river, he skipped up the steps to the front door, threw it open—and froze, staring at the sunset-clad figure beyond.

"Kai? What are you doing here?"

Kazutai Katani, head of House Kazutai—and Takami's elder brother—turned to face him, flicking his orange-and-white fan open and closed in that way that said he was annoyed. "And greetings to you as well, little brother," he replied airily. "I came to see how you are getting on."

Behind him, another man appeared, looking mortified—and terrified, as well. "I am sorry, my lord," Moto stated, bowing deeply. "Lord Kazutai insisted upon waiting inside, and I did not feel it was my place to refuse."

"And in that you were correct, good Moto," Katani agreed, not even glancing back at the servant. "Now fetch us some tea. My brother and I have things to discuss."

Takami stepped inside and closed the door behind him. "Do we? I cannot imagine what." He did not wish to argue while standing in the entryway, however, and so led his brother instead into the small sitting room to their left.

He watched as Katani's sharp eyes took in the elegant furnishings, the polished teak floors, the delicate patterns in the rice-paper panels of the door, and the lush landscape beyond, displayed to good advantage with both outer walls drawn back from the corner. "You've done well, little brother," Katani said, helping himself to a seat upon one of the low couches placed around the little central table. "It is a fine property and will do our family very nicely."

Takami had been lowering himself onto the opposite couch but stopped mid-motion. "There is no 'our family,' Kai," he corrected, not bothering to moderate the sharpness of his tone. "I am no longer part of House Kazutai, remember?"

"Really?" Katani made a show of examining his perfectly lacquered fingernails. "I do not recall granting you permission to abandon our bloodline."

"The emperor did," Takami replied crisply, seating himself at last. "Would you care to gainsay him?"

But his brother brushed that aside. "He granted you your own house, which was a great kindness," he allowed, speaking as if it had merely been charity rather than in any way deserved. "But House Fujitai is merely a branch of House Kazutai, naturally." He sniffed at Takami, or more precisely at his attire. "You'll need to change that, of course. Blue and orange clash so terribly."

"Kai—" Takami started, leaning forward, intent upon stopping whatever his brother was scheming before it got started. But he only received a sharp-edged smile in return.

"Now, Taki, let's not fight," Katani insisted, using the pet name that always made Takami feel like he was five again. "After all, we wouldn't want word of any discord to get back to the emperor, would we? Or any repeat of the past?"

"Don't," Takami warned, but his voice came out too soft, too weak, more a plea than a command. Just as his brother had no doubt intended.

"I believe I saw stables when I arrived," Katani continued instead. "I do love to ride. You remember, don't you, Taki?"

Takami found himself unable to answer, even as his brother smirked and stood, brushing off his elegant robes.

"I will send Iri over to take measurements and begin preparations," Katani stated. "Don't worry, I'll let you keep one of the better rooms for yourself. Oh, and Mother and the girls say hello. I'll tell them you'll stop by for dinner some night soon."

And with that he swept out, leaving Takami to collapse back on the couch and curse his own weakness, his greedy brother, and the dark secret that still bound them together.

CHAPTER ELEVEN

The others were polite enough to wait until Narai had nibbled some food and taken several sips of his favorite jasmine tea before asking anything.

Shizu Yokori led off, as usual. "How did it go?" Her little silver fork snagged another candied water chestnut, her favorite.

Narai smiled around his cup. "Perfectly." He took another sip, savoring the delicate floral scent and taste, the heat on his tongue and throat. "Two tan per person." He nodded at Fujiko Oritano, sitting to his left. "You were exactly correct in your estimate."

His friend and fellow merchant beamed. "I knew it! They were never going to accept the idea of removing limits entirely, and two is a significant improvement." She arched a brow at Jiro Masute, across the table from her. "And you thought they'd settle on four!"

He shrugged, his long, silky hair floating around his thin shoulders. "Yes, yes. You win. Again." He withdrew a gold coin from his robes and flicked it toward her. Yokori snatched it with all the speed of a viper, but Masute had already turned back toward Narai. "How do you read them in general?"

Narai set his cup down and considered before replying, steepling his fingers before him. "It is a very strong group," he stated at last. "The emperor has chosen well. Two from the nobility, but neither from a previously major house, though of course both will experience significant elevation from their new appointment. Two from the merchants, including myself. Two from the military, his two Taikoros, both women and both new to their posts. And then three commoners—the first matekai in centuries, the first buhiyo in all Awaihinshi...and of course our close and dear friend Kagiri."

Yokori scowled. "Yes, yes, but what do you *make* of them?" she demanded, raising chuckles from the others. She could always be counted on to cut to the heart of a matter with that sharp tongue of hers.

But Narai did not mind. She kept him on his toes, which was valuable indeed. And their interests had always aligned, as it did with the other two—formerly three, before Kagiri had made an example of Eien Kawatai. Pushing that dark memory aside, he focused on her question.

"Master Eijiri is the one we have to watch out for the most," he began. "Though his interests have always been tightly focused on his own house and the gem trade in general, he is sharp and has as much experience navigating the politics here as I. He also seems to have no personal agenda, though that could change if gems become directly involved."

He frowned, toying with his cup, running a finger around the delicate edge. "The other I worry about is Seikoku, the young buhiyo. She has no formal training, little education, but nothing gets by her. And she has a way about her, a grace even when being blunt, an ability to remain calm and clear and level-headed. Her priority is her town, however, and they will always come first." He allowed himself a small smile. "Them and Noniki, now a matekai. I suspect she loses objectivity where he is concerned."

"He was always a hothead, as I recall," Masute remarked. "Surely we can turn that impulsiveness to our advantage?"

Narai shifted, trying as always to ease the pain in his hip and grimacing as he did. "He has changed," he explained once he'd resettled himself. "He is still passionate, still plainspoken, but that rage is gone. Though if she were at risk, or their friends, or his brother, I suspect he could be goaded into action still."

"And the others?" Yokori prodded. "What of the two nobles, for example? We know nothing about them!"

"No, but they could be useful," he answered. "Fujitai Takami was born and raised here and knows the city and its ways but never concerned himself with politics. He was the second son of a minor house, and all his attention is on the water. He is earnest but could be led." He smiled. "Heiayuki Futoba is from the provinces, only newly arrived. She knows little of Awaihinshi. And though she was already head of her house, they were a branch of the Ieuyuki. She is desperate to shake off that connection and restore her family's honor. That, and her compassion, could easily be exploited."

Masute sniffed, reaching for a dumpling and laughing as he snatched it just before Oritano could. "And the warriors?" he asked around the mouthful. "They should be easy to manipulate."

Narai tapped his forefingers against his chin. "I would not count on that, no. Neither of them has much experience at giving counsel, it's true, but they are both soldiers, and loyal to a fault. They'd react aggressively to any perceived threat, and they with-hold their thoughts unless pressed." He allowed himself a slow smile. "They can be played against each other, however. And the Honjofu leader, Shizumi, has an additional weakness. Kagiri."

"Oho!" That was Oritano, slapping her leg. "Our young friend has found himself a lover? Good for him!" She probably meant that, though none of them would ever doubt she had ulterior motives as well. They all did, after all.

"I do not know if it has gone that far," Narai corrected. "But there is interest there, on both sides." They all knew what that meant. It was potential leverage, not only against the Taikoro but against their own former pawn turned master…turned who knew what now.

Not surprisingly, it was Yokori who asked: "And how are the two of you managing together?" There was no question as to who she meant.

"Fine," Narai allowed. "He watches my every move, waiting for me to do something questionable." He smiled. "But he is still a boy, and he thinks like a warrior. I think like a merchant."

They all raised their cups to that. Yes, things were progressing nicely, Narai decided as they continued their meal, shifting to talk about their upcoming plans. The empire was in good hands, including his own, and he would see it flourish.

If he and his friends prospered from that connection as well, what was the harm in that?

CHAPTER TWELVE

Noniki dreamt.

He was floating over the land, with no sense of body, only thought and spirit. It was much like when he'd meditated, only now he was soaring higher, farther, leaving Awaihinshi behind to drift across the Edishu and then the Wagata, following the mighty Tonawa south and then east before turning south again to follow the Rumiri instead. Miniri stretched out before him, much of that region dry and dusty but broken here and there by patches of green. Up ahead he could see the shoreline and the sea beyond, but even as he worried about becoming lost over that vast stretch of water Noniki felt his headlong rush slowing. He was also skewing slightly to his right, and not through any choice of his own.

Something was drawing him in that direction.

There was a town below, no more than a half dozen rough buildings among as many lean-tos and canvas tents, but as he descended Noniki thought it looked as if a mighty storm had swept through the place. Temporary structures had been tossed about and even the more permanent ones had been misshapen, as if a giant hand had shoved them away. What could have done something like this?

He saw no people about, which was equally odd. And no blood, no signs of battle. The place was simply shattered and empty, like a cracked snail shell after the owner had already vacated.

In the dream, Noniki longed to touch down, to feel the earth beneath his feet, so that he could investigate this strange destruction more fully. But instead, whatever had drawn him here pulled him away again, heading north and west but at a far slower pace and much closer to the ground.

Even so, it seemed mere minutes before he found himself amid another wrecked village.

Still he could not stop, and up ahead Noniki spied a third town, though from a distance this one looked intact and full of life.

Between it and him, however, was something else. Something he'd thought never to see again.

When he'd first encountered Kaemusei, that force had presented itself as a swirling cloud of blacks and whites and grays, with bursts of color shot through it.

What lurked up ahead was similar. Smaller, perhaps. With more color, though only a single shade, of vivid light blue. Yet it was a whirling ball of energy, just as the Silent Change had been.

But the Silent Change was gone. Noniki had dispersed and dispatched it.

What, then, was he looking at now?

He woke with a start, and it took a moment to remember where he was and why. Then he shifted, his bed creaking from the motion. A breeze drifted in through the small window overhead, and Noniki remembered. He was in Sorainasei. He was safe.

But he also knew something else for certain.

That had been no dream.

"For now, we must continue to make do with you four," Kagiri told his taishos as they all gathered around the desk in his office, standing since there were only three seats and five people—six if you counted Fuko Miyosi, who stood in one corner, quill and writing tablet in hand, ready to jot down any orders or questions or other notes. "Taisho Daishin, Taisho Masagi, as you two have the most experience you will divide the final gyunao between you if we have need to deploy all our forces." He smiled. "Fortunately, we are not currently at war with anyone, that I'm aware." Masagi Matsu smiled politely at the attempted joke. Daishin Nishoji looked like he was trying to understand it—and failing miserably. Soma Yamani might have been carved of stone for all the response she showed. At least Tsuneto laughed! And the stocky little soldier looked the part now, too, since both he and Yamani had been properly outfitted as befitted taisho in the aiashe.

Kagiri was starting to ask how his generals thought they should deploy their troops for the time being when someone knocked on the doorframe. It was several quick, impatient raps, and Kagiri found himself grinning as he hurried to answer, waving Miyosi off. Sure enough, it was his brother standing without, breathing heavily from no doubt running here.

"Niki!" His amusement at the interruption vanished at once because his little brother was drenched in sweat, his simple clothes clinging to him, his hair plastered down. "What's happened? Are you all right?" Kagiri's thoughts went to the last time his brother had looked so fatigued and so concerned. "Are we under attack again?"

Noniki shook his head. "No." He glanced up, meeting Kagiri's eyes. "At least, I don't think so." He glanced into the office. "Sorry to disrupt your meeting, but this can't wait."

"Of course. Come in." Kagiri stepped aside, shutting the door again after his brother had entered, and ushering him to join them around the desk. "I don't believe you've met my generals..." he started, but his usually genial brother was ignoring the four soldiers. His attention had gone straight to the massive map mounted on the wall behind them.

"Yes," Noniki was muttering to himself as he stepped past them to study the image of Rimbaku displayed there. He raised his hand, tracing the Tonawa to its juncture with the Rumiri and then down that river's length to the southern coast. "Somewhere in here," he said, splaying his fingers so that they and his palm covered much of Bezenkai, his thumb nearly grazing the spot that was Ginzai on the map. He glanced back at Kagiri. "This is where the trouble is."

Masagi coughed politely. "Begging your pardon, Rojiri," he stated with a bow, because of the course the elegant officer knew who Noniki was. "But there isn't any trouble there. There can't be. That whole region is nothing but dirt and the occasional rice farm or fishing village. And the southern fortifications are there to prevent any possible incursion from the sea."

"Yet I felt it," Noniki insisted, still focused on Kagiri alone as he lowered his hand and turned back toward them fully. "There's something there. Something dangerous. And it's coming this way."

Daishin was frowning. "Could it be the Higinasi?" he asked. "They've never troubled us before, but their kingdom lies to the south, perhaps they skirted along the shoreline to sneak up the river? Or perhaps it is raiders from the sea?"

Noniki shook his head. "Nothing so mundane, I'm afraid," he replied. "It held hints of Kaemusei, but it is not the same." His eyes appealed to Kagiri. "It is there, though. I am sure of it. And it is a threat, a serious one."

Kagiri nodded. He trusted his brother with his life and always had. Noniki's strange new powers only meant his brother was aware of more in the world, not less. "Who is in charge of the southern fortifications?" he asked his officers. "I know Atsumi Izo had been handling the placements there." Atsumi had been one of the Taisho when Kagiri had inherited the role of Dogenriku, but the tall, stylish nobleman had proven too arrogant to take orders from a mere commoner, and Kagiri had stripped him of his rank and position.

Interestingly, it was Soma who answered. "I believe Issa Kiso Akinari is still in charge there, sir!" she stated crisply. When Kagiri raised an eyebrow she added, "I served under him during the campaign against the Kindichi. He's a good man, sir, loyal and competent."

"Very well." Kagiri tapped his chasai against his leg, considering. "I assume the fastest way to get word to Issa Kiso is by boat, or do we have homing pigeons?"

Miyosi cleared his throat. "Unfortunately, sir," the clerk explained, never meeting Kagiri's eyes, "those fortifications are too new for pigeons to have been raised there yet. The command staff should have several from here to send us messages, but we have nothing that could go to them.

All of his generals nodded—but Noniki grinned, some of his usual cheer returning.

"I believe I can come up with something a little faster than a boat," he offered. Now approaching the desk, he frowned, searching its contents before pulling out a blank parchment and a quill. "Write a message to him," he instructed, pushing the writing implements toward Kagiri. "Hand it to me when you're done."

Kagiri nodded and, taking his seat, penned a quick order instructing the colonel to dispatch a shotao into Bezenkai, checking for any disturbances. "I don't know entirely where to send him, or what he should look for," he warned as he wrote, "but if there's a problem, hopefully they'll spot it." Finishing the letter, he took up his ahaiinko, mixing ink and pressing the engraved end into that dark puddle, then transferring the official seal to the document. Blowing on the whole thing to dry it, he offered the page to Noniki.

"Thank you." Taking the letter, Noniki laid it flat upon the desk again. His hands moved quickly, folding this part and that, and after a moment he held up a neatly done paper bird, much like the ones they'd learned to make as youths to delight the smaller children. Not pausing to admire his handiwork, he carried the urigani figure to the room's outer door, which Tsuneto quickly slid past to open for him. "Issa Kiso Akinari," Kagiri heard his brother whisper to the paper figure. "Along the southern shore. Find him, wait for his answer, and then return here once you have it."

There was a sudden breeze, carrying the scent of fresh flowers and grass—and the paper bird flexed, rustling, and rose from Noniki's hand with a fluttering of its folded wings. Wobbling at first, it quickly straightened and took off into the early morning light, its flight so swift it was soon out of sight.

"That will reach him by noon," Noniki promised, turning back to them now that he was empty-handed, and he laughed at the look on the assembled taishos' faces. "I am sorry to have shocked you all," he said, seeming more his usual self now that he'd addressed his concerns. "I'll let you resume your meeting."

Kagiri showed him to the door. "I'll let you know as soon as I hear anything," he promised, seeing his brother out.

"Thank you." Noniki's eyes were still shadowed, and his face more somber than usual. "I am not imagining it, Giri. Something is coming."

"I believe you," Kagiri assured him. "And whatever it is, we'll be ready."

Returning to his generals, he found Daishin still standing as if stunned, Masagi doing his best to look unimpressed—and failing—and both Soma and Tsuneto looking thoughtful. "If only there were a way for us to do what your brother just did," Tsuneto commented. "Think of how quickly and easily we could transmit orders and receive reports!"

Kagiri laughed. "Yes, that would be helpful," he agreed. "But, since we can't, let's focus on what we can do for now, hm?" Still, he clapped the recently promoted general on the shoulder to show he appreciated both his willingness to innovate and his speaking up with ideas, before diving back into the matters at hand.

A part of him, however, remained focused on the map hanging behind them, and the paper bird now winging its way south—and wondering what that magical messenger would find.

CHAPTER THIRTEEN

"**S**ir! Sir!" Makino Tsunaka burst into Kiso Akinari's office, something small and fluttery cradled in his cupped hands. The junior lieutenant hurried across the room and carefully, almost reverently, set the item down upon Akinari's desk.

"What is this, exactly, Tsunaka?" Akinari asked his subordinate, but gently. Tsunaka was a terrible soldier, but that was not entirely his fault, given both his lack of coordination and his family's lack of funds to purchase him adequate aishone. He was a decent man, however, if a bit high-strung, and an excellent clerk. None of which explained the urigani bird the shosa had just placed before him.

"It just arrived, sir!" Tsunaka hurried to explain, his words tumbling over themselves as they did when he got excited. "Came in through the hall window!"

"Through the...?" Akinari studied his clerk, trying to decide if this was some elaborate joke, but he'd never known the man to kid about aiashe business, and he seemed sincere enough now. Puzzled, awed, maybe even a little afraid, but sincere. "You're saying it blew in from outside?"

Tsunaka shook his head vigorously. "No, sir! It flew in! Under its own power!"

Akinari tapped the paper figure, and only years of training kept him from jumping when it shifted, folding in its wings just like a real nesting bird. How was that even possible? As he and Tsunaka watched, the paper unfolded itself, settling down flat before him—and he caught his breath, seeing the seal at the bottom.

"This is from the Dogenriku himself," he declared, quickly reading the letter. "Summon my shosa at once!"

Tsunaka bowed, then saluted, then stumbled away, already calling for messengers as he fled the room. Behind him, Akinari sighed, then used the relative quiet to read the letter a second time. What it said made little sense in and of itself, but when combined with the strangeness of the message…well, he had little choice but to take it seriously.

"We have received word," he stated a short time later, "of a new threat originating in Bezenkai, not far from the Rumiri. The Dogenriku has instructed us to investigate and to report back at once with any information we can gather about it."

His two majors—the other two were both out on patrol and could not be reached in time for this meeting—stirred and glanced at each other. Predictably, it was Makino Tsunaka who spoke first.

"What manner of threat, sir?" Makino asked, stroking his narrow mustache. "Raiders? Bandits? Rebels?"

"We don't know," Akinari admitted. "Though the letter suggests that it may be more…eldritch in nature."

He was unsurprised to see Makino smile, an arrogant, unfriendly expression. "Eldritch, sir? Has the new Dogenriku perhaps been imbibing too much rice wine?"

Beside him, Haga Emitsu chuckled. "From what I heard, he may not be old enough to drink tsekuri!" The two men smirked at each other, and Akinari found his temper rising, as it often did when forced to deal with the pair. Why, in the First Emperor's name, couldn't he have sober, competent officers instead of these two preening martinets?

He allowed a bit of steel to enter his voice as he snapped, "Shall I inform our lord commander, then, that you choose to disbelieve his word and flout his direct order?"

Both men straightened, faces paling as they realized they had gone too far. "No, of course not, sir!" Haga managed, saluting. "I will send out a bantao at once!"

"A shotao," Akinari corrected, and took some pleasure in the way his major's eyes widened. "Dogenriku's orders."

"Of course, sir. A shotao, led by one of my finest. To patrol Bezenkai along the Rimuri, seeking any signs of possible trouble." Haga was capable of performing his duties when pressed, and now at Akinari's nod he did a credible about-face and marched from the room.

Makino shook his head. "Better him than me," he muttered, offering a lazy salute before exiting as well.

Only once they'd both gone did Tsunaka, who'd been standing in the corner, clear his throat. "Why didn't you tell them about the letter, sir?" he asked. "About the magic?"

Akinari sighed. "Because they just would have jeered more, and questioned my sanity and yours," he answered. "Haga will send a shotao, as ordered. That is enough."

A part of him wished he could go himself, but of course that was impossible. He had far too many duties here. Still, if there was anything out there, Haga's men would find it. Even as he thought that, however, Akinari felt that sinking feeling in his gut that often warned him of trouble. He'd already known that the Dogenriku would not have sent such a message, in such a fashion, for an idle rumor. His instincts merely confirmed the fact. The threat was real.

"Where're we going, exactly?" Haru asked, strapping on his jin-gaso and checking his chokoto in its scabbard.

"Wild goose chase, from the sound of it," Tamura answered, already swinging into his saddle. "But orders're orders, so it's off we go."

"Nice day for it, anyway," Yatsu offered from his own horse. "I don't mind getting out of the fort for a bit."

"Easy for you to say," Tori grumbled next to him. "You don't have to ride in front. I'm the one getting bugs in her teeth."

Haru laughed. "Serves you right for being such a good rider," he teased. "You get to ride with the chuisu while we're back here with the rest."

Tori pulled a face, which only made the others laugh more. Especially when Sechimi rode up and called, "Shotao, fall out! Tori, you're with me!"

The platoon moved out, twenty riders in all, loosely grouped in bantao of four or five—except for Sechimi and Tori, who rode out in front of the rest. "I wish you wouldn't single me out like that, sir," Tori grumbled as they exited the fort, their horses snorting at sheer pleasure from being let loose on the plains once more, dust pluming beneath their hooves as they galloped ahead.

The lieutenant could have taken offense at such rank insubordination. Instead she just favored Tori with an indulgent smile. "I don't do it because you're the only other woman in the first unit, you know," she chided gently. "I do it because you really are the best rider we've got. After me, of course."

Tori's grimace twisted into a smirk. "Oh, really? *After* you? We'll see about that!" Tapping her heels to her horse's flanks, a laugh of pure joy exploded from her lips as she shot ahead.

"Disrespect!" Sechimi hissed, but she was laughing too as she raced to catch up and the rest of the unit followed behind.

They'd been riding for an hour, slowing to a walk in order to preserve the horses' strength, when they spotted the first village. "That's Onokura," Tori said, shielding her eyes. "Good aragei and heioki there."

Beside her, Sechimi rolled her eyes. "Spoken like a true soldier, thinking with your stomach," she teased. But her laughter ceased and her smile faded as they rode into Onokura, and she felt her stomach twist upon seeing the devastation there. "Some kind of fire?" she muttered. "But not the buildings—that looks like storm winds."

"Those people were burned, all right," Tamura agreed, the rest of the squad having caught up to them. "Oil, maybe? Killed first, then burned?"

"No," Sechimi corrected grimly. "Look at their positions. Those people were running when they burned. Flame arrows, could be. Taken away when they left to cover up what'd happened."

They rode through the village without another word, everyone taking great care to keep their horses from stepping on any of the twisted, blackened bodies strewn across the one wide dirt road. "We'll come back and bury them properly later," Sechimi promised once they were beyond the grisly site. "But for now, I want whoever did this."

Around her, her soldiers nodded, and it was with fresh purpose that they set out once more. No one thought it a wild goose chase now.

They passed through three more villages, smaller than Onokura but otherwise much the same, before Haru, who had the sharpest eyes, called out, "Someone up ahead!"

"How many?" Sechimi asked at once, drawing her naritaba from its sheath at her horse's side and laying the weapon across her lap, ready for use.

"I'm just seeing one," Haru reported. He frowned. "Not enough dust, though, even if he's walking."

Sechimi glanced at her soldiers. "Everyone at the ready!" she ordered. "We don't know who this is, could be a survivor, could be a scout—could be bait. Stay alert, and attack at the first sign of a threat!" Whatever had killed those villagers had done so too quickly for them to escape or fight back, so she wasn't taking any chances.

As they neared, she saw that Haru had been correct. It was a single man, on foot, walking at a decent pace but not running. And there wasn't any dust rising beneath his feet. How had he managed that?

"Hello!" she called out as they drew closer, close enough for her to see his wild hair, long beard, and frayed clothes. "Do you need help, sir?"

The man stopped and turned to face her. "Help?" he replied, his voice deep and echoing. "We all need help. This whole land needs help. It is dying, decaying, in the final stages of ruin. It must be swept clean and planted afresh."

Something in his eyes made Sechimi pause. They were alight, the way she'd seen in only the very fervent—or the very crazed. "Sir," she said, slowing her horse a few paces from him. "Are you responsible for the deaths of those villagers?"

He laughed in reply. "Death? You cannot kill that which is no longer truly alive."

"Sir!" It was Haru, hissing at her from one side. "Sir, look at his feet!"

Sechimi glanced down at the man's feet, in their cracked, worn-out old boots—and felt a chill ripple through her.

She could see air between his boot soles and the ground.

"By order of the Emperor, I am placing you under arrest!" she declared, swinging her naritaba around and down, its sharp edge halted inches from the man's throat. "Resist and we will be forced to attack!"

He laughed at her, despite the blade hovering near his neck. "Resist? Oh, yes, I believe I shall resist. And I acknowledge no emperor. Stand aside or perish." His words were measured, cold, with a trace of mockery, and Sechimi did not bother to respond.

Instead she tightened her grip and swung.

There was a crackle of heat, a flash. Her naritaba melted away before it could brush the stranger's skin. Whatever had caused that swept up the weapon and over her hands and arms. Sechimi screamed as her limbs disintegrated.

Her shotao attacked. There were screams and cries, arrows and spears and swords.

The man grinned, baring yellowed teeth—and a wind flung the entire platoon back. Horses were bowled off their feet, crushing their riders beneath them. Weapons spun away. Blades snapped.

The burning had spread to Sechimi's chest, and down to her legs.

Tamura charged—and burst into flame.

Haru fired an arrow—and was flattened by a boulder slamming into him from the side.

Tori and Yatsu swept in from either side—and turned to ice, shattering from their own momentum.

Sechimi felt lightheaded. Her vision was blurring, darkening. She could no longer draw breath.

The last of her soldiers died as she did.

Standing over them, the man studied the bits and pieces that had been a full shotao. "Disgraceful," he sniffed, and a wave of fire spread out from him, turning them all to ash for the wind to carry away.

Then, with a scowl, he turned and started across the plains once more.

CHAPTER FOURTEEN

Futoba was bone tired as she left Aihiri, so much so that she barely noticed passing through the pale yellow gates separating Atsani from Motohiri. It had been a long day, going over timing on the push to expand people's rice-farming rights and also their plans to start buying back people's aishone.

She'd known that being a Rojiri would involve a great deal of deliberation, of course. Well, she'd suspected as much, at least once the position had been offered to her. But she hadn't expected such lengthy and detailed deliberations! Kishin Narai in particular seemed a very devil for details, wanting to nail down every possible permutation to make sure everything would be absolutely clear, with no room for disagreement, confusion, or error. That was good, she supposed, but now the sun was already setting and she just wanted to go home and eat something, have some hot tea, and put her feet up.

Home. It still felt strange calling the estate here in Awaihinshi that. Futoba had grown up in eastern Yunigiri, not far from Obanari. She had only been here to the fabled City of Polished Light a handful of times as an adult, initially with her father and then once or twice on her own after he had passed and she'd taken up the leadership of their house. Most of the time, their estate here had sat empty save for a few servants dedicated to maintaining it, and when she'd arrived it had just been her and her personal maid, Hana, because she hadn't been sure how long they'd be staying.

Or whether they'd be allowed—or able—to leave.

When Futoba reached the estate's front gates tonight, however, she found them flung wide open, a small caravan of horses and wagons filling the small courtyard beyond. Her heart raced, a thrill jolting through her, and she was suddenly awake and alert. Restless with newfound energy, she dodged the heavily laden animals and all but ran up the front steps and into the main house.

"Mama!" She had barely crossed the threshold before a bundle of dark hair, blue silk, and sticky flesh barreled into her legs. "We're here!"

"You are?" Leaning down, Futoba scooped her daughter up in her arms and then spun around, peering past the giggling five-year-old. "Where? I don't see you!"

"Right here, mama!" Inomi reached out with both grubby hands and grabbed Futoba's cheeks, dragging her mother's face to hers. "I'm here!"

"Oh! Inomi! *There* you are!" Futoba's heart soared listening to her daughter laugh, the absolute best sound in the world. She spun again, and this time spotted the short, stocky man waiting by the main sitting room's door, an even smaller child cradled in his arms. With two steps Futoba had closed the distance and was hugging her husband and son as well, with both Inomi and little Kiyo squealing happily.

"I am so happy to see you," she told Iefusa when she finally pulled back enough for them all to breathe.

"And I you," he assured her, his voice as soft as ever but the sparkle in his eye assuring her it was true. "But I should warn you—"

Whatever else he'd meant to add was interrupted by a loud, "My lady!" as Arima stomped into the hall. Futoba's otanui was as short, gray, and growly as ever, but she'd known the sturdy housekeeper long enough to know the woman was glad to see her again.

"Arima," Futoba replied warmly. "Thank you for coming. I know it's a long journey."

Her most senior servant waved the thought aside. "It's a good thing I did," she sniffed, sweeping her eyes about the hall. "This place is an absolute shambles! But never fear, my lady, I'll soon put it to rights."

Behind her, Futoba spotted Natsu cringing against the

archway to the kitchens and sighed. She'd have to speak with the woman after this. Natsu had been the housekeeper here and had done a perfectly acceptable job, especially since it had only been her and a few other servants in residence. But with Futoba now settling here permanently, she'd felt she needed not only her family but Arima, and the irascible otanui had high standards indeed.

But her head housekeeper was speaking again, and Futoba dragged her attention back to the woman. "There is another matter I'd hoped we might speak on," she was saying, and off to the side Futoba saw her husband nod. So this was what he'd meant to warn her about! "In your study, perhaps?"

"Of course," Futoba replied, handing her daughter back to Iefusa and following after her housekeeper—almost as if Arima were the one in charge and she were a servant about to be disciplined. She repressed a sigh. Some things never changed.

The study was one of Futoba's favorite rooms here, with its polished wood floor surrounding a simple tatami mat under the low desk and seat cushions, its handsome paper-globe lantern hanging overhead, and most of all the expansive openings along both outer walls, looking out onto the home's private garden. She was happy to see that her desk from home had already been set here, and her favorite cushions, making it far less like someplace she was visiting and far more her own space.

She was, however, surprised to see two people standing at attention before the desk—especially since, after a second, she recognized them both.

"Koma. Maki. How are you both?" They both bowed deeply, of an age with Arima and just as worn and wrinkled—but also just as hale and alert.

"As well as can be expected, my lady. Thank you." That was Koma, who, like her cousin, had been an otanui and, like Arima, tended to speak her mind. Her husband was the quieter one, but solid and dependable as a tree trunk, and good at balancing numbers. He had been chituju, and a good one.

The problem, of course, was where he and his wife had both

been employed. It was a household Futoba had been more than a little familiar with. After all, she'd been related to them by blood.

That same house was the reason she had returned to Awaihinshi.

"They've been turned out, my lady," Arima cut in. "All of them, tossed out on the street like so much rubbish. And after a lifetime of faithful service!"

Futoba nodded, moving behind her desk and settling onto the cushion there to give herself time to think and formulate her reply. "It is awful," she agreed at last. "But you do understand why, I hope? House Ieyuki was found guilty of treason! Ieyuki Nagao was executed for it!"

"And what's that to them?" Her otanui demanded fiercely. "*They* didn't commit treason!" She turned her glare on her sister and brother-in-law, who both obediently dropped to their knees and pressed their foreheads to the floor.

"We are loyal servants of the empire, my lady," Koma stated from that position. "We always have been."

"It's not right for them to be punished for something they didn't do," Arima said firmly, hands on her hips as if she expected Futoba to argue. "And to lose their livelihood, their home, because of something their former lord did. Many of the others have crept back, squatting in households they once proudly upheld, but Koma and Maki could not bring themselves to stoop so low. As if they were common criminals or beggars, and not people who had served faithfully."

Futoba sighed. Fighting with Arima was always like trying to walk forward against a hurricane. "It is not right," she agreed, fingering the chain she wore, and her housekeeper relaxed her belligerent stance just a little. "Koma, Maki, you are welcome here—as guests for now, but if Arima can find suitable employment for you, of course I'm happy to take you on. Family looks after each other."

Arima beamed, or as close to it as she ever got, and bowed deeply. "Thank you, my lady. I knew you would be as compassionate as ever." She gestured for the other two to rise. "Come on, let's get you settled. Dinner'll be ready within the hour," she called back over her shoulder as she hustled her relatives from the room.

Futoba slumped a little after they left, but perked up again at a soft, familiar footstep. "I see you survived," Iefusa teased as he crossed the room and sank down beside her, putting an arm around her and hugging her close. For a moment Futoba just closed her eyes and breathed in his scent, which was always a mix of parchment, ink, sandalwood, and the berry-scented wash Inomi liked for her hair.

"I did," she acknowledged eventually. Another sigh escaped her. "And she's not wrong. Why should those two suffer for something Nagao did, when they had no part of it, no say in it, and probably no knowledge of it?"

"But you're worried that's not the end of it." As always, it was like he could read her mind.

"It's not," Futoba agreed. "How can it be? What about everyone else from the estate? All of them will be suffering the same fate. Are we to take them all in?" The actual members of House Ieyuki had either committed honorable suicide or gone into exile, but only the most tyrannical of lords would require such from their servants. Yet the aiashe had no doubt emptied the estate of everyone, regardless of position.

Another thought occurred to her, and she pulled back to meet her husband's eyes, as kind and concerned as ever. "Iefusa, it's not just House Ieyuki. Half the great houses revolted against the emperor. Amani, Orita, Yoshino, Domo, Etsuya—they're all gone! Half of Atsani is empty right now, and all of those servants, all of that staff, has nowhere to go!" Arima had said many were hiding out in their former homes. Futoba pictured that, whole compounds filled with the no longer employed, people whose skills were all geared toward serving others and who now had no one to serve. How would they survive?

His grip on her tightened, just enough to provide additional reassurance. "You can't be responsible for all of them," he told her, but deep down Futoba knew that, this time, her husband was wrong. True, as the head of House Heiayuki, she need only concern herself with those from House Ieyuki, since until recently that had been her allegiance as well. But as a Rojiri? She had to think about everyone in Awaihinshi, and in all of Rimbaku.

Besides which, she had the sneaking suspicion that if she didn't find some way to help all of those displaced servants, no one would.

CHAPTER FIFTEEN

Takami was startled from his gloomy thoughts when the paper bird sailed into the room.

He'd been dwelling on his impending doom, as he'd begun to see it. Yesterday he'd returned home to find Iri, House Kazutai's otanui, inspecting the place, complete with measuring tape. The tiny housekeeper had terrified him in his youth and was still frightening now, with her wizened features and black-bead eyes. The fact that she treated him exactly the same, like an unruly child who could barely be trusted to listen, let alone obey, only made matters worse.

"The master will require a full inventory," she'd informed him in her reedy little voice. "Then he will determine what will remain here, what will be removed to the old house, and what will be disposed of."

Takami had gathered every ounce of his authority and courage to state, "He is not the master here! I am!"

Iri had merely tutted and waved him away, scuttling past to measure the study. "This lacks the southern exposure the master prefers," she'd stated with that cold note of displeasure Takami remembered so well. "It will not do. We will convert the corner room for his study. You may keep this for your own use."

"How generous," he'd muttered. But not loud enough for her to hear.

He'd despaired, however, and had been sunk in a fugue ever since. Kai was treating him exactly as he always had! It was like he'd never been promoted by the emperor, never been made Rojiri, never been granted his own house. But how could he make them listen if they refused to hear anything he said, and simply proceeded with their own desires over his objections?

*I could order the Honjofu to...*he started, but that thought died halfway. What would he ask the empire's elite soldiers to do? Bar a lord of the realm from entering his brother's home? He really *would* be a child then, if he had to issue such a ridiculous command! And that was assuming they would even comply—more likely Shizumi would tell him her warriors were not meant for such frivolous squabbles.

So it was with some relief that he spotted the paper bird sailing in through one of the windows set high in the council chamber's outer wall, and watched it glide across the room to alight upon the conference table and somehow unfold itself into a flat, completely uncreased sheet of parchment.

Noniki and Futoba were also present, and both had watched the odd progression and regression, the former with pleasure, the latter with unabashed curiosity. Once the letter—for there was writing upon the paper, in two different hands—had ceased moving, Noniki leaned forward and snatched it up.

"Hm." The young wizard was frowning when he glanced up from reading it. "I had best let Kagiri know about this."

He rose from his seat, and Takami found himself standing as well. "May I join you?" Anything to keep from being alone with his thoughts, and these days Futoba seemed distracted as well.

Noniki smiled. "Of course." Together they exited the room and traveled down the hallway, stopping at another door across the way. Noniki knocked upon it without hesitation. "Giri?"

Takami heard motion from within, then the door slid open, revealing the Dogenriku. "Niki! What is it?" The tall young warrior's eyes landed on Takami. "Hello, Takami!" Though not as effusive as his brother, Kagiri had always been friendly toward him, which Takami appreciated. Especially since, if the rumors he'd heard were true, Kagiri could kill him a dozen ways before he drew another breath.

Doing his best to ignore those thoughts, Takami shrugged, indicating his shorter companion, who held up the parchment. "I have word from the south," Noniki said, and followed when

Kagiri gestured for them both to enter and join him by his desk. Takami had not seen the Dogenriku's office before, but looking at it now, he approved. It was plainly furnished, very clean and functional, but with good space and light and an entire side wall open to the walkway and gardens beyond. *Southern exposure,* he thought bitterly. *Maybe I should tell Kai. Let him try to claim* this one!

He concentrated on the current matter—which he knew nothing about. "What is occurring to the south?"

It was Kagiri who answered. "Niki sensed something dangerous down there, somewhere in Bezenkai near the Rumiri. He asked me to send some men to investigate." He was perusing the letter as he spoke, a scowl growing as he read. "The commander there, Kiso Akinari, reports that he sent a shotao, as instructed. They've not returned, nor sent anyone back with word, and his other scouts have seen no sign of them. They've simply vanished." He was in full glower now. "How can a score or more of trained soldiers just disappear?"

Noniki was shaking his head. "It's my fault," he said. "I told you the threat was real, but I should have warned against checking it. I'm so sorry, Giri."

"Not your fault," his brother assured him. "It's a soldier's job to confront danger. This was clearly more than they bargained for, that's all." He frowned. "I just wish we knew what we were facing."

Takami had been studying the large map framed on one wall. "I could send a boat down there," he offered now, turning to face the two brothers. "A cuioburi, small and fast. Not to fight whatever this may be, just to get a sighting and then return to tell about it." He traced a finger along the rivers that crossed Rimbaku. "From the Edishu to the Tonawa to the Rumiri." He smiled, as he always did when he thought about sailing. "The currents are swift at the center of each, and the winds strong. An experienced captain could make it down there in three days." For an instant, he thought about offering to go himself, but knew that was just the child in him, wanting to run from his troubles. He was no longer that scared little boy, however. He was a man, and a Rojiri, and the Dogenkaishu. He had responsibilities, and he would not shirk them. No matter how much he might wish to.

"It could be dangerous," Kagiri warned. "If whatever is down there can wipe out a full shotao, it can easily handle a single boat and a handful of sailors."

But Takami had already decided on his course of action and was not about to be gainsaid. "I am not sending anyone to fight whatever this is," he promised. "Not even to get too close to it. Just to sail within sight, close enough to tell us something. Is it an army? A monster? A storm? Even knowing that much would be helpful, yes?"

The brothers glanced at each other, then nodded. "Tell whoever you send to steer well clear," Noniki urged him. "Whatever it is, it is dangerous, and this only proves it." Taking the letter back from his brother, he whispered something to it before presenting it to Takami. "Give this to your captain," he explained. "Once he's spotted the danger, have him write down what he sees. The bird will find its way back to us."

Takami accepted the parchment with a nod, but inside he felt a spike of concern. There was only one reason the young matekai would give him this enchanted paper for the task: He feared anyone they sent might not be able to return themselves.

As with the aiashe, however, the aikaye knew the dangers. They too had signed on for such risks.

At least, that is what Takami told himself as he bowed and let himself out of the Dogenriku's office. He left the two brothers behind and made his way to his own offices, then out of the compound and across the imperial grounds. He was headed to the gates that would take him all the way down to the outer walls, and the docks that projected beyond them.

There he was sure to find at least one of his daiso, whose names he had not yet learned. Takami figured the captains would best know which kogashiri or chudai could be trusted to perform such a mission quickly and carefully.

But he hoped Noniki's fears would prove unfounded. He didn't want his first official act as Dogenkaishu to cost the empire one of its ships and the crew that manned it.

Takami felt a certain tension leave his body as he stepped through the final set of gates, leaving the blue walls of Mazihini behind him and stepping out onto the long docks. A spray of water struck his face at once, carried by the breeze, and that particular salt tang made his heart rejoice, as did the sight of the sun slanting across the water, turning its edges silver and gold against various shades of blue.

He was home.

The guards stationed along the dock reminded him, however, that this was no pleasure trip. And that this was not the main dock off the city's southern gate. Awaihinshi had three sets of docks, in fact: those to the south were the largest, where the majority of boat traffic went, while the little cove west of that was the smallest and only for the royal family, the Rojiri, and the nation's generals and admirals. He was standing on the third set, in between the other two and equally as large as the main dock but reserved for the aikaye.

His docks.

Takami was glad he had detoured to collect the chasai from his office. While all the men here were Navy and thus under his command, they did not yet know him, and he saw several start at his sudden arrival, turning and raising yanoi and chokoto to bar his path. Then they noticed the baton and immediately stiffened, saluting and clearing a path for him.

He would eventually come to know all of them by name, and for them to know him by sight, but for now this would suffice.

An officer approached as he neared the first of the ships anchored along the docks, the edges of her maikiro silvered to denote her rank. A daiso, he saw, and a woman, tall and slim, dark hair tugged back in a tight knot, face and eyes intent and serious.

"Dogenkaishu," she stated, loud enough for her voice to carry across the docks, making sure everyone there knew who he was as she saluted crisply. "I am Enotaba Harukano, one of your daiso. I am currently the ranking officer on duty here on the docks. How may I assist you?"

Takami considered her carefully. Female officers were rare among any of the nation's military forces, he'd noticed, so for her to have risen to even that rank meant she was either well-connected, talented, clever, or some combination thereof. He could see clear intelligence in her gaze, but no arrogance, and her question sounded genuine, the statement before that merely one of fact. So he rewarded her with a warm smile, and was pleased to see her stance unbend ever so slightly.

"Greetings, Daisho Enotaba. I am pleased to meet you, and I apologize for arriving without notice. This is not a surprise inspection, though I have no doubt if it were, I would be well satisfied with the results." Her chin rose, as did the corners of her lips. There was pride there, but of the sort he appreciated, pride in a job well done. "I have an urgent matter, and I require your assistance, as I do not yet know my officers as well as I would like."

He stepped closer to her and lowered his voice, not to keep his intent secret but to show that this was a conversation for them and not for the entire docks. "There is trouble of some sort in Bezenkai," he informed her. "Somewhere near the Rumiri. I wish to send a scout to see if we can discover anything about it. A single cuioburi, not to face this danger but to identify it and report back. I need one of your most reliable for this, and they must set out at once." He frowned, remembering something else. "Actually, I will require two ships, on two different fact-finding missions, but this one is by far the most urgent."

"Of course." She stroked her chin, eyes roaming the ships arrayed along the docks, before nodding once. "I know just the person. This way, sir." And she led him quickly down the long, planked walkway to a cuioburi nestled among two others, the trio of sleek scout ships looking like resting hawks compared to the slower, bulkier hozaiburi opposite them. Men bustled about the trim little ship, engaged in the endless list of tasks required to maintain a boat, but all of them went to attention as Takami and his guide approached. One stepped forward, a slight man with the bowed legs and weathered skin of a life at sea.

"Dogenkaishu, sir. It is an honor!" the man announced, saluting. His voice was rich but raspy. "Chudai Nakori Enyo, at your service."

"At ease, chudai, and thank you," Takami replied, waiting until the lieutenant had shifted his stance to a more relaxed one before continuing. "I need you to undertake an urgent scouting mission down the Rumiri." He explained the task and then offered up Noniki's enchanted letter. "The moment you have ascertained the danger, write it upon this. Then"—he hesitated only a second— "tell it to return here." He saw the man's confusion—and that of Enotaba beside him—and sighed. "Yes, I am aware of how it sounds. The matekai himself has placed an enchantment upon the paper. It will return here of its own accord, no matter what happens." He fixed Nakori with a sharp eye. "Understand that a shotao of aiashe were already sent to investigate—and have since disappeared. The danger is very real, so do not approach any closer than necessary and send the letter back immediately, then follow it at once. Is that clear?"

Nakori's face had borne a faintly amused expression at the first mention of enchantment but that had vanished upon hearing the rest and his nod was without mockery. "Yes, sir. We will take care of it." He saluted again, then turned and started shouting orders. Within minutes the quick little ship was casting off its lines and backing out into the Edishu.

"Sir?" That was Enotaba, her voice low. "What sort of threat is it? Should we be prepared for a larger excursion?"

Still watching the cuioburi raise its sails and get underway, Takami nodded. "I do not know its nature yet, but yes, I think we will need to be ready." She saluted, and he knew she would make sure the fleet was prepared for whatever happened.

With magic in the mix, Takami hoped that would be enough.

CHAPTER SIXTEEN

Even before he knocked, Shizumi knew it was Kagiri at the door. She'd come to recognize the rhythm of his steps, steady and unhurried, and his silhouette through the panes, tall and lean. *Stop it*, she told herself yet again. *He's a peer, that's all. A fellow warrior. A fellow Rojiri. A friend, even.*

Yet, as always, her heart lifted at the sight of him approaching.

Some of that joy faded, however, when she slid the door open and found not just him but his brother Noniki and their fellow counselor Takami. It was dampened even further when she saw his expression.

Normally, Kagiri had a certain calm warmth about him, comforting in a quiet, relaxed way. Now, however, his eyes were shadowed and his jaw set. The two with him bore similarly somber expressions.

"What is it?" she asked, standing aside and waving them inside.

"We have a problem," Kagiri told her with his usual bluntness, a trait she both shared and appreciated. "And I think we're going to need your help."

He handed her a sheet of parchment, which she quickly perused. "There's a problem in Bezenkai?"

"There is," Noniki agreed. "Giri sent a shotao to investigate, and they never returned."

"So I sent a small boat, just to scout," Takami put in. "The captain was only supposed to spot the danger and report back, using this enchanted letter. That was four days ago." He pointed to a spot near the paper's bottom edge, a dot Shizumi had assumed was just an accidental ink drop. "That was all he managed to write."

She frowned, examining the mark more closely. "It's not even a real character, just a scratch, and barely that."

The young noble nodded. "I know. But the instructions were to write down what he saw, then send the letter back." He ran a hand through his hair, looking unusually unsettled for someone normally so calm and collected. "I think he wanted to make sure it got back to us at all, but couldn't send it without writing something, so he did that just to get the magic to work."

Shizumi nodded, offering the letter back to Kagiri, but it was Noniki who accepted it. "So there's something down there dangerous enough to take out a full troop and an entire boat crew." She couldn't help breaking into a quick, sharp grin. "When do we leave?"

All three men stared at her. "What? I assume that's why you're here, because you want me and my Honjofu to deal with whatever this is?" She shrugged. "That's fine, I can be ready in ten minutes." Even though she'd been stationed back here in Aihiri for several weeks now, she kept her bakiro packed and ready to grab at a moment's notice. That was the soldier's life, after all.

Kagiri glanced at his brother and Takami before turning back toward her, his face oddly sympathetic. "I was hoping you'd detail a bantao to accompany more of my men," he told her gently. "I'm going to ask Hibikitsu for permission to send a full reitao this time, but I would feel better knowing some of your warriors were there to take point." He was clearly trying to smile, and not quite managing it. "But you can't go, any more than I can."

"What?" She glared up at him—of all the times for him to be so much taller than her! "Of course I can! It's my Honjofu!"

"Yes, which is exactly *why* you can't go yourself," Takami put in. "You need to be here, directing operations. We don't even know what's out there yet, so it makes no sense for you to risk yourself in the field."

Noniki was nodding. "Imagine what would happen to your warriors if you went and didn't make it back," he pointed out. "We're still hoping this is just a scouting mission." His tone, expression, and stance said otherwise, however.

Shizumi didn't care. She glared at all three of them equally. "You want to speak with the emperor?" she snapped at Kagiri. "Fine. So do I. Let's go see what he has to say."

Without waiting for a reply, she stormed out of her office and down the hall.

By the First Emperor, if Hibikitsu didn't agree right away to let her go, she'd make him agree!

Hibikitsu frowned down at her—he'd still been in the throne room, so she was kneeling just before the dais. "Absolutely not," he stated, his voice calm and not at all angry but also completely certain. "I will not allow it."

"Your Majesty—" Shizumi started, but stopped when he held up a hand.

"No. I'm sorry, Shizumi." He sounded like he meant that much, at least. "But I can't afford to lose you. That goes for you as well," he added, looking to her side where Kagiri also knelt. "I only just assembled a proper Rojiri and appointed both of you to your leadership roles. If you both got yourself killed facing some unknown threat all the way down south, that would all fall apart."

"Sire." That was Noniki, who was kneeling on Kagiri's other side, with Takami beyond him—it was a mark of Hibikitsu's preoccupation with their news and their subsequent requests that he hadn't yet thought to bid them stand. "I do think the threat is real, and should be dealt with sooner rather than later. Already it's been nearly a week since I first sensed it, and it can only be drawing nearer with each passing day."

The emperor nodded, stroking his chin. "Yes, I—oh, get up, all of you!" He paused a moment while they rose to their feet. "I agree, we cannot sit by and let whatever this is creep closer and closer. Kagiri, you have my leave to send a full reitao to deal with the threat. Shizumi, you may send a bantao with it, to take charge of the expedition in conjunction with Kagiri's officers. But neither of you are going with them."

She opened her mouth to argue. The look he leveled at her stopped any words from emerging. This was not friendly, casual Hibikitsu who sat around the council table with them, eating a nafti and idly wiping the juice from his chin with the hem of his sleeve, which was worth more than most villages. This was the emperor of all Rimbaku, and he had given her a direct order. She could only dip her head and bang her fist against her chest in salute. "Yes, your Majesty."

Kagiri did the same, and after a moment more Hibikitsu released them. He had been hearing reports and petitions when they'd begged a moment of his time. Courtiers, bureaucrats, and others still stood outside the throne room, patiently waiting their turn. Shizumi turned on her heel and stalked out. She'd barely gotten through the wide double doors before Kagiri caught up to her.

"I'm sorry," he said, reaching out as if to lay a comforting hand on her shoulder but stopping just shy of doing so. She appreciated both the gesture and the restraint, but was still too furious to acknowledge them, or him, so she kept right on walking. "I know it's awful," he continued, those damnably long legs allowing him to keep pace with her easily. "You know I wish I was going, myself."

She nodded, but then another thought struck her, the logical follow-up to what had come before, the reality behind the emperor's edict, and she froze as if her feet had been nailed to the floor.

"Shizumi?" This time he did touch her shoulder, his concern clear in his face and voice. "What's wrong?"

Despite all her years as a soldier, all her encounters with danger and death, all that time learning to cope with risk and battle and violence, Shizumi found herself crying as she finally turned to face him fully. "Who will you send?" she asked, her voice hoarse, and cursed her own weakness but could do nothing to abate it.

Kagiri frowned. "I don't know," he answered slowly, as if her question made no sense to him—or, she guessed, as if he could not see the connection between that and her obvious anguish. "Daishin Nishoji, most likely. He's solid, dependable—and not too creative, so I won't have to worry about him getting any clever ideas about attacking a clearly superior force." He was watching her closely, warily. "Why?"

She shook her head, not sure he'd understand but knowing she owed it to him—and to herself—to try. If only Kohori were still here! The older Taikoro would have known without her having to say a word. Now she forced them out, though her throat had suddenly gone sandpaper-dry. "Taisho Daishin is a good man," she agreed carefully. "But you are not close. My Honjofu is smaller, so much smaller. I have only three officers. Do I send Norio Shinjuru, who helped keep our unit together after Fujibuki was murdered? Or Akino, part of my own bantao, who I trust more than almost anyone else in the world—except for Geniji, who I trust even more?" She wiped at her cheeks with the back of her hand, angry at herself for such a display, though she saw no criticism or condemnation in Kagiri's eyes, only sympathy. "If whatever this is has already killed so many, I may well be sending one of them to their death!"

He nodded. "Yes. You may be." She was grateful that he didn't try to downplay the risk or ignore it. "But how would your going have been any better?"

Ah, of course. She had to remember that, for all his amazing skill, the young man beside her had never been a proper soldier, never led anyone into battle. He had, he'd revealed to her once after a training bout, been raised in a fishing village and been working as a server in a bar before he and his brother had fallen in with merchants and wound up breaking into the Tawasiri, where he'd gained his fighting prowess. She did not think any less of him for that, but it did mean he had not directly experienced battle the way she had. "When I lead my warriors into battle," she explained, "I am taking the same risk they are. That is acceptable to me. But this—you are asking me to send one of them off, possibly to their death, while staying here! That is the coward's way! Real warriors lead from the front!"

Kagiri's smile was as kind as ever. "They do," he agreed. "When they can. But sometimes, it seems, being a leader means letting others do the fighting for you. And, yes, take the risks for you, too. Do you think any of your officers would argue that you should be going with them?"

She had to shake her head at that. "No. They understand how the chain of command works." She scowled up at him. "But I still hate it."

He nodded. "I'd be willing to bet they know that, too. And appreciate it. I would."

Takami and Noniki joined them, and a part of Shizumi wondered if they'd deliberately hung back in order to give her and Kagiri a moment alone. "I can ferry both your soldiers down there," Takami offered. "With that many going we'll have to use the gotaiburi, which are a bit slower, and we may need to sail down along the coast instead of taking the rivers, but it'll still be a damn sight faster than walking."

"I will try sensing this thing again," Noniki told them. "Perhaps I can at least give you an idea where to start looking." His broad, handsome face was thoughtful as he added, "I may be able to offer some limited protection, too. Without knowing exactly what this threat constitutes, I probably can't do more than that, but perhaps it will help."

Shizumi nodded. "I'll speak to my officers and decide which one to send," she assured the three men with her. "They can be ready to leave by dawn."

"I'll brief Daishin and send word to gather the regiment," Kagiri said. "They'll be ready by dawn as well."

"Then I'll get the boats prepared," Takami promised. "They'll be waiting at the docks."

They parted ways, each heading off to handle their own preparations, and Shizumi forced herself to focus on logistics, thinking about which warriors to send and what they'd need.

Perhaps, if she kept busy enough, she wouldn't notice the fear and guilt twisting in her belly quite so much.

CHAPTER SEVENTEEN

Iraku was fidgeting again, and Seikoku had to resist the urge to slap his shoulder to make him stop.

"I still don't see why I need to be here," the boy—though he was not that much younger than she was, if she were being honest—muttered, and Seikoku sighed.

"Because I want you here," she told him. "And because you weren't doing much of anything else."

That produced more grumbling from him, but he couldn't very well argue the point. His older brother was starting to settle in as one of Sorainasei's gardeners and groundskeepers, but Iraku had no interest in farming or gardening, and little patience for it. Bringing him with her today had been a spur-of-the-moment decision when Seikoku had seen him sitting on the compound's front steps, just staring off into space while the other residents all went about their daily tasks. Still, if nothing else, it had forced him out and about. And having an extra pair of hands might prove useful.

Assuming they wound up with anything to carry.

The older woman beside Seikoku sniffed. "I still do not think this is wise," Senkousa Medeiko stated in her rich, honeyed voice, no doubt striving for stern correction but sounding more like she was whining. "The Relicant Way has worked for centuries now. Surely throwing all of that aside, tearing down generations of tradition and stability...well, it simply seems foolish, is all."

That produced a snort from the young man with them. "Spoken like somebody who makes a living off people using the bones," he said with a grin, and their hostess's mouth shut with an audible snap, bursts of color appearing on each cheek.

Yes, bringing him was proving useful already.

Before he could taunt the woman further, or she grow angry at the barb, Madam Medeiko straightened, her head swiveling toward the tent flap exactly like a hound catching a scent. "Come in, come in," she called, and a hand shifted the flap aside. It proved to belong to a middle-aged woman, her hair as gray as the Bone Reader's and pulled up into a similar bun, her clothes as worn and bleached of color as their owner.

"Begging your pardon, Senkousa," the woman began, her eyes touching on Seikoku and Iraku before returning to the heavy woman between them. "Only, I saw the announcement that was posted, and it said to come here, so I thought…"

She trailed off, and Seikoku deliberately shifted to draw her attention, then offered a gentle smile. "You were hoping to sell your aishone to the emperor?" The woman nodded. "Then you have come to the right place. My name is Seikoku. I am one of his Rojiri." The visitor's eyes widened at that, though her mouth remained set in a narrow, distrusting line—until Seikoku displayed the carved jade pendant she wore. Hibikitsu had presented one to each of them, as both a token of his appreciation and a proof of their position. "Why don't you show us what you've brought?" she urged, letting the heavy seal drop back beneath the collar of her shatage.

The woman nodded and took a hesitant step forward, the flap sliding shut behind her. As if that had sealed her fate, she covered the rest of the distance in a rush, arriving breathless at the little ivory-inlaid table before Medeiko. Then, revealing a small pouch clenched tight in her hands, the woman emptied its contents onto the tabletop.

The minute she saw the bones, the Senkousa became all business. "Hm," she said, her long, lacquered nails reaching for the first of the fragments and stopping just shy of touching them. "Your mother? No," she corrected herself at once. "They are too steeped with age. Your grandmother."

"Yes," their first customer agreed, looking pleased. "She was a clever woman, learned in herbs and poultices and other remedies. My mother used her bones only sparingly and passed the rest to me when she died, along with her own."

Seikoku could hear the dismissal in that last phrase and knew with a pang that it was the exact reason their plans had to succeed. The grandmother's bones were still valuable, but the mother had never learned much on her own—after all, why should she, when she had *her* mother's knowledge to draw upon? So, though she had left her bones to her daughter, they were all but worthless, and that would continue to happen with each successive generation. People were too dependent on their early ancestors, and those were a finite resource. When the last of the ancient, valuable bones had been consumed, what would be left besides a society where no one knew how to do anything on their own?

Unless they changed that culture now, while they still had time to do so.

"I can give you two gold for them all," Medeiko was saying, and the woman gasped, her lips parting in a sudden, surprised smile.

Seikoku frowned briefly, however, and caught the Bone Reader's eye, shaking her head ever so slightly. "Are you sure, Senkousa?" was all she said, however.

Medeiko was no fool—one of the reasons Seikoku had chosen her, along with the fact that she was well known in Mazahini, just as Futoba's selection was in Bejinuri, where she was today. Now Medeiko tilted her head, as if reconsidering. "Very well, three gold," she amended, making it sound as if she were being generous.

In fact, Seikoku suspected the woman would have then sold these same bones for at least four gold, maybe five.

Fortunately, she was not the one buying them. Not today.

Instead Seikoku reached into her sash and drew forth three gold coins. "There you are," she said, offering them to the woman, who snatched them away, then bowed as if embarrassed by her haste. "Thank you and take care." The happy customer nodded and hurried out, bowing again and again until the tent flap hid her from view.

Seikoku realized with some regret that she had not even learned the woman's name. Though perhaps that made things easier. She knew all too well, from her own years fencing stolen goods, that anonymity could be a blessing.

Medeiko had already begun reaching for the bones, but Sei-koku tapped her hand with a finger—not hard, but enough to serve as a reminder. "Iraku," she said, "please gather them up and hold onto them for me."

He scowled at her—his skin was beginning to even out a little in color as he got more sun, but his hair was still as black-and-white as ever. "Why me?" he complained. "I can't even use them!"

She offered him her sweetest smile, which caused him to blush and duck his head. "Exactly. Who better to trust with such things than someone who cannot be tempted by them?" Iraku and his brother were Mukanichi, "untouched," born without even a drop of the Relicant Touch. That had made their lives an utter torment growing up, she knew, as they'd been outcast by most, forced to take any work they could find and beg when they could find nothing.

She thought it fitting that he should now be entrusted with a treasure beyond imagining.

Medeiko sniffed again, her eyes narrowing as she watched him scoop the bones into a large bag with no more care than if he were clearing a plate after someone's lunch. "It is such a waste," the Bone Reader lamented. "Are you sure I cannot buy them off you? Even just a few of those could prove useful for some people." She tried on a sly smile. "We could split the profits. No one else need ever know."

Seikoku did her best to look shocked. "Madam, are you suggesting I betray our beloved emperor's trust? Surely you could not mean such a thing!"

She barely stopped from laughing as the older woman's face drained of color. "Oh, no, of course not!" the senkousa protested quickly, waving her hands about frantically, her usual calm arrogance shattered. "I am a loyal servant of the empire!"

"Good." Seikoku drew a trio of copper coins from her pouch and set them carefully on the table. "There is your commission for this first sale."

Now it was Medeiko who grumbled, but the coins disappeared when someone cleared their throat from outside the tent. "Yes, come in, come in!" she called, the consummate professional once more, and Seikoku did giggle a little this time before giving their newest customer her full attention.

She suspected it was going to be a very busy, very rewarding day. She hoped Futoba was having similar luck. Seikoku also expected she'd be glad she'd brought someone young and strong along to help carry back all the bones they would have collected by the time the sun set.

CHAPTER EIGHTEEN

Geniji lay back in the hammock, arms behind her head, and closed her eyes. "This is the life!" she exclaimed.

Leaning on the rail near her, Diritan groaned. "Easy for you to say. Anything I've eaten in the last week is now floating in the water behind us. I think I've left a trail all the way back to Awaihinshi."

The big Honjofu laughed at that, not bothering to glance his way. "You need to get out more," she advised. "A few more of these trips and you'll be as comfortable on a boat as you are on land."

"So, not at all, then?" Kori offered from where he sat perched on a nearby barrel, chuckling at his joke. Which was good because at least it meant *someone* was amused.

The three of them, along with Masai, Reiko, and Nioko, were lounging upon the forward deck of the lead gotaiburi, enjoying the breeze as it and the two boats behind it carried them and several hundred aiashe down the Tonawa. They'd been lucky that the boats, big as they were, were still narrow enough to take the river. Otherwise they'd have had to hug the outer coast, which would have taken longer.

It didn't help that they weren't sure what they were looking for, or where it would be, exactly. But so far it had stayed close to the Rumiri, and Geniji suspected she'd find it still in that vicinity. Once they were on that river she'd order her bantao to don armor again, but for now she saw no reason to give up the rare comfort of wearing only hosode and ponmei.

She had worried a little about this mission, her first as a gunso in charge of her own unit. Especially since she wanted to reward Shizumi's faith in her.

Of course, at the moment that just meant keeping Kori from annoying the others so much they threw him overboard. But Geniji knew that would change, and soon.

Sure enough, the following day as they sailed down the Rumiri one of the sailors shouted down from the top of the center mast, "I see something up ahead, on the western shore!"

Geniji and her Honjofu immediately turned to that side, straining to study the terrain. If only Isano were here! But she'd felt she couldn't take *all* of Shizumi's old bantao and so had left the sharp-eyed archer behind.

After a moment, Nioko pointed. "There!"

Peering at the indicated spot, Geniji finally saw several thin, dark plumes of smoke. "Is there a village over there?"

Masai, who'd grown up in Bezenkiri, nodded. "We're almost level with Ginzai but that's a lot farther in, so it'd have to be Magojifu."

Geniji considered that. "Whatever the trouble is, it's still following the river," she said. "That's good for us—if it'd struck out across the countryside, we'd have to ditch the boats and pursue on foot. But it's working its way up north, which means we've passed it." Twisting about, she spotted the kogashiri in charge of the boat and the small fleet, a man named Kouiji Nofasa. "Back it up!" she ordered.

He laughed at her. "Boats don't work that way, gunso. Best we can do is angle toward the shore, then turn her around and start back upriver—but we'll have to break out the oars for that, since the wind and current are both going south. Slow going and hard work."

"Put us to shore, then," Diritan pleaded. The burly Honjofu was still feeling queasy. "We'll intercept on foot."

Nioko nodded. "We'd be less noticeable that way," she agreed. "Scout ahead while the army marches behind."

They were all looking at Geniji, and she suddenly understood why Shizumi preferred fighting to giving orders. Bones, it was tough being in command! Still, she shouldered it. "Right, good plan. Put us on the western bank, soon as you can." Then she grinned at her unit. "Gear up. We're on the hunt."

Everyone got ready, which didn't take much—Honjofu traveled light for a reason. By the time the boat had angled across the river and come to a rest against a soft, sloping bank there, her bantao was good to go.

"Anchor here and wait for us," Geniji instructed as her team easily navigated the narrow gangplank down to dry land. "If we're not back in three days, head back to Awaihinshi and report." That should give them plenty of time.

The boat's commander nodded. "Good luck."

She grinned at him, hefting her naritaba. "We're not the ones who'll need it."

A full day later, though, Geniji was shaking her head. "That can't be right."

"It is," Nioki insisted, and Masai nodded. "It's just one man."

"Not even a particularly big one," Masai put in. "No armor or weapons, either."

"Well, those troops and ships and villages didn't disappear themselves," Kori argued, grinning. No one so much as cracked a smile in return, though, and he quieted with a grumble.

Geniji was thinking. "We've seen some strange things, the last month or two," she reminded the others. "People burned to death with their eyes gone, flying skeletons, angry clouds—and then there's the new Rojiri, the one who's a wizard and the other who fights like ten akatai together." *The one my best friend is sweet on,* she added but would never, ever say aloud. Except to tease Shizumi if she knew no one else was in earshot. And she was unarmed.

"So let's not assume this stranger's some kind of pushover, or that we have the wrong man. We go in quiet and careful, assess the situation, and make sure the army's ready to back us up." The others nodded, even Kori, and she left them to go find the head of the aiashe contingent.

Taisho Daishin Nishoji was conferring with his own officers but paused when she approached. "Gunso Geniji," the solid general called out, saluting. "What are your orders?" One of his taisu made a face, quickly smoothed away, but Geniji didn't take it personally. It had to be strange to see their general taking orders from a mere sergeant, but of course she was Honjofu, and they'd been given the lead on this expedition. She appreciated that Daishin himself seemed to have no qualms about it.

"We've spotted a man we believe may be the threat in question," she told him openly, speaking as one leader to another. "My bantao will investigate, get close as we can before engaging. I'd like your aiashe right behind us, though, in case things go sour." She frowned, though not at him. "If he is the one we're after, he's already destroyed several villages, one ship, and an entire shotao, so we need to treat this seriously. If we attack, we do it full force, no hesitation and no quarter."

He nodded. "Agreed. We are ready."

"Excellent. Then let's get to it." She saluted him, which he returned. Then Geniji went to gather her team and go engage the enemy.

"He really doesn't look like much," Reiko commented as they crouched behind a low hill, spying on the man just over the rise. "I could snap him in half, easy as a dead branch." The big warrior made a twisting gesture with his huge hands.

Nor was he wrong. Studying the man, Geniji could not see what all the fuss was about. He was tall, certainly, but thin with the look of long starvation. His clothes hung loose on him, faded and frayed, though she was close enough to see the handsome patterning they'd once displayed. His hair was long and wild, as was his beard, and his hands were empty and completely unadorned.

Yet something about him reminded her of a brewing storm:

the air crackling with tension, the colors more vivid, a certain sharp taste to the world.

The man was clearly dangerous.

"Weapons at the ready," she instructed, shifting her grip on her own. "If he comes quietly, fine. If he lifts a finger, hit him with everything we've got." Glancing over her shoulder, Geniji saw the army arrayed down the hill behind them, and Daishin nodded.

Even so, she felt oddly exposed as she stood and marched over the hill, her five teammates arrayed behind her.

The man stopped and turned to face them. Had he heard her, or just somehow sensed their presence? Either way, it was unnerving. "More warriors," he stated, and his voice was creaky from disuse, rusty as an old nail, but deep and with an odd echo, as if he were speaking from a vast cavern. "And where is your bone magic, then? Your abominable use of your ancestry? Your despicable desecration of your own past?"

Geniji was glad she'd instructed her team not to bring aishone along. They had been slowly weaning themselves off the use of bones, following Shizumi's lead, and so she was able to honestly hold up her free hand now, splayed and open. "No magic here," she called out. "Just us."

She was close enough to see his eyes narrow, and the brief nod that followed. "Well. Good, then. You are not so horrible as the others. What do you want?" The way he said it, and his stance as he waited for her to reach him, was that of a king addressing a supplicant. There was certainly something regal about his nature, his expression—and his deepset, glittering gaze.

"I need to know if you're the one who's been destroying villages around here," Geniji replied, doing her best not to react to the authority in his tone. She was Honjofu, answering only to her Taikoro and the emperor himself, and this ragged stranger was neither of those. "And if you're responsible for a missing shotao and a missing cuioburi."

He laughed, but it was a bitter, hollow sound. "They were wrecks already, devoid of any true life," he answered, a snarl twisting his features into something barbaric and terrifying, like a demon clawing through his skin. "I have cleansed them, as I will cleanse all this land, purifying it of its filthy practices so that fresh life may rise up again, wholesome and true."

He tilted his head, considering her, and Geniji was now close enough to see his face clearly. Bones, he was practically a skeleton himself—but lit somehow from within, like a lantern burned inside, gleaming out through his eyes and his very pores. What *was* he?

"You were tainted, but no longer," he declared, and it felt as if a death sentence had been lifted, a judgment rescinded. "You and yours may join me, if you wish. Or merely stand aside, and no harm will come to you."

The tightness all around intensified, Geniji's hairs standing on end, and she gulped. This was the point where she'd be seeking cover from stray lightning, if she weren't so sure it was all centered around the odd man ranting before her. As it was, the threat was clear, and she had no choice but to respond.

"I appreciate the offer," she replied, having to shout as the wind suddenly picked up. "But I can't let you hurt anyone else." With a wave of her hand, she summoned the army, which marched forward to line the ridge behind her. "Surrender yourself now, or we will be forced to attack."

She saw the yellow gleam of his teeth as he bared them. "Typical," he sneered. "You fear what you do not understand and seek to stop that which is only right and good. Very well, you seal your own fate." A spark leapt from his outstretched hand, straight at her head, and Geniji reflexively shifted back, batting it away with her spear.

She wasn't sure who was more surprised, her or the stranger, when the spark was knocked aside, its angry, buzzing glow quickly fading into the surrounding sunlight.

"What? How?" the man demanded. If he had been annoyed before, he was incensed now. "You have no magic!"

No, but I know someone who does, Geniji thought. *And luckily, he did something to us before we left.* At the time, she'd thought it silly and pointless, the Rojiri named Noniki visiting them with

Shizumi before their departure and waving his hands over each of the bantao in turn—she'd felt a light breeze wash over her skin, like a soft reminder of sunlight and summer, but that had been all.

Now she was grateful, knowing in her bones that the gesture had somehow saved her from a grisly fate. Presumably the same one that had befallen those aiashe and aikaye and villagers.

Thinking of them, Geniji felt anger wash away her fear. Threat confirmed, guilt admitted. That left only one recourse.

"Attack!" she shouted and charged the man, her naritaba held high, blade catching the sunlight.

She saw the shock on his face, as if no one had ever dared confront him in this way before. But that quickly gave way to an arrogant sneer, much like any noble confronted with something he considered beneath him.

"I have no time for this," the man declared, waving a hand— and a massive gust of wind shoved Geniji back, her feet skidding on the ground as she struggled to maintain position. "If you insist upon fighting, I will give you someone to fight."

She saw, through the windborne grit nearly blinding her, as he held out both arms, head back and eyes closed but hands turned down toward the ground rather than up at the sky—

Then the ground began to buck and crack, as figures rose from the earth.

"Oh, great, these again," Geniji muttered as the skeletons formed, bones coming together into strange configurations that towered over her. She recalled the battle over Awaihinshi all too well and readied herself, mentally shifting her tactics toward bludgeoning and bashing.

But then dirt and grass and mud and rock flowed upward as well, wrapping around the monstrous figures. Those elements somehow transmuted themselves, becoming something resembling flesh and scale and skin, and suddenly she was facing an army of bizarre creatures but ones that looked as alive as she was.

Standing in their midst, the man crossed his arms over his narrow chest and smirked down at her—when had he become so tall, or was he simply no longer standing on the ground? "Let us see how you fare against *my* army," he declared.

Then a thing built like a horned giant with four arms was lunging for her, and Geniji was too busy fighting to think about anything else.

CHAPTER NINETEEN

Hibikitsu was not used to being touched. In his more bitter moments, he reflected that an emperor and a Mukanichi had that in common, the lack of physical contact with others, though of course his lot in life was far kinder than those unfortunates. Thus he started slightly when Takami's hand closed gently around his wrist.

"Do not fight it, sire," the young noble advised, close enough that his soft voice could be heard despite the rush of the wind and the lapping of the waves. "This is not a battle. You do not need to win. Instead, think of it as a negotiation. Feel the way the water wishes to take you. If that is the way you wish to go, then lean into it, let it guide you."

"And if it is not?" Hibikitsu asked, glancing up at his instructor and squinting against the sun behind the other man, diluted only slightly by passing through their ship's single sail.

Takami smiled. "Then you let it lead for a time, until you can ease into a different direction. Forcing the issue will only make it more difficult."

Hibikitsu laughed. "Much like a negotiation indeed!" He eased his grip on the tiller and felt it shift beneath his palm, the little boat leaping forward as the water carried it swiftly from Awaihinshi. Droplets caught him on the cheek and he laughed again, shaking his head to keep them from his eyes.

He had forgotten how much he enjoyed sailing!

But the last time—also the first—he had been a passenger on a takaneburi. He had helped where he could, but only by coiling ropes or wiping down the deck. The ship's captain had handled all the navigation, the actual sailing.

Hibikitsu was eager to learn how to do such things for himself. Not that he would have much opportunity, as emperor, to sail his own boat. But the knowledge could still be useful. Plus it was one more thing he would be able to do himself, without any aishone.

And who better to teach him than his new Dogenkaishu?

He had offered Takami the job because Kagiri and the others had seen the young noble sailing a chayaburi and had commented on how comfortable he'd seemed, how at one with the water. They were on the same sort of quick little sailboat now, and Hibikitsu was loving it. It reminded him of a paper kite, so light and agile, dancing across the waves.

He was not sure his Honteno bodyguard was enjoying their outing quite as much, but she was being a good sport about it. And at least she was not getting sick, the way Diritan had on their travel down from Tabichi that time.

They stayed out on the water for a good hour or more, and Takami proved to be an excellent instructor: clear in his explanations, patient in his training, and happy to sit back and let his emperor do all the real work, learning by doing, while always staying close enough to step in should there be any real need. By the time they turned back toward the royal docks, Hibikitsu thought he could at least keep from drowning himself and most likely make it all the way across the river without falling in.

"You did very well, sire," Takami assured him as he helped dock, perfectly judging the distance so the chayaburi barely bumped up against the pylons before coming to a halt. "Another session or two and you'll be ready to take her out all on your own."

"Not on his own," the Honteno warned, leaping easily across and looping the mooring rope around the pylon. Then she grinned. "Taikoro'd have my head, I let that happen." Her name was Dairamu, and she was proving to be pleasant company, cheerful but not boisterous.

Hibikitsu laughed as he hopped onto the dock beside her, eschewing the hand she offered. "Well, we wouldn't want that, would we?" He turned back toward Takami, but the Rojiri was staring at something off to the side, his brow furrowed. "Is there a problem?"

"Hm?" Takami shook himself and offered a wry smile. "No, your Majesty. No problem. I saw a ship returning, though, and I think it's one I sent to investigate something. If you'll excuse me?" Hibikitsu nodded, and the young noble stepped onto the dock and then slipped past them, making for the gate at the end which would let him back onto the Royal Way. He could exit through the first door inside, Hibikitsu knew, and then cut across Mazihini to reach the aikaye's docks.

"I suppose he'll tell us what that's all about when he's ready," he muttered now, before following Dairamu toward the gate himself.

As it turned out, he did not have to wait very long, because Takami caught up with them before they'd passed through Sakiriti, the sides and roof of the enclosed tunnel shifting color to match the walls of the city tier beyond. "Sire!" the young noble gasped, out of breath from racing after them. He held a scroll, which he offered up, red-faced and panting. "I think you should read this."

Hibikitsu took it and, unrolling the top, began to read. He began frowning after only the first few lines and was scowling by the time he reached the end. "You are sure of this?" he asked, coiling the paper back up but not returning it.

Takami had recovered himself by now. "I am, sire. I had my suspicions, which is why I sent a boat to either confirm them or disprove them." He shook his head. "I'd have preferred to be wrong."

"So would I," Hibikitsu agreed. "Yet, since it is so, better to know it now." He sighed. "Steps will have to be taken."

They walked the rest of the way in silence, as he thought through what would need to be done and how best to do it. He was a little surprised not to be enraged at the news he'd just received. Not that long ago, he'd have been screaming and cursing and breaking everything in sight. Now he felt more disappointed than furious. It was a promise broken, and a blow to his hopes for the future, but hopefully not a fatal one.

Upon reaching Aihiri, the Royal Way depositing them partway across the manicured grounds and within sight of the palace, Hibikitsu turned to his two companions. "Send word for all my Rojiri to attend me in the throne room at once." When Dairamu hesitated, he sighed. "I am literally a dozen paces from my own front door, and several of your fellows standing outside them," he pointed out. "If that is not safe, nothing is. Now go." She saluted and took off at a sprint. Takami followed, though at a fast walk, and Hibikitsu headed indoors to change into more formal attire, as the situation would require.

A short time later, he sat upon his throne, leaning forward in the lacquered seat to peer down over the railings at the nine men and women gathered below. Kagiri, Shizumi, and Reizei were still in their armor, and all three bore nihono—traditionally, no one was to carry blades in the emperor's presence, but after being attacked twice in this very room Hibikitsu had decided to waive that rule where his three trusted commanders were concerned. Takami was still in the light hantien and ponmei he'd worn for their boat training, since he'd hardly had time to change. Seikoku and Noniki were dressed equally simply, while Eijiri, Narai, and Futoba wore fine robes, as befitted successful merchants and the head of a noble house.

"Thank you for assembling so quickly, my Rojiri," Hibikitsu began. "We regret the need, but there is an urgent matter we must address." Several of them straightened slightly, and he knew they had picked up on his use of the royal "we." This was not to be an informal conversation.

He held up the scroll Takami had provided. "We have here disturbing information regarding certain recent activities." He frowned, tapping the scroll against his knee. "As you are all aware, we recently amended an ages-old prohibition against individuals being allowed to farm more than a half tan for personal use." They all nodded, as well they might, since it had been they who had proposed the idea. "This allows our people the opportunity to grow rice not only for their own families but potentially to sell and thus earn from." His hand tightened around the scroll, and he forced it and his voice to calm, though his words still emerged sharp as razors. "Yet it seems some have taken advantage of this new ruling—in Hochiro, in particular." Out of the corner of his eye, he saw one of the assemblage stiffen. "Nor is it some random stranger, or some distant lord. No, one of those closest to us has abused our trust and acted for their own personal gain. Is that not so, Kishin Narai?"

The merchant froze, but only for a second before bowing as best he could, given his bad hip. "I apologize if you feel that to be so, your Majesty," he began smoothly, his face as genial as ever. "It is true that I completed some business in that area recently, but I do not feel it was excessive, or a violation of any sort."

But Hibikitsu unrolled the scroll, running his finger down its contents. "You have bought shares in a dozen small farms in the past week," he pointed out sharply. "All contiguous, so in effect forming a single unbroken concern, but still held in the original owners' names and so each allowed two tan by the new rule. Is that not so?" When Narai began to reply, Hibikitsu held up his hand. "Is it not so?" The man nodded, and he continued. "And you are not alone in this matter. Similar stretches were purchased by one Shizu Yokori, a Jiro Masute, and a Fujiko Oritano. All close confederates of yours, are they not?" The merchant did not respond. "The second you had secured our consent on your proposal, you and your friends began buying up land," Hibikitsu stated. "Together, you now own a large stretch of the most fertile land in that valley—enough for you to control the price of rice between you, squeezing out not only any small farmers but also the nobles, who will be unprepared for such well-organized and ruthless competition."

Kagiri was scowling at Narai and took a step forward, causing the merchant to shrink back at once, face twisting in pain—and possibly fear. "Damn you," Kagiri said, his soft curse as devastating as any scream. "I thought you were sincere for once, in your desire to serve. But you only ever serve yourself."

"I have broken no laws," Narai replied, lifting his chin but not quite meeting his young accuser's eyes. "I have only done as many others will do, now that Your Majesty has wisely and generously righted an old wrong."

Hibikitsu rose to his feet. "You have not committed a crime, no," he agreed, though he knew his face and tone were hard as stone. "But you have violated our confidence. You have worked to engineer a situation for your own profit and done so in an under-handed fashion. We cannot and will not tolerate such behavior from one close to us, nor one involved in the guidance of this nation." His words rang out across the throne room, empty save them and the Honteno by the doors. "Kishin Narai, you are hereby stripped of your rank as Rojiri. You will return to us the medal-lion given to you, and the robes provided to you, and you will take yourself from our sight, never to enter our presence again."

The merchant's face twisted, and for a moment Hibikitsu thought he might protest. But then he glanced at Kagiri, loom-ing on his left, and Shizumi, who had stealthily positioned herself to his right. With a short nod, Narai lifted the medallion from around his neck and held it out. Noniki took it from him. With that done, Narai bowed and, turning, made his way slowly, pain-fully, but with tattered dignity toward the throne room doors. The guards pulled it open for him and closed it again once he'd passed through, sealing the merchant from the room forevermore.

"I am sorry, sire," Kagiri said, sinking to his knees before the dais. "This is my fault. I brought Narai to speak to you in the first place."

Noniki moved to stand by his brother, patting him on the shoulder. "We all voted to include him," he said gently. "And we all knew he was crafty. We just thought he'd use that craftiness for the good of the nation, and not just for himself."

Hibikitsu nodded, sitting back down. "I do not blame you," he promised the young warrior. "I, too, thought him a good match."

"Will you overrule the land purchases?" Seikoku asked. "I'm assuming you can."

He considered that. "No, that would be petty of me, like throw-ing a tantrum after someone beat me at a game. I must be better than that." He grinned. "Though it's possible the ferries along the rivers there will be put to use carrying troops and supplies right around the time of the next harvest, making it both more difficult and more expensive to ship rice from those farms."

The others nodded, and a few of them chuckled as well, which made Hibikitsu feel marginally better. One of those who'd laughed was Futoba, and that reminded him of something else. "Futoba," he called, and she turned immediately, dropping down to abase herself. "Yes, yes, get up." He couldn't be too angry at her for showing such respect here in the throne room, he knew. "It occurred to me," he told her now, "that you are still occupying your family's old estate in Motohiri, is that not so?"

"It is, sire," she answered, returning to her feet. "I had not been there for many years, but it is still well-maintained and quite comfortable."

He smiled. "I am glad to hear it, but I wonder if you would not be happier a little closer to Aihiri? There are several fine estates now available in Atsani, any one of them fit accommodation for a Rojiri. You could even take that which had belonged to the Ieyuki, which I assume you are familiar with?"

She shuddered slightly, tugging on a delicate chain around her neck. "That is most generous of you, sire," she assured him, bowing deeply. "I would not be comfortable in that place, however. We are still struggling to make it clear we have no further association with that ill-fated house."

"Oh. Of course." He grimaced. "I am sorry, that was thoughtless of me. One of the others, then. Any one you like."

Futoba smiled. "You are very kind. I hope you will not think me ungrateful if I take time to consider it?"

"No, not at all." He rose to his feet. "Is there any other pressing business, since we are all here?" No one replied, and he leaped over the railing, landing lightly on the polished floor beyond. "Very good. Shizumi, perhaps you have time for a training session? I feel the need to work out my frustrations over recent events."

She saluted. "Of course, sire. The yard in ten minutes?"

He nodded, and the others all bowed before filing out. Hibikitsu watched them go. He was sad that his Rojiri were once again incomplete, but more upset at Narai's actions. Was it so difficult to find an honest man, one willing to set the empire's needs above his own? At least he still had the others. But thinking of the merchant had his blood boiling and Hibikitsu quickly retreated through the throne room's small side door into his private study, there to strip off his court robes. A few bouts with Shizumi, trying to master swordwork with only his own skill and strength, should help burn off that anger in a more productive fashion.

He would also need to remember to thank Takami for looking into the situation. Otherwise the matter could have become a good deal worse.

CHAPTER TWENTY

"**D**amn it all!" Narai hurled the cup across his sitting room, where it shattered against one of the columns, leaving a gash in the lacquered wood and a smear of tea to drip down. "How dare they?"

"How dare they?" Yokori repeated, brows raised in her narrow face, a smirk playing upon her thin lips. He had sent word to the others at once, and they had gathered here promptly to discuss and commiserate, although he seemed to be getting very little of the latter at the moment. "The emperor and his Rojiri? How dare they, indeed! Who do they think they are, other than the ruler of our nation and his royal advisors?"

Narai glared at her, but she did not back down, and after a moment he was forced to chuckle and shake his head. "Yes, all right, fair enough." He lowered himself onto the couch—gone were the days when he could flop down without a care, thanks to a certain tall, emerald-armored warrior. "But we did nothing wrong! We merely took advantage of the situation—"

"Which we could not have done without your position, since that was the only way we knew about the arrangement in advance," Masute finished for him, leaning back in his chair and stroking his long hair. "You can hardly blame them for finding it a conflict of interest."

"Well, you can, since we were hoping they would not," Oritano argued cheerfully. "But we knew it was a risk. *You* knew it was a risk. The rest of us really had nothing to lose."

Yokori disagreed. "We could still lose a great deal," she snapped. "If the emperor decides to be vindictive. He could void the sales, seize the property, claim our goods, any number of punitive measures!"

On that front, at least, Narai felt he could reassure them. "He will not. Hibikitsu is not that sort. He would consider it beneath him to respond in such a manner." He stroked his short, neat beard and sighed. Truth be told, he admired the young emperor and the advisors he'd assembled and had been honored to be included among them. But yes, he had known there was a chance this latest scheme would have repercussions.

"Ah, well. What's done is done." He reached for the fresh cup of tea Oritano had poured him, and took a long, steadying drink. "Thank you. We may need to be wary when the harvest comes, in case they do decide to punish our ambition in some way, but we will weather that when and if it occurs. We should be able to turn a tidy profit regardless."

"Of course, now we are back to where we were before," Masute pointed out. "Begging scraps of information off Kagiri, when he can spare a moment to remember us."

Narai shook his head. "No. We will not hear from him for some time. He found my naked ambition...unsightly." A part of him went cold and he rubbed absently at his wounded hip, fearing the young warrior might punish them further, in much the way he had back on the road when he'd discovered their previous treachery. But surely this, while distasteful to his eyes, was a far lesser crime, if it was even one at all? No, Narai decided. Kagiri had other matters to focus upon. He might not be happy with them and might shun them for a time, but he would not seek to harm them further. Like the emperor, he would see such behavior as beneath him.

Yokori was scowling into her own cup. "So we are back to where we were even before our travels, then," she stated heavily. "Not that our acumen is not sufficient to the task, but it was certainly pleasant having the advantage of foreknowledge."

He considered that, drinking his tea and letting the hot liquid soothe him. Finally, he said, "Though I no longer have access, there were certain things discussed and even set into motion which we could still make use of." He had already imparted those same plans and ideas to the others. They were, after all, in this together, bonded by mutual self-interest as well as many years of shared ventures, both failed and successful.

His friends all regarded him with sharp eyes and eager faces. "You are now convinced to move forward with the project, then?" Oritano asked, watching him closely as she perched on the edge of her seat. "When Yokori proposed it, you had certain reservations."

"I did, but now those seem less significant." He smiled. "It was always a clever scheme. And with my departure from that post, I no longer have to worry about the same conflicting interests as before. Besides, though they may be displeased with us over some aspects of it, I still see no reason for the Rojiri to object. We will be serving the desires of the emperor, after all, and aiding him in working toward his larger goal." He laughed. "We will simply be making a tidy profit in the process."

The others shared his amusement. "That is the best way, for a merchant," Masute agreed, raising his cup. "Doing good for others—and making money for ourselves while we do."

"Hear, hear," the others agreed, and the mood was much improved as they drank and ate and discussed how best to proceed. Narai was feeling a good deal better about his dismissal by the time they had worked out all the details. And if a small part of him thought, "They will regret sending me away like that," well, that only provided an additional delight to the overall prospect.

CHAPTER TWENTY-ONE

Reizei was, of all things, fighting with her desk when she heard the commotion.

Her leg had been acting up again—she was pushing it too hard, the imperial physician had reprimanded primly, insisting on walking the grounds several times a day—and she'd finally given in and stretched it out full length, her foot extending past the desk, her heel resting on the carpet beyond. Ah, that was better!

But then came a lot of noise out in the hall and in the yards. What in the First Emperor's name was going on?

She sat up, pulling her legs back in so she could turn and stand—and hissed in pain as her wounded limb bumped against the desk's sturdy wooden base. Bones, that hurt!

Reizei had gotten banged up before, of course. You didn't get through even the basic training of an aiashe, much less the far more advanced training of a Honteno, without taking some bruises, some sprains, even a few breaks. This one was by the far the worst, though. She'd been lucky, too. An inch lower and the arrow would have embedded itself in her knee, most likely rendering her incapable of ever bending that leg again. It had struck her in the thigh instead and missed anything vital.

Yet it still hurt. And far worse when it rained, or when she pushed it too hard. Like now as she limped to her feet, cursing up a storm, and grabbed up her cane so she could hobble to the door like an old man.

Throwing the barrier back, Reizei almost collided with Itamon. "What in the nine hells is going on?" she demanded.

Her chuisu had an unusually worried look upon his broad face. "You need to come see," was all he said, which was also not like him. Itamon could stretch ten words into twenty or even fifty, every time.

Now he just turned and hurried away, though he was kind enough to stop and wait for her at the corridor's end. Cursing still but mostly under her breath, Reizei did her best to keep up.

They emerged from their wing of the compound to find a swirl of confused soldiers, servants, and courtiers on the grounds beyond. "Enough!" Reizei shouted, banging her cane against one of the porch columns. The racket was enough to get the crowd's attention, and they quieted. "Whatever is going on, if you are not directly involved, move aside!"

She lumbered forward, sweeping about her with her cane like it was a yanoi, and people melted back as if the sturdy tool could in fact cut them down. Her Honteno quickly took the hint, Itamon and Manari forming up to flank her, several of the others falling in line behind.

Thus it was a small column of warriors who finally crossed the grounds halfway to the Royal Gate—and stopped there, staring at the sight before them.

Reizei frowned, studying the trio of men and women staggering from that passageway. They looked familiar, though she couldn't put names to them. She had seen all of them before, however. She was sure of that. And seen them here, which made sense, given their black armor. They were Honjofu.

And clearly they had been in heavy battle—and, given their long faces, lost badly.

The sound of rapid footsteps came up behind her. Guessing what it meant, Reizei twisted to the side just in time for Shizumi to rocket past, followed by several of her warriors. Bones, the woman was fast! Kagiri followed, far enough back to give the Honjofu's commander her space but near enough to provide support if needed. At times Reizei found the two of them so sweet it made her teeth ache.

"Geniji!" Shizumi pulled up short before grabbing the big woman leading the sad little cluster, hand raised to clasp or hug or help support. "What happened to you?"

"Hey, boss," Geniji—Reizei remembered her as boisterous but never mean—said, grunting a little. She had one arm draped over another warrior's shoulder, and there was blood all down the side of her face. It was impossible to tell if that black armor had similar streaks, but Reizei could see it was badly dented, as if the woman had been caught in a rockslide. "So, we found the guy."

"It was a man?" That was Kagiri, who had joined them, and Reizei eased forward to participate as well. After all, Aihiri was *her* domain.

Stop putting on airs, a voice in her head warned. *You don't need to prove anything, and you're driving away all your allies every time you try.* Reizei ignored it, focusing on the conversation instead.

Geniji nodded, groaning at the motion. "Yeah. One guy. Skinny as all get out, too. And filthy, like he'd been living in a cave or something." She shook her head, then winced. "Anyway, I asked him to come back, real nice. He said no."

The one supporting her, a short, burly fellow, snorted. "Seemed pretty insistent on that, in fact."

"What did he do?" Shizumi asked. She indicated Geniji's wounds, and those of the others. "Those aren't from a sword. And where's Reiko? Where are Kori and Masai?"

"Gone." That was from the third Honjofu, a slim woman with narrow features supporting Geniji's other side. "Stomped flat, beaten to a pulp, torn apart." She shuddered. "It was horrible."

Kagiri frowned, then scanned their surroundings. "We should take this someplace quieter," he suggested. "See to your wounds and hear the full story." His eyes landed on Reizei, as cold as ice, and she forced herself not to scowl back.

Instead she said, "I would like to be there as well, if you'll permit, Taikoro Misataki. This threat concerns us all."

Shizumi spared her only a glance before nodding brusquely. Both of them were still angry at her, then. Lovely.

You deserve it, the voice reminded her. *You were an idiot.* Reizei snarled inside her own head for it to shut up. She was well aware how badly she'd botched that encounter. That's why she was trying to do better.

And why she'd sought help.

Itamon and the others were waiting a short distance back, and Reizei waved him over. "Fetch Essa Jimouen. Have him come to the Honjofu barracks at once." Her lieutenant saluted and raced off.

Then Reizei followed the others back to the buildings behind her, cursing the dirt and grass when it caught at her cane or her wounded leg but determined not to slow them down.

"I've never seen anything like it," Geniji insisted. She was breathing a little easier now that they'd pried her damaged deo off her, tossing the crumpled breastplate to the side. Jimouen Muhimoto had arrived, as crusty and overbearing as ever, and had fussed about while his two assistants cleaned the Honjofu sergeant's wounds. The burly one, Diritan, was favoring one side, and Nioko had several long, nasty gashes on one arm and shoulder, but their gunso had taken the brunt of it. At least, of the three who'd survived.

"The things we fought here, those were bad enough," the big woman continued, glowering at the doctor as he pushed her arm down so he could inspect her wounds more easily. "But these, these weren't skeletons. They were alive! Or at least they looked it, though I swear they were still stone for all the good our weapons did." She shuddered, then cursed as Jimouen poked her in the side. "I already know where it hurts, thank you!"

"Good, then you know how to bind it effectively?" the doctor shot back. "How to keep from getting rot or infection, how much to restrict movement so it can heal? No? Then keep quiet!"

"You say he took out the entire reitao," Kagiri repeated, shaking his head. Without his helmet, he looked so young. "Or at least these creatures of his did."

All three Honjofu nodded. "We'd have been done for as well," Diritan offered, "if it hadn't been for the matekai. Your brother, I mean. Whatever he did before we left, it kept us alive."

The woman, Nioki, sighed. "Even that couldn't save the others.

When something like a mountain gorilla but three times bigger jumps on you, or when a giant tiger with fangs longer than my forearm tears your belly open, or when a four-armed giant flings you against a mountainside, there's only so much magic can do."

Shizumi hung her head, and Reizei felt for her. She knew only too well what it was like to lose comrades who were also your friends. When the former Rojiiri had turned traitor, more than half the Honteno had died holding them at bay. Every single one of those had been someone she'd worked with, trained with, fought with, laughed with, ate with, for more times than she could remember. But no more.

"Did he say what he wanted?" she asked, forcing herself not to flinch as the others turned to look at her. "He isn't doing all of this just on a whim."

The three battered warriors all frowned. "He said…he was impressed we had no aishone," Geniji recalled. "He talked about cleansing the land, starting over."

Diritan nodded. "He said he'd leave us alone if we stayed out of his way. I think he may've even meant it."

Kagiri scowled. "Let him cleanse the land by destroying everything in his path? That's hardly something we can allow." He rose to his feet, as always exhibiting that fluid grace that was the mark of a true warrior. "We need to tell Niki. And the emperor. We'll have to act before this gets any worse."

Shizumi stood as well. "Agreed." But she shook her head when her Honjofu moved to follow her lead. "No, you three have done enough. Stay here, let the good doctor tend to your wounds, and rest."

Geniji tried to argue and yelped when Jimouen poked her again. "Stop doing that!"

"Sit still!" he snapped, then pointed a bony finger at the other two. "And you're next!"

Reizei eased herself to her feet and followed Kagiri and Shizumi out, back onto the barracks' front porch. They did not try to prevent her, but they did not glance back or include her, either. Nor did they slow their own quick, uninjured pace.

Your own fault, the voice reminded. "Yes, I know," she snarled under her breath. "Leave it!"

Not that she expected that to work. Maniko Kohori had spoken her mind when she was alive. Dead, she apparently had even less reticence.

That was Reizei's own fault too, however. She had foolishly started down this road.

Now, trailing behind her fellow Taikoro and the Dogenriku, she wondered if there was any way to stop what she'd begun. She wished she could ask for their advice, warrior to warrior.

But it seemed she'd already burned that bridge, and Reizei wasn't sure she could repair it, or build a new one. She'd always been better at cutting through things. That's what had made her such an effective warrior.

It didn't help her much as a leader, however. And using Kohori's bones felt like it was only making matters worse.

CHAPTER TWENTY-TWO

Noniki was in the council chamber, chatting with Takami and Futoba, when his brother burst in. "Niki!" Kagiri's face was set, his jaw squared in that particular expression Noniki knew meant "we have a problem and we need to deal with it *now*."

Shizumi was right beside him—it amused Noniki how two such puissant warriors could be so clueless about romance, to the point of not realizing each other's interest—and looked equally grim. And Reizei limped in after them like a broken shadow, looking none happier.

"What's happened?" Noniki asked, rising to meet them. "Is it your expedition? Did they—"

His brother nodded. "They found him, yes. And he wiped them all out."

"Wait, he?" Noniki's stomach twisted as he took in the rest of that statement. "All of them?" He glanced at Shizumi, and she managed a wan smile.

"Three of mine survived—thanks to you." She pounded her fist to her chest in salute. "I am in your debt."

Noniki waved that off. "I did what I could. I'm sorry it wasn't enough. But what happened, exactly?"

He returned to his seat and the other three followed, settling around the table. Only Eijiri and Seikoku were missing to make the Rojiri complete. But this was no ordinary deliberation, no casual exchange of lofty ideas. No one interrupted as Kagiri and Shizumi took turns repeating what the three wounded Honjofu had said. By the time they'd finished, Noniki felt as somber as they looked.

"Very well," he declared, pushing his chair back and climbing to his feet. "This has gone on long enough. Time for me to see this stranger for myself."

In less time than it took to blink, his brother was standing beside him—as was Shizumi. "Not alone," Kagiri insisted. "If you're going, we're going with you."

Noniki smiled and clapped his brother on the shoulder. "I wish you could. But I am not going by boat or by horse, and I doubt this method is one you can use, even with those ancient memories of yours."

Shizumi was frowning. "You mean to use magic to—what, spy on him?" When he nodded, she did as well. "Good. Then we will spy with you. Three sets of eyes are better than one."

"I—" He started to say that it didn't work that way, then stopped. Because, in all honesty, he wasn't sure that it didn't.

He'd intended to set his soul questing, in much the way he'd done while meditating before. Only this time, traveling much farther, well beyond the city, all the way down into Bezenkai. He didn't think he could do that with two warriors clinging to him like children at their mother's skirts, not when they couldn't separate soul from body on their own.

But maybe he could. After all, he'd still barely scratched the surface of what magic could do. Could he take their souls with him? Would he have to form some kind of bond first, spirit to spirit? Or put their bodies in a trance? Perhaps focus their thoughts on the intended destination, then use that direction as a target and fire them like an arrow along that path? Or—

Kagiri cleared his throat and smiled when Noniki turned to him. "You were getting ahead of yourself, hm?"

That made him laugh. Yes, perhaps he was. What's more, he'd been outsmarting himself, to boot. Because if there was one thing Noniki was starting to understand about the magic, it was this—

Thinking about it, devising some sort of method or plan, was exactly the wrong way to go about it.

He didn't plan the magic. He just tapped into it, doing what felt right.

In this case, that meant holding out his hands. Kagiri took

his left at once, and Shizumi quickly latched onto his right. Then Noniki began slowly turning in a circle, dragging the pair along with him. They hesitated at first, but after a few stumbling steps the warriors joined hands as well, and now all three of them were skipping about like little kids. They spun and spun, growing dizzier and dizzier, the world beginning to lose focus around them as everything but their trio began to blur.

And then Noniki felt himself drifting upward.

It was different from before. Then, he had felt only the world around him, with little sense of self. Now, Noniki could still feel himself, his consciousness, his soul. It was as diffuse as before, but not endlessly so. Instead it spread out like a ball, forming a faint sphere that was Noniki.

And floating within it, like two droplets trapped inside a soap bubble, were Kagiri and Shizumi.

Noniki saw them as sparks of light, both bright and clear. His brother's light had an odd, overlapping halo about it, almost like a prism, fuzzy at the edges but clean at the center. That had to be the effect of those past warriors, the Gensaiba matekan, who had latched onto Kagiri and eventually merged with him. Shizumi, by contrast, was a single light, without complication or confusion. More than most in Rimbaku, she had never even blurred her soul with aishone—as Mukanichi, she couldn't have, even if she'd wanted to.

The two lights bobbed within the protective shell he'd woven around them and twisted about each other in the process, like a dance.

Or a courtship.

Putting that thought aside, Noniki focused on his task. He rose up through Awaihinshi, passing through the roof and out into the open sky.

Then, with no transition, he was sailing across Rimbaku, speeding southward so fast the ground below them blurred in passing.

Shizumi let out a small cry, but one of wonder and joy. Kagiri gave a soft grunt, echoing her emotions. Noniki could hardly blame them. This land really was beautiful.

But up ahead, he could already see a dark stain, like a scorch mark upon the very earth. It stretched back down, running south until it faded from view. That was fine. He was after the endpoint, not the beginning. He concentrated, focusing on the start of the blemish, and zoomed toward it, stopping and hovering just before reaching the devastation.

Because that's exactly what it was.

To either side, the land was rich and fertile, green with grass and vines and stalks, thick with flowers and fruits.

But directly ahead of him, Noniki saw only destruction.

Something—someone—had carved a path right through the territory, burning away every trace of life as they passed. The ground still smoked behind them, and here and there the black soil was marred by gray and white flecks.

Ash.

Stomping down the broad pathway came an army right out of a child's nightmares. Giants and dragons and great raging beasts, all larger than the biggest man, all trumpeting and roaring and screaming, all laying about them with tooth and claw, fang and wing, crushing anything in their path.

And at their head marched a solitary man.

Tall, as Kagiri had said, Noniki judged from his aerial vantage point. Narrow. Disheveled, and far more than that. There was something almost dusty about him, about his faded clothes and untamed hair and beard. It took a moment for Noniki to realize the man was floating over the ground rather than walking upon it, and he felt a strange frisson of fear and delight at the sight, for he knew what it meant, what he'd already begun to suspect—

He was no longer the only matekai in Rimbaku.

Then the stranger stopped, his monstrous army lumbering to a halt at his back. He straightened, shifting his weight from side to side—

And tilted his head back, shielding his eyes and turning in a slow circle.

Until he was looking straight at Noniki and his two passengers.

"What have we here?" he asked, his voice an echoing creak. "Sentries, sent to spy on me?" He sniffed, his face wrinkling from the action. "And whose trace did you consume to work such a feat, hm? I want none of your filthy presence. Begone."

He swept his hand toward them, though they were well out of reach. But a gale echoed his gesture, the wind rising from nowhere. It slammed into Noniki, sweeping him back like a stray leaf, tossed and turned by the current. He struggled to stay put, to anchor himself in place, but it was no use. The flurry was too strong for him. He was flung out toward the sea, Kagiri and Shizumi tumbling inside his expanded essence, all three of them left dizzy and breathless.

For a moment, Noniki felt chilled with fear. What if they got caught up by the waves somehow, and were unable to make their way back to their bodies? But then he forced himself to relax. Returning was not a matter of travel or direction. It only required letting the natural state reassert itself.

Noniki stopped struggling and, at once, his spirit was tugged back toward Awaihinshi. Toward his body. He did not resist, and in an instant he found himself standing on his own two feet again, staggering, his hands still clasped by his two companions.

"Are you all right?" That was Futoba, who was by his side, guiding him back to his chair. "The three of you were swaying, eyes open but not seeing. Then you all gasped and shook and almost fell."

He let himself be seated and focused on calming his breath and his mind. Kagiri and Shizumi had returned to the table as well, where Takami and Reizei had waited, and for a moment no one spoke.

Shizumi finally broke the silence. "That was…"

Noniki nodded. "Yes."

They had found the threat. And he understood now exactly why he'd been unable to sense the man's presence. He was indeed a fellow matekai, and a powerful one.

All of which boded ill for them, and Rimbaku.

CHAPTER TWENTY-THREE

The great council chamber was silent and Kagiri slumped in his chair, drained by that strange experience. It was like he had been soaring through the air, free as a bird, light as a cloud! Yet at the same time, there had been a tremendous strain upon him, such that he now felt as if he'd run the length of Awaihinshi and back. He could see that Shizumi felt much the same—they had held extended martial bouts often enough for him to know how she looked exhausted.

It was his brother he was most worried about, however. Noniki did not look merely tired. He looked stunned, his eyes unfocused, his jaw slack.

"Niki?" Kagiri put a hand on his shoulder and got no reaction—no flinch, no smile, nothing. "Are you all right?"

After a second, when he feared his brother had not been heard at all, he nodded. "Yes." The response was little more than a breath, but Noniki said it again, slightly stronger. "Yes." Finally he turned toward his brother, managing the same sheepish grin as when he'd been caught out at something. "I'm fine, Giri. Truly. Thank you."

But he shuddered as he said it. Still, he was responding, at least, which meant they could focus on the bigger problem again. "Who was that?"

Noniki shook his head slowly. "I don't know."

"A wizard." That was from Shizumi, and she shrugged when they both looked her way, though even that motion lacked her usual energy. "Had to be. Already destroyed an entire reitao on his own. And a boat. And who knows what else." She grimaced. "And he tossed us aside like a cracked cup."

His brother was nodding. "Yes. He was matekai."

Kagiri frowned at him. "I thought you were the only one."

"So did I," Noniki admitted with a rueful chuckle. "Evidently we were wrong." He sighed. "But beyond that, I have no idea. No idea where he came from, no idea what he wants."

"We know where whoever you saw must be going, though," Reizei offered softly, as if afraid to insert herself in the conversation. "Here. Where else?"

That certainly made sense. And anyone approaching Awai-hinshi with an army at his back—especially such a bizarre yet powerful army as that!—was someone Kagiri did not want coming any closer. "We need more information. Such as his name, to start. And where he gained that magic. And what he has planned."

His brother straightened a little. "Yes. Yes, we do. Perhaps—" A pitcher of water stood to one side on the table, along with a pitcher of wine and several cups. Ignoring the rest, Noniki took up the first pitcher and poured some of its contents onto the table in front of him, where it formed a shallow pool. Then, setting the pitcher aside, he held both hands over that watery disc.

Kagiri felt a soft breeze ruffle his hair. It had a cool, crisp scent, like the first taste of winter. The water filmed over, turning to ice before his eyes. Its surface turned cloudy, then cleared. In that circle he saw sky and sun and earth, as if he were looking through a window from someplace high up. He thought he recognized the landscape as the place they'd just been—part of them, anyway. The view shifted, sliding forward, and for a second he caught a glimpse of massive figures and a tall, slim one in frayed and faded robes floating above them.

Then the ice cracked, shattering into a thousand tiny shards and lumps.

Noniki sat back. "No good," he said, pouring more water but this time into a cup he quickly drained. "I cannot see him. No doubt he is blocking it somehow." He scowled at the bits of ice. "I didn't even know you could do that."

Thinking about the stranger, Kagiri had a thought. "His clothing looked old, didn't it?" he asked. "Old and worn out." The two who'd seen the same man nodded. "But not just normally old, not like Mother Utu's shawl. His looked ancient. Like relics."

"It did," Shizumi agreed. "And his hair—he looked as if he'd lived in a cave for a few decades."

Kagiri was following the notion that had sprung into his head. "What if it was longer than that? A good deal longer? What if he were as old as his clothes?" He looked at Noniki. "What if he had magic because he was from before the Cataclysm?"

The other two had all been quiet until now, but Futoba let out a strange gasping squeak. "That's impossible!" she insisted. "That would make him hundreds of years old!"

Noniki was considering, however. "Perhaps not impossible," he said softly. "Unlikely, yes. But with magic, the unlikely can easily become a reality." He was studying Kagiri now, and suddenly grinned. "You have an idea."

"I do." Kagiri laughed. "Possibly a useless one. Certainly an odd one—if not utterly ridiculous. But maybe, just maybe, it will help."

"What are you talking about?" Shizumi asked. "What are you going to do?" She was watching him closely, as fierce as ever, and Kagiri had the overpowering suspicion that, if he said he was going to jump from Aihiri and try to hit the river far below, she'd insist upon going with him. That was why he smiled at her now, and tried to act nonchalant, even though head, heart, and stomach were suddenly all in knots.

"It's nothing to worry about," he promised her. "I'm just going to have a little chat. With myself."

Then he closed his eyes and concentrated on the voices within.

When Kagiri had first emerged from the Tawasiri, he'd been alarmed to discover that he heard voices now. And not just random ones, or stray lines that could easily be faulty memories. No, he had heard six distinct voices.

The six Gensaiba matekan, the sorcerers' blades.

He'd thought he'd gone mad. The voices had been quick to assure him otherwise, though that had hardly been comforting. It was when he'd discovered his new martial prowess that he realized they spoke true. He had not lost his mind. The voices were real. And they were now bound to him—permanently, it seemed.

Slowly, as they'd traveled here, Kagiri had learned to assert himself, to tame those voices so that they could only offer advice and knowledge without attempting control. And, as he'd become more confident, more skilled, the voices had faded. He rarely heard them anymore.

Which didn't mean they were not still available. They had just been submerged into his larger self.

Now he intended to draw one back out.

Closing his eyes, Kagiri concentrated on the first Gensaiba who came to mind. Nikiyu Sinchu. Slim, soft-spoken, and lightning fast. "Nikiyu," he called out in his head. "Can you hear me? I'd like to speak with you, please."

He felt a strange rushing sensation, as if he were falling from a great height, and a presence below, waiting to receive him. Kagiri tried to scream, to rise up, anything to avoid the encounter, but it was no use. He plummeted directly into that phantom embrace.

And opened his eyes upon a world of wonders.

Kagiri recognized the room at once, with its tall, black-framed windows and its graceful arches, the floor intricately tiled, the walls carved in decorative bands, weapons and armor hung on racks to either side, benches alongside, and a broad table at the center bearing food and drink.

He was back in the Tawasiri. And not the ancient, empty, haunted relic the tower had become. No, he was seeing it as it had been before, when the Gensaiba and their matekai were still alive.

Back in the days before the Schism.

What's more, he recognized the five others sitting or standing or pacing nearby, three men and two women, each wearing a fine but understated kitoro over casual ponmei with plain but comfortable woven sandals. It was the Gensaiaba matekan.

Except there should have been six of them.

Kagiri ran through the faces and names imprinted in his mind. There was Geido Shinen, as big and boisterous as ever. And Shito Kibi, not beautiful but invitingly friendly. Onyoku Jeizen, light and quick, with a tidy little beard tracing his strong jaw. Bushiki Kenin, short and stocky. And Komu Setsui, lovely and calm.

Which left out Nikiyu Sinchu, narrow, quiet, and disapproving. The very one Kagiri had called on for help.

"Here you go," Shinen was saying as he thrust a handsome goblet at Kagiri. "Drink up. Might as well, hm? Not much we can do until they're done." The big man held up his own cup, and they clinked together in toast. "To beauty, fame, and glory everlasting," Shinen proposed, and Kagiri found himself matching the statement word for word, though he was sure he'd never heard it before.

But it seemed part of him had.

"It sounds bad," Setsui commented from where she lounged on one of the benches, fluttering her long, delicate lashes. "The worst yet."

The others all nodded, several of them with a grimace. Kagiri tried to ask what they meant, but no sound emerged from his mouth. Instead, he found himself sipping his wine as if he had no control over himself.

Then he did speak, but only to say, "There must be something we can do. Before this becomes a problem."

Except that wasn't Kagiri's voice.

He had heard those soft, disapproving tones before, however. When he'd encountered all six Gensaiba, both in the Tawasiri and after, in his own head.

It was Sinchu, the one warrior missing from his view of the scene. So this, then, was the answer to his plea. Rather than speaking *to* Sinchu, he was now speaking—and seeing, drinking, walking—*as* him.

Kagiri wished he could talk or move independently. He wanted to ask things, to interrogate the gathered warriors. He also wanted to drag himself over to a window so he could get a better view of what lay beyond.

Nothing worked. He was evidently an observer, trapped in Sinchu's body here just as the Gensaiba were all trapped within him back home.

But what a time to be trapped! Because the air itself felt alive with promise, carrying hints of sugar and spice and music. The tiled floor thrummed beneath his feet. The fruit and cheese and bread laid out on the table practically glowed with invitation, and he could hear the water and wine splashing and sparkling in their decanters and pitchers.

Then Jeizen reached for a nafti—and the mottled green and gold fruit leapt into his outstretched hand. A tap with his forefinger and the skin split neatly, revealing the crisp white flesh within, which then divided itself into tidy slices.

But how? Jeizen was an expert at hand-to-hand fighting. He was no mage!

Yet, as Kagiri watched, several of the others performed similar feats. Nothing large, just tiny little tricks, yet things no one in his time could do, save Noniki—and now this deadly stranger. And surely, if they had been wizards, he would have felt that when he'd absorbed their spirits? There was nothing arcane in him, Kagiri was sure of that.

Perhaps, then, the magic was not in the Gensaiba, but in the air, the food, the world.

Maybe this was what life had been like before the Schism. Full of magic for everyone.

He wondered what had happened. The stories they'd heard when they were young had said nothing about the cause, only that it had destroyed all the magic in the land.

Clearly, whatever it was hadn't happened yet.

Kagiri tried again to speak to the others, to ask them why they were gathered, why they were worried, if they knew anything about the stranger.

He could not. All he could do was watch the drama playing out before him.

A shout drifted down from somewhere, along with a shower of dust from high overhead. "Definitely bad," Kenin agreed. "When even Honei is shouting? That's a problem."

Kagiri remembered the one glimpse he'd had of Bushiki Honei, after Noniki had separated Kaemusei back out into the wizards that had formed it. The matekai had smiled as if he wanted to laugh at everything around him, but not in a mean way, or a belittling one. And that cheerful figure was shouting loud enough to shake the tower above?

Kibi rose to her feet. "Maybe we should intervene," she suggested, her broad face creased with concern.

Kagiri found himself—Sinchu—snorting. "And what good would that do? They'd just cast us out and go right back to it."

But Shinen stood beside Kibi. "We have to try," the big man urged. "We can't just sit here."

Setsui grumbled, as did Sinchu, but they did not argue. The two of them fell in with the rest as they turned and headed towards the stairs leading upward.

Those in front had managed only to set their feet onto the first step when Kagiri found himself falling to his knees. The others tumbled down around him. "Do you…feel…that?" Jeizen gasped, clutching his chest.

Kagiri did not, but he felt Sinchu nod. "What…is it?"

"It's…" Setsui started to answer, but collapsed before she could finish, her jade banezhan tumbling from her thumb. It shattered when it hit the step. The others fell as well, goblets and fruits dropping from their hands, all of them going limp in a tangled heap. They were more than just unconscious, however—their eyes were open but unseeing, their chests utterly still.

Kagiri lay with the rest, though he himself did not seem affected. Only the body he was guesting in.

Then something plucked him from that cooling form and he found himself growing dizzy, as if he were falling again.

When he opened his eyes, he was still at the table, the other Rojiri watching him closely. Most of them looked confused, but Noniki smiled. "What did you see?"

Unfortunately, Kagiri wasn't sure how to answer that. Or that whatever had just happened would prove to be any help.

CHAPTER TWENTY-FOUR

Futoba was in many ways relieved to arrive home and find a trio of supplicants waiting to speak with her.

She had witnessed the events in the council chamber today with mixed apprehension, confusion, and terror. That there was something dangerous approaching was abundantly clear from the tense battle-readiness of the three military commanders present, and from the unusual gravity shown by the normally relaxed Noniki.

The problem was, Futoba really didn't understand any of it.

From her perspective, Shizumi, Kagiri, and Reizei had rushed into the room with stories about lost boats, downed soldiers, and an army of monsters. Noniki had reacted as if this were all very serious, however, and had announced his intention to see for himself.

Only, he had never left the room.

Instead, he had taken Kagiri and Shizumi's hands, spun the three of them in a circle, stared into space in a daze—and then all but collapsed where he stood.

Apparently, that had been enough.

Futoba had heard the old tales of magic from before the Schism, of course. She had loved them as a child, the stories of matekai raising castles from the ocean, leveling mountains, diverting fires around whole villages, and so on.

But they had never been real. Just ancient fables.

In the time she'd been back, she had seen several things she would have considered torn from those legends: an army of winged skeletons (though she had not yet been in Awaihinshi during that failed attack, she had seen enough wreckage and remains, and heard enough firsthand accounts, to accept it as true); an estate whose entire appearance had been changed overnight; a paper bird that flew of its own accord.

This had been both more subtle and more frightening, because there had been no outward signs of magic. Yet she could not find it in herself to doubt something important had happened.

That had been followed by Kagiri losing himself in his own thoughts, sitting at the table still as a statue with his eyes unfocused on the world around him. He had emerged from that state with a gasp, looking badly shaken. Then he had imparted another myth, a tale of the Gensaiba matekan, gathered in the Tawasiri while their matekai argued and quarreled above them.

All of that had been too strange to comprehend. People asking to speak with a Rojiri to request some favor was far more understandable, a recognizable situation, and though she was tired, Futoba agreed to see them at once.

They had been waiting in one of the sitting rooms, and she joined them there rather than having them brought to her study. They were all women and rose to bow deeply as she entered. All three wore robes of a sensible cut and good cloth, neither too fine for the city's lower regions nor too cheap for its middle ones, and all three looked to be of or approaching middle age, with their hair in respectable buns or coils.

The one to the right Futoba recognized, though it took her a moment to place the face.

"You are Senkousa Utami, are you not?" she asked, and the woman in question beamed, the expression not quite matching her thin face and close-placed eyes.

"I am, milady, yes." Utami's voice was as rough as the last time they'd spoken, though Futoba had realized quickly that it was not any form of illness or a sign of displeasure, just her natural tone. "How kind of you to remember."

Futoba laughed at that, gesturing for them to sit again on the couch they'd just vacated, while she herself sank gratefully into one of the chairs opposite. There was tea on the low table between them, and Natsu, who had been waiting to one side, was already pouring her a cup. "I could hardly forget, after we spent nearly the whole day together," Futoba said with a smile. "Thank you, Natsu." She took a sip, savoring the rich blend—Iefusa always teased her about how he liked the floral teas and she the robust ones. "I do not believe I know your friends, however."

Utami dipped her head. "My pardon, milady. Please allow me to introduce Senkousa Medeiko and Senkousa Wani." Both women bowed. Medeiko was short and solid, with a lined face and gray hair but a warm smile. Wani was younger and prettier than her two companions, with surprisingly blue eyes.

Futoba frowned at the first woman, though just in recollection. "You worked with Seikoku, did you not? In Mazihini?"

The woman's smile widened. "I did, milady, yes. I was honored to assist her in your new endeavor." Her voice was rich and warm. "Wani here is based in Sakiriti, and we have already recommended her to aid you both when you expand to that level."

Sipping her tea, Futoba considered the trio. Three Senkousa, each from a different tier of Awaihinshi, and two of them already assisting in the empire's buyback program. "Is that why you've come, then? To put her forward? But you said you'd already done that."

The three glanced at each other, and Medeiko took up the answer. "No, milady. We are here for another reason entirely, though it follows from the first, in a way." She sighed. "Are we given to understand, from your recent actions, that the days of the Relicant Way are numbered?"

Futoba used the action of drinking to give herself time to consider an answer. The emperor had not been reticent about his intentions, but there had been no public announcement yet. Still, the more perceptive could certainly put the pieces together and see where the empire was headed. "Yes," she admitted finally. "The emperor's intention is to wean his people from dependence on aishone. Whether that means they will no longer be used at all is another matter, but certainly they will no longer be the cornerstone of our culture."

She tried to read her guests' faces. She had just told them

outright that their livelihood was doomed, and with it their position, for Senkousa were held in high regard, thanks to their gifts. Medeiko did not look upset, only thoughtful. Utami seemed more mournful. Wani's eyes had narrowed, but her face remained placid, neutral.

"We understand," Medeiko assured her. "And, while it will reduce us personally, how could we not, as loyal subjects, wish to see the empire grow stronger and more vibrant?" She leaned forward slightly, lowering her voice a little as if sharing a confidence. "But that is why we have come, milady. We understand that, before too much time has passed, our current occupation will likely cease. We will need a new way to survive and perhaps even thrive, and we hoped we might request your help in such."

Futoba set her cup aside. "I am listening and will help if I can and if it is not inappropriate," she promised.

That earned smiles from all three. "I have an interest in herbs," Utami announced. "Wani in flowers, both the growing and the arranging of such. And Medeiko, Medeiko is a surprisingly fine painter." Her friend dipped her head at the compliment.

"We have taken inspiration from Sorainasei, milady," Wani put in, speaking for the first time. Her voice was high and thin, a mismatch to her beauty. "And hoped to follow their example."

"You wish to establish a community of artists and crafters?" Futoba considered. "That seems a reasonable goal, and a laudable one." She tilted her head. "But surely you do not require my assistance for that?"

Utami cleared her throat. Wani looked away. But Medeiko lifted her chin. "We would like to petition to be granted ownership of one of the vacant estates in Atsani," she stated boldly. "We have some money saved, the three of us and a few others, enough to pay taxes and cover any repairs required, but of course the estates themselves are not for sale. They can only be granted by the Emperor himself."

Now Futoba understood. "And you would like me to champion your request to him." That made sense—if the petition came from one of his Rojiri, Hibikitsu would certainly consider it. And, in all honesty, probably grant it as long as there was no clear reason not to.

Nor did she see any issue with the request herself. If anything, it was a good and noble cause, aiding these Senkousa in transitioning to a different life that did not involve aishone. And giving them one of those estates would also show the empire's gratitude for the services they had rendered all these years.

She even had the perfect estate in mind. One to which she had some claim herself, and thus more than the usual influence in distributing, perhaps. Doing so might also help settle another concern she'd yet to address.

She smiled at them, and all three visibly relaxed. "I think your request is a fine one, and I would be happy to present it to His Imperial Majesty, with my strongest recommendation. I would ask just one thing. The people who were employed at those estates, many of them have remained there in secret, as they have nowhere else to go. I would ask that, if you find any such, you do your best to either welcome them and include them in your own plans or to help them find other homes and positions."

Wani clapped her hands, and Utami's eyes filled with tears. Medeiko retained her composure but her smile was wide indeed as she inclined her head. "Thank you, milady. Utami had said you were kind, and I see it is indeed so." She produced a small scroll from her sleeve and set it on the table. "If it pleases you, here is our petition. We are happy to provide any other details you might require, of course. And naturally we would assist any unfortunates we found on any estate we were granted."

"I will look this over right away, and let you know if there is anything else," Futoba promised as the three Bone Readers rose. "And, if not, I will instead contact you as soon as the emperor makes his decision."

They all bowed deeply, murmuring their thanks and appreciation, and then filed out, leaving her to think about the idea. She liked it. She suspected the other Rojiri would as well, and Hibikitsu himself. The remaining major families would be incensed, of course, but would be powerless to prevent it. And it should make life easier for Seikoku and her residents, as they would no longer be the only such settlement in Atsani. Plus the other former Ieuyuki servants might find a new life there, with new employers or perhaps even as equal partners.

Of course, that brought another matter to mind, and she frowned, a little of her good mood deflated. The emperor had offered her one of those empty estates as well, which was most generous of him—and entirely in keeping with what she had seen of his character. Accepting would be a visible boost in the honor of her house. A larger estate would also require more staff, meaning she could offer some of those displaced servants a position herself.

Yet she was unsure whether she should accept. In fact, something in her gut told Futoba she should turn down the proffered gift. She just was not sure why.

For the moment, however, she could focus on the Senkousas' request. That seemed a good deal more straightforward. Her own choice could wait.

Right now, Futoba decided, getting to her feet, she would go find her family, hug them all tight, and then see what Arima had prepared for dinner while hearing all about their day. Everything else could wait until morning.

CHAPTER TWENTY-FIVE

"**Y**our Imperial Majesty! What an unexpected pleasure!"

Hibikitsu was too well trained to curse or make a face, but it was a near thing. Instead he turned and smiled, bowing at the small, silver-haired woman hurrying toward him, her plump and bespectacled scribe trailing behind he as usual.

"Lady Nihoro. Master Makono. We did not know you were here and hope we are not intruding upon your solitude." In truth, he had *not* known they were here in these gardens and would not have ventured into them if he had, for he had done his best to avoid the pair of Fyushan guests. Still, they had been granted the freedom of Aihiri, and so he had been bound to run into them outside the throne room eventually.

"You can hardly intrude upon your own demesne, sire," Nihoro said with a dry little laugh, a hint of gentle chiding in her tone. "Yet we appreciate your generosity, as always." She ventured a smile which caused even more lines to appear across her face like webbing. "I hope we are not the ones intruding upon you, for I know how much your time is in demand and that this must be a rare moment of quiet for you."

That had definitely been a subtle yet pointed dig at his not having met with her since her arrival, and Hibikitsu ducked his head, openly acknowledging the hit.

"You are as perceptive as you are diplomatic, Lady," he stated. "And we apologize for any perceived slight, for in truth none was intended. We have, as you so aptly noted, been much engaged with other affairs of late."

"Oh?" Her dark eyes were as bright as a Hakichuekai's as she leaned a little closer. "I hope there has not been any trouble? Is there anything I might do to help, either as a representative of my Mistress or as my own humble self?"

Hibikitsu was too familiar with courtiers and nobles not to recognize the naked curiosity displayed on her face—and too experienced to succumb to it. "No trouble beyond the usual matters of governing an empire," he replied with an airy tone. "More tedious than difficult, as we are sure your own Empress could relate. We appreciate your kind offer, however."

The little emissary was far too skilled to look put out at having her inquisitiveness thwarted. "Of course," was all she replied. Then she brightened again. "However, I do have good news, Your Majesty. I have recently received word from my Mistress." Her bow this time was deeper, more formal, as was her following statement: "She has bid me thank you for your kindness in hosting myself and my aide, and for your generous offer. As I fully expected, she is both delighted and appreciative of your desire to be neighborly and would like me to begin negotiations with you as soon as is convenient."

Hibikitsu bit back a laugh. His Honteno had been watching the three sets of emissaries very closely and would have reported had Lady Nihiro received any messages. She had not. Noniki had also assured him that there was no magic of any sort around the woman or her scribe companion. Thus this claim of a recent update was a ruse, as had been the initial request to wait here for such a missive. But that was fine and expected. He was sure the woman had been given detailed instructions before she'd left her own country, and part of those had been to dole out information as she felt necessary, at whatever pace she deemed most appropriate. Now, however, he merely nodded.

"We are pleased to hear that, and happy to continue improving our relations to one another," he replied. "We will consult with our Rojiri and find a time to sit with you and start such discussions as soon as is feasible."

That was a fairly standard response, promising little, but her smile was as bright as if he had just agreed to give her starving nation the food for free. Oh, she was very good at this game,

Hibikitsu admitted to himself. Rilani had chosen her ambassador well! "Thank you, Your Majesty." Nihiro bowed deeply yet again. "I will await your pleasure." She backed away, still bowing, and her scribe moved with her, mimicking the motion, if with less grace. That one was a mystery, and Hibikitsu had discussed the man with his advisors more than once since the pair's arrival. While unassuming and thus far completely nonverbal, Makono Takari seemed almost too placid, too harmless, to be believed. There was also an odd delay in his response to protocol—when his mistress bowed, it took him several seconds, and sometimes a pointed reminder from her, to follow suit. Shizumi, who was perhaps the most suspicious of the Rojiri, had wondered if the man might not be more bodyguard than clerk. Still, as long as he caused no trouble Hibikitsu had little reason to object, and the pair was closely observed at all times.

With them departed, he was free to roam the gardens once more. And, as had often been the case of late, Hibikitsu found his steps leading toward one spot in particular. It was just behind the warriors' practice grounds, a walled space rich with flowering trees and bushes. At one end it boasted a hidden door leading into a small section dominated by a shallow pond surrounded by flat stepping stones and barely trimmed trees with narrow resting ledges along the sides. This had once been his mother's favorite place, her own private refuge from the world. When she had died, while he was still very young, the sheltered location had been mostly forgotten—until a certain young Honteno had found it and made it her own.

It was this little garden that Kohori had frequented most over the years, particularly once she'd risen to Taikoro and needed someplace where she could go and not be disturbed.

And it was here that she had died.

Standing by the pond, Hibikitsu closed his eyes and breathed in deep, taking in air gently scented by pine and cedar and fresh water. It was a calm place, restful and untamed. He had seen at once why his loyal guard commander had liked it so much. And, though the part of him heavy with grief had wanted to tear it all out and wall the space up, sealing it off forever, a wiser, calmer voice had prevailed. One that he fancied sounded like Kohori herself.

That voice had said, "Do not blame this place for my death, sire. And do not destroy its beauty because I met my fate here. Instead, come here to remember me, and to know that I was happy. May its peace serve you as well as it did me."

And it did. He found that, being here, he could forget his troubles for a few minutes. Forget he was emperor, even. Here, in this moment, he was just Hibikitsu, a young man standing in a tiny private garden.

That could not last, of course. But it was with renewed calm that he exited the spot, carefully closing the hidden door again behind him. And he was glad he had, because he had taken only a few steps from it when a trio appeared around a short distance ahead, a man and two women, all clad in green and blue and white.

For an instant Hibikitsu considered diving back into the little garden, shutting the door behind him, and praying they had not seen him yet.

That was an unfit response from an emperor—or any decent gentleman—however, and so instead he put on a pleasant if noncommittal smile and stepped forward to greet them.

"Lord and Lady Yakami." He dipped his head as they bowed and curtsied, as graceful and handsome a couple as ever. His eyes flicked to the younger woman behind them, her jade-hued kitoro patterned in the Higinasi wave crest. "Your Highness."

She dipped into a smooth curtsy, her face calm and composed. "Your Imperial Majesty." This was the fourth time they had met, including the first in his throne room, and Hibikitsu had yet to see even a flicker of emotion from Ogawa Tsuni. He had once wondered aloud if she might be some clever marionette, so still were her features. Kohori would have slapped the back of his head for such rudeness, and it would have been well deserved, but he had been alone at the time and so had only his thoughts to reprimand him. One would certainly expect a princess to have been carefully and thoroughly trained, yet he could not help hoping for some signs of life and independent thought.

Especially since her brother, the king of Higinasi, had sent her here with the express purpose of marrying Hibikitsu!

"We hope you are finding your time here pleasant," he stated now. "And we regret that we have spent so little of it together, due to the constant needs of the empire."

It was Lord Yakami who answered. "Of course, sire," the diplomat replied smoothly. "We are only too aware of how much rests upon you and are grateful for any moments you might spare us, as we appreciate your generous welcome."

"Your estates are lovely," Lady Yakami added, glancing around at the gardens that currently surrounded them. "And so very different from our own home. Is that not so, Your Highness?"

All three of them turned toward the princess, who responded with a quick nod. "It is. I have never seen such flowers and trees, Your Imperial Majesty. They are quite beautiful." Her voice matched the rest of her, Hibikitsu thought, being pleasant but unremarkable, the tone careful and each word clear without being overly crisp. Her eyes were a pleasant shade of gray-green, but seemed too dull to him, lacking any real interest in her surroundings or their conversation.

Nonetheless, he answered with a smile and an acknowledging nod. "That is most kind of you, princess. We are sorry we have never seen the flowers of your homeland but are sure they are exquisite."

"We have in fact brought a few specimens, as a gift," Lord Yakami cut in. "Perhaps, when you have the time, Her Highness might show them to you and instruct you in their care?"

It was a clearly concocted excuse to get the two of them alone, but there was no way Hibikitsu could refuse it without insulting his guests, or their nation. "Of course," he replied, bowing to the trio. "We would be delighted to receive them and would appreciate your wisdom on how best to maintain them."

They all nodded and smiled and bowed or curtsied as well. Then Lady Yakami spoke—Hibikitsu had noticed how she and her husband worked perfectly in tandem, taking turns in conversation, each supporting the other. He wondered if their marriage was as perfectly balanced and harmonious in private. He hoped it was. "We have taken enough of your time, Your Imperial Majesty, so we will withdraw and grant you your privacy once more, with your permission and our gratitude."

He bowed his approval of their extremely polite and considerate request, and watched as they turned to depart, the couple moving as one and Ogawa Tsuni following in perfect obedience in their wake. Was the princess truly that docile, he wondered. Did she have any thoughts and feelings that had not been scripted for her by the Yakami or by her brother and king? He was both curious and frightened to find out.

At least, Hibikitsu thought as he began walking the gardens alone once more, he had not encountered the Yatamoran delegation out here as well. If he had, he was not entirely sure he could have resisted the urge to scream, or simply to run.

CHAPTER TWENTY-SIX

Takami raised his hand with the rest. "Aye," he said, though privately he still had some misgivings about gifting such valuable property and gaining nothing tangible in return. Those might be holdovers from his own upbringing, however, and so he forced them back down. After all, who was he to say that someone should not get a second chance at happiness?

Hibikitsu looked around the table, glancing at each of his Rojiri in turn. All had their hands raised. "Very well," the emperor stated at last, tapping his forefingers against his chin. "I agree. I think it is laudable of these women to think of their future and to plan for a brighter day when their current services will no longer be required. I am happy to gift them the former Ieuyuki estate as a token of our appreciation and a chance for them to start again."

Futoba bowed from her seat, a skill Takami had also mastered as a youth. "Thank you, sire," his fellow noble said, her low voice rich with emotion. "If you would not mind, I would like to convey the news to them myself."

"Of course." He smiled. "I will have a scroll prepared, officially awarding them ownership, and delivered to you." He started to stand but stopped midway from his chair. "Was there anything else we needed to discuss at the moment?" At the murmurs of "No, sire," he completed his motion and stepped away from the table, lifting his sword from the polished surface and sliding the legendary nihono back into his sash. "Excellent. Then I will bid you all a good day." He accepted their bows and salutes with a nod and made for the door, Reizei beating him there to open it for him.

"That went surprisingly well," Noniki commented once the emperor had gone. He grinned at Seikoku. "I think Sorainasei has broken down any resistance he might've had to the idea."

The young buhiyo laughed, a rich, warm sound that once again had Takami envying his fellow Rojiri for the obvious affection she directed toward him. "It is hard to deny one collective when you've already allowed another," she agreed with a dimpled smile. "Speaking of which, I'd best be getting back." She paused before leaving, however, and glanced over at Takami. "Tomorrow is Dayabei," she reminded him. "Will you be there?"

"I will," he promised. Then a thought struck him. "We should invite our new neighbors. I'm sure they'd be interested in attending as well."

This time it was him Seikoku shared a laugh with, and Takami had to explain to the others once she'd gone, Noniki escorting her out. "The few remaining old houses in Atsani were...less than thrilled about a town appearing in their midst. They evidently have a weekly meeting to discuss matters of the tier. Neither of us were originally informed, but once we found out we've made a point of attending."

"And now you'll bring a pack of senkousa with you." Shizumi laughed, pounding the table. "Oh, they'll love that!" Still chuckling, she stood and nodded at Kagiri. "Spar?"

"Of course." He was out of his chair and following her from the room a moment later, and Takami resisted the urge to laugh at the look on the young warrior's face. Why should he decry someone else's attachments? He was merely jealous that he had none.

That thought brought his mood back down, and he pushed back, standing and bowing to Futoba and Master Eijiri. "I think I've been too long from the waves," he explained, and both nodded as if they understood. Perhaps they did. Regardless, Takami hurried from the chamber, from the compound, and from Aihiri itself, taking the Royal Way down through the city until he'd reached Mazihini and exited into that level. There, however, he had a decision to make.

Did he head to the aikaye's docks, to check in on his officers and sailors and take one of the cuioburi out for a brief sail? Or did he make his way to the public docks beyond there and rent a chayaburi for the afternoon so that he could go out on the water by himself? He was sad that he had no boat of his own, but of course all of his had belonged to House Kazutai, and naturally his brother had not allowed him to take any when he left.

His brother. Takami's hands balled into fists at the thought of Kai. He'd returned home last night, after a long day of meetings and discussions and poring over ledgers, to find Moto nearly in tears. He'd discovered why when he'd entered his bedchamber.

It was his father's eto-riantzu.

Takami had recognized the sturdy wooden cabinet instantly, of course. He had seen it all his life, stationed in the corner of his father's room, with its slatted sides and the brass plates at its corner joints. Though it had wheels, he had never seen them used. When his father had passed, the chest had gone to his elder brother, along with everything else.

He'd known at once what its presence had meant.

Sure enough, Moto had been wringing his hands. "I'm sorry, lord!" his retainer had wailed. "Iri barged in with it and I couldn't stop her!"

"No, of course not," Takami had agreed. "It's not your fault, Moto." Nor had it been. His sole servant could hardly be expected to stand up to House Kazutai's fearsome otanui, after all.

But the chest's presence was a clear message. Kai still intended to claim the estate as his own, right down to taking Takami's own room.

He'd started to turn away but had stopped as a new thought had intruded. What did the chest contain? He'd never known. With trembling fingers, Takami had flipped the latch and slid the door panel aside—

—and then had twisted and stumbled away, struggling to breathe and not retch.

Inside had been a burned and blackened saddle, the family crest barely visible in the damaged leather and wood. Another message, and no more subtle than the first: Do not resist or I will destroy you.

Takami had slept in the sitting room that night and suspected he'd do so again tonight, or else move to a different room. He couldn't bear to be in the same space as that thing.

Now his mood was completely spoiled, and with a growl he turned away from the water altogether, stomping through the crowds to make his way back up toward Atsani one painful level at a time. Perhaps that would at least exhaust him enough to sleep without dark thoughts circling and tormenting him all night.

Takami was indeed exhausted by the time he passed through the yellow gates and stepped into Atsani again. It was late now, daylight shading down into dusk, oil lamps beginning to brighten along the road, and lights coming on in the few other occupied houses on this tier. Music and laughter could be heard as he passed Sorainasei, and for an instant Takami considered stopping off there. Surely his fellow Rojiri would welcome him and invite him to dine with them and all their loud, uncomplicated friends. That would be rude of him, however, and so he sighed and walked on, alone as always.

A moment later he was surprised to pass more lights, however, and did pause, for this estate had belonged to the Yoshino, and they were no more. Yet there was a definite glimmer coming from beyond the closed gates, and Takami noted a banner flying above them as well. He was certain that had not been there before. He could make out a butterfly, which matched the Yoshino crest, but no other details in the twilight. Strange.

Past that was his own estate, and he was relieved that there was no commotion there, and no one waiting but Moto. He knew his brother was deliberately drawing things out, torturing him with the endless waiting for the doom they both knew was coming, but for now, at least, Takami welcomed the quiet.

The following night, Takami did present himself at the karo's small office by the gates. As previously, he found Wakiza Yukane, the karo, seated behind his desk, with Watane Yatahei and Sunao Iensen already occupying the chairs before it. In a clear act of disdain, the karo had chosen not to provide additional chairs as requested, forcing anyone else who attended to stand or lean against a wall. Or, if you were Seikoku, perch atop a table.

No matter, however. Takami smiled and nodded to the three gentlemen as he entered—and opened the goji he'd been carrying, setting the folding stool down beside Lord Watane. "I hope I am not late?" he asked as he sat.

Wakiza sputtered—he'd noticed the governor did that a great deal when confused or confounded, which was often—and Sunao scowled, but Watane smiled. "Not at all," he answered. "Welcome." Of the three, he was far and away the least objectionable. Perhaps it was their shared interest in the water, for the man had been Dogenkaishu before him. After the previous meeting Takami had made a point of complimenting the other lord on the state of the royal navy, and they had spent a few moments happily discussing boats and their captains.

A noise made them all glance back toward the door, just as Seikoku strolled in, a similar stool tucked beneath her arm. Trailing her was another woman, older and heavier, with a lined face and a gray bun.

"Good evening, all," Seikoku said as she placed herself at Takami's side, opening the stool and slipping onto it in a single smooth motion. "I would like to introduce you to Senkousa Medeiko. She and several of her colleagues have been granted ownership of the former Ieuyuki estates."

The other woman nodded hello and sat on Seikoku's other side, producing more muttering and scowling and an elegant seated bow from Watane. "We hope to be good neighbors to all," she said in a smooth voice which did nothing to alleviate the other two lords' obvious frustration.

More footsteps echoed out front, however, and all of them looked as an unfamiliar pair entered. They were both dressed in proper robes of pale blue silk marked with a speckled black-and-white butterfly similar to the yellow-and-black striped butterfly of the disgraced Yoshino, though the young man wore his kisoni loose over the maikiro of an aiashe. He clearly deferred to the older woman at his side, however, and Takami was quick to offer her his own seat.

"Thank you," she said, bowing to him. "I had not realized seating would be in such short supply." She was older but unbowed, of middling height, with sharp features and sharper eyes. "I am Makino Ebira, head of my house. This is my nephew, Makino Horeki." He bowed to the assemblage, showing no strain or limit of movement from his armor.

"That is all well and good, Lady Makino," Lord Wakiza stated, his face red. "But this meeting is for residents of Atsani only."

She nodded. "Yes, we are aware. We have recently reclaimed our ancestral home here in this tier. It had previously been usurped by a rogue branch of our bloodline, the Yoshino. We have since disowned them, severed all ties, and taken back what was ours."

Lord Sunao leaped to his feet. "You lie!" he shouted down at her, his face purpling with rage. "House Yoshino was the forebear, and you but a cadet branch! You have no right to be here!"

The younger Makino interposed himself between the bellowing noble and his aunt, and Takami did not fail to notice that the young man's hand had gone to the nihono at his side. "Are you questioning the honor of my aunt and our house, sir?" he asked, his tone mild, almost bored, but his eyes cold. "If so, I must insist upon satisfaction by combat."

Now it was Sunao who sputtered; despite his size, Takami had already pegged the man as a bully. Sure enough, when faced with someone not cowed by him and a potentially real threat, the arrogant lord backed down. "You have proof of your claim, then?" was all he managed as he stepped away, sullenly returning to his seat.

"Of course," Lady Makino replied with a small, smug smile. "I would be happy to provide such to the emperor, should he request it. Now, I understood these meetings were to discuss matters within our neighborhood. Shall we begin?"

Watching her, Takami could not decide if he was appalled or impressed. The claim was a complete lie, of course—in that, Sunao had been correct. But there were few who could prove that now, with House Yoshino destroyed. Nor would Hibikitsu wish to stop someone willing to step in and fill the gap that house's betrayal had left—rather, he was likely to applaud House Makino's bold move and allow them to remain there, provided they demonstrated their worth.

Whether Lady Makino and her kin could do so remained to be seen, but one thing was certain—they would irk Sunao and Wakiza to no end in the meantime.

CHAPTER TWENTY-SEVEN

That night, after the meeting ended and she'd said her good nights and made sure everyone else had gone to bed, Seikoku did something she had not done in a long time, back in another life:

She broke into a house.

It was not terribly difficult, despite being so out of practice. Slipping from her own bedchamber, she stole into the night, soundless on slippered feet. All of the lights had been doused, shrouding the estate in darkness, and Seikoku slipped from shadow to shadow, using the trees and bushes to disguise her approach. Her destination was a tall, broad but single-storied building, with a wide, gently angled roof that flared out at the corners. Her target was the rear of that structure, which faced a second, smaller building behind it. Seikoku stilled once she'd reached the last bush, considering her options.

Then she launched into a sprint across the garden there.

The house had a broad porch running all the way around it, linked in places to smaller side buildings, and the whole was raised up on sturdy posts. She could have gone straight for the room she wanted, as there was a sliding door there allowing easy access to the porch and gardens, but she knew entering that way would make too much noise. Instead she leaped up, using the porch's flexible planks as a springboard to propel her higher—and caught one of the roof's supports. Swinging her legs up well over her own head, Seikoku was able to pop up onto the roof itself, her slippered feet finding steady purchase on the esuge shingles.

Just below the roof and above the door were a pair of short, wide windows for ventilation. It was a small matter for Seikoku to slide one of those open—it made a small hiss but nothing too noticeable—and slip through, diving forward and flipping over to land on her feet on the tatami mats inside.

She straightened—only to find a man standing there, watching her.

"Well done," he complimented her. "Very quick, very quiet. I can see why you were such an excellent koshitsu."

"Please," Seikoku replied, standing straight and flicking her hair back from her face. "I was an *exceptional* koshitsu."

Then, with a giggle, she stepped forward, into his outstretched arms. Their lips touched, and she forgot all about sneaking and stealing and concentrated on other illicit things.

"I still don't see why you need to sneak in," Noniki said when they eventually parted enough to catch their breath. "It's not like the others don't know about us."

"I know." She laughed, giving him another quick kiss before sliding free of his embrace and moving to drop cross-legged onto the edge of his low bed. "It just feels...odd to flaunt it, somehow. We're all so close, we've been through so much, I just feel funny about it. I'm sorry, Niki."

"Hey." He sank down next to her, taking her hands in his. "Don't be. I wasn't trying to make you uncomfortable. And I get it. I'm not sure I want Kanai teasing me about it, or Isoro blushing when I walk by—or Minawa trying to give me advice."

Seikoku shuddered. "No, definitely not that!" The older woman who helped her run Sorainasei was likely to be as earthy and blunt about that as she was about everything else. "Besides," she added, leaning back on her arms and studying him from under her lashes, "it's not like you need any help figuring out what to do."

"No?" He grinned at her, which always took her breath away. Then he waved his hand toward the door. She felt a flash of warmth and smelled a hint of flowers, and knew he'd warded the room, both to keep anyone from bursting in on them and to keep sounds from traveling beyond its walls. That done, Noniki leaned in and kissed her soundly. "I do think I have an idea what to do next."

She smiled, even though she could feel her own face flushing—along with other areas. "Oh, do you? Prove it."

So he did.

Shortly before dawn, a drowsy but very contented Seikoku slipped from her lover's room and made her way back to the side building she shared with Isoro, Kuma, and the other unmarried women. That was something she'd pondered more than once in the last few days, though she'd yet to mention it to Noniki. What would they do once their relationship became more public? Would she move into the center building with him? But Kagiri had the other bedchamber there, which could prove awkward for all concerned. Or would she and Noniki move to the third building, which was all couples? Or perhaps claim one of the smaller buildings not connected to the others, and make that a private home for the two of them? How would their friends feel about being separated like that?

Bones, why were relationships so complicated?

For now, however, she would continue to sneak in and out. If nothing else, it helped keep her skills sharp. And she always slept well after a night of such clandestine work…among other things.

She was smiling as she snuck back into her own room, stripped to her hosode, and slid under the covers of her bed.

The next day, however, Seikoku was not smiling.

"Something is wrong," she said, studying the books that lay open before her.

"We're off to a slow start, I agree," the taller, thinner woman beside her commented, perusing the same pages and the tallies inked upon them. "But we knew that might be the case. It's a massive change, and most people need time to adjust to such things."

She knew her friend and fellow Rojiri was right about that,

but still Seikoku frowned. "It's not that," she insisted. "Look." She tapped a finger on the figures at the top of the first page. "These are from the day we started the process." She moved to the next row down. "And these are the second day. Not even half as much."

Futoba looked unconcerned. "We expected that," she reminded Seikoku. "We'd made the announcements a few days before, so we had people preparing and gathering and waiting to stop in as soon as we opened the doors. All those people came the first day."

"Yes, I know, and that's fine. But look here." Seikoku tracked her finger down the page. "The numbers rise, little by little, day after day. That's because word started spreading. A lot of people waited until they knew it wasn't some sort of trick. They watched others go in with bones and come out with hard coin. That gave them the courage to try it for themselves."

The young head of House Heiayuki nodded. "Just as we thought they would."

"Right. But look here." Seikoku indicated a spot on the page. "The numbers stop going up—and then they start going down. Little by little, but they're falling each day. Why?"

"Perhaps we've reached the limit?" Futoba suggested. "We knew not everyone would want to sell us their aishone. This was merely the first attempt."

Seikoku continued to stare at the rows of numbers. "I think it's more than that," she said finally. "I don't think the city has run out of aishone, and I don't think everyone who's left doesn't want to sell theirs. There's something else going on."

"What?" Futoba asked.

"I don't know yet," Seikoku admitted, pushing the book away and getting to her feet. "But I intend to find out."

Not quite sure where she was going yet but knowing she thought better on her feet, Seikoku headed out of Aihiri, exiting the compound by the main gates rather than the Royal Way. She wended her way along Atsani's broad central street until she stood before the sun-and-sky gates of her own home.

But she didn't go in. Whatever the answer was, it wouldn't be there.

Think, she told herself. *If the people are no longer selling us their aishone, what are they doing with them? Keeping them? Hoarding them? Destroying them?*

Or selling them to somebody else?

That was it, she realized, feeling the rightness in her blood. It had to be. The citizens of Awaihinshi were still selling their aishone—just not to the Rojiri or the Emperor.

Now the question was, who *were* they selling them to? And why?

Think like a thief, Seikoku thought. That was essentially what was happening here, after all. Someone was stealing the aishone out from under their very noses.

Fortunately, she happened to be an excellent thief.

The first place she went was a certain modest storefront down in Mazihini.

"Ah, Rojiri Seikoku!" Medeiko said as she entered. The Bone Reader bowed deeply. "I was not expecting you today, but of course you are always most welcome."

"Thank you, Senkousa," Seikoku replied, accepting the proffered chair and the cup of tea that followed. "I hope you and others are settling well into your new home?"

The older woman nodded. "Very much so, thank you. We are deeply grateful to the emperor, and to both you and Rojiri Heiayuki."

"We are happy to help, and to reward you for your long and faithful service." They both sipped their tea after that, until the bell outside tinkled, indicating a customer. "Please ignore me," Seikoku said. "I will just sit here with my tea."

"Of course." Medeiko then raised her voice. "Enter!"

A young woman stepped inside, her clothes simple and sturdy

and caked with flour. A baker, then. Approaching bashfully, she started upon seeing Seikoku there, but a friendly smile set her more at ease. "I apologize for intruding," the woman began, clutching her hat in her hands. "Should I come back later?"

"No, of course not," Medeiko replied with a warm smile and that rich voice of hers. "Please, sit. I take it you have brought something to sell?"

The woman nodded, sitting cautiously on the fine cushions and producing a small pouch from her jacket. "Yes. Here. These were from my mother and her father. They were bakers, too."

The senkousa accepted the pouch and weighed it in her palm before undoing the ties and shaking the contents out onto the little table between her and her customer. "Yes, very fine," she agreed, nudging the bone shards apart with one long, lacquered nail. "I can give you four—no, five gold for them." Her eyes flicked toward Seikoku when she named the amount, but that seemed more than fair for the number, size, and quality of the aishone, even generous, and so she merely nodded back over her tea.

"Oh!" The woman looked thrilled. "Thank you!" She accepted the coins, tucking those back into her jacket before stumbling to her feet. "Thank you!"

As the woman left, Medeiko swept the bones back into their pouch, tying it off and adding it to the lacquered little kune mato tucked into the corner beside her. Then she made a notation in the ledger atop the safe. All very proper and businesslike.

Except that Seikoko noticed the way the Bone Reader's long, lacquered nails had lingered on the tabletop—not tapping but pressed down ever so slightly. As if something were concealed beneath them.

Watching the strange gesture, she still nearly missed it when Medeiko brought her hand back to her lap—and, in doing so, dragged whatever was under her nails across the table and over the edge. The older woman slid something out of her sleeve, a small paper envelope, and scooped up whatever was there.

Which Seikoku was willing to bet was at least half the bone shards their visitor had just sold them.

The envelope disappeared back into its hiding place and Medeiko made a show of marking down the sale in her ledger. But, despite her care at holding her arm just so in order to block a view of the page itself, Seikoku still caught enough of a glimpse to know the woman had written down that she'd spent two gold, not five. She'd been incredibly smooth about it all, completely nonchalant. Most people would never have noticed.

But then, most people weren't trained thieves.

Seikoku lingered for another hour or two, and there were five more customers during that time. Each time, Medeiko made a generous offer.

And each time she carefully divided the bones unevenly and hid the larger portion away, only a few bits and pieces going to the iron safe and the rest disappearing up her sleeve or into her belt. Then the Bone Reader entered the sale as smaller and less valuable.

That explained the low sales numbers. Medeiko was taking in more than twice what she claimed. But where was she getting the money to make such expansive purchases, when she wasn't taking it from what the emperor had provided to run the program? She was essentially operating at a loss each and every day, paying more than she should and only getting a fraction of the money back from the emperor. It didn't make any sense.

Unless the goal wasn't so much to make money, at least not in the short term. The reduced sales were lowering their confidence in the program, and no doubt making Hibikitsu question the wisdom of continuing. But how would that help anyone, either?

Ah, but it would help the Senkousa, if he decided to cancel the project and let people continue using aishone as they always had. The Bone Readers would remain a critical part of society.

Only, now they had a fancy estate in Atsani itself. Wealth, respect, influence—no wonder they didn't want things to change.

By the time Seikoku said her good-byes and headed home, she was absolutely certain Senkousa Medeiko was deliberately undercutting the emperor's new bone-buyback program. The only question was, was the Bone Reader doing this just to get even, to slow her eventual retirement, to make some money before the end, or for some other reason entirely?

And where was Medeiko getting the money to fund these secret extra purchases? Was she spending her own gold just to destroy the buy-back program? That seemed counterintuitive if she was hoping to profit off this somehow. If it wasn't her gold, though, whose was it?

All of these were important questions, and Seikoku vowed that she would not stop until she found the answers.

CHAPTER TWENTY-EIGHT

Shizumi was staring at the monthly food bills, hoping if she glared at them long enough they would somehow resolve themselves and save her the trouble, when Geniji slid the study door open and poked her head in. "You want to see this," the big woman warned, her tone weighty. Shizumi was at her side in an instant.

"What's happened?" she demanded, but her friend shook her head, leading her down the hall and through the connecting door into the next section of the compound, which belonged to the Rojiri. They bypassed the main council chamber, however, and instead headed toward a door Shizumi already knew well.

The one belonging to the Dogenriku.

She reached out to knock—and nearly punched a timid-looking man with a round, soft face and watery eyes as he pulled the door open before she reached it. He yelped and jumped back, then quickly recovered himself and bowed.

"Taikoro! I was just about to come find you! Please!" He stood aside, and Shizumi stepped past. Kagiri was perched on the front of his desk, and his smile when he saw her brightened her world at once, but his eyes remained serious.

"I was just about to hear Kahei's report," he explained, gesturing toward the wiry little man beside him, "but wanted you to hear it as well." The other man wore the uniform of a gocho, Shizumi saw, and it showed signs of hard wear, as did his dirt-streaked face. But he stood straight and saluted when she approached.

"Taikoro, it's an honor," the man declared. His eyes widened slightly at seeing Geniji looming behind her, but then he smiled. "Glad to see you made it, gunso."

Shizumi could feel her friend's grin. "You too."

That recognition gave her a piece of the puzzle. "You were with the force Taisho Daishin commanded."

The soldier nodded. "Yes, Lord Commander!"

"We know about the stranger and his army of monsters," Kagiri said. "Geniji reported as much." He didn't mention that they'd seen it for themselves, but Shizumi could hardly blame him. She barely believed it, and she'd been part of the magical excursion. "I thought the entire reitao had been wiped out."

The man—Kahei—shook his head. "No, sir. We lost a lot of good men, and it all happened so fast most of them didn't even manage to draw their blades. When the taisho realized what we faced, he called the retreat."

A part of Shizumi railed against fleeing a battle, but that was pride and youth talking. The older, wiser part of her—the part that had been a commander long before being made Taikoro—understood. When facing a clearly superior force, throwing lives away needlessly was not only wasteful, it was stupid. Far better to retreat, regroup, and reassess.

Kagiri nodded. "How many survived?"

"About half," the corporal admitted, scowling. "The taisho knew we couldn't survive another direct conflict. But he didn't want to just leave those monsters rampaging about unchecked. So we shadowed them. Once he was sure where they were headed, he dispatched me back here to report." He puffed out his chest. "I'm the fastest distance runner in the entire army, sir."

Kagiri smiled. "I believe it. Daishin did well to send you, and to follow the stranger. What path did he take, and where is he going?"

Kahei glanced up at the map on the wall, then at his commanding officer. Receiving a nod, he skirted the desk and jabbed a gloved finger at the image of Rimbaku. "He left the Rumiri," he explained. "Cut across this valley and started following this smaller river instead." They all watched as the corporal traced the river up—and directly to a town marked just below a lake. "He's heading here. Muraito."

All of them nodded. Shizumi and Geniji had been through

that town on their way to join their former commander, Fujibuki Haro, down in Nariyari. And she remembered that Kagiri had said he and his brother were from a small fishing village near Ginzai, which was a little way below Muraito.

"Is that his destination?" the tall Gensaiba asked now, scratching his chin. "Or is that just the next target in his path?"

Above Muraito was the lake, which was fed by an offshoot of the Tonawa. And that mighty river led up to the Zinyang—but before that it crossed paths with the Edishu. Within sight of Awaihinshi itself.

"He's coming here," Shizumi stated, feeling the truth of that in her bones. "He may not be in any rush, but this is his real destination. It has to be."

Kagiri met her gaze. "Agreed." He straightened. "The question is, what are we going to do about it?"

"Absolutely not." Noniki shook his head so hard he'd have whipped them in the face with his hair, if he had much of it. "He'd destroy you in an instant."

"Niki—" Kagiri started, but his little brother cut him off.

"You saw what he did! And you really want to go up against that!" He turned toward Shizumi. "You agree with me, right?"

She shook her head, shifting just a little closer to Kagiri—and pointedly ignoring the chuckle that rose from Geniji, who was leaning against a column near the door. "Your brother is right," she answered. "We have to stop him. And we need to do it fast."

"And how do you plan to do that, exactly?" their young matekai demanded. "He's already slaughtered hundreds of people!"

"Your magic—" she said, but didn't get any further, as he laughed.

"My magic! I barely know what I'm doing!" he stated in what was nearly hysterics. "This man, whoever he is, he's a true matekai. I'm just a pretender, a raw recruit. I wouldn't stand a chance against him, and that goes double for both of you."

Shizumi wasn't ready to believe that. "You protected Geniji and the others."

"From a casual attack, and even that was as much luck as anything," he told her. "If you're talking about charging him, my help would be like holding up an umbrella as you're being engulfed by a tidal wave." He shook his head again, though at least he was a little calmer now. "Go after him and you'll die. Simple as that."

Kagiri looked at her, and Shizumi knew her gaze mirrored his own. And what she saw there wasn't fear; it was frustration.

"We have to do something," she insisted. But this time she shifted her attention away from the plainly dressed, plain-spoken matekai—and focused on the taller, much more elegantly dressed man seated at the table's high end. "Sire, if we don't act now he'll destroy Muraito the same as he did those smaller towns. And he'll keep coming until he gets here and does exactly the same thing."

Hibikutsu considered. "Can you stop him?"

Shizumi shared another glance with Kagiri, but finally they both shook their heads. "Probably not, Your Majesty," she admitted. "But maybe we can slow him down until Noniki can come up with some way to defeat him properly."

The young matekai moaned, burying his face in his hands. "I can't! I told you! He's so much stronger than me!"

Kagiri draped an arm over his brother's shoulder. "You're stronger than you think," he said. "Always were." His eyes moved to the emperor. "Shizumi's right, though. We need to get out there and stop him ourselves."

Hibikitsu frowned. "As I've already said before, I don't wish to lose you."

"And I have no desire to be lost," the Gensaiba answered with that quiet calm of his. "But if it is our lives versus those of all the people in this city, I know which one I'm willing to sacrifice to save the rest."

Shizumi nodded. Taikoro or not, she was still a soldier. Putting her life on the line to protect the citizens of the empire was part of the job.

"Things will only become more difficult if he makes it to

Muraito," she warned. "Not just because there are more people, either. He'll be harder to catch inside the city. The buildings are closer together, so fire can jump quickly from one to the next. And he won't be hemmed in at all, not with all the rivers below and the lake above. Strategically, he couldn't have asked for a better location for a fight. Which is good for him and far less so for us."

Kagiri turned back toward the map—they'd asked his brother and the emperor to join them in his study rather than adjourning to either the Rojiri meeting room or the throne room because of that painted image. "He has not reached the city yet," he pointed out now. "If we hurry, we could get there before him and set our forces in that valley. He'd have to fight through us to reach it."

But Shizumi saw another way. "What if we stationed ourselves here instead?" she suggested, moving quickly to his side and tapping a spot to the east of the river. "We've already seen that he's hostile. If he knows we're there, he'll come after us."

"Which will draw him away from Muraito." Kagiri smiled down at her. "Smart. Then even if he gets past us he'll be on the wrong side of the river. Since his real goal is here, he'll most likely ignore the city and just march past it and along that side of the lake."

Hibikitsu was considering their proposal; that much was clear from the look on his face, which was more resigned than rejecting. "I still do not see why the two of you would need to go yourself," he began, then stopped, shaking his head. "No, that is untrue. I do not like that you would go, but I do understand. And, although I might not have even a few months ago, I would now do the same, were I in your shoes." He sighed. "I could order you to stay here, you know."

"You could," Shizumi agreed. "And we would obey you. But you would potentially be dooming all the people of Muraito as a result."

He scowled at her, though she could see it was more chagrin than anger. "I never should have promoted you," he claimed, but the grin that followed belied that. "Very well. How much time will you need to prepare?"

Shizumi started to answer but stopped and nodded at Kagiri

to go ahead. "A few days," the tall warrior replied after a moment's consideration. "I'll need to gather my troops, instruct my officers, coordinate travel with Takami—and I have a feeling there's something else I need to do, something important." He didn't elaborate on that last part, and no one pushed him. It wasn't his way to be mysterious, so they all knew he'd tell them when he could.

For her part, she could have her Honjofu ready to travel in a few hours, but she wasn't about to show him up like that. So she simply added, "We will be ready as well."

Hibikitsu nodded. "All right. But if we receive more information in the meantime, either about some better way to combat this threat or about it being too dangerous to even consider, you will cancel those plans at once."

They both saluted. "Of course, sire. We have no intention of throwing our lives away."

Shizumi knew that wasn't strictly true. As warriors, they would throw their lives away if necessary.

They wouldn't do so without cause, however.

And, if that did have to happen, they'd make damn sure whoever took them paid dearly for the privilege.

CHAPTER TWENTY-NINE

Hara Kuriko was not pleased.

Admittedly, she rarely was. She had high standards, after all, as befit the senior Otainui to the Emperor himself! She was responsible for all of Aihiri—or, at least, the main building—and it was her duty to keep everything absolutely perfect for His Imperial Majesty. Naturally, then, she demanded excellence. Sadly, she rarely received it.

Right now, however, she was even less happy than usual.

Frowning, Kuriko ran a finger along the raised lip of a painted wall panel. Her fingertip came away darkened with dust. Disgraceful! She would be speaking rather firmly to her staff about this!

Her internal tirade was cut short, however, by a sound from nearby. Not the steady thump of booted feet as the Honjofu made their rounds, however. No, this had been a softer noise, more like a slippered footfall.

But it had come from the door off to the side, which led into the Imperial dining room. And, since they were currently between meals, there should not have been anyone in that private space.

Moving with some care herself, Kuriko sidled over to the door and slid it aside just enough to peer into the room in question. Sure enough, she spied a man within, dressed in simple ponmei and a hantien. He was not one of hers, and she doubted he worked for old Yosuke Fujita, the imperial groundskeeper. Who was he, then, and what was he doing in the emperor's own dining room?

The man, who was neither tall nor short, heavy nor slim, young nor old, straightened slightly, and a hint of light filtered by the outward-facing screens caught upon his cheek and brow, though much of him remained shadowed. Still, it was enough for Kuriko to recognize him, and fury quickly flooded through her, replacing her curiosity and faint unease. Slamming the door open, she stomped inside and directly over to the startled figure, glaring up at him.

"You!" she declared, hands going to her hips. "I remember you! I already had to run you off once! What are you doing back here?" She noted the braided cords around his neck and waist, and the faint outline of something behind his back. "Are you going to tell me that you're making another delivery?" she demanded. "Because your tray is clearly empty, which means your business in the kitchens has already concluded. Now you are simply trespassing."

The man—she remembered his name, Hajime, but simply couldn't be bothered to use it—twisted his hands together, glancing all around him as if for someone to come to his aid. "I'm so sorry, Madam Hara," he said, the words emerging quick and breathless, his eyes wide. "I keep getting turned about in this place, it's so big! I meant no harm!"

"So you say," she sniffed, not willing to give him any leeway. "Yet this is the second time I have found you here, so it seems you know your way at least to this room. A room you should never have entered in the first place."

He shook his head. "It's right off the kitchens," he mumbled, glancing down at his feet. "That's all."

Kuriko did not buy that for an instant. She had dealt with far too many troublemakers, nuisances, rebels, and liars in her time not to recognize dissembling when she saw it. This Hajime might act the fool, but he had not merely blundered into this room. Twice.

"I will speak with Muiada," she stated at last. "Whether you continue to make deliveries here is up to him, but if so, you will do so only as far as the porch. You are no longer welcome within these walls, and I will instruct the Honjofu to throw you out should they ever catch you inside again. Now leave at once, before I have them begin that practice this very day."

She turned away, the matter done, but stopped at a strange hiss behind her. It sounded more snake than man, but surely no such reptile had ever been allowed on these premises! Glancing back, she saw the noise must have come from Hajime, who was now scowling down at her, his face darker than ever.

"Meddlesome little woman!" he snapped, the words emerging in a cold, thin rasp. "It was not your time yet!"

Kuriko had no idea what he meant, but she could hear the threat inherent in his statement. Twisting about, she bolted for the door—but a long-fingered hand came down upon her shoulder, halting her flight as easily as a child might restrain a mouse.

"No," the dessert maker told her in a dark whisper. "Your arrogance and interference have determined your fate."

His fingers dug into her, causing a burst of pain to blossom through her kitoro as if he had pierced her skin there. Glancing down at the offending limb, Kuriko noted distantly that it seemed inky, like a blotted painting, with smoke or shadow rising along its edges. The entire room felt darker now. Shadows had crept up over the outer wall, blocking the light.

And, in the burgeoning dark, she saw Hajime's eyes glow a fiery red. The rest of him had melted back into the shadows, nothing but a vague shape amid the dark, but those eyes were bright as embers.

So were his teeth as he smiled. And those looked very sharp.

Kuriko opened her mouth to cry out, to call for help. But a hand clamped over her face, pinning her jaw shut. Only a muffled squeak emerged.

The pain in her shoulder was intensifying. Now it felt like that whole area was on fire, the agony radiating out into her arm and up along her neck.

She would have screamed from it if she'd been able.

"You have no one to blame but yourself," Hajime told her—if it was even still the dessert maker, grown so tall and thin in the dark. "Remember that."

Then the pain reached her head, gripping her tight. Kuriko tried to pull free, but it was no use. She could feel her thoughts growing fuzzy. She couldn't breathe. Her lungs were on fire as well. Hands and feet were tingling. Everything felt heavy. Everything hurt. Everything was burning.

She hoped she would not leave a scorch mark on the rug.

Dai Yi straightened, removing his hand from the dead woman's mouth as her body burned, the fat melting away into oily black smoke, the bones twisting. Removing his claws from her shoulder, he still maintained enough of a grip to keep the tiny housekeeper's corpse upright.

With the other hand he plucked her eyeballs free. The rest of the body he let drop to the floor. It struck light as a leaf, with only the slightest whisper of sound.

This was not how he had intended things to go. He'd wanted to scout the building a bit more, figure out the best access and exit points, possibly find out something about the emperor's schedule, his daily routine. But Hara Kuriko had stumbled upon him and had not been willing to leave it alone.

Dai Yi had intended to take Yamana Muiada, when it was time. But this would be even better. The head chef had the freedom of the kitchen and work areas, while the otainui had the run of the entire compound.

But why did she have to be so diminuitive?

With a sigh, he popped both eyes into his mouth, gulping them down.

He did his best not to shriek in pain himself as the transformation began.

It was always easiest to become someone close to his own height and build. But Dai Yi had at least a double handspan over Hara Kuriko. The magic practically bent him in half as it forced him down into her shape and size. The pain was excruciating.

Fortunately, he had trained long and hard for this mission. Pain would not defeat him.

After a minute, "Hara Kuriko" brushed off the front of her kitoro. Why was everything here always so disordered and unclean? Didn't her staff know to do better?

She frowned down at the small, wizened body by her feet. And who was going to clean this up? Her, evidently. Typical.

Glancing around the room, she saw nothing she could use—but

remembered there was an ancient riantzu, a relic from an emperor several generations ago, out in the hall beyond. Yes, that would do nicely. Listening carefully and hearing no one around, she slipped out long enough to grab hold of the cart and wheel it back into the dining room.

At least this time her staff had done as they were told! The cart's wheels had clearly been oiled recently and made hardly a squeak as she moved it, shutting the door behind her.

The real Kuriko's body barely fit inside, and Dai Yi had to push and shove limbs into place. But "barely" was still good enough.

Returning the cart to its rightful place, she suddenly felt eyes upon her. Looking up, Dai Yi met a dark-eyed gaze very similar to his own.

At the end of the hall stood three tall, slim gentlemen in long, close-fitting robes of yellow and black. Their dark hair was pulled back in identical tight braids, and there was little difference in either features or expression. Nonetheless, it was the middle figure Dai Yi focused on, making a quick, sinuous gesture with his right hand.

The man dipped his chin, ever so slightly, before turning back the way he'd come. The other two followed suit without a word, and a moment later Dai Yi was alone in the corridor once more.

With a small smirk, Hara Kuriko marched to the hall's other end. The imperial kitchens lay beyond, and she intended to scold Yamana Muiada about letting his pet dessert maker roam about so freely.

It was a good thing she'd spotted the man. Otherwise, who knew what sort of trouble he might have caused?

CHAPTER THIRTY

Daishin Nishoji paused the conversation with his officers as one of their scouts came running up. "Taisho!" the woman called even before she'd skidded to a stop and saluted. "The stranger and his army are continuing apace!"

"Thank you, soldier," Daishin told her. "Dismissed." He faced his officers again, and the regional map laid out on the folding table between them. "He remains on course, then."

Glancing about him, he noted the eager expressions on some of the younger officers' faces. "Chusa Ichiro," he said. "Your thoughts?"

The young noble saluted crisply. "Sir!" he shouted, despite their faces being mere handspans apart. "We should marshal the troops and attack! Traditional pincer movement, half around the front to distract, the other half from behind to strike by surprise. We could eliminate the threat in moments, sir!"

One of the others, equally young, was nodding, and Daishin looked to him next. "Taisu Mori," he said. "You concur with this assessment, and this proposal?"

"Sir!" Mori's salute was, if anything, even sharper than Ichiro's had been. "Yes, sir! This is our chance to destroy the invader once and for all! It is the army's duty and honor to protect the empire in this way!"

The other two officers, both more seasoned and from less influential families, shook their head. "Issa Tomoko?" Daishin asked. "Your thoughts?"

Tomoko, who was at least a decade older than Mori and Ichiro, snorted. "We hit them with our full force, plus the Honjofu, and lost half our men in the blink of an eye," he pointed out in his surprisingly melodic voice. "Now you want us to try again, but on our own and with half those numbers? He'd slaughter us all in a heartbeat."

Beside him, Morita nodded. "We wouldn't stand a chance," he agreed, not bothering to wait for Daishin to call on him but instead sneering at the two younger officers. "Apologies if that dashes your hopes of a dramatic victory and the accolades that would follow such a feat."

Mori reddened. "You insult me and my house—" he began, but Daishin pounded a fist on the table to get his attention.

"There will be no challenges to duel here," he warned, glowering at each of the four in turn. "Save the fighting for those things that killed half our brothers." He shook his head. "While I admire your confidence," he told his two younger officers, "I do not share it. No, Tomoko and Morita are correct. Without some sort of assistance, we would not stand a chance against that barbaric horde, even without the stranger's dark magic. Our only hope is to shadow him and to be ready if any of his men or creatures step outside his protection. But we certainly cannot count on that."

He dismissed them to see to their troops and relay the news that they were to continue with their previous assignments. Then he left the camp, marching up the low rise ahead. Just below its peak he dropped down, first to a crouch and then onto his belly. Withdrawing his spyglass from its leather case at his belt, Daishin crept forward another pace or two before raising the device to his eye.

The stranger's image seemed almost to jump out at him, as if the man had deliberately turned to face him. He still looked haggard as a beggar, Daishin thought, and wild as a Mukanichi or a mad beast. Yet there was a clear power about him, almost a glow, and not just from the way his feet seemed to skim over the ground or the legion of strange, monstrous figures he led.

That inhuman army was part of the problem, of course. Daishin switched his focus to them. No two were alike, it seemed, though in the massive jumble it was difficult to tell. Particularly since their coloration matched the terrain so closely—without the spyglass it looked as if the ground itself were rippling and rolling, like the stranger was walking through ever-shifting valleys and hills. Daishin could see them clearly now, but still it was difficult to focus on any one of them well enough to make out exact features.

Whatever they were, they were big, powerful, and implacable. He'd watched them tear through his men without pause, without hesitation. Like beasts—or trained killers. He wasn't sure how intelligent they were, whether they were closer to trained animals, tamed natural forces, or disciplined soldiers. The inexperienced like Ichiro and Mori would say it did not matter, that the foe was the foe and needed to be defeated regardless. But Daishin knew better. Putting down a stampede of maddened boars required entirely different tactics from defeating a squad of trained warriors. Different equipment, too.

Until he knew what category applied to those foes, any attempts they made were almost certainly doomed to failure.

Was he a coward, then, as those two youths had implied, for holding his men back from an attack he knew could not succeed? Or merely a realist?

Daishin knew which he preferred to believe. He was also fairly certain his new Dogenriku would agree. Though as young as Ichiro and Mori, possibly even younger, Kagiri had impressed him as eminently sensible and as having an admirable concern for the safety of the troops in his care. He would never approve of throwing lives away, particularly when there were other options available.

So, for now, Daishin would restrain his more hotheaded officers. They would continue to shadow the stranger and his unnatural forces. They had been lucky so far that the man's march had taken him on his current trajectory, for no towns or villages lay in his path. Daishin had seen the reports of what had happened to those he had entered previously, and that was when the man had been traveling alone, without his bizarre entourage.

Of course, at the current pace and trajectory they would reach Muraito in less than a week. And that city had more people in it than all the previous towns combined.

Daishin hoped he would have orders from the capital or some personal revelation before then. Otherwise he might be forced to give in to his junior officers' urgings and put his men in this madman's path, in the hopes that their deaths would at least allow some of those townsfolk to survive.

Kishin Narai raised his cup, clinking it against those of his friends. They were sipping a very fine tsekuri Fujiko Oritano had brought, as they had some cause to celebrate. The rice wine was lovely, delicate with a sharp edge that highlighted rather than obscured its flavor, and he savored it as it burned its way down his throat.

"The initial stages have gone even better than we'd hoped," Oritano reported once they'd all emptied their cups. "We may need to adjust our timetable if that pace continues."

"That would be good," Shizu Yokori commented, blotting her lips with a silk square. "The longer this takes, the more likely it will be noticed."

Jiro Masute laughed. "And what if it is?" he asked, flicking his hair back. "We are breaking no laws."

Narai frowned. "True," he agreed. "Yet we all know that laws can be changed. It depends upon how our plans are discovered and how they are taken once they are. It is possible we will have their goodwill, since in a way we are aiding them—but we cannot assume that and must prepare for a far less favorable response."

The others all nodded. "We have taken every possible precaution," Yokori reminded him. "Though no plan is foolproof, still we have covered as much as we could think of." Her smile was as sharp as ever. "And between us, we can think of a great deal."

Oritano giggled, the potent drink making her even more cheerful than usual. "We are our own Rojiri, dispensing excellent advice and then acting upon it ourselves," she stated, and Narai knew it was partially meant as an attempt to assuage his still-wounded pride.

He appreciated the effort, even if mention of his recent post stung, so he smiled to disguise that pain. "Yes," he agreed. "If the emperor had been willing to listen to me more, we could have been of great assistance now and in future. As it is, we will continue to act upon our own recognizance. Our efforts will be lauded by history, at least."

"And our pockets will be full while we appreciate such retroactive commendations," Yokori added, refilling their cups from the elegant little bottle.

"With the former, I am more willing to wait for the latter," Masute said, taking his cup and hoisting it in salute. "To full pockets!"

The others joined suit. "To full pockets!"

Tsekuri had never tasted so sweet, Narai thought, as when it was shared with good friends over even better news.

Medeiko glanced about her as she stepped out of her shop, though she was not sure why she bothered. No one suspected anything. She was sure of it.

Nonetheless, she took a roundabout route as she walked through Mazihini, clutching her bakiro close to her chest. It was early evening, and the street was full of people leaving off their day's labors and returning home for the evening meal, meeting with friends, or gathering last-minute supplies for the night and the day ahead. Many of them knew her on sight and nodded or smiled as they passed, but no one stopped her.

Few had cause to speak to a Senkousa unless they had bones to sell.

Making her way to a particular tavern, Medeiko checked behind her again before ducking inside. No one seemed to be paying any attention.

Nodding at the woman behind the bar, she headed toward the back, taking the last booth there. The place was dimly lit, only small lanterns on each table providing a soft glow around them, and she found herself mostly in shadow as she sat. It was a simple matter to pull the pouch from her bag and set it on the bench beside her.

Feeling around under the seat, Medeiko found a similar pouch, though smaller. When she extracted it, it jingled. It felt nice and heavy as she placed it in her lap.

The pouch she'd brought, which was a bit lighter and made a dry, rustling sound as its contents shifted, she placed where the smaller one had been. Then she switched the new bag into her bakiro. She rose and exited without ordering a drink. The place was starting to fill up, enough that the server would probably never remember her having been there.

Relieved now that the hard part was over, Medeiko slowed her pace slightly. It was a long way up to Atsani, but she was in no particular hurry.

She hoped her peers had been equally successful with their own endeavors, but she would find out soon enough.

They had yet to name their new home, but Medeiko was pleased to think that they were all working together to make sure it prospered right along with them.

CHAPTER THIRTY-ONE

Kagiri was beginning to hate sleeping.

Each night, as soon as he lay his head upon his pillow, he fell under its spell, so completely that, when he woke in the morning, he was still lying in the exact same position.

And each night, once he was asleep, he dreamed.

Growing up, Kagiri had rarely remembered his dreams. Little snatches here and there: an image or two, a word, a color, a feeling.

Now he remembered each one clear as the vase in the corner of his room, its clean white porcelain all but glowing in the dawn light. Each dream was so vivid, so complete, so understandable, it felt as if he'd lived it.

And each dream was of the same place. The same time. The same familiar tower where his whole life had changed.

That first time, he had brought it upon himself, he knew. He'd gone into his head, sought out the remnants of the Gensaiba matekan, and begged them to help him, to show him what he needed to see.

The times since then, however, had been against his will. Kagiri had tried asking them to stop, tried ordering them—tried begging them.

Yet here he was again.

He had already experienced this scene through Nikiyu Sinchu, then through Geido Shinen, then Onyoku Jeizen and later Bushiki Kenin. Each time, he had lived the same encounter—their last in life. All of them in the tower together, waiting uneasily as their matekai quarreled somewhere above them.

Each time, the warriors had decided to intervene. But something had struck them down before they could do so.

That invisible blow killed the Gensaiba and sent Kagiri hurtling back into wakefulness, to sit up gasping and sweat-soaked, the others' demise still cloaking him in its pain and grief.

Now, it seemed, he was doomed to relive it yet again. He struggled to wake up, to shift his thoughts, to think about something else, but it was no use. Already he could see the tower rising up before him, its glossy black stone carved into intricate bands, the sea smashing against the thin path to the left, a wall of brambles rising to its right, open air behind the tower and the little plateau that held it.

He had forgotten how breathtaking a sight it was. And how eerie. Nothing else was quite like it.

This was the first time he had dreamed about arriving here, and Kagiri wondered about that change even as he felt himself ride up to the tall, peaked door.

It was also the first time he—inhabiting whichever Gensaiba it was this time—was with someone other than their fellow warriors.

"Hello, the tower!" That shout rose from the woman riding beside him, her broad face set in a warm, easy smile. Kagiri knew at once who it was, both because he had seen her image once before, when Noniki had teased what was left of her soul out of the swirling mass of Kaemusei, and because she looked like a slightly bigger version of Shito Kibi, the Gensaiba's master of the blade. This, then, was Shito Daiko, Kibi's cousin and wizard, and they had obviously arrived together, as most of the Gensaiba and their matekai would.

The door creaked open, revealing a tiny woman shadowed by a massive man. "Took your time," the woman declared, stepping out into the sunlight, though her brilliantly blue and orange robes nearly overpowered that simple illumination. Her oversized companion laughed, and Kagiri knew him as much by that deep sound as by his face. Geido Shinen, and Geido Isami with him.

"Who else is here?" Kibi asked as they drew up to the tower and swung down. Kagiri automatically took both reins, leading the horses off toward the tower's side, and Shinen hurried down the steps to assist her. He slapped her on the back in greeting, and Kagiri felt his host stumble a little from the exuberant gesture.

"Thank the spirits you're here!" Shinen rumbled as they tied the horses to posts and undid their saddles. "It has been only Kenin and myself, and you know how he is. Getting even a word out of him is like trying to pull salt from the sea."

Kagiri/Kibi laughed. "Just the two of you?" they asked, brushing down their horse. "Where are the rest?"

Her big friend shrugged. "No idea. Hope they get here soon, though. Yours and mine and Kenin's, that's a dangerous combination."

Was it? Kagiri wondered. Why? He gleaned hints of an answer from his host's mind: something about alliances, enmities, and differences of opinion, as well as factions within the matekai. That would explain the shouting that came later.

By the time they'd finished tending the horses, the two wizards had vanished into the tower. Kibi and Shinen followed, climbing the broad steps to the same room Kagiri remembered so well, with its tall windows and arches, its decoration, its racks and benches, and of course its enticing buffet. As Shinen had said, Bushiki Kenin was already there, short and stocky, standing with his feet well apart and his arms behind his back, a stern scowl on his face.

"Kibi," he said, dipping his head at her as she entered.

"Kenin." No love lost there, clearly! Although part of it, Kagiri gathered, was simply the wrestler's way.

Footsteps rose toward them, and all three turned just as a slim man with a tidy little beard came charging up the stairs. "Knew I'd find you all here," he said, panting a little from the exertion. "And already partying without me." He waggled his eyebrows at them.

"Jeizen." Kibi nodded. "That just leaves Setsui, Sinchu, and Segei."

"Our three S's," Onyoku Jeizen quipped, walking over to join them. "No offense, Shinen."

The big man chuckled. "None taken."

"I'm here," a delicate voice announced, and they all glanced toward the stairs, and the lovely young woman standing upon the last of them, a serious expression adding gravity to her beautiful features. "And I saw Sinchu reining in as I came upstairs. But don't expect Segei."

"Why not?" Kenin asked, and only then nodded hello to the new arrival. "Setsui."

Komu Setsui dipped her head, a tiny smile playing on her lips, before responding. "Juroji told me. They're not coming."

"Not coming? It's a moot!" Shinen stated. "They have to come! It's the rule!"

Jeizen snorted. "A rule made by whom? The matekai? If they made it, surely that means they can break it just as easily. I, for one, would hardly blame them for avoiding all this." He swept the wine goblet he'd just filled in a sweeping arc, taking in not only the room but the tower sections that rose high above them.

"True," Kenin agreed. "But without Fukuru, it will only get worse."

That received a chorus of nods and muttered agreements, including from Kagiri's host. And when Nikiyu Sinchu joined them a few minutes later, the lean little man confirmed those suspicions in his very soft voice. "Bezaitin said it was true," he agreed. "The Taido have chosen not to answer the summons. They will not be attending."

Above them, the shouting had already begun.

"Here you go," Geido said, filling a goblet and handing it to Sinchu. "Drink up. Might as well, hm? Not much we can do until they're done." They were the same words from Kagiri's first visit to this past event, and from there it all unfolded exactly as it had each time before. Up to and including everyone's sudden and dramatic demise upon the steps that led higher into the Tawasiri, to where the gathered wizards apparently fought each other.

Kibi's body hit the tiled floor, the last of her breath stilling in her throat, and Kagiri felt himself being pulled out of her and tossed back into his own time. He woke gasping for air, his sheets drenched, his whole body twitching from sheer relief and shared trauma.

All the while, his mind was racing. What had he learned this time that he hadn't before? He had not gone any farther forward, which made sense. But he had started earlier, outside the Tawasiri itself. He had seen the others arriving, greeting each other, worrying about this meeting and its outcome.

Except for the Taidos. Taido Segei was the Gensaiba's strategist, the finest tactician among them, and good enough with a blade to almost challenge Kibi.

And his wizard? The Gensaiba within him grudgingly gave it up now, a single name that rolled off the tongue but sent fear jangling through every nerve:

Taido Fukuru.

The voice of reason, he had felt one of his hosts think of that particular wizard. Without him, "it will only get worse," Kenin had said. Yet Taido Fukuru had chosen not to attend.

Taido Segei had survived whatever had struck the Tawasiri, Kagiri knew. The young warrior had gone on to gather all the disparate groups throughout the kingdom, uniting them under his own Higeibara crest.

He had forged an empire, the Relicant empire of Rimbaku. Hibikitsu was his direct descendent.

But what exactly had happened to the magical half of that duo?

How had Taido Fukuru vanished from history?

CHAPTER THIRTY-TWO

Noniki startled into wakefulness. Beside him, Seikoku stirred. It was barely a twitch, but he knew somehow that she was already fully alert and keeping herself still to listen.

"Someone's at the door," he whispered, though of course that wasn't necessary.

She frowned—their faces were mere inches apart, and any other time he would just sit and marvel at the beauty of her, the perfect shape of her jaw, her cheek, her nose, her eyes. At this particular moment, however, they had other concerns. "I don't hear anything," she replied, her own voice kept low but conversational.

"No," he agreed. "Me either. But the ward is set to respond when someone encounters it." He waved it away, letting the normal sounds without rush back in—and any they made flow outward—and now they could clearly hear the tapping, soft but insistent.

"Niki, you there? Niki?"

"Coming!" Noniki called back, rising to his feet and accepting the robe Seikoku handed him with a smirk and a swat on the rear. He was chuckling as he crossed the room, pulling the garment around himself, and slid the door open.

Kagiri burst in the second there was enough space to do so. "Niki, I—" He stopped, frozen mid-word, eyebrows rising and cheeks flushing, and Noniki smothered a laugh. Evidently his normally hyper-observant warrior brother had just realized they were not alone. "Sorry," he muttered, his whole face now scarlet. "I didn't realize— I should've—"

"Don't stop on my account," Seikoku drawled from the bed. She'd somehow acquired Noniki's shirt and was wearing it, sitting upright and cross-legged, the blankets still covering her legs.

"Yes, well—" Though still obviously flustered, Kagiri finally pulled himself together enough to continue. "I know who the stranger is. Or at least, I think I do."

Noniki frowned, but there was no way he was not going to ask. "Who?"

"Taido Fukuru!" His brother declared triumphantly.

Noniki waited. When nothing more was forthcoming he asked again, "Who?"

His brother repeated the name. "One of the matekai," he added after a moment. "The last one. He didn't attend the meeting."

"Taido?" That was from Seikoku, who had joined them by the door. She'd also managed to don her own clothes again—when and how had she done that without either of them noticing? *That's what you get, falling for a thief,* he told himself. "Isn't that the emperor's house?" she asked now. "Starting with Taido Segei?"

A thief, and cleverer than you, Noniki amended, not for the first time. Because now that she said it, he remembered. "Of course! And when you first met him," he reminded his brother, "didn't the Gensaiba in you recognize Hibikitsu as the First Emperor?"

Kagiri nodded. "They did. He looks just like him, apparently. He wasn't there, either. At the last meeting, I mean."

He'd related to them the memory he'd experienced before, in the council chamber, so Noniki understood the reference. "This Fukuru, he was Segei's master?"

His brother frowned. "Not exactly. The Gensaiba protected the matekai, but it was more than that. Closer to a partnership than a master and servant. They looked out for each other, complemented each other. Besides which, they were always kin, either siblings or cousins, so they had that bond and that sense of familial duty." He shrugged. "But they were paired, yes. Which is why neither of them were there. Fukuru declined to attend."

"And you think the man you saw was him?" Seikoku asked. "Wouldn't that make him hundreds of years old, though?" She cocked an eyebrow at Noniki. "Tell me you're not going to outlive me by centuries."

He laughed and gave her a quick hug. "Wouldn't dream of it,

and I doubt you'd let me, anyway." Then he sobered again. "It could be possible, though. I still don't know enough. If he *is* that old, it'd explain why he could do things I'd never even imagined." He shook his head. "If only we knew more about him."

Kagiri nodded. "When I tried asking the Gensaiba, that's what triggered the memories, but I don't think there's much more they can tell me. They didn't really know him. And Segei wasn't with them, so I don't have any connection to his spirit."

"Connection to his spirit," Noniki mused. "I might have something that will help." He turned and crossed the room, stopping at the tanu there. From its top he retrieved one of his few ornamentations: a thick jade ring, its milky green surface unadorned. Seikoku had given it to him when they'd first reunited, and he wore it upon his thumb, but Kagiri had since revealed its true purpose—and its original owner's identity. Now he cradled it in his palm as he rejoined his lover and his brother.

"You said this was part of a set, worn by a matekai and his Gensaiba," he reminded Kagiri. "And Hibikitsu had the other half, the kanashi inherited from Taido Seigei. Which means this—"

"Must have belonged to Taido Fukuru," his brother agreed. "Smart. Can you use it to, I don't know, connect with him somehow?"

Noniki considered that, but Seikoku was already shaking her head. "You said he was powerful," she reminded him, "and more experienced by far. So if you did link yourself to him, wouldn't that leave you open to attack? Like tethering yourself to a tiger."

He nodded. "Possibly so, and best not to risk it. But I may be able to draw something from the ring itself, without ever going near the man." He lowered himself to a cross-legged position on the floor, then waited as they joined him, one on either side. Sitting there, just the three of them, Noniki felt a rush of warmth. These were the two people he cared about most in all the world, and having them near him, with him, was a tremendous source of comfort and strength.

He hoped it would be enough.

"Objects have no memories of their own," he explained, holding out his palm at eye level so they could all see the ring resting upon it. "But they are still porous, in a way—they can absorb the thoughts and feelings and memories of those around them. Particularly intense ones. I may be able to read some of those from this, gaining a sense of the man who once wore it."

He focused on the jade ring, but at the same time he let himself drift, his eyes not seeing the object as it was now. Rather, he opened himself to whatever else the accessory carried, whatever images and thoughts had clung to it over all these years.

At first, nothing happened. Then, slowly, an image began to form over his palm. He heard Seikoku curse softly, but remained in the moment, and the vision came into sharper focus.

It was a man.

Looking at the face, there was no mistaking. This was the same man they'd seen in Bezenkai. The man they now knew for certain was Taido Fukuru.

He no longer looked quite the same, however.

The face floating above them here looked calm, even mellow. He was lean but clearly healthy, his cheeks cleanly shaved, his hair tidily tucked back into a knot, his eyes alert but, if not warm, at least not cold. Receptive, Noniki would have said.

It was difficult to reconcile that with the haggard, disheveled man who'd ranted at them before brushing them aside.

Kagiri evidently felt the same. "I'd say the centuries haven't been kind to him," his brother said quietly.

"No," Noniki agreed. He focused further, seeking any other information from the ring. What he received was a welter of impressions. "I'm getting flashes of emotion," he reported to his two companions. "Tolerance. Patience. Forbearance. And, increasingly overshadowing the rest, frustration. Fatigue. Disappointment, mixed with anger and regret."

That was all the ring could offer without him trying to use it as a springboard to reach its former owner himself, so Noniki lowered his hand, letting the image fade.

Kagiri was nodding. "In my memories, the Gensaiba were surprised he didn't attend," he recounted. "And said that, without him there, everything would be a great deal worse."

"It certainly sounds like he was the peacekeeper of the group," Seikoku said. "Or one of them, anyway. That would explain those emotions, including the last few. He got fed up trying to keep his friends from fighting, especially since it never seemed to help for long." She sighed. "I've had a small taste of that and it made me want to tear my own hair out—or somebody else's. If he had to put up with that for years, I can see why he'd eventually snap."

"Do you think he caused the Schism?" Kagiri asked. "Maybe it finally got to be too much for him, and he blew up at everyone and everything?"

Noniki pondered that but finally shook his head. "No, if that'd happened, he likely wouldn't have survived it." Which reminded him of something else, something they'd encountered not that long ago. "Kaemusei."

The others understood at once. "You said it was all the matekai—all those who were in the Tawasiri, anyway," Seikoku remembered. "But all jumbled up together, nothing but a mass of hunger."

He nodded. "That's what I would've expected for someone who set off some sort of magical cataclysm. If the matekai fought in the tower, not just with words or fists but with magic, and it kept escalating—"

"Eventually they'd explode?" Kagiri asked. "What about what I feel at the end of these memories? All of the Gensaiba just collapse like puppets with their strings cut."

Noniki could guess what that meant. "When I work magic, I draw upon the world around me," he answered. "If I were facing another wizard, we would both be doing that. The longer we fought, the farther we'd have to reach for power. And if we weren't being careful, we could pull that from everything around us indiscriminately."

"Meaning they drained the life force of their own kin, their friends and partners, in their feuding," Seikoku summarized. "That's what killed them. And then it was all too much and it exploded, causing the Schism." She tapped her lower lip, forcing Noniki to concentrate heavily on the subject at hand, lest he become distracted. "So what about Fukuru?"

Noniki thought he had an answer to that. "He must have been shielded somehow," he guessed. "From detection like he is now, but also from someone draining his magic. When the Schism occurred, it wiped out all the magic in the land—except for Kaemusei, which was trapped in the Tawasiri until you accidentally freed it, and Fukuru. He may have been frozen somewhere as well." He sighed. "When we put Kaemusei to rest, what magic had been tied up in it flowed back out—and as the only other matekai, some of it may have trickled back to Fukuru. Enough to awaken him."

His brother sagged. "This is all my fault, then. If I had never gone into the Tawasiri, Kaemusei would never have emerged and Fukuru would still be wherever he's been all this time."

Noniki reached over and gave him a one-armed hug. "Someone would have entered there eventually," he pointed out. "And it was my own encounter with Kaemusei that gave it enough magic to find direction and purpose again—and awakened my skills in return. So no, don't blame yourself."

"At least now we know who we're dealing with," Seikoku put in, and both brothers smiled at her, grateful for the reminder.

"We do," Kagiri agreed, getting to his feet. "I will inform Hibikitsu—and Shizumi. She and I will set out tomorrow for Bezenkai. I've already sent word to Daishin Nishoji to expect us, and what we plan." He smiled down at Noniki, offering both him and Seikoku a hand up. "This is why I needed to delay, though. I'm sure of it. I had to have enough of the memories to tell you who he was."

"Which you did, and I thank you," Noniki replied, accepting the hand and hugging his brother once they were both on their feet. "I will do what I can from here—and I'll work on ways to shield you and Shizumi and the others before you go, as well."

"Thank you." Kagiri returned the embrace. When he stepped back, he was grinning. "I'll restore your privacy for now, though." He'd ducked away and slipped out before Noniki could hit him.

He turned to find Seikoku there, and they hugged as well. "Can you beat him?" she asked. They both knew who she meant.

Noniki wasn't about to lie to her. "I don't know," he admitted. "But I suppose I'll have to."

Because he'd realized something else, something he hadn't mentioned. Just as the ring and its matching hairstick had been linked, so too had Taido Fukuru and his Gensaiba. That link had been stretched with each successive generation, but it was still there.

Which meant the crazed matekai was coming for Hibikitsu. And Noniki was the only person who could get in his way.

CHAPTER THIRTY-THREE

Shizumi sorted quickly through the bakiro's contents, long experience letting her ignore any potential embarrassment at thumbing aside smallclothes. After a moment she turned away from the sturdy carry bag, toward the tall young man waiting anxiously beside her.

"You did a good job," she assured him. "Everything you need, and no unnecessary weight. Nicely done."

Kagiri rarely smiled, but when he did it was a burst of sunlight on a dreary day, a rainbow after a storm. She felt herself flush in the glow of that expression, but couldn't bear to turn away from it, or the obvious gratitude shining in his eyes. Gratitude and perhaps more?

"Thank you," he told her, as earnest and softspoken as ever. She liked the way his words were rarely hurried, as if he thought about each and every one before he let them spill forth. Her own reticence was usually just because she could never think of anything to say that did not sound foolish or obvious! "When Niki and I left home, we didn't have anything but the clothes we were wearing, a fishing net and some hooks, a few days' food in a sack, and a handful of brass coins." He laughed. "And can you believe the Gensaiba, for all their skills, never had to prepare for a long trip or a hard march? Their idea of preparing for this trek was to make sure I brought enough wine!"

"Comes from working with a wizard, I suppose," she replied. "If you can get anywhere in a heartbeat, you don't really worry about forgetting your hantien or your heavier boots."

They both laughed, and for a moment just enjoyed standing there together. She was always so comfortable around him! And, at the same time, not. When they were sparring or talking or eating, she could treat him as just another warrior, like Geniji or Isano. But then she'd get distracted by how long his lashes were, or the planes of his face, or that little hint of a smile on his lips. That was something she definitely didn't do with her old squadmates!

Eventually Kagiri reached across and tugged the bag's drawstrings shut, closing and buckling the flap over it to keep the contents safe from wind and rain. "I suppose we need to deal with the rest now."

She sighed. "Must we? Can't we just go, and let all that sort itself out?" She knew better, of course, and was already following him to his study door, but couldn't stop herself from complaining about it, just a little. The look he gave her was sympathetic, but he didn't slow his pace and neither did she, moving quickly down the hall and through the junction separating the Rojiri's realm from that of the Honteno.

It was a bad sign that Shizumi felt herself tense as they crossed that threshold, as if she were entering enemy territory.

"Enter," the low, sharp voice called when Kagiri knocked. He slid the door open and waved Shizumi through first, closing it again after he'd stepped through.

She was pleased with herself for keeping her hand off her sword, at least.

"Taikoro Atukai." She dipped her head, one equal to another. "We wished to speak a moment about contingencies before we left."

"Taikoro Misataki." Reizei's tone and expression were just as formal as hers had been, her nod also a match. "Dogenriku Kagiri. Yes, you are both leading the forces to engage the enemy in Bezenkai. What can my Honteno do to assist you?"

Shizumi was watching the red-clad woman closely and thought she spotted a wince after she'd spoken. Was that at the thought of helping them? Or was it from hearing how she sounded, so distant and officious?

So unlike Maniko Kohori.

That thought was unworthy of her, however—Shizumi herself knew exactly how it felt to follow in someone's footsteps and bear those expectations, good and bad. She did her best to ignore the flicker of annoyance and instead launched into what she and Kagiri had already discussed. "We are good as far as the assault itself, thank you. It was more the matter of Aihiri we wanted to discuss." She saw Reizei's brow furrow and hurried on before she could be interrupted. "I will be leading a chotao of my Honjofu, fully half my forces. Kagiri is bringing a second reitao. That leaves a hundred of my warriors here and another thousand aiashe down in their barracks in Mazihini. I've already instructed my chuisu, Norio Shinjuru, to offer you any assistance you might require, and of course to defer to you as far as the compound and its protection."

"I've done the same with Masagi Matsu, the taisho I'm leaving in charge of our forces here," Kagiri added. He grimaced. "Truth be told, he'd not be my choice to command in my absence, but he's also the general I least want in the field. He'll do as he's told, though."

Reizei had listened to all of this with a stony expression. Her nod now was curt. "Thank you for notifying me, and for your consideration. But I assure you, my Honteno have the matter well in hand. We will not require any outside assistance."

That was the last straw for Shizumi. "Bones, woman!" she snapped, stepping forward and leaning on her rival commander's desk to glare down at the woman. "We're just trying to help! Why don't you get the stick out of your ass and see that!"

Reizei bolted to her feet, though she had to lean on the desk as well, given her wound, and scowled right back at her. "What I see is people trying to encroach on my territory!" she shouted in Shizumi's face. "People who don't think I can do my job well enough, so they feel they have to step in and do it for me!"

"That's not—" Shizumi started, but a calming hand on her shoulder made her cut off mid-shout.

"That is not how it is," Kagiri offered, his voice unruffled. "We are only trying to help and to work together. Think about how Kohori would have responded to us just now. Can you not see the difference?"

"Of course I can!" Reizei cried, and Shizumi was shocked to

see tears streaming down her rival's face. "Do you think I can't hear her shouting at me right now? Her pointing out what a mess I'm making only makes it worse!" Her eyes widened, as if surprised at her own statement, and she twisted her head for a second, her eyes darting to the wall behind her—

And the tall, graceful urn in the alcove there.

The urn containing Kohori's aishone.

"Oh." Shizumi couldn't stop herself from gasping. "Oh, Reizei, you didn't!"

Reizei collapsed back into her chair and buried her face in her hands. Her palms were wet with her own tears when she glanced back up at the pair standing above her, towering there like a set of stern judges. Weighing her actions and condemning them.

"What else was I supposed to do?" she cried. "I can't do this on my own! I was never going to be good enough—not for you, not for the emperor, not for anyone!"

Not even for me, she admitted silently.

Kagiri sat and half-gestured, half-tugged Shizumi to do the same, taking the two stools placed before the desk for reporting subordinates. "You felt inadequate," he said, his voice soft and even gentle. "Like you couldn't possibly measure up, given what she had been. And you had her bones, so you thought you could at least gain some of her insight, her wisdom, to help guide you."

She nodded, gulping to get her racing heart back under control. "But it didn't help. I could hear her voice, but all it did was tell me what I was doing wrong. I already know that!" She hiccupped out a laugh, waving at her two disapproving visitors. "Look at us! She was friends with you"—that was to Shizumi, still staring at her—"and got along fine with you"—to Kagiri. "I've gone and made you both my enemies in under a month!"

"We're not your enemies," Shizumi said, but it sounded automatic, neither feigned nor felt. The Honjofu commander frowned, as if noticing that herself, and repeated it more slowly, with more emotion. "We're not your enemies." She leaned forward. "We're really not, Reizei." She offered a tentative half smile. "We're all new at this, you know."

"I nearly threw up." Reizei shifted her gaze to Kagiri, as did Shizumi, and he ducked his head a little but then straightened and continued, a bashful smile on his lips. "The first time I had to address my troops. I was so nervous I was almost sick from it." He shook his head. "The Gensaiba were amazing warriors and I have all their skills but they were never soldiers. They didn't follow a chain of command. I have absolutely no idea what I'm doing with any of this." He returned her look and included Shizumi as well as he added, "I've been trying to watch you two to get ideas of how to handle all this."

Shizumi laughed. "The first time I led a bantao," she stated, "we ran into a freak snowstorm. Got blown off course, spent two full days buried in a snowdrift because I was too proud to admit I might've lost the path. I still have spots on my arm from the frostbite."

Reizei found herself laughing as well, and the other woman didn't bristle at it, sharing the humor instead. "I was still new to the Honteno," she related after a second, "when we got our first disturbance up here. Everyone on high alert, all nerves and tensed muscles, weapons drawn and ready." She chuckled, remembering. "Turned out to be a pokanu escaped from the gardens into the palace. I nearly put an arrow through it."

All three of them were giggling now, picturing one of the tall, gaudy birds running around the halls, Reizei and the other Honteno chasing it with bows and spears.

When Kagiri spoke again, his voice was kind but thoughtful once more. "When I first became Gensaiba," he told them, leaning forward a little, "I had all their voices in my head. They were so loud I couldn't hear my own thoughts, only theirs. In battle, that was fine, even good—I was just a scared boy from a little fishing village and they were the greatest warriors in the land, so I let them take control. But the rest of the time, I still heard them constantly. I thought I might go mad."

"How did you deal with it?" she asked. Because clearly he had somehow.

He smiled. "Little by little, I learned to push them down. Their voices faded. Now I have to actively seek them out if I want to hear them. I still have their skills, but my thoughts are my own."

Shizumi nodded. "I'm Mukanichi," she reminded them bluntly, "so I've never had anyone else's thoughts or skills. But I do know exactly how empty that can feel, like you can't possibly compete with those who have something more." Kagiri reached out and took her hand, and Reizei thought her fellow Taikoro looked surprised at that but quickly smiled and accepted the gesture. They had always been good together, since the first time she'd seen them, and Reizei found she was pleased for them. And why shouldn't she be?

"I'm sorry," she told them now. "Kohori was amazing. She wasn't just my commander, she was my hero. Now here I am, trying to fill her shoes. I just feel like I can't possibly measure up to all that. It made me testy, territorial. I took it out on you two, because I saw you as rivals and you're both so poised, so in control." She shook her head. "I made a fool of myself."

Kagiri laughed. "The first time I met with my taisho, I hid on the roof until my own clerk talked me down," he confided. "And then they basically bullied me and walked out."

Shizumi nodded. "I still can't make heads or tails of the budget reports," she admitted. "I stare at figures for this much rice and this much beans and this much pork and I just have no idea what I'm doing." Her smile was warmer this time. "We're all just figuring it out. But we can do that together."

Reizei felt herself smiling back—and relaxing, for what felt like the first time since she'd accepted this position. "I would really appreciate that." She glanced back at Kohori's urn. "And I'm done with that. I'll still look at it, and still wonder what she'd do, how she'd handle something, but I'll let my own memories of her answer, rather than hers. She deserves better than to be used as a crutch to shore me up."

"So do you," Shizumi told her. "You've not been a Taikoro

long, but you've been a Honteno longer than I've been a Honjofu, and you were one of her lieutenants. You know how to do this. You just have to trust yourself."

"You're right." Reizei knew she was telling herself that as much as her guests. "All right, let's start over. Thank you for thinking of me, and of Aihiri, and for making arrangements to provide help if I need it." She stood and bowed to them both. "I hope you fare well in the south, and that once you both return we can find ways to work together better in future."

They both stood as well, and Kagiri offered her his hand. Shizumi did the same. "We will," he promised as the three of them stood there, all connected. "After all, us warriors need to stick together, right?"

She laughed, as did Shizumi, but it was a good laughter, a cleansing one.

And Reizei knew, without any need for aishone, that Kohori would have been laughing right along with them.

CHAPTER THIRTY-FOUR

Futoba was already halfway through Atsani when she thought to stop in at the new compound. It had been more than a week since the Bone Readers had taken possession of the former Ieuyuki estates, after all. And, as she had facilitated the transfer, should she not play the role of a dutiful neighbor and make sure they were settling in properly?

The massive iron gates, still bearing the imprint of a swallow in flight though at least the gold paint had been scraped off, were slightly ajar, which Futoba found surprising. Surely, even here, the Senkousa should be worried about their safety, being a group of women alone? But perhaps they kept the gates open as a sign of welcome, the way Sorainasei's seemed to be always open for visitors during the day.

Regardless of the reason, Futoba chose to slip through without announcing herself. She wasn't entirely sure why, other than to get a more honest look at how the group was faring.

What she saw made her stop mid-stride and nearly choke as she forgot how to breathe.

Futoba had visited this particular estate many times in her youth, and then a handful more as an adult. She was well familiar with its layout: the winding path through the fields from the gates to the gatehouse barring the main compound; the wide courtyard beyond that; the main house, with its inner courtyard and meditation pool; the kitchen garden to one side; the barracks in one back corner and servant quarters in the other, with pens and fields in between. It was a competent, functional design, more efficient than attractive, though of course the grounds and the house were grand and lush.

What she saw before her now bore little resemblance to those memories.

For starters, the gatehouse was being expanded, both widened to cover the entire front and heightened with a second level. At the same time, it looked like the servant quarters had been pulled down but the barracks were being rebuilt for some reason. The main house, at least, looked largely intact, though it was in the process of being repainted and its roof reshingled. There were workmen everywhere, most of them in nothing but torito and hos-ode, carrying timbers and slats and bundles of reeds and other construction materials. The entire place was abuzz with activity.

But why? She understood the need to remake a place in her own image, separating it from its past in order to give it a brighter future, but this seemed excessive. Why not just repaint, perhaps file the swallows off the doors, and be done with it?

Also, where had they found the money? Senkousa were widely respected and usually at least moderately well off, but these renovations would cost more than the three women she'd met could possibly have. Especially since they all worked the lower regions rather than the highest ones, and so presumably had not been able to save up as much. Futoba thought she recognized a few faces among the men and women she saw working, so perhaps a few of the former Ieuyuki servants had been put to such tasks, but the rest were clearly trained in construction techniques, meaning they had been brought in from outside. Such people would not take jobs on promises or reputation.

What truly concerned her, however, was the work on the guard-house and the barracks. That did not look like simple redecorating. Why expand those unless you were expecting to be attacked by someone—or looking to attack in turn?

All of this bore looking into, and Futoba straightened with a sigh. So much for merely checking up on them!

Glancing about, she did not see any of the Bone Readers nearby, which also struck her as odd. But one of the workmen had a wooden writing tablet he was consulting, so Futoba made for him instead.

"You there!" she called as she approached. "Hand that over!"

The man started, glancing her way. He was solidly built, his hair beginning to gray but his eyes still sharp, and they narrowed as she neared. "Excuse me? Do I know you?"

"You do not," Futoba replied crisply, "but I am Heiayuki Futoba, one of His Imperial Majesty's Rojiri." She held up her imperial seal of office, watching his eyes widen as he took in the carved jade emblem. "Is that your work order?"

He nodded and mutely handed the tablet over. Futoba scanned it. The barracks were not being rebuilt so much as reinforced, she saw—a doubled outer wall, a raised floor, bars on the windows, and an iron door. Why? Were they making it into a prison?

Equally interesting was the signature at the bottom, authorizing the work and covering the expense: Fujiko Oritano. Futoba knew that name, though it took her a second to place it. Once she had, however, she all but growled. Something was definitely sour in all this.

"Rojiri Heiayuki!" The warm voice carried across the courtyard, and she turned to find Medeiko hurrying toward her, Utami and Wani right behind. "What a pleasant surprise!"

The sturdy Senkousa's face was creased in a welcoming smile, but Futoba refused to be lulled this time. "What is the meaning of all this?" she demanded instead, waving the tablet toward the rebuilding efforts. "Why are you crafting a stronghouse at the back of the estate? What do you intend to store there? And why is it being paid for by one Fujiko Oritano, a known associate of Kichin Narai—who was, until very recently, one of my fellow Rojiri?"

Medeiko had reached her now and fluttered her hands in what was no doubt meant to be a calming gesture. "I am sure some of this does appear strange to you," the Bone Reader admitted, her voice low and calm, "but we can explain. Why don't we all sit down and have some tea and discuss it?"

A hand reached out and snatched the tablet from her, and Futoba turned to find Utami there on her left. Wani was now on her right, and the construction foreman had moved up behind her. But Futoba straightened to her full height, which allowed her to peer down at them all. "I doubt there is much you can do to explain this away," she replied in her iciest tone. "And I find I do not wish to enter that house with you at this time." An image came to her of a ledger with decreasing numbers, and she frowned. "You are storing aishone there, aren't you?" she accused, eyes locked not on Medeiko but Utami. "That is why you need the added security. But not your own bones, and not those the emperor purchased. You are up to some other game, and Narai and his partners are behind it all."

She had known that Medeiko would not give anything away—the woman was slippery as a quisuin—but Utami was far less polished. Sure enough, the thin Bone Reader gasped, staring at Futoba like she was an akatai drawing out all her secrets.

Medeiko, however, merely smiled. "You are perceptive as well as kindhearted," she noted, her tone somewhere between complimentary and matter-of-fact. "Yes, we plan to stockpile what aishone we can. That way, if anything should happen to the emperor's own stores, we will have ours in reserve. Surely you agree that we should not simply toss away all of our history, our heritage, our memories?"

"I do," Futoba admitted. "But that does not explain why you are doing this in secret, or why those particular merchants are involved?" *It does explain why we are taking in fewer aishone than expected,* she thought, but decided not to state out loud. Yet. She was, after all, still surrounded.

"We can discuss that," Medeiko offered. "That and many other things. This is a time of great change, Rojiri Heiayuki, as you yourself know only too well. For those who are thoughtful and careful, such times can be exceedingly rewarding. Why do we not discuss how we may help each other toward that end, to everyone's benefit?"

Futoba considered playing along, but she had the feeling once she entered that house, she might not be able to leave. Thus she drew herself up in her haughtiest manner. "I thank you for your invitation, but I believe I have seen more than enough for today. I will take my leave and consider what you have said."

She turned—and found Wani there, very nearly in her face. "Apologies, Senkousa," the pretty Bone Reader said softly, reaching out and grabbing Futoba's wrist. "But I'm afraid we cannot allow you to go just yet."

The others also moved in, and Futoba thanked the First Emperor that she had grown up with male cousins and had learned roughhousing simply in self-defense. Now she twisted her hand free from Wani's grip, ducked under Medeiko's lunge, and twisted around, outside the little circle. That still put them between her and the exit, however, with more workers noticing and heading this way. Which meant it was time for something more drastic.

Accordingly, Futoba stepped forward herself, wrapping her arm around Medeiko's neck and pulling the shorter woman back against her.

"I will be leaving now," she declared over the Bone Reader's head. "I would advise you to stand aside."

Despite her current predicament, Medeiko laughed. "What will you do?" she asked. "You have no weapon, and I am a poor shield. Surrender yourself and we will treat you as kindly as we can."

In response, Futoba drew the slim chain from around her neck. A small golden globe hung at the end, its latticework as fine as hairs. She held the globe against the other woman's cheek. "Tell them what this is," she warned. "You are a Senkousa, you cannot fail to feel it so close to you. Tell them."

Medeiko had stiffened reflexively as the globe had neared her, trying to shrink away from its touch. "There is a single shard of bone within," she said, her usually honeyed voice rough with fear for once. "It...it is that of a master assassin."

"Correct." Futoba brought the tiny sphere back toward her own face. "It has been in my family for generations, a weapon of last resort. If you attempt anything, I will swallow it. I am Suponichi, those deadly skills will become mine before you can blink. You may be able to take me despite that, but it will require all of you, and many of you will lie dead at my feet before we are done. Starting with you." She tightened her grip enough to make the Bone Reader gulp for air. "Decide your fate."

Then she popped the globe into her mouth, pinned between her teeth, and waited.

The moment stretched on in silence. Then she felt her captive nod jerkily.

"Let her go." Medeiko's voice was a mere rasp. "Stand back and let her go."

The others backed away, not without frowns and scowls of their own. But they were pale and shaking as well. None of them were warriors, nor did they have any of those aishone to hand, it seemed. They were outmatched and they knew it.

"We can still work something out," Utami pleaded, though she did so from out of arm's reach now. "Please!"

Futoba did not bother to answer. Instead, after checking that the path behind her was clear, she released Medeiko, shoving the woman away from her and into her friends.

Then, spitting the globe back into her hand, Heiayuki Futoba, Rojiri and head of her house, abandoned all dignity, lifted the hem of her robe, and raced for the gates.

She did not stop until she was not only out of the compound but well down the street. Then she finally slowed, hung the pendant back around her neck, and caught her breath.

The question was, what to do next?

Fortunately, she saw a light up ahead, from the lamps affixed to another set of gates. But these were carved into the image of the sun bursting forth from behind a cluster of bright, fluffy clouds.

Sorainasei.

With a quickened pace and a glance back over her shoulder, Futoba made for Atsani's other community—and hoped its mayor would be at home, and willing to help.

CHAPTER THIRTY-FIVE

Seikoku listened as Futoba explained what she'd seen and what she'd surmised. "I'm impressed," she admitted once the taller woman had finished and slumped a little—they were sitting on a bench in the gardens, since it afforded them a comfortable spot and some privacy but also fresh air. "That was quick thinking on your part, with the aishone."

The noblewoman tugged the thin chain, a nervous habit Seikoku had noticed before. "I inherited this from my father when I became head of house," she said, pulling the little sphere out to dangle it from her fingers. "I never thought I'd have to use it or even threaten to." She shuddered. "I still can't believe I did that."

"I can." Seikoku couldn't help but laugh at her companion's horrified expression. "What I mean is, you're strong-willed and resourceful. I'm not at all surprised you didn't let them intimidate you—or worse." Her thoughts returned to what Futoba had just told her. "I knew Medeiko was up to something," she mused. "I caught her siphoning off aishone the other day, and I suspected she had a backer somewhere supplying the money to purchase those. I had no idea it was Narai and his cronies, but it fits, I suppose."

Her friend—and they *were* friends, Seikoku thought with some surprise—nodded. "From a purely business standpoint, I can hardly blame him. Let us do the work of getting people to sell, then buy up all the best ones for yourself? Of course, if we're not able to stockpile any ourselves, we'll probably have to drop the initiative altogether, but by then he'll have a tidy little aishone treasury. He could sell them to the throne, dole them out, whatever he wants."

Seikoku scowled. "You're right, it does make sense. And it's all legal. Just underhanded and despicable." She sighed. "We can't let them get away with it, obviously."

"No," Futoba agreed, straightening. "Absolutely not. We trusted him as one of us, and even though he's been dismissed from that position—for exactly this sort of behavior—he should still show some honor. And the Senkousa, we relied upon them. I helped them gain that compound!" A grating sound emerged as she ground her teeth together. "In some ways, this is all my fault!"

"No, it's not," Seikoku told her firmly. "They'd have done this anyway, I'm sure. Narai would have just stored them in some stockhouse somewhere." She smiled and rose to her feet. "At least this way we know exactly where to find them."

Her friend stood as well. "What are you going to do?"

Seikoku laughed, glad that she'd recently confided in the other woman about her past profession. It had slipped out one night while they were going over details, but it was good not having to hide that part of herself, especially at a time like this. "Well, first I'm going to make sure they really are stashing aishone in there. It wouldn't do anyone any good if we charged in accusing them of that, only to find they were keeping aged tsekuri in that building, would it?" She tapped a finger to her lip. "Once I've confirmed that, we'll figure out what to do next." A part of her thought she should simply steal them all back, but Futoba must have divined that from her expression because the noblewoman shook her head.

"If they are there, best to leave them be," she warned. "Since they really did purchase those aishone legally, we'd only make things worse if we took them." A grin cracked her long face. "Though I would love to see Narai's expression when he found an empty storeroom. And Medeiko's." If the noblewoman had ever felt any distaste for associating with a known—though fully pardoned—thief, she had clearly gotten past that.

"I won't take anything," Seikoku promised. "You go home, spend time with your family, relax a little. I'll stop by in the morning and we can discuss our options."

The other woman nodded and let herself be led back to the

central courtyard and from there to the front gates. "Thank you," she said once they'd stopped there at the entrance. "I knew you were the right person to ask."

"Of course," Seikoku replied warmly. "We're friends. And we're in this together." Acting on impulse, she hugged the taller woman, who stiffened only a second before returning the gesture. Futoba seemed far less glum when she finally pulled away and stepped out into the street beyond.

For herself, Seikoku was actually struggling to tamp down her rising anger. How dare those women take advantage of their trust like this? And the emperor's? Their selfishness and greed could endanger the entire program, which in turn risked dooming the kingdom to the same stagnation they were trying to prevent! She had half a mind to strip the entire complex bare of all valuables, then find some way to turn the women out on the street, penniless and homeless.

That was unworthy of her, though. She thought of what Noniki would say. "Don't stoop to their level," she could see him warning, his handsome features as earnest as ever. "But don't let them get away with it, either."

Well, she wasn't sure how she'd manage that trick yet, but she'd figure something out. She and Futoba would. Together.

First, though, she had a late-night excursion to plan. How convenient that the new compound was only a few doors away!

The next morning, Seikoku presented herself at the gates to House Heiayuki's compound. She had not yet had time to explore all the tiers of Awaihinshi and decided that she liked Motohiri—it was similar to Atsani, with no shops or stores, only residences, but a little busier, the street a touch narrower, the estates slightly smaller and closer together. There was a restrained, elegant bustle about the place, as befitted the home of the major merchant houses, and everyone she saw on her walk over seemed to have a clear purpose and destination. Some of them nodded politely to her as they passed. Others did not, no doubt seeing her simple clothing and deciding she was not important enough to warrant their attention. Seikoku didn't care to correct them. Anyone like that was not worth her own time, anyway.

House Heiayuki's estate proved to be narrower than Sorainasei but still quite lovely, with handsome old esuge lining the walk. Like her own home—and how strange to think of it as such—a single large building dominated the compound. Unlike Sorainasei, however, she quickly saw that this central structure truly was a home, and a large one. The first evidence of that came as she climbed the broad, shallow wooden steps, only to have the front doors swing open and a small figure dart out and barrel directly toward her.

Seikoku reacted instinctively. Crouching, she spread her arms wide, catching the little girl mid-step and then standing and twisting to spin them both around. The girl's initial shriek of surprise turned to utter delight, and she was giggling when Seikoku set her back down again.

"That was fun!" this new acquaintance declared, peering up at Seikoku from a mass of tangled dark hair. "You're really pretty."

"Thank you, so are you." Which she was, especially when she smiled. There was something of Futoba in her eyes, too, and that connection was confirmed a second later, as the head of house herself appeared at the door above, red-faced and out of breath.

"Inomi!" she called, stopping at seeing the girl and Seikoku together on the steps. She recovered quickly, however, and bustled toward them, scooping the girl up. "Please don't run off like that," she pleaded. "You need to let Hana comb your hair out!"

"No!" Inomi protested, pummeling her mother—Seikoku assumed—with chubby little fists. "It hurts when she does!"

"That's only because it's so tangled," Seikoku assured the girl. "I'm sure if you tell her that, she'll be as gentle as she can. And after it's all nice and clean and untangled, she can put it up for you, and then it won't be in your way or get caught on anything." She turned and showed off her own short braid, tilting her head to make it sway back and forth. "See?"

Inomi stared at her with wide eyes. "Can I have mine like that?"

Futoba smiled. "Of course, sweetie. Let's go tell Hana, okay?" She turned, balancing the child on her hip with what struck Seikoku as years of practice before glancing back at her. "I hope you don't mind."

Seikoku laughed. "Not at all." She followed them up and into the house, winking at Inomi and making her giggle. The interior was just as she'd thought from the outside, elegant enough but also warm and homey, and she liked the place right off.

Futoba handed the little girl off to her maid, providing instructions on the braid, and then gave Seikoku her attention once they were alone on the entryway. "I'm so sorry about that. Inomi can be...opinionated."

"Don't be," Seikoku assured her. "She's adorable, and I don't mind at all."

Her friend's face relaxed into a fond smile. "She is, isn't she? And she knows it, which is the trouble. This way." She led the way into a handsome study, eschewing the desk to seat herself on one of the wide, colorful cushions before it and motioning for Seikoku to do the same. The outer walls were already open, allowing the early morning light to seep in along with the scent of flowers and trees from the gardens beyond. "Would you like some tea?"

"Thank you, that would be nice." Seikoku took a second to admire the room while her hostess rang for tea. "Your home is lovely."

Futoba smiled—she seemed more relaxed here than in Aihiri, which Seikoku could completely understand. "Thank you. It still feels a bit strange living here full-time, but we're beginning to make it our own again." An older woman appeared with a tray containing tea and small plates of tukaiono, sliced fruits, and ujiro. She placed those on the low table by the cushions. "Thank you, Koma." They waited while the woman poured them both cups, then bowed and left the room. "What did you find out?"

Seikoku took a sip of her tea—it was excellent, richer and more robust than she might have chosen for herself but a fine way to wake up and start the day. "You were absolutely right," she said finally, setting the cup back down and taking a slice of pickled radish with the little fork set out for that purpose. "They are keeping aishone there, and they have quite a collection already." She savored the flavor of the tukaiono, its saltiness both offsetting and enhancing the tea's smokiness. "So, what do we do about it?"

A brief, almost mischievous grin lit her friend's face for a moment, showing exactly where Inomi had gotten that from, but Futoba's voice was still serious when she answered. "I have been considering that, and I believe I have an idea. We will need some assistance, including some action from the emperor, but in the end this may actually accelerate our plans, rather than slow or prevent them."

She explained what she had in mind, and when she'd done Seikoku laughed along with her. "Yes, that should do quite nicely," she agreed merrily. "And I have just the people to help with those other aspects." She drank more of her tea. "But first, I believe you told me you had two children? Might I beg to meet the other, and your husband as well?"

Futoba was a quiet woman, reserved and often serious, but her smile now was as bright as the sun as she called out and asked Koma to have her family join them.

The next two days were busy ones. Hibikitsu had agreed to their plan at once and also assured Futoba he did not blame her in any way for what had developed. "The danger of being a good person with a kind heart and a strong sense of duty," he'd told her, "is that you expect others to be the same. But I would rather believe so and occasionally be disappointed than go through life assuming the worst in everyone."

That had been well put and had made Seikoku think about her own attitude toward people. Not so long ago she had been a thief and a grave-robber, and though she'd deliberately targeted those she found dishonorable, there had never been any shortage of victims. She had treated most people as reprehensible, requiring them to prove themselves otherwise.

Meeting Noniki had changed all that. Not just him, with his inherent goodness, but the journey they'd started together after his return. Traveling from Ginzai to here with Kanai, collecting like-minded folk along the way, had opened her eyes. There were still plenty of good, decent people in the world, and hearing Hibikitsu say it, Seikoku knew he was right. She no longer assumed everyone was awful—instead, she gave them the benefit of the doubt more often than not. If they disappointed her, as Narai had, she was done with them. But at least she didn't automatically assume that they would.

Some of those worthy people were gathering now, as they did at the end of every day, to eat together in Sorainasei's main hall. But today many of them had been engaged in different activities than their usual wont.

Jitu Kanai was laughing as he entered with Otokai. "I kept asking why I couldn't simply buy my aishone back," the sturdy potter was telling the quiet, cany horsetrader as they approached Seikoku and the long tables. "'But I just sold them to the Senkousa a few days ago, surely she still has them!'"

His companion chuckled. "Nicely done. I was a bit less subtle. I bought a round of drinks at one of the taverns, telling everyone how I'd sold my aishone for four gold but, when I went to buy them back, it only cost me two, so I had money to spare." He grinned. "I did wonder aloud at how there were fewer than I remembered but passed that off as being too deep in my cups."

Seikoku hugged them both. "Thank you," she told them. "You both did brilliantly."

Nor were they the only ones. She'd enlisted several of her friends to visit Mazihini, Bejinuri, and Sakiriti, both the Senkousas' establishments and stores, markets, and taverns in general. And all of them were, in one way or another, spreading the tale that the Bone Readers were buying aishone not for the throne but for themselves.

Bright and early the next morning, Seikoku and Futoba visited the Senkousas' compound together. They brought three pairs of Honteno with them as well, just in case.

"Rojiri!" Medeiko came hurrying from the main building once a guard had been sent ahead with word of their arrival. Two others Futoba quietly identified as Utami and Wani were right behind her. "What a pleasant surprise!" Seikoku did not miss the panicked look the older Bone Reader shot at Futoba but acted as if she hadn't noticed.

"I wish it were, Senkousa," she said instead, with as much regret as she could feign. "Unfortunately, we have a grave problem. It seems people have almost completely stopped selling back their aishone. Numbers have plummeted lately. We were hoping you might be able to explain why."

The older Bone Reader was a clever woman and put on an expression of polite confusion. "I had noticed the same, Rojiri," she confessed, bowing low. "However, I'm afraid I do not know the reason behind it."

That much, at least, was probably true. And Seikoku took some pleasure in nodding to Futoba, who stepped forward. "I *do* know the reason," the tall noblewoman declared, her resonant voice ringing out across the space, making the handful of other women nearby stop to listen. "It has become known to the citizens of Awaihinshi that you have been purchasing aishone for yourself, rather than simply acting as a broker for sales to others."

A gasp rose from several of those attending, and Wani paled. "We rely upon our reputation for objectivity," the pretty Bone Reader whispered. "If that falls into question..."

"Then no one will avail themselves of your services," Seikoku agreed. "Because you are no longer disinterested parties. You are now potential buyers yourself and must be assumed to be acting in your own best interest, not that of your customers."

Utami was gaping like a fish. "You have ruined us!" she accused in a rough voice.

"Us?" Seikoku faked ignorance. "The Rojiri had nothing to do with this." Her voice sharpened. "Nonetheless, it *is* true, is it not?

You have been siphoning off aishone, setting aside half of each purchase intended for the emperor and keeping them for yourself. Keeping them there, in fact." And she pointed at the building in the compound's back corner.

The two flanking Senkousa both stuttered and gasped, but Medeiko's eyes only narrowed, her stance and expression still calm. "What do you want?" she asked, her rich voice low.

Futoba faced down the shorter woman. "From you? Nothing," she stated coldly. "Except that you comply with the law, as every good citizen must." And she handed Medeiko the scroll she'd brought.

They both watched as the Bone Reader unrolled it and read, her composure leaking away as she did. "What?" she finally managed, glancing up at them. "This is...you cannot be serious!"

"What is it?" Utami asked. Her friend handed her the scroll, but Futoba explained it to save her the trouble.

"The emperor has decreed that any business stockpiling aishone must pay taxes on such as an Imperial good," she said, again projecting so everyone could hear. "And any individual or group thereof that possesses more than the specified amount of aishone will be treated as a business for that purpose." That had been her idea, and it was a brilliant one. Any normal person with their own aishone would not be affected, only those who were collecting them to trade or sell.

People like the Senkousa.

"We cannot pay that," Medeiko stated flatly. "But you already know that, don't you?"

Seikoku offered the woman a tight, predatory grin. "Perhaps you can appeal to your sponsors to pay it for you." She was watching for the other woman's eyes and mouth to tighten, and nodded when they did. "No, I thought not. That was the arrangement, after all, hm? That they would put up the money, and dictate how the aishone might be used after, but not be associated with your actions in any way, so as to avoid any consequences should you be discovered? Which you now have."

The lead Bone Reader bowed her head. "What must we do?"

Again Seikoku let her friend have the satisfaction. This had been her plan, after all. "You will surrender the aishone you have collected to the throne," she announced, her tone making it clear this was not a negotiation. "Whatever monies you have left did not come from us, and surely your sponsors will not wish to come forward to claim it. It is yours to keep. As is this estate...provided you demonstrate the capacity to maintain it properly, and to pay the associated taxes. Otherwise, you will forfeit it as well and relocate."

All three Senkousa nodded glumly. They stood aside as one of the Honteno retreated to the gate, returning with a pair of men leading an ox-drawn cart. They would oversee the removal of the aishone to the Imperial vaults, but she suspected they would have no further problems. These women knew they had been beaten.

Turning, she bowed to her friend. "Rojiri Heiayuki, shall we return to Aihiri? I am sure there is much for us to do there."

Futoba bowed in return, though a smile flickered at her lips. "Why, yes, Rojiri Seikoku," she agreed. "I think that would be best. There is nothing more for us here."

Together, heads held high, they exited the compound, leaving the Bone Readers to stare after them.

CHAPTER THIRTY-SIX

Takami listened along with the rest as Seikoku and Futoba explained what had happened with the Senkousa, and with their own former colleague. "Are you sure they didn't break any laws?" Reizei asked once they'd finished, leaning forward in her seat with a clink of armor. "I'd be happy to have them dragged back here in chains to explain themselves."

Hibikitsu had been listening attentively, but now he sighed. "No, I am certain they stayed just within the letter of the law," he replied, tapping his fingers against his jaw. "Narai is too clever to make such a mistake." He shook his head. "I'd hoped the Bone Readers were sincere in both their desire to help and their wish for a new life, but of course not everyone will be. We cannot prevent that. Still, it is disappointing."

"Do we really think they'll toe the line after this and be good citizens of Atsani?" Noniki asked. "Especially now that they don't have income from their former occupation and have just lost the funding from their new one." It was strange to see him without his brother, but of course both Kagiri and Shizumi were already en route to Bezenkai, leaving the council table decidedly lopsided.

"We cannot be certain, no," Futoba replied. "But our other choice is to assume the worst, and I'd rather be guilty of optimism than negativity." She seemed glum but determined, which Takami could understand. After all, it was obvious she blamed herself for being fooled.

He could relate to that all too well.

"I agree," Hibikitsu assured her. "We will all observe to see what they do next, but I hope this truly does set them on the path toward new lives with new and even more rewarding goals."

That was their only business for today, and the others soon dispersed, returning to their homes or offices and their other duties. Takami lingered, however, mainly because he did not want to go home.

He wasn't sure how long he'd been sitting there when someone cleared their throat. Glancing up, he found Seikoku and Futoba standing on the table's other side, watching him closely.

"Are you all right?" Seikoku asked gently. "You've seemed troubled lately, and it has only grown worse with time."

"We just want to help, if we can," Futoba added. Her earnestness and their shared compassion broke the last of Takami's reticence, and he slumped in his chair.

"Thank you," he told them. "But I'm not sure anyone can help at this point." He explained about his brother demanding control of the estate, and of House Fujitai in general. "…and there's nothing I can say or do to stop him," he concluded.

Futoba was nodding. He was not surprised she understood—she was the head of what had been a cadet house, no doubt she'd had plenty of people trying to steal control of it from her, and even more trying to discount her house now that it was no longer connected to the Ieuyuki. Seikoku, on the other hand, was pacing back and forth, frowning mightily.

"Why can't you stop him, exactly?" she asked. "Sorry, I'm just… couldn't you just tell him to leave you alone, or not let him in, or something?"

In his mind's eye, Takami saw the burnt saddle again. "I can't." It was clear, however, they were not going to take that for an answer. "Even when we were younger," he explained heavily, not meeting their eyes, "Kai was…imperious. He bossed around everyone he could, including our mother." He frowned, flattening his hands atop the table to avoid pounding it instead. "I was never sure if our father simply did not notice or actually approved of such behavior. He could be…demanding, as well."

Futoba opened her mouth but Seikoku quieted her with a gesture and simply waited for Takami to continue.

"Kai has always loved to ride," he went on, forcing the words

out. "I have always hated it. The smell, the height, the precarious-
ness, the jostling, all of it. My love was, and is, the sea. But we
had only the one servant tasked to mind us both, so we could only
engage in one or the other." He tapped the table with a knuckle.
"So we always went riding." The next part was the hardest, but he
had come this far, and these were his friends, his colleagues. They
deserved to know.

"One day, I'd had enough. I reasoned that, if the stables were
damaged, we would have to go sailing instead." He studied his
own hands intently.

"So I set it on fire."

Futoba gasped.

"Three horses died," he recounted, speaking each word slowly
and carefully. "And one stablehand was badly burned. Kai told
our father that a lantern must have been knocked over somehow.
He has held it over me ever since."

"You worry that, if you stand up to him, he will reveal the truth,"
Seikoku surmised. "But how old were you when it happened?"

He grimaced. "I was ten. He was fourteen."

"You were just a child! Children do stupid things."

Takami dared to glance up at their faces. In them he saw surprise, anger—but no revulsion. No horror.

No pity.

"But if he tells the emperor..." he started.

Futoba straightened, her jaw resolute. "Then you tell him first,"
she stated. "And have him issue a writ, confirming that House
Fujitai is its own master, not beholden to anyone."

For an instant, Takami dared to hope. Yes, that might work!

But Seikoku was already shaking her head. "You cannot go to
the emperor with this," she warned, and though her tone was soothing, her face was equally set. "You cannot involve him at all."

"Why not?" Futoba asked, turning to her. "It would solve
everything!"

"It would solve nothing," the young buhiyo countered, her eyes
never leaving Takami. "Your brother is a bully. You cannot stop
a bully by threatening him with someone bigger. That only delays

the inevitable and leaves you reliant on the other person to keep you safe. You have to do this yourself."

He considered that. She was right. He knew Kai too well to think he would ever stop just because someone else said to. How many times in their youth had he bowed to their father's commands—and then found a way around them afterward?

"But how can I stop him?" Takami asked. "I've never been able to keep him from doing anything he wants!"

Seikoku offered him a firm nod and a small smirk. "You were never a Rojiri before," she pointed out. "And you never had friends like us, either."

She pulled out a chair and sat. After a second, Futoba nodded and did the same.

Takami studied them both—and felt a smile breaking out. "Very well. Let us think of ways to convince my brother it is in his own best interests to leave me alone."

They stayed up late into the night, discussing and planning and scheming. The next morning it took several cups of very strong tea before Takami felt ready to face the day. He'd rather have gone back to sleep, but knew it was best to deal with things now, before he lost his nerve. Accordingly, he had Moto find him a pair of strong men and paid them to carry a package for him. Then he set out with them and their burden in tow.

House Kazutai was in Motohiri, one tier down. Takami had always liked the level in general, with its walls a soft peach hue and its streets quieter than the lower levels but still possessed of some life. There were people out and about now, but they all moved aside to let him and his retainers pass, and soon enough he was standing at the gates of his childhood home. They were shut—Kazutai had never been the welcoming sort unless he stood to gain by it—and Takami rapped on a particular petal. A second later, it slid aside so the man within could peer out. His eyes widened when he saw Takami standing there.

"Hello, Uhei," Takami said. "I am here to see my family."

"Of course, lord!" Uhei closed the panel, and an instant later the gates swung open. "Shall I announce you?"

"No need." Takami sailed past the startled servant and made his way down the path toward the main house. The compound had not changed any in the weeks he had been away, and he felt strange being within it once more, but squared his shoulders and refused to let that sway him from his course of action.

Someone in the house must have seen him, because he was still a few paces from the steps when his brother emerged. "Taki," Kazutai called out. "I do not recall summoning you." His eyes flicked past Takami to the two with him and widened upon seeing what they carried.

"Good morning, brother," Takami replied, not stopping until he was at the steps. He gestured for the men to set down their load and leave. "I've brought you Father's chest. Much as I appreciate the thought, I have no need for it."

Gazing up at his brother, Takami saw his eyes narrow and his nostrils flare. "You seem to be laboring under a misapprehension, little brother," Kazutai stated through clenched teeth. "It is not for you, but it does belong there. The rest of my things will follow shortly."

"No." Takami enjoyed watching his brother's eyes widen at the tone of that single syllable. "They will not. You are not welcome in my home, Kai. Nor are your things."

There was a small commotion from the house, and several more people emerged to cluster behind and around Kazutai. One of them was a woman, middle-aged but still handsome, with knowing brown eyes. Beside her were two girls who shared some of her features, just as he and Kai did.

"Taki!" The younger of the two hurried down the stairs and threw herself into his arms. "I've missed you!"

"And I you, Yodo," he assured his little sister. "And you, Uji. And of course you, Mother."

Their mother smiled at him, though not without casting a quick, fearful glance at his brother. "You look tired, Takami."

"I am, a little," he admitted. "But I expect I will sleep better tonight."

Kazutai had had enough of this family reunion. "You will sleep when and where I tell you," he hissed, descending the steps to glare at Takami from mere inches away as Yodo hurried back to the safety of their mother. "I am head of house here!"

"Here, yes," Takami agreed. "But not Fujitai. That is mine."

"You are a cadet house only!" Kazutai roared, his face purpling with rage. "Nothing more!"

Rather than respond directly, Takami withdrew a scroll from his sleeve. "Do you recall the tales of how Matsutano founded this house?" he stated to no one in particular. "How he had been cast out of his village with nothing more than a spear, a fishing net, and a single white flower with orange leaves?"

His brother snorted, contempt momentarily derailing his fury. "We are all familiar with the story, Taki."

"Ah," Takami said, "but did you know it is not entirely true? Matsutano was not from a village at all. He was a second son and set off to seek his fortune when his brother inherited all." He grinned at the obvious parallel and offered the scroll to his own brother before adding the last bit, the truly important part:

"All of House Etsuya."

"What?" Kazutai snatched the scroll and hurriedly unrolled it, scanning the contents. His face went from crimson to white as he read. "This is a lie!"

Takami shrugged. "You can see it there for yourself. Our original ancestor, Matsutano, was a younger son of House Etsuya. Which means House Kazutai is itself a cadet branch—of a house that has since been disbanded for treason."

That last word hung in the air, echoing in the sudden silence as everyone froze. He let it sink in fully before drawing himself up and meeting his brother's furious stare.

"So, Kai, what will it be?" he asked softly, the words just for the two of them. "You can force the issue, try to claim that my house falls under yours, but I will expose the truth of our origins and we will all suffer together." He shrugged. "Or you can walk away. The secret will remain ours alone. And that of the friends I've entrusted it to, of course."

He waited, not pushing but not backing down, either. Just watching his brother's face as he thought the matter through. Finally, however, Kazutai snarled and turned away, making the only decision he could that would let him keep what he already had, if nothing more.

"Fine," he grated out. "Fujitai stands alone. You owe me nothing."

"Precisely." Takami shifted to look up at the three ladies of the household and bowed deeply. "Mother, sisters, it would please me beyond measure if you would consent to join me in my home and make it yours as well."

The girls both clapped their hands with delight. His mother had not moved, however, other than to shift her gaze to her elder son. The question hung in the air, heavy despite being unspoken.

"Go, if you want!" Kazutai bellowed, crumpling the scroll in his hands. "Get out and don't come back!"

That was all she needed to hear. With quiet dignity Takami's mother led his sisters to him and returned his bow with one of her own. "My son," she said softly, "we would be delighted to live with you as part of your house." The girls hugged him, and he them, and his mother as well.

But Takami was not quite done yet. "Anyone else who wishes to join House Fujitai," he announced, loud enough for all there to hear, "you are more than welcome."

The first to move was Kame, which was no surprise, as she had been Takami's mother's maid since before he was born. Furi, the girls' principal maid and teacher, was right behind her. Uhei approached from the other side, Toro beside him, and a few others followed.

With each new defection, Kazutai's fury grew. He was practically frothing at the mouth as he eyed them all. "Traitors, the lot of you!" he shouted. "Abandoning your house!"

"Following a member of the old house to his new one, rather," Takami corrected. He drew dignity around him like a heavy cloak. "They have granted me their allegiance, and I will honor them for that. I, Fujitai Takami. Head of House Fujitai, Rojiri to the Emperor, and Dogenkaishu of his aikaye. Farewell, brother. I doubt we will meet again."

And with that, Takami turned on his heel and marched out, his mother beside him, his sisters skipping around them, and a half dozen servants following in their wake. With each step, he felt lighter and lighter, until he was sure his feet must be barely touching the ground. He had woken yesterday morning shrouded in gloom, fear, and dismay, in a large estate with no one but Moto for company. Now he was free, his own man, and tonight the house would be filled with family and staff. After speaking with Futoba last night, Takami also had plans to reach out to some of the other former houses in Atsani, or rather to the servants who'd remained. He would fill some of his vacancies with those worthies, jobless through no fault of their own.

When the emperor had granted him lands and titles, Takami had found them empty and cold. But now, at last, House Fujitai would become a real home.

CHAPTER THIRTY-SEVEN

Hibikitsu was seriously considering gnawing off one of his own limbs. Though he wasn't entirely sure how practical that would be in this particular situation. Still, it worked for trapped animals, did it not? And that was exactly how he was feeling at the moment.

Trapped.

He had retreated to his private study, one of the few places he knew no one would dare enter without his express permission. But he suspected he would be approached the moment he exited.

It was as if the Yatamorans could somehow track his movements from a distance. He would be walking down a corridor or passing through one of the gardens and suddenly they would be there: all three of them, Hu Yongian and his twin shadows, tall and slim and as emotionless as a tree trunk yet with a strange eagerness as they pounced, determined to "educate" him in the backwardness of his own nation and the superiority of theirs.

If he had to listen to another lecture from them, he would probably scream.

"What do I do about them, Kohori?" he asked aloud, the words echoing around the otherwise empty study. He was not just speaking of the Yatamorans, of course. There were also the Fyushans and the Higinasans. Three sets of dignitaries, each with their own agendas, their own goals, but each determined to claim as much of his time and attention as possible.

He would very much like to avoid them all.

"Stop behaving like a petulant child," he admonished himself. He was the emperor, for bones' sake! He could hardly go off and sulk just because he had to speak to someone when he'd rather not!

Yet he did not feel it was entirely unreasonable of him to wish for a little peace and quiet, on occasion.

"Then make them be quiet," he could almost hear Kohori say. "You're the emperor, are you not?"

"Yes, but I can't very well order them to leave me alone," he replied aloud. Or rather, he could but would risk angering his neighboring nations if he did. No, he needed some way to gain a brief respite without giving anyone reason to complain.

"If you were married, you could foist some of them off on your wife." He could practically see his friend and bodyguard's smirk at the suggestion.

He wasn't married, of course. But perhaps the notion still had merit.

Rising to his feet, Hibikitsu slipped out of the room, taking the private back passage which led to a twisting tunnel and, from there, to the Rojiri's council chamber. He had rarely used this route, feeling it was beneath him to spy on his own advisors, but now it allowed him to reach their meeting room without being seen.

He'd hoped to find one person in particular and nearly laughed for joy when, upon sliding back the secret panel in the wall, he spotted a stocky man with a wide face and neat beard, handsomely attired in fine satin robes and an embroidered cap.

"Your Imperial Majesty!" Master Eijiri bowed deeply as Hibikitsu entered and shut the panel behind him. "I was not expecting you!"

"I was, however, looking for you," Hibikitsu replied with a smile. "I was hoping you might do me an enormous favor."

The master merchant bowed again. "I live to serve, Your Majesty."

"Yes, yes, thank you." Hibikitsu set a hand on the older man's shoulder. "Have you actually met the Yatamorans yet?"

"I have not, no," Master Eijiri admitted. "Does this concern them?"

"It does." He searched for the words to put this diplomatically. "They are very…insistent upon claiming some of my time."

"I see." The merchant's lips slid up in a small smile. "And you wish for me to divert some of their attention?"

"Exactly!" Hibikitsu clapped the startled councilor on the back. "I'm sure you can come up with something to discuss, yes?"

Eijiri stroked his beard, the light winking off the many rings he wore and the gems in his ears. "Of course, sire. I would be honored."

"Excellent." Hibikitsu stepped to the room's outer door, opened it—and nearly jumped as three tall figures loomed up before him. How did they do that?

Fortunately, he was able to control himself and turned his motion into a slight nod instead. "Ah, Ambassadors," he said. "Just the men we were looking for. We don't believe you've been introduced to Master Eijiri yet. He is one of our most trusted advisors."

The three Yatamorans swept into the room, gliding silently past him, and bowed to Eijiri. "A pleasure," Hu Yongian stated. Hibikitsu was not entirely sure the other two *could* speak, as he'd never heard any sound from them.

"And for me as well," Eijiri replied, bowing back. "I had hoped to meet with you, in fact. I am a gem merchant by trade but also by interest, and I was greatly impressed by the jewels you so graciously presented His Majesty." He was referring to the large chest full of gold and gems they had brought as a gift when they'd first arrived. "I would like to know how such items are collected in your country, and what significance they play in your culture."

Hibikitsu slipped out of the room, shutting the door behind him, and let out a small, happy sigh. First Emperor bless Eijiri! That took care of one delegation. Now for the other two.

Heading to the gardens, Hibikitsu soon found his second target, another trio. "Lord and Lady Yakami," he said, nodding hello. He'd thought he might find them out here—they seemed to prefer it to the palace. "Your Highness."

"Your Imperial Majesty." All three bowed, though it was Lord Yakami who spoke. "Lovely to see you, as always."

"And you," he replied, stepping in a little closer and lowering his voice, "though we will admit that this is not entirely a social call. We had actually hoped you might help us with a rather delicate matter."

"Oh?" Lady Yakami raised one perfectly shaped eyebrow. "We would of course be happy to help in any way we can, sire."

"As you may know," he started, "the Fyushans are guesting with us as well. A Lady Nihiro and her assistant. They have come to negotiate the purchase of grain and other foodstuffs, which their kingdom desperately needs. Yet we have little experience in such transactions. Your nation, however, often trades with others. Would you perhaps be willing to speak with her and begin such talks on our behalf? We would be most grateful."

The handsome couple exchanged only the briefest of glances before bowing again. "We would be honored to assist you, Your Majesty," Lord Yakami replied. "We will seek out Lady Nihiro at once."

Hibikitsu watched them go, as graceful as ever. He was so pleased with himself that he was completely surprised by the low chuckle that erupted behind him.

"Oh, that was well done, sire." It was the princess, and she was watching him closely. Only the faintest of smiles showed on her lips, but her eyes sparkled and her cheeks dimpled. "Very clever indeed."

He recovered and bowed. "Thank you, Your Highness," he said, unable to stop from grinning. "I was rather taken with it, myself." He only realized after he'd spoken that he'd referred to himself in the casual sense, but they were alone and they were both royalty. Besides, it felt right.

"And the Yatamorans?" she asked. "Surely you would not distract only two out of the three?"

"Also occupied," he confirmed. These were the most words they had exchanged since her arrival, and, Hibikitsu thought to himself, by far the most intriguing. Perhaps she was not so docile and bland after all!

She nodded as if approving. "And what will you do with yourself, now that you have this sudden moment of freedom?" There was a teasing tone to her words that he quite liked.

He gave the matter some thought, as he had not in reality planned that far ahead. "I believe I will go riding," he declared at last, and smiled at the small sigh that escaped his companion. "Do you ride, Your Highness?"

Her smile this time was fully visible. "Whenever I get the chance, Your Majesty. I am happiest out of doors, and most of all when in the saddle." She ducked her head after that, as if embarrassed by her sudden lack of decorum, but glanced up again when he laughed.

"Then perhaps you might like to come with me," he said, offering her his arm. "I will introduce you to Shisi, one of my closest friends. Though perhaps we will need to stop in the kitchens along the way—he is most likely cross with me for not visiting recently, and a nafti will go a long way to soothing him."

This time it was she who laughed, a happy little chuckle. Her dimples were now in full evidence, and her eyes bright as she set her hand on his elbow. "I would be delighted, sire."

"Please," he told her as he led the way through the gardens and toward the stables where his faithful steed no doubt waited impatiently. "It is Hibikitsu."

Her answering smile was warmer now. "Then you must call me Tsuni."

They continued to chat as they walked, and Hibikitsu discovered he was warming to the idea of a political alliance with his nearest neighbor.

CHAPTER THIRTY-EIGHT

Kagiri peered down at the figures tromping through the valley ahead. Even from this distance they appeared to be close to his own size. "This could be...challenging," he admitted.

Beside him, Shizumi snorted. "Yes, and the ocean could be deep," she replied, staring at the same horde. She shook her head. "How can we expect to stand against that?"

She didn't suggest backing down, however. Neither of them did. They both knew why they were here and what would happen if they failed. So he did his best to smile at her, striving for some of his brother's former bravado. "We are the finest warriors in Rimbaku, remember? What hope do they have against us?"

That made her laugh, as he'd hoped it would. "Oh, yes," she agreed. "Perhaps we should offer them the chance to surrender, then. It seems the least we can do."

Neither of them moved, watching the strange army. It did not march, nor was it in orderly lines. It was more a loosely aimed rampage than anything else, Kagiri decided. Like a strange, hideous menagerie brought to life, set loose, and herded all in one direction.

He had no doubt, however, that their lack of cohesion did not in any way reduce their capacity for violence.

"Do you see him?" he asked, studying the writhing mass of creatures. He could not make out the man they'd seen, the sorcerer. Taido Fukuru.

Shizumi shook her head. "He could still be down there somewhere," she pointed out. "Or he could be using this as a diversion, drawing our attention so he can slip past us."

Not that it mattered. Whether the matekai was there himself or not, his creatures were.

And they were headed straight for Muraito.

Shizumi stirred first. "We should get ready."

He nodded, but put out a hand when she started to move. "If we live through this—" he began, but she stopped him, taking his hand in hers.

"We will," she promised.

Kagiri smiled at her fierceness. It had impressed him from the first. Only later had he come to know her sharp mind, her keen wit, her coiled energy. "*When* we are through this," he amended, tightening his clasp slightly. "There is much I would discuss with you."

She smiled back, the emotion bringing the planes of her face to life. "And I with you." Then, rising up on her tiptoes, she kissed him, a surprisingly gentle gesture from such a hardened warrior. They lingered there only an instant, their lips brushing together, before she turned and slipped free, shooting him a knowing smirk as she started back down the ridge toward their troops.

With a strangled curse and a short chuckle, Kagiri followed.

An hour later, they stood with the officers of both aiashe and Honjofu arrayed around them, the regular soldiers gathered in a larger circle enclosing the smaller group. Once he was sure everyone was there, Kagiri reached into his bag and pulled forth the item Noniki had given him as they were preparing to depart.

"It's...a light?" Shizumi's gunso Akino muttered. "Sir."

Kagiri smiled. "It is indeed." In fact, it was a very handsome atorido, its four sides each done in a fine geometric pattern, carvings incised at top and bottom, and the whole thing carved of esuge, the wood's natural red tones gleaming beneath the lacquer. As with all hanging lanterns, this one had a ring set in the knob rising up from the center of its sloping roof, and he held it aloft by that, displaying it so that all could see. The sun's rays struck it, catching on the gilded edges—

—and then the lines cut out of the pattern began to shine,

growing brighter and brighter as the lantern started to glow of its own accord.

"Draw your blades!" Shizumi shouted, and the air rang with a thousand hisses and clangs as sword and spear were bared and raised. The weapons gleamed in the lantern's light, as did the edges of breastplate and helmet, guard and greave.

Even after the lantern dimmed, those items continued to shine.

"My brother the matekai has granted us aid," Kagiri announced in his loudest voice, intended to carry to every soldier present. "His magic cannot make us invincible, but it will grant us strength. It will help shield us from harm. And it will let us do harm to those who endanger our land and its people. We will not let them hurt anyone else!" He held his own nihono high. "For Rimbaku!"

"For Rimbaku!" A thousand voices bellowed in reply.

"Good speech," Akino commented as officers began shouting orders and the soldiers began forming into ranks once more. "Short and to the point. I like it."

Kagiri nodded to the man, handing the lantern to an aiashe to be set somewhere safe now that its work was done. "So glad you approve." Shizumi had warned him about the Honjofu's dry wit, but that was something he could handle all on his own, without any help from the Gensaiba.

The upcoming battle, however, might require all the help he could get.

Shizumi had been issuing orders to her own warriors but now she returned, tightening the straps of her karute. "Ready?"

He made sure his own was on correctly, then set the menatu in place, leaving only his eyes uncovered. "Ready." She was tensed, eager for action, and he frowned. "Remember, even if you see him..."

"Yes, yes, do not engage directly," she said, and he knew she was scowling behind her mask. "I am well aware."

Noniki had made them promise. "My magic should keep him from attacking you directly," he'd said, "but not if you get in close and draw his full attention. So don't."

Hibikitsu had agreed. "You are to target his army only," the emperor had reminded them. "Pick the fight you can win."

Whether they *would* win remained to be seen.

There was nothing for it now, however, but to mount up, sound the charge, and ride into battle.

"Are you okay?" Shizumi asked, and Kagiri realized he'd let his mind wander for a moment.

"Fine," he replied. And though he could tell she was not entirely convinced, she still nodded and signaled for the attack to begin.

Kagiri knew he *should* be fine. He was the Gensaiba, after all. The combination of six of the greatest warriors this nation had ever known.

The problem, he realized as they rode out, was that they had all been amazing fighters—but none of them had been leaders. He was not worried about how he himself would fare. He had confidence in his own abilities. It was his soldiers. They were trusting him to lead them to victory and to keep them safe as much as possible. But he had no experience in such things, and nothing to draw upon. What if he got it wrong?

A hand on his arm pulled him from his thoughts. "Lead by example," Shizumi told him, as if she'd somehow read his mind. "Show them what it means to be a great warrior. The rest is just common sense, sharp eyes, and caring what happens to each and every one of them." She clearly spoke from experience, and he nodded, feeling marginally better.

They came charging down the ridge, a flood of soldiers and warriors, his aiashe mingled with her Honjofu, with the two of them in the lead. Shouts and screams filled the sky, and the creatures below paused, glancing up at the unexpected commotion.

Kagiri and Shizumi hit the first of them like a tidal wave smashing into the shore.

His sword lashed out, lopping the head off something like a snake-man. Hers sheared the wings off a bat-warrior. Enhanced by Noniki's magic, the steel cut through stone-hard skin and flesh as if it were autumn wheat.

Behind them, their warriors shouted, emboldened by the sight of their leaders' success. They collided with the monsters, and the battle truly began.

It was utter chaos. Kagiri was glad they were facing nonhuman foes, though. He could slash and cut and stab anything that did not resemble a regular man, woman, or horse. Shizumi rode to his left, Akino and the archer Isano beside her. On his other side were Mori Yukeno and Ichiro Tamori, the two young men evidently eager to redeem themselves. Soma Yamani commanded the forces to the left side, and Tsuneto those to the right. Daishin guarded the rear—Kagiri had assured him that this was in no way a criticism or a punishment, merely that the stocky general had been fighting and marching longer than the rest of them.

Noniki's magic was a wonder. The creatures were not made of normal flesh, yet sword and spear cut them just as easily, while regular deo and makiro, karute and jingaso, withstood blows that should have crushed them.

Not that the monsters were rendered harmless. Many of them were like regular beasts but massively oversized and with elongated claws, fangs, bristles. Others were giants with three or more arms. Then there were strange amalgams of different animals, often with human-like arms as well.

As Kagiri watched, one enormous creature covered in what looked like stone fur grabbed up a soldier. The man screamed as the monster took each arm by the wrist, and each leg by the ankle—

Then it roared, bunching its shoulders and arms, before yanking them apart.

It was still howling its victory when Kagiri's sword took it through the throat.

Still, they were winning. The monsters seemed a bit slow of thought, able to react instinctively but not to plan—or to group together. Whereas Shizumi's Honjofu were exceptionally well-trained. His own aiashe were not as polished, or as clever, or as nimble—but they followed orders well, they stuck together and protected one another, and they knew how to attack a single opponent all at once.

When the first monster dropped to the ground, all semblance

of life wrung from its flesh, a wave of despair washed over the creatures. Kagiri understood. It was the realization that, for all their size and muscle, even these creatures would not last forever. Mortality had a way of shaking even the strongest soul. And whatever caricature of life these creatures possessed, it was enough for them to cling to it as desperately as any man.

"There!" Shizumi pointed, and Kagiri followed the direction of her arm to see a tall, slim man, wildly disheveled, floating in mid-air on the other side of a winged lion with a barbed tail. It was Fukuru, and evidently he had not seen them yet.

We're not supposed to engage him, he thought to himself. They'd promised Noniki. But one look at Shizumi's fierce gaze told him she'd had the same realization:

Noniki wasn't here. They were. And Fukuru was right there in front of them.

How could they not make the attempt?

Without a word, he and Shizumi both turned and loped toward the distracted wizard. Kagiri curved around to the left, while she headed to the right. They timed it perfectly and lunged together, their blades striking him full in the chest.

Or at least they would have, if a fiercely cold wind hadn't whipped around them at the last second, whisking their weapons to one side, freezing their breath mid-air, and lifting them up to wriggle impotently like pinned butterflies.

The man, Fukuru, twisted about and smiled directly at them.

"Ah, the leaders of this little play army, I assume?" His voice had an echoey sound, as if it were emerging from a dark well, and Kagiri shivered at it. Nor was he alone in that reaction. Deep within him, what was left of the Gensaiba reacted as well. They had all known this man, interacted with him—but hearing him now, Kagiri felt their surprise, their confusion, their concern.

Even their fear.

Meanwhile, Fukuru was studying them both, a frown upon his long, gaunt face. "No bones?" he muttered. "That is promising. Still, you stand in my way. And you know what they say, cut off the head of the snake..." He made a dismissive, chopping gesture, as if his hand were a cleaver and he were enacting the very fate he'd just described. And, indeed, Kagiri felt a fluttering across his throat.

But nothing more.

The matekai's frown deepened into a scowl. "Not again!" he raved. "The others are gone! None are left to oppose me!"

Kagiri couldn't help grinning at that. One was. His brother.

As if he'd spoken that aloud, the wizard focused suddenly upon him. "You!" he howled, lunging forward until his long nose brushed Kagiri's own. "You know who did this! Who? Where is he?"

"Awaihinshi." Kagiri started, for that answer had not emerged from his own lips. But beside him Shizumi wet her lips and spoke again. "Our matekai is protecting us. He is with the emperor, in Awaihinshi."

"Awaihinshi." Fukuru repeated the name, twisting his lips around what was apparently an unfamiliar word. "Very well." With a shrug his winds vanished, dumping the two warriors to the ground. Then, without another word, the wild matekai rose higher, a column of air carrying him off into the sky.

Off toward the nation's capitol, where Noniki and Hibikitsu waited unsuspecting.

"Why did you do that?" Kagiri gasped, sitting up. He felt as if he'd been pummeled repeatedly by several large and angry men.

Shizumi looked as if she felt the same. She shook her head, and he saw nothing but understanding in her gaze—that, and a fierce resolve. "Your brother is the only one who can face him," she pointed out, also struggling for breath. "And this way, we have only his creatures to defeat." Pushing herself to her feet, she held out a hand. "Shall we?"

Kagiri let her haul him upright. She was correct, of course. He knew that. Strategically, it had been absolutely the right move. But that didn't mean he wouldn't fear for his brother until they could make it back to Awaihinshi themselves.

A fist bigger than his head came sweeping down, and he dodged it reflexively, chopping it off at the wrist. Of course, they still had to fight their way through an entire army of monsters first. Best to focus on that, for now.

CHAPTER THIRTY-NINE

The instant she felt the wind pick up, Reizei knew something was wrong.

It had been a calm if cloudy day, the air still and thick with impending rain, the trees and bushes of the imperial compound blurred by a thin fog. The emperor was riding Shisi around the enclosure, the Hibinasan princess astride a dappled gray mare at his side. She rode well, Reizei noticed, confidently but not aggressively, treating her horse well but making it clear she was in charge. Admirable traits in any arena.

The pair were laughing as they rode, the emperor looking more relaxed than Reizei could recall seeing before. Possibly even happy.

Her shout shattered that mood, but it couldn't be helped.

"Sire!" She lacked the stature to pull him from his horse or the speed to catch the reins, so instead Reizei charged out into the paddock, waving her cane above her head. Hibikitsu saw the gesture and reined in Shisi at once. "We need to get you back inside! Now!"

He didn't need to ask why. Already the temperature had dropped from pleasantly warm to chilly and the fog had vanished, leaving the air clear but the sky darkening above. It felt like a thunderstorm—but there had been nothing on the horizon just moments before.

Dismounting easily, he offered the princess a hand, though she showed equal grace at relinquishing her seat. Reizei hurried the two of them back to the palace, Totsu and Onomi falling in beside her as they stepped through the outer doors. "Take them to the throne room and let no one else through," she ordered, and the pair saluted before guiding the pair of royals away. The emperor's study was closer and smaller but it opened onto one of the private gardens. The throne room had only two entrances, and both could be barred.

With them safely away, Reizei turned her attention to whatever was coming. Dairamu had just emerged from the barracks and sprinted over. "What is it?"

Reizei liked the woman, who'd been a Honjofu before transferring to the household guard. She was sturdy and reliable, and normally quite cheerful, though her present mood echoed their situation, being tense and somber.

"I don't know yet," Reizei admitted. "But I fear the worst. Summon the others, all those on duty."

Dairamu nodded and quickly retraced her steps. By the time she re-emerged, another dozen Honteno behind her, it was cold enough for Reizei to see her breath misting before her in the crystal-clear air. This was not natural.

Up above, lightning flickered. Thunder rumbled. One cloud was darker than the rest, a narrow streak against the heavy blanket. And it was drawing closer.

"Be ready!" Reizei shouted over the increasing wind plucking at her hair. "Let no one past!" She unlimbered her bow and nocked an arrow.

Then that streak dipped down like a waterspout. And atop it she saw a tall, wild-haired man, riding it as Hibikitsu had his horse mere moments before.

The tip of the strange cloud touched down, sending grass and dirt flying. Then it vanished, leaving the man behind to stride toward them across the damaged lawn. "Stand aside," he ordered, his voice as rolling as the thunder. "Or be destroyed." He sounded neither angered nor concerned, not even exhilarated. If anything, his words were casual to the point of boredom.

"Turn back!" Reizei called in return. "None may enter save by permission of the emperor!"

The man sneered at that. And kept walking toward them.

Reizei drew back, sighting along the arrow's length. "This is your last warning!"

Still he drew closer.

She fired.

Despite the wind, her arrow flew straight and true—and caught fire mid-air, burning to ash mere inches from the man's chest.

Before she could draw again, he was upon them.

"For the emperor!" Manari shouted, bringing his nihono down in a vicious arc. The others echoed his cry, stabbing and slicing from the sides and even over Reizei's shoulders.

The ground itself rose up in a wave as if it were water, blocking spear and sword alike. Then bursting outward, blinding and choking them with dirt and rock. Reizei stumbled back, gasping and wiping at her face to clear both lungs and eyes. The man was only a blurry shadow, but she stabbed toward him nonetheless.

A mighty gust lifted her clean off her feet and slammed her back against the palace's outer wall. She slid to the ground with a groan, wincing as her injured leg struck first. All around her, her Honteno had been tossed aside like so many leaves.

The stranger barely spared them a glance as he stormed past, the palace doors flinging themselves open at his approach. He passed within.

"No!" Reizei grabbed her cane and struggled to her feet, hobbling after the man. "Stop!"

Surprisingly, he did—but only so he could spin about and spear her with a sharp, deep-set gaze. "You," he said. "I can smell it on you. The bone magic." The sneer on his face matched the disdain in his voice.

"Yes," she admitted, faltering to a stop. "I did use it. But not anymore."

"Why not?" he demanded. "Why not wallow in it like the rest of these people?"

She wasn't sure why they were standing here discussing this, but for every second they did, that was another second he was not attacking the emperor, so she replied. "Because it made me weak," she admitted. "I knew it would, knew it was weakness to use it in the first place. But I felt so hopeless, so lost, I figured I couldn't feel worse." She hung her head. "I was wrong."

He nodded. "This much I understand. But is that not your way, all of you? To borrow from the dead rather than creating for the living?"

"It was," Reizei agreed. "But we're trying to change."

For an instant, as he studied her, she thought that might be enough.

Then he shook his head. "It is too late for such paltry efforts," he declared. "This soil is too weak to bear fruit. But I will raze and replant." He resumed his trek down the hall, long legs covering the distance rapidly. By the time Reizei realized he'd moved on, he was nearly to the throne room's outer doors. Totsu and Onomi stood there, yanoi in hand, the weapons crossed to bar entrance. Both recruits looked capable, even fearsome in their red armor, but Reizei could see their hands shaking on the hafts.

The stranger shook his head. "Mere children." Then, with a wave of his hand, he sent the two young Honteno crashing to the side. Another gesture and the doors flew open.

Unable to stop him, Reizei hobbled after, determined to protect the emperor if at all possible. Even if that meant throwing herself between him and this man. It was exactly what Maniko Kohori would have done, and for once she didn't need any bones to tell her that.

CHAPTER FORTY

Even from inside the throne room, Hibikitsu could hear the commotion outside. "You need to get to safety," he tried telling Tsuni again. And again she shook her head, not angrily but with quiet determination.

"If you stay, I stay," she insisted.

"He is coming for me," he explained, because who else and what else could it be? They had already guessed that the renegade wizard would eventually make his way here. They just had not expected it to be so soon.

The room's wide double doors burst inward hard enough to slam against the walls on either side, cutting off further discussion. With a growl of his own Hibikitsu thrust the princess of Higinasi behind him and, hand on his sword, strode forward to confront the tall, intense figure marching toward him.

All the while, a part of him couldn't help wondering where Noniki was.

In the gardens of Sorainasei, Noniki suddenly blinked and looked around. Something had startled him out of his daily meditation. But what?

There was an unseasonable chill to the air, he noted. And a sharp tang, like lightning. Yet the sky remained clear—except behind him, where a single dark cloud hovered.

Directly over Aihiri.

Bolting to his feet, Noniki ran for the compound's front gates. The enemy was here! He had to reach the emperor in time!

Fukuru stormed into the shadowed room, fuming at the ostentation displayed there with its carved pillars and stained-glass windows and mosaic floor. No other guards sought to bar his path, and he was unobstructed in his approach toward the slim figure waiting directly before the dais. It was a man, young and clean-shaven, in rich robes with a jeweled crown nestled atop his dark hair. One hand rested atop the handle of a nihono shoved through his sash, and a woman stood behind him, equally young and just as elegantly attired.

"You must be the ruler of this wasteland," Fukuru called out as he closed the distance. "The so-called master of this tragic wreck."

To his credit, the man did not flinch. "I am Hibikitsu, emperor of all Rimbaku," he replied, his voice strong and oddly familiar. "And you are Taido Fukuru, last of the matekai of old." The woman's eyes widened at hearing his name. Interesting.

"The last matekai, yes," he agreed. "The last remnant of old Ritakhou, awakened once more and dismayed at what has become of his home. But I will right this sinking ship. I will restore this land to what it once was." He glared at the so-called emperor. "Your services are no longer required."

He heard a steely hiss as the man drew his sword, leveling its mirror-bright blade at him, chiseled tip aimed at his throat. "It is you who are no longer required here," this Hibikitsu replied. "Begone, lest you meet your long overdue end."

Fukuru laughed—such effrontery!—but the sound died in his throat as his steps carried him near enough to see the weapon properly. He knew that blade! "Where did you get that sword?" he demanded.

Then he looked past it—and froze. Because the face of the man holding it was also achingly familiar. "Segei?"

Hibikitsu found that, oddly enough, he was not surprised.

He remembered a similar encounter involving a furious warrior, though that one had proven to be a misunderstanding and had led to a newfound ally and friend. But that intruder, too, had been stunned upon seeing him, and had called him by the same ancient name.

And this unwelcome visitor hailed from the same time as that one's attendant spirits and carried many of the same memories.

Perhaps he could use that to his advantage.

Still, he could not bring himself to lie. "I am Taido Segei's descendant," he admitted instead. "And you are not the first to say that I greatly resemble him. I take that as a great compliment and honor. After the Schism that destroyed this land's magic and nearly doomed it, it was Taido Segei who brought the survivors together, uniting them into a single people and reforging the kingdom. He was Rimbaku's first emperor. I carry his blade Kosshiki in remembrance."

The intruder—Taido Fukuru, an old legend brought to life—shook his head, wild hair flying about him. "The Schism?" he murmured with that odd echo. "I know nothing of this."

Hibikitsu lowered his sword, though he kept it at the ready. "There was a cataclysm," he explained. "Something to do with your fellow matekai, I now understand. They fought? Drawing all the magic into themselves for that purpose? And then it exploded, leaving the land broken."

The ancient wizard nodded slowly. "Yes. That...I did not attend the moot. I was weary of their constant arguing. I stayed in my tower, and I felt something happen. Then there was nothing until I awoke." His eyes, which had been staring off into the distance, refocused on Hibikitsu, all but glowing in their fury. "To find a shattered shell where once there had been life and joy! You have wrecked my home!"

"I am attempting to restore it," Hibikitsu countered. "You could help tremendously with that. You remember what it was like before—use that knowledge and your power to help us return to that former glory!"

Fukuru tilted his head, staring at him with the intensity of a raptor peering down at its prey. "No," he declared after a moment. "You are beyond saving. All of you are. I must rid this land of its taint—of *your* taint—and start afresh."

He lifted his hand, also aglow. Hibikitsu raised his sword, knowing it would not be enough but determined to go down fighting. Behind him, Tsuni cried out. He hoped the mad wizard would recognize her as an outsider, not part of Rimbaku at all, and spare her. If only they'd had more time together!

The light increased. Fukuru's hand still glowed, but it was not just that. The sunlight slanting in through the stained-glass windows was now blinding as well. What had happened to the storm clouds? The wizard stabbed forward—

—and his incandescent fingers bounced off the colored beam from the window like a branch thrown against a sturdy wall.

"No." The word carried across the room, emerging as it did from the short, sturdy figure standing by the open doors. Hibikitsu sagged with relief.

Noniki had arrived.

Hurrying down the aisle, Noniki thanked the First Emperor he had not been too late. It had been a near thing, but his winds had carried him up and into Aihiri just in time. Now he studied their intruder as he rushed to stand beside his friend and liege.

Seen in person, Taido Fukuru was even more emaciated, more wrung out, more feverishly manic than he had realized. The man's eyes were bright, the skin of his face taut, sweat standing out upon his forehead. His hair spread outward as if lifted by static. He radiated energy, an almost visible aura that crackled and spat like an angry fire as he turned to glare at Noniki.

"You!" he shouted. "I saw you before! How dare you interfere? Begone!" He swept a hand at Noniki, winds whipping along behind to toss him aside and batter him against the far walls.

But the winds were old friends now. Noniki bade them quiet

and they obeyed, wrapping around him in a calm and cooling breeze. "My name is Noniki," he stated. "I am the matekai of Rimbaku. It is you who are unwelcome here, Taido Fukuru. You have outlived your time and overstayed your welcome. Please depart in peace, lest we be forced to treat you harshly."

"You, a matekai?" The gaunt wizard laughed. "I think not. You are barely a pup! I was a full twoscore in my power before the end!"

And, just like that, the battle was joined.

Hibikitsu staggered back as he felt the forces collide, the two men before him struggling with powers he could not see but could sense in the air all around them.

Taido Fukuru was all rage and power, pummeling Noniki with fury and the massive confidence of an established master.

At first, his friend looked overwhelmed. But in their time together Noniki had demonstrated a tremendous will and, with it, an inspiring calm, a gentle but unshakable strength.

Slowly but surely, he began to fight back.

Noniki had been stunned by that initial onslaught. This relic of a wizard wielded such immense power! And he had been a wizard longer than Noniki had been alive, not even counting the centuries of sleep. How could he compete with that?

A bolt of lightning crashed down upon him, tearing through the vaulted ceiling in a cascade of tiles and wood and plaster. Though nearly blinded by its fury, Noniki shielded himself and the two behind him, using that same sunlight he'd employed before. The gentler light diffused the glowing bolt, spreading its energies across the room in a harmless wave.

In response, Noniki gathered the moisture from the air, swirling that around his opponent in a watery chain.

Fukuru laughed. "Is that the best you can manage?" the older wizard taunted. He flexed, freezing the water and then shattering it into a cascade of icicles flung from him like a thousand loosed arrows. "Pathetic!"

Raising a bubble of heat to melt the frozen missiles before they could strike, Nonik wondered if the ancient matekai might be right.

"No," Noniki told himself. "I won't accept that. I cannot. Too much depends upon this for me to fail."

Rallying his strength, he pushed back, sending not just a bubble of heat but an entire wave, like all of summer had struck at once. It washed over his opponent, stifling him, burning away the air and leaving only dust in its wake.

Fukuru stumbled, raising a fluttering hand to his neck. Noniki could see the ancient mage's throat working as he struggled to swallow, to breathe. The man's eyes, already bulging above his sunken cheeks, widened further as he staggered. Yes!

Then, with clear effort, the older wizard swallowed. His eyes slid shut, tears dripping down his cheeks.

And as Noniki watched, those tears swelled. They grew to the size of grapes, then plums. They spilled off Fukuru's chin, now as big as melons.

They splashed on the floor, and exploded into a tidal wave. It flung Noniki back against the wall, drenching him. The force of the waves pinned him there, the water freezing into icy bonds, holding him wriggling off the ground like a trapped insect.

Noniki summoned his strength, raising heat as before, and melted his way free. He dropped to his knees, gasping for air, shaking his head. That had taken all of his might.

Meanwhile, Fukuru was gliding toward him like a strange beast, elegant in his skeletal stride, seemingly fully recovered from his own earlier weakness.

How could Noniki hope to compete with a man such as this?

Hibikitsu could see his friend falter, his confidence shaken. Taido Fukuru was a force to be reckoned with, driving all before him. How could calm, gentle Noniki stand against that?

But that thought sparked a recent memory, from one of his training sessions with Shizumi.

"I am smaller than you, slighter than you," she had pointed out after besting him at the blade yet again. "You are stronger and have a longer reach. How, then, am I able to defeat you?"

He had mulled that over before venturing, "You turn my own strength against me?"

"Correct." Shizumi did not smile much, but she had rewarded him with a tight nod. "Power is good. Finesse is better. Know how to use your own strengths and those of your opponent to your own best advantage."

And he knew, instantly and without a shred of doubt, what lay at the core of his friend's power. "Noniki!" Hibikitsu shouted to him now. "It isn't about who's stronger! Your gift is your bond to the land!"

Hearing those words, Noniki was struck as if that lightning had indeed transfixed him. Not in pain, however.

In understanding.

He forced himself upright, facing his rival across a mere body length, no more. Yet as he drew a deep breath Noniki began to feel himself renewed. More than that, he felt re-invigorated.

"You were a master of this land," he told Fukuru as the ancient matekai hurled fire and ice at him. But Noniki let those mingle together, the twin onslaughts canceling into a fine, warm mist. "You wielded its magics." This time the wizard threw wind and water at him, a hurricane in miniature—at Noniki's touch, however, it quieted and joined the mist, sprinkling the room with a welcome shower.

"But you were a tyrant," Noniki continued, knowing he was right as he spoke the words. "You took from the land."

He held out his arms, palms up—and sunlight washed over them all, evaporating the rain like a fond memory. "I am one with the land. I do not take from it by force. It gives itself to me freely, as I give to it in return."

He gestured, and Fukuru's next attack fizzled at his fingertips. "You cannot defeat me. Surrender, depart, and do not trouble us again."

Fukuru stared. How was this upstart, this child, able to defeat him? How was he able to counter every attack so effortlessly? Did he not know who he was facing?

"I am Taido Fukuru!" he shouted, his words shaking the columns and beams of this great room. "I am the last and greatest wizard of Ritakhou! I will never accept defeat!"

And he wrenched at the twisted, faded world around him, yanking free what magic he could find still lurking there and hurling it at his arrogant would-be rival.

Noniki felt his opponent drawing power and sighed. So much for a peaceful resolution.

With a wave of his hand and a push of his will, he reversed the flow. Fukuru shrieked as the magic was pulled from him and into the land instead.

"Give up," Noniki advised again. "Please."

But the ancient matekai only struggled harder.

It was no use, however. The more he pulled, the quicker his power drained away.

And that had been all that was keeping the centuries-old wizard alive.

As Noniki watched, powerless to stop it now, the already gaunt figure wasted away, narrowing as the magic reclaimed flesh and bone.

With one last, echoing cry, Taido Fukuru, last matekai of Rita-khou, vanished into the sunlight.

The burst of energy that followed knocked Noniki off his feet.

Hibikitsu shook his head and rose, turning to help Tsuni back to her feet. "What was that?"

Noniki was standing as well. "I think—" he started, but stopped as the air itself began to glitter.

And sing.

Yes, it was singing, Hibikitsu confirmed, looking around in wonder. Dust motes danced among the sunbeams, and from them rose a faint but definite melody, delicate and lovely.

"It's beautiful," Tsuni whispered beside him, and he smiled, taking her hand.

Yes, it certainly was. But he still didn't understand.

Fortunately, it seemed someone did. "It was Fukuru," Noniki said softly, face upturned to the light, a serene smile spreading across his face. "He was the last remnant of the old kingdom. When the Cataclysm happened, much of that power must have seeped into him. It's what kept him alive, but it's also why Rimbaku had no magic of its own—it was all stored away, bottled up in one unconscious wizard. Now that he's gone, the magic is free and flowing back into the land." He turned to Hibikitsu. "Do you realize what this means?"

Slowly, Hibikitsu nodded, a grin stretching his cheeks. "Yes." He laughed and spun Tsuni around with him. "We no longer need the Relicant Way. Rimbaku has magic once more. We're free!"

CHAPTER FORTY-ONE

After regaining a semblance of his customary dignity, Hibikitsu insisted upon taking Tsuni back to her rooms. "There is still much to be done, and I'm afraid I will be occupied for a while," he said as he led her from the throne room. "And I am certain Lord and Lady Yakami, having seen and heard the commotion, will be worried for your safety."

She frowned but only slightly, then nodded. "I will not delay you from your duties," she promised. "I understand those all too well." A quick, shy smile chased the frown away. "But I hope we may ride again soon?"

He felt his own lips rise in response. "We will," he assured her. "As soon as I am able, I promise."

She pulled her hand from his, though gently, and curtsied. "Then you must see to matters," she stated. "I know the way back to our suite and will be perfectly safe now that you have dealt with the danger."

It was not I who defeated the wizard, Hibikitsu thought, but chose not to say, for he had no desire to dim the warm glow in her gaze. Instead, he merely bowed and watched her go for a moment before turning back.

But the throne room was not where he needed to be right now. No, far better to find his Rojiri, reveal what had happened, and discuss how to use this to the nation's best advantage. In one way it was a shame Tsuni had been there to witness the event—she was, after all, the princess of a neighboring nation, though Hibikitsu was sure he could trust her not to reveal anything unless her brother the king questioned her directly. Still, there were also the Fyushans and especially the Yatamorans wandering the halls, and both of those kingdoms would be quick to capitalize on this information if they could.

Still considering options, Hibikitsu made his way down the hall to the next turning and took a right there. That would take him to the Rojiri council chamber. Noniki would follow soon, he was sure. Kagiri and Shizumi were away, of course, but he would send for Takami, Futoba, Seikoku, and—if he was not still there—Master Eijiri. Together they would have enough wisdom to figure out where their kingdom went next.

Intent upon those thoughts, he nearly collided with someone coming from the other direction. Perhaps the only thing that saved either of them from injury was that the newcomer only came up to Hibikitsu's chest.

"Ah, Madame Hara!" he exclaimed, backing up reflexively. The little woman who ran his household was terrifying, after all. "I apologize, I did not see you there! Are you all right?"

"Your Majesty, it was entirely my fault," the tiny otanui replied, bowing deeply. She still looked exactly as she had in his youth, her tidy chonmage the dark gray of a storm cloud, her face deeply lined, her eyes small and dark and bright like a bird's. "But I am glad I found you. There is something I am afraid you must see."

"Oh?" He frowned, looking past her down the corridor, where a door marked the transition to the area that was his destination. But Hara Koriko had faithfully served him and his father before him. "Yes, of course. What is it?"

"It is here, in your dining room," she replied, turning toward the partially open door beside them. The same door she must have just emerged from, Hibikitsu realized. No wonder he had not seen her! "And I fear I must apologize, for I am at least partially to blame."

Unsure what she meant, he let her guide him into the room, shutting the door behind them. No lanterns were lit and the outer walls were shut, only dim light filtering in through the screens so that the entire space was cast in shadow. "What is the matter?"

The diminutive housekeeper stepped up beside him. "It is right there, sire, that corner of the rug. Do you see?"

Squinting in the dark, Hibikitsu bent over to study the indicated area. "No, not really. Did something spill?" This hardly seemed worth the bother!

"Yes, something did." Madame Hara's voice sounded strange suddenly, higher than normal and oddly raspy. "And will again." Those words came out in almost a hiss.

Had the room grown even darker? And colder? Hibikitsu could see his own breath. But the mad wizard was no more. What was happening here?

Straightening, he turned—and ducked instinctively as something lashed out at him from the darkness. Something that swooshed through the shadows. A blade.

Or claws.

Yanking Kosshiki free, he brought the blade up. But he could not see who or what had just attacked him.

Which was why he missed the swipe that carved open his side, parting silk and flesh with equal ease.

Gasping in pain, Hibikitsu swung in that direction. His sword cut nothing except air and shadow.

But the shadow hissed as if angry at the intrusion.

"Poor little king." Those words emerged from the hissing like snakes from a cave. "All alone. Where are your warriors now? Your wizard? Your pretty princess?"

"Leave her alone!" Hibikitsu roared. He stabbed into the dark, but Kosshiki caught on nothing solid.

"I will," the voice promised. "But you will not." A pair of fiery orbs appeared, poised near the height of his crown.

Hibikitsu thrust at them with all his strength.

Kosshiki struck something and stopped dead. For a second, he thought he must have impaled the owner of those eyes.

Until the sword was ripped from his grasp.

"No!" He punched instead, and felt his fist graze something, eliciting a grunt. Yes, there!

Then he was struck in return and sent reeling back into the table.

Another blow landed, driving the air from his lungs.

A third clawed bloody furrows into his chest.

Hibikitsu screamed and threw himself at his unseen assailant. He felt a body there and wrapped his arms tight around it.

Arms tightened around him in response.

He could not breathe.

His lungs were on fire.

So was his flesh.

The world swam about him.

He felt lightheaded.

Try as he might, he could not stay awake.

Hibikitsu, Emperor of all Rimbaku, slumped as consciousness fled, and his life along with it.

"At last." Dai Yi felt the body he held shudder out its last, its warmth already fading. Before the vital essence could escape, he loosened his grip, letting the emperor's fresh corpse fall back against his one arm.

With the other hand he plucked Hibikitsu's eyes from their blackened sockets. Those the shadow assassin tossed into his mouth, swallowing them in two successive gulps.

The magic took hold, and he grimaced, falling to his knees. At least that let him lay the body down. It was already shriveling into a burnt husk.

The transition was easier this time—the emperor had been a decent height!—and after a moment he straightened, then rose carefully to his feet.

Hibikitsu dusted his hands and glanced around. Peering easily through the receding shadows, he spotted his faithful sword and retrieved it, wiping the ancient blade clean before restoring it to its sheath at his side.

He frowned down at the body before him. *That* would not fit in the riantzu! Ah, but tall vases occupied each corner of the room, decorative fronds waving above each one. Scooping the remains up easily, he strode to the nearest vase and dumped the true emperor's corpse inside. Perfect!

Then, crossing to the door, Hibikitsu took one last glance around. Nothing looked amiss. Nor did he. He was as calm and put together as ever.

Inside, however, Dai Yi was crowing with glee. At last he had fulfilled his mission!

The emperor of Rimbaku was dead. The kingdom now belonged to Yatamoro.

CHAPTER FORTY-TWO

Seikoku couldn't help it—she shivered a little as she entered the throne room. "I don't exactly have the best associations with this place," she whispered to Noniki beside her.

He had one arm around her waist and squeezed gently. "I know. Mine are a mix, too. But the emperor asked us to come."

She nodded and let herself be led down the wide aisle, past the handsomely carved pillars, and up to just before the lacquered railings separating the dais from the rest. Hibikitsu sat upon his throne, gazing down on them, and for an instant he seemed another person entirely, his face strange and stern, his eyes cold.

Then he shook himself a little and smiled. "Our Rojiri," he announced in a clear and carrying tone. "Thank you for attending us." Futoba and Takami were there already and turned to nod hello as she and Noniki joined them at the front, while Reizei occupied her customary place against one wall, but Seikoku's attention was focused upon the three men standing to their right, tall and severe in their high-collared robes.

What were the Yatamorans doing here?

"Yesterday was a momentous occasion," the emperor continued, "and it has led us to consider how best to guide our nation into a bright and prosperous future. To that end, we have determined that—"

But whatever pronouncement he had planned was cut short as a red-clad soldier burst into the room. "Your Majesty!" Seikoku recognized the man as Reizei's lieutenant Itamon, and his broad face wore a wide, happy smile as he prostrated himself before the dais. "Your pardon, sire, Taikoro, Rojiri, but ships have been sighted turning onto the Edishu, and they bear imperial colors! The fleet returns!"

"What?" That was from Takami, who stepped forward to confront the Honteno. "That's impossible! Bezenkai is three or more days from here. They only set out five days ago. Even if they'd found nothing and turned back at once, they would still be at least another day away, and most likely more."

"Nonetheless," Itamon insisted. "I saw them myself. They are your ships, Dogenkaishu."

Hibikitsu was frowning but brightened as the two men turned back toward him. "If this is so, it means our Rojiri Kagiri and Misataki have returned," he stated. "This is excellent news! We must go forth and see for ourselves."

"Your Majesty." That came from one of the Yatamorans, the one in front. The only one who ever spoke, as far as Seikoku could tell. "Perhaps it would be wiser to remain here, above it all, and have them come to you. That is the prerogative of leadership, after all."

For a moment, Seikoku thought the emperor would follow the suggestion. But then, with a glare at the ambassador, Hibikitsu shook his head. "Nonsense," he declared, rising to his feet. "We wish to go and meet them, and so we shall. *That* is the true prerogative of leadership."

The Yatamoran inclined his head, but not before she caught a flicker of anger upon those narrow features. Which was odd. What right did he have to dictate the emperor of Rimbaku's actions?

Hibikitsu hopped over the railing, landing soundlessly upon the floor below. Nor did his feet make any noise as he strode toward the main doors. Seikoku found that strange as well. She had always been impressed with the young emperor's poise and presence, and he was certainly not clumsy, but right now…right now he was moving as she would.

He was moving like a thief.

Over the years of her dangerous profession, Seikoku had developed a good instinct for danger. That sense was screaming at her right now. Something was very wrong here.

But she did not know what, exactly. All she could do for the moment was follow the emperor out of the palace and toward the Royal Way. Still, she took a second to whisper, "Stay alert," to Noniki. He frowned but nodded, and she felt a warm rush at the way he looked at her. He had no idea what was going on, but he trusted her.

She didn't know either but was certain the two of them could figure it out and deal with it somehow.

Down at the aikaye's docks, sailors were bustling about, and several were already catching ropes from the tall ships pulling into various open berths. On the first of those Seikoku saw a pair of familiar figures, one tall and emerald-armored, the other short, slight, and all in black. She felt and shared Noniki's relief at the sight. His brother and their friend had both returned safely.

"Quite the reception!" Kagiri joked as he easily navigated the plank from ship to dock. "Were you worried we'd damage your ships, Takami?"

The head of the Navy laughed and clasped hands with him. "Not at all. But thank you for bringing them back intact, nonetheless."

Noniki was next and hugged his brother. "How are you back this soon?" he asked when they parted. "Not that I'm complaining!"

"We don't rightly know," Shizumi admitted from next to Kagiri. Nor did Seikoku miss how close they stood. It looked like perhaps the two warriors had finally reached an understanding. Good.

"We were fighting Fukuru's creatures," Kagiri explained. He grinned and clapped his brother on the shoulder. "Your gift was greatly appreciated, by the way. The wizard himself abandoned them and headed here—"

"He has been dealt with," Noniki assured him.

"We thought as much," Shizumi put in, "when his monsters suddenly collapsed. They simply fell apart, reverting to so much dust and dirt."

"We turned around and started back here," Kagiri continued.

"I remember saying, 'if only we could get there faster,' though I know we were all thinking it." He shook his head. "Next thing you know, the shore started speeding past, so fast it became a blur. I thought maybe it was something you'd done."

"No," Noniki replied. "But I think I know how it happened." Seikoku nodded. He'd told her about the battle with the old wizard, and what had occurred after. Reizei had been there as well, and the head of the Honteno was walking easily without her cane today, her wound completely healed. This seemed little different. After all, if magic was back in the world, why couldn't a fleet of ships sail home in a single day?

Hibikitsu had been hanging back, allowing the happy reunion and listening to the explanation. Now he stepped forward. All eyes turned to him at once, and Kagiri and Shizumi both saluted. "Your Majesty," Shizumi stated.

"Taikoro Misataki," he replied with a regal nod. "Dogenriku Kagiri. Welcome home." He smiled, but Seikoku thought it lacked his usual warmth. "Your absence has been deeply felt."

The Yatamorans had traveled down with them, and now the one—Hu Yongian, she remembered—gave a little cough. "Perhaps it would be best to continue this back in your palace, Your Majesty," he suggested, and Hibikitsu frowned for an instant before smoothing the expression away.

"Yes, very well," he agreed, exactly like a petulant child. "Let us return." He turned about, facing back toward the city once more—

—and, just for an instant, as the sun's rays beat down upon him, Seikoku saw his shadow split in two.

Half was soft-edged in the harsh light.

But the other half was sharp and dark, and too angular by far.

It was gone almost before she'd registered it, but Seikoku shivered despite the warm day and fought down a wave of intense sorrow.

Because suddenly, remembering tales she'd heard from two of her friends, she knew exactly what had happened. And it was truly horrific. There was little to be done about that now, however.

The question was, how to deal with the result?

"Your Majesty," Seikoku said as they exited the Royal Way and stepped onto Aihiri once more. "Though I know they must be tired, perhaps Kagiri and Shizumi could give you and your Rojiri a more thorough accounting of their expedition? In the relative quiet and comfort of our meeting chambers?"

She saw the Yatamorans start, their leader opening his mouth to protest, but Hibikitsu cut him off, a smirk forming on his lips. "Yes, that is an excellent idea," the emperor stated. "Let us adjourn there. *Your* presence is not required." That last was said pointedly to Hu Yongian and his two followers.

"But, sire—" the ambassador began, only to have his words cut off with a raised hand. There was little he could do but bow. "Of course. We await your pleasure, Your Majesty." The three of them departed in a visible huff.

As they crossed the lawn toward the Rojiri's council chamber, Seikoku slid beside Shizumi, who was toward the rear of the little group. "I seem to recall hearing about a thing that you did," she whispered to the Honjofu's leader. "You and Kohori. In the throne room, against an impossible enemy."

"Yes," the other woman responded just as quietly. "Why?"

Seikoku looked pointedly at their ruler's broad back. Shizumi's eyes widened, then narrowed. She nodded.

When Seikoku moved away to rejoin Noniki, Shizumi matched pace with Kagiri—and whispered something to him. Ever the consummate warrior, he did not outwardly react.

"What's going on?" Noniki asked her, keeping his words just between them.

Seikoku wasn't sure how much she could say without alerting their target. "Treachery" was what she came up with. "Be ready." He squeezed her hand in response.

They entered the large, beautifully painted room, and Hibikitsu immediately moved toward the seat at the head of the long table. But she intercepted him before he could sit. "Sire," she began, bowing and gesturing toward the middle, and then the ornate lantern hanging overhead. "Perhaps you would be more comfortable here, by the light?"

"Not at all, but we thank you," he replied, settling into his seat. He drew the scabbarded sword from his sash and set it down atop the table. So many of those gestures were familiar, but now that she was watching for them Seikoku could see they were not quite right. There was something forced about them. Something staged.

Like he was trying to act as if everything were still normal.

"Would you care for some tea?" she asked next, stepping over to the cart an alert servant had wheeled in before they'd even reached the room. Without waiting for an answer Seikoku selected a delicate cup and poured it full of the steaming, fragrant liquid. Then she turned, stepped toward the emperor—

—and pretended to stumble, flinging the cup's contents full at his face.

"Ahhh!" Quick as a cat, he hurled himself backward, sending the chair crashing to the floor. He did not fall, however. Instead he flipped over and rolled to his feet, landing in a crouch. His face was scrunched in fury, his hands extended, fingers hooked.

And his eyes glowed a deep, sullen red.

"Get him!" Seikoku shouted. "Niki, the light!"

Even as Kagiri and Shizumi dove forward, loath to draw weapons against the mere semblance of their friend and liege, Noniki gestured toward the lantern. It bloomed like a flower, showering them all in a glow brighter than the sun outside and far more concentrated.

"Hibikitsu" hissed, hunkering down and shielding his face with his arms. Beneath him, his shadow tensed—then vanished, driven out by the blinding light.

Kagiri and Shizumi immediately grabbed him, each to an arm, and hauled him to one of the other chairs, slamming him down into it. Reizei had caught on by now and tugged off her sash, which she used to tie him up.

"You cannot do this to me!" their captive howled. "I am the emperor!"

"No," Seikoku told him. "You are not. You're one of those shadow assassins. Where is the true emperor?"

He glared at her—and then broke into a nasty, leering grin, showing off sharpened teeth. "Gone," he replied, his voice shifting, growing higher but also raspier. "I am all that remains."

Sadly, Seikoku suspected that much, at least, was the truth.

CHAPTER FORTY-THREE

Noniki stared at the man bound before them. "No!"

But even as their captive laughed, he knew. He could sense it. Hibikitsu had always had a bright, clean energy about him, like a great fire deeply banked yet leaking out enough to captivate. This figure, though outwardly he looked the part, felt dark and oily, like his very essence was slippery.

"What have you done with him?" Kagiri demanded, slamming the man back against the chair. "Where is the emperor?"

Shizumi laid a hand on his arm. "He's gone," she warned, her voice heavy with grief. "If this one is anything like his predecessor, he killed the real Hibikitsu, burned his body almost to ash—and then ate his eyes to absorb enough of his shape and memories to pass." She shuddered and Noniki remembered that she had seen all of this before, shortly before he and Kagiri had arrived—when another shadow assassin had tried for the emperor.

This one, however, had succeeded.

"It was the Yatamorans." Reizei's face was twisted in anguish and rage. "They're behind this."

Seikoku nodded. "You saw the way they spoke to him. Like he was the servant, and they the master. This was their intent all along."

The man in the chair, the one wearing their friend's face, laughed. It was a harsh sound, jangling against Noniki's nerves. "And what will you do about it?" he taunted. "Nothing! Because I contain all that is left of your precious friend, and you will not risk losing even that much. Fools! Cowards! Weaklings!"

Kagiri spun about, and for an instant Noniki thought his brother might attack the imposter anyway. After a tense heartbeat he sagged against the table instead. "It's true," he admitted. "If even a shred of Hibikitsu survives in there, I cannot risk it." Of course, of them all, Kagiri would understand that the best. After all, the Gensaiba lived on in him, too.

Across the table, Reizei was studying the ersatz emperor. "You swallowed some of him when you ate his eyes," she said slowly. "How much, I wonder? Is it like aishone? There were moments you really acted like Hibikitsu."

Noniki found himself nodding and stepping forward, his eyes and senses all focused upon their captive. Yes, Reizei was absolutely right. "Hibikitsu," he called, using voice and magic together. "Hibikitsu, can you hear me?"

The bound man snarled and glared, but Noniki was listening with more than just his ears. And he thought he'd heard something in response.

"Hibikitsu," he tried again. "I know you are in there. Come forth, my friend. Speak with us. We are here, your Rojiri."

He could feel that something, slightly closer now. A strong presence, bound by an even stronger sense of responsibility. Hibikitsu had one of the strongest senses of duty he'd ever seen, and it was that he used now to reel their emperor back in.

"Hibikitsu. Please. We need you here. Your people need you. Your kingdom needs you."

Their captive took a deep breath—and, as he let it out, the shape of his face shifted, losing that exaggerated angularity he'd displayed when attacking them. The glow in his eyes disappeared as well, leaving them clear, dark, intelligent, and more than a little confused.

"Noniki?" Hibikitsu said, his voice shaky. "What's happened? I feel strange." He shook his head. "I remember Madame Hara wanting me to see something…then an attack…bright eyes…." He shuddered, glancing down at his bonds—and froze, as shadows began to rise like smoke off his trapped limbs. When he spoke again, his voice was somber.

"I didn't survive, did I?" It was not really a question.

"No, sire," Noniki admitted. "It was another shadow assassin.

He killed you and stole your identity." He forced himself to smile. "But perhaps he got more than he bargained for."

The emperor's brow furrowed. "I don't understand."

But some of the others evidently did. "You're like a caterpillar," Seikoku suggested, stepping up beside him, her smile bright and hopeful. "You're encased in a cocoon now, but you could emerge and be free."

"It's a duel," Shizumi added. "You and him. Only one of you will make it out alive—but that can be you."

Kagiri nodded. "You can still feel him in there," he said quietly. "But don't let him drown you out. Overwhelm him instead. Make your voice stronger. Assert yourself."

Noniki reached out and cupped the trapped man's head between his hands, one palm against each temple. "You can live again," he urged. "You just have to want it badly enough."

"I do want it," Hibikitsu promised him, hope dawning on his face. "I do. I want to live."

He did. Noniki could feel it. And he wanted that for his friend and ruler, too. They all did.

The question was, would that be enough?

Hibikitsu found himself in shadows.

He could see nothing around him, no ground, no walls, no sky. Nothing but murky darkness. It pressed in on him, thick and cloying, smelling faintly of fresh smoke and old blood. He coughed, and the shadows burrowed into his chest, wrapping around his heart. His eyesight dimmed, his breath failing, his heart stuttering to a stop.

Just as it had before. The last time he had died. Killed by the same assassin who sought to eliminate him now.

Well, he would find that the emperor of Rimbaku was made of sterner stuff than that.

Closing his eyes, Hibikitsu slowed his breathing, forcing his body to quell its panic. After all, he understood instinctively that he had no real body here. Only his mind and his will.

And those no assassin could ever break.

He drew a breath, let it out, drew another. The shadows receded somewhat, leaking back out of him. He could feel them hovering nearby, however. Watching. Waiting.

Intensifying.

"So." The word was a mere hiss of sound, like a blade across glass. "The little emperor thinks to survive. You will not succeed, little man. You are already dead. You are only a memory now."

Opening his eyes, Hibikitsu found himself staring at a man, his features only faintly visible. He was tall, taller than Kagiri, and slim, as skinny as the mage Fukuru had been. Every inch of him was angles, sharp as blades. His face was perfectly smooth, his hair a glossy black even against the dark, but his narrowed eyes glowed red as coals.

"You murdered me," Hibikitsu accused, his hands bunching into fists.

The tall man—a Yatamoran by his features and complexion—nodded, a sneer twisting his thin lips. "I did. You are mine now, just a tool for my use."

But Hibikitsu shook his head. "No. I am Hibikitsu, Echo of Victory, emperor of Rimbaku. I will not be your tool." He remembered what his friends had said, though that brief moment since his death felt like a dream. "This is a duel only one of us can win." Somehow, Kosshiki was suddenly in his hand, the shadows shrinking back from the gleam of its naked blade. "And I do not intend to lose."

He slashed out, hard and fast, his sword sweeping down and across. His foe blinked, hands raised as if to block, and cried out as Kosshiki cut deep, splitting him from shoulder to opposite hip.

Then he laughed as the wound vanished utterly.

"You are just a fragment, a stored echo," the man declared, grinning down at Hibikitsu. "I am Dai Yi, shadow assassin. And you are within my body, my mind, my soul. I am in complete control here." He waved a hand and the shadows thickened, wrapping around Hibikitsu like a dozen squid, pulling his arms back painfully. He cried out as his limbs spasmed and his sword fell away, vanishing from view. It was as if the entire world were bearing down upon him, crushing him. Everything dimmed.

Until a sound reached him:

"We are with you."

It was Noniki's voice, but also Kagiri's, Seikoku's, Shizumi's—all of them. His advisors, his allies...his friends. Supporting him. Lending him strength.

Hibikitsu gritted his teeth. He tensed, twisted, and tore free of his bonds.

"No!" he shouted, his words echoing in the emptiness, the sound giving the world form around him. His footing improved. "I am my own man!"

He lashed out with a kick, his foot striking Dai Yi in the gut and sending the tall man stumbling backward. Hibikitsu leaped after, punching the assassin in the jaw and rocking his head back. He knew he couldn't let up for even a second. "I will be free!" he shouted.

But when he swung again, Dai Yi caught his arm. "You will be swallowed up," the assassin replied with a snarl, his nails digging into Hibikitsu's wrist and sending jolts of pain lancing up his arm. "Just like all those before you."

As he said that, the ground seemed to shake beneath their feet. Hibikitsu thought he saw a flicker of surprise in his opponent's eyes. What had that been?

"I have killed and consumed many," the assassin continued. "And will take many more before I am done. You are merely another victim along my path."

The world trembled again. But they were in the man's mind. So what was causing those quakes? They sounded angry, Hibikitsu decided. Like their surroundings were crying out against the killer's statements. Against his recounting of his past victims.

And perhaps that was it.

"You kill, and take in part of each victim's soul," Hibikitsu reasoned out loud. "Which means they are still a part of you, even now. And you may be stronger than any one of them—but are you stronger than all of them together?" He glanced around him, at the dark. "Come forth!" he cried. "Together, we can revenge our-selves upon this monster who murdered us all!"

The shaking this time nearly knocked them both off their feet. Dai Yi lost his grip on Hibikitsu's arm, flailing to keep his balance—and then cried out as a hand emerged to grab his wrist instead. A hand belonging to a small, sturdy figure with lined features and a tidy hair bun. "Murderer!" Hara Koriko cried. "Defiler!"

Another hand latched on, this one belonging to a man who stepped forth. Hibikitsu thought he looked vaguely familiar. "I was happy in my shop, with my desserts," the man exclaimed. "You murdered me just to get into the palace!"

Next was a tall, blocky woman with a crescent scar upon her cheek, dressed in the armor of a chuisu. "You killed me so you could enter the city unnoticed," she accused, wrapping a thick arm around Dai Yi's throat. "Now I will have my revenge!"

Others emerged from the shadows, men and women alike. They each grabbed hold of their killer. And then began to pull.

Dai Yi screamed as his former victims tore pieces from his body, flesh for flesh. With each loss he seemed to fade, losing solid-ity and color. Yet still he stood, even after the last of them disap-peared with their grisly prizes.

But the shadows had receded somewhat as well, and, casting about, Hibikitsu had spied a familiar gleam at his feet. Reaching down, he scooped up his sword, shifting his grip before charging forward. "For Rimbaku!" he shouted.

His killer cried out as Kosshiki pierced his chest, spearing him through the heart. Yet the man grinned, through now-bloody teeth. "You cannot win," he whispered, his eyes still burning bright. "This body is mine. You are only a momentary visitation, soon gone."

Hibikitsu could feel the truth of that. Already he felt some of his strength fading, his senses darkening once more. Soon he would be washed away. Unless he found a way to anchor himself here, to take root and force the assassin out instead.

Something about that thought resonated with him, like a

plucked string. Yes. An anchor. Roots. This monster had killed him but had swallowed his soul before it could fade completely away. And he was here now, thinking and feeling and breathing. Here inside Dai Yi—but also, through him, in his kingdom. In Rimbaku.

A land whose magic had just been re-awakened.

That magic was still everywhere, in everything. Even moreso in him, Noniki, and Reizei, who had been there when Fukuru had released the magic into the world once more.

The assassin had his shadow magic, but Hibikitsu had the magic of his kingdom, his empire, his home. He was also the latest to be dragged into this body. It had been molded to match his essence, which gave him some degree of control. And he still remembered what it was to live as himself. More than anything, he wanted to live, to love, to learn—and to be here for his people.

He channeled all that desire, that need, that obligation, into his will to live—and into the magic that had imbued him and was all around him. "Let me live!" he screamed.

He felt the magic surge up in response. It wrapped around him, filling him with light and warmth and strength.

And, grabbing hold of that power, Hibikitsu channeled it into his arms—and twisted his blade, slicing it through Dai Yi and splitting the shadow assassin in half.

This time, the man did not laugh. Nor did he recover. Instead, his lower half crumbled away, fading and taking some of the shadows with it. His upper half began to fade as well, and Dai Yi glared at Hibikitsu, mouth working as if he wanted to scream or curse but unable to do so before his face vanished as well.

His eyes were the last to go, their glow lingering in the final wisps of shadow before they too went out, leaving Hibikitsu to drop to his knees, alone.

He closed his eyes and felt the bounds of this body rushing in upon him as his soul expanded to fill its every nook and cranny.

He had won.

The others jumped when their captive threw his head back and screamed—as smoke flew from his mouth, dissipating as it emerged. When he finally sagged back against his bonds, Noniki could sense nothing left but the man they all knew and admired, even loved.

"It is done," he told the others, stepping back and leaning against the table. "The emperor is restored."

Shizumi had not backed away. "Are you certain? I want him back too, but what if he is only pretending, lying in wait? Can we trust him enough to let him resume the throne?"

But Noniki was sure. "I can feel his soul," he replied. "It is—it is like a plant cutting. The assassin stole a piece of Hibikitsu and grafted that piece onto his own soul so that he could assume his identity. But now that piece has grown stronger than its host and supplanted it. None of the original growth remains. Only one soul resides within, and it is wholly Hibikitsu's."

What he did not tell them just yet was that, while the soul was their friend's, the body was still that of a Yatamoran darakada. Some of those strange abilities might still linger. But he would instruct Hibikitsu in their use, if that were so. And who knew, they might even come in handy someday.

Of course, that raised another question, and Futoba was the one who spoke it aloud. "What are we going to do about the ambassadors?" she asked. "I think we all know they were a part of this."

Everyone nodded, but Noniki smiled. "We will let the emperor decide their fate," he said.

After all, who better to do so than the man they had conspired to kill and replace?

CHAPTER FORTY-FOUR

Hibikitsu regained consciousness a few minutes later, and Kagiri watched him closely but could see nothing that did not match the man they knew, the emperor they followed. The friend they loved. Neither did the others, and without a word of discussion they all stepped back as Noniki released the bonds and helped their former captive to his feet.

"Thank you." Hibikitsu looked around, meeting each of their eyes. "Thank you for believing in me." He appeared earnest, and he moved with his usual dignity and poise—but none of the cat-like grace his killer had displayed. Kagiri still worried, of course. But Noniki was certain, and he trusted his brother.

They all bowed or saluted or both as the emperor departed, Reizei accompanying him. That done, Kagiri sank back into his chair. "First Emperor preserve us," he muttered.

As if that had been some sort of summons, he felt his consciousness slipping away, fleeing into his own mind and the experiences of the other personalities still trapped there.

"Not again!" was all he had time to think before the world shifted around him and he found himself once more at that fateful tower of old.

He was just arriving, not by foot or on horseback but atop a large, beautifully woven carpet. Sitting behind him was the man causing the rug to float through the air, his large eyes closed, his long face intent. Komu Juroji was a brilliant scholar and delighted in experimenting with his magic, as evidenced by their strange conveyance, but Kagiri could tell that his current host trusted the bookish wizard completely.

If Komu Juroji was here, that meant his host was none other

than Komu Setsui. Indeed, what little Kagiri could see of himself was slim and willowy, with straight, silky hair tucked back behind her ears and long lashes obscuring the view with each blink. He had no doubt that if he glanced at a reflective surface, he would see the Gensaiba's master archer's beautiful features peering back at him.

As they landed, the carpet settling onto the ground before the Tawasiri's front doors, Juroji turned to her. "Matters are at a boil," he said, his voice high and sharp. "They could well bubble over. If that happens, it could escalate quickly, even catastrophically. Give me your hand."

Without a word, Setsui did so, and her cousin grasped it—and pulled free the jade banezhan there. "What are you doing?" she asked as he clasped the thick ring in both hands.

"Offering you what protection I can," he answered. Kagiri saw the accessory glow brightly, then fade, though when Juroji offered it back he could still make out a glimmer deep within. "If you find yourself in danger," the matekai instructed, "break the ring. It will shield you from what comes next."

Kagiri wanted to ask more, and suspected his host did as well, but Juroji was already rising to his feet. She had little choice but to follow. A handsome woman with strong features was by the door, evidently having arrived shortly before, and had turned back to wait for them, a smile on her lips.

"Juroji," she said as they approached. "Setsui. Jeizen has already headed up to join the others. Shall we?" Juroji nodded and the two matekai ascended together, Kagiri/Setsui following behind but stopping at the Gensaiba's gathering place while the pair continued upward. At the first landing, noises out the window prompted her to look, spotting a slim pair riding up. Nikiyu Bezaitin and Nikiyu Sinchu.

Setsui reached the edge of the Gensaiba's common room just as Kibi was saying that they were only waiting on her, Sinchu, and Segei, and Jeizen made a comment about "our three S's."

"I'm here," Kagiri heard himself call out. "And I saw Sinchu reining in as I came upstairs. But don't expect Segei."

The rest went as remembered—right up until they mounted

the steps that led to the matekai's meeting chamber. When his host felt that first spasm in her chest, she tugged desperately at her ring, yanking the heavy jade from her thumb. "It's..." she started to say, but collapsed. Fortunately, the ring fell from her grip as she did, hitting the step and bursting like an overripe fruit.

As the only one still fully conscious, and being partially detached, Kagiri felt the magic explode out of the ruined jewelry and envelop the warriors laid out there on the stairs. It formed a bubble around them, its surface iridescent as the sheen on a soap bubble. Outside that sphere, the world began to shake, fixtures and furnishings and even architectural elements shattering as the wizards above began to let loose upon one another, tossing magic back and forth in a battle like the world had never seen. Yet, fragile as it appeared, Juroji's spell held. It kept those within it safe.

Unfortunately, they were already dead.

The magic he'd cast could not bring them back—perhaps if he'd known, but he'd only sought to protect them, not resurrect them. Instead, his enchantment did the only thing it could do under the circumstances, striving to fulfil the purpose for which it had been created: it bound the Gensaiba matekan's spirits together, both to each other and to the tower around them. It kept them from fragmenting, from dissipating, from fading away or moving on.

Unknowingly, it trapped them in the Tawasiri. The Cataclysm destroyed their bodies. Time eroded away the rest, leaving only bones and then dust. Yet their spirits, their souls, remained.

So, too, did the matekai. The wizards had sucked all of the magic from the land in order to fight one another and had ultimately killed each other—except that their magic was too great for them to die completely.

Instead they passed into a semiconscious state, flesh gone but minds and souls remaining. Without a spell like Juroji's, however, they lost all cohesion, their identities bleeding together into a jumble of emotions and magic.

They became Kaemusei.

Their Gensaiba, meanwhile, remained distinct, each mind still intact. But, bound to the tower itself, they had no way to leave its confines, and nowhere to go if they did.

Until Kagiri stumbled in through the doors.

Except—Kagiri felt something click in his head. He had entered the tower for the first time that day…and yet, in another sense, he had already been here. Six times. Or one time, six ways. He had been here with the Gensaiba. He had watched the Cataclysm happen, and not just as an ancient memory.

And he'd been here just now, inside Setsui, as her cousin's magic bound them all together.

Kagiri's mind swam. Was that even possible? He was alive centuries after them!

But to them, this was now. And in a way, they were right.

It was magic, after all. Who said he couldn't be in two places—two times—at once?

But if he had been here in the tower with them this whole time, that meant…

He would have shaken his head, or buried it in his hands, if he could.

It meant that his going there hadn't been random. And that his surviving had not been sheer luck, either. He had lived through the experience, not gone mad, emerged as the Gensaiba with all of them inside his head, because he had already been bonded with those ancient warriors. Just now.

The thought of it made his head hurt.

But at least he knew the rest of the story now. He knew what had happened to them. He knew what had caused the Cataclysm.

When he blinked and opened his eyes, he was back in the Rojiri chamber, still seated. No one was staring at him, so he suspected he had not been lost within the vision for as long this time.

He also wasn't gasping for breath. He had not emerged in a panic. This had been a gentler transition.

Kagiri was almost certain it would be the last. He had finally seen and learned what the Gensaiba had wanted him to gather from these visits to the past. He now knew how they were all connected.

The Gensaiba were finally at peace within him. Now, more than ever, their spirits had faded back. Though still there should he need them, Kagiri knew they were little more than helpful memories now.

There was a nudge at his side, not quite an elbow to the ribs, and a low, familiar voice asked, "Are you all right?" Kagiri could feel the coiled energy there, the restlessness barely contained. So different from his brother now, but in some ways so like him in their youth. Yet this was controlled, disciplined, like a cat ready to strike but patient to wake.

It was one of the many things he admired about the woman beside him. Admired and much more.

"I am," he answered honestly. "Truly. Thank you." He knew from the question that, even if the rest of their friends had not noticed his momentary absence, she had. There was very little that escaped her.

Which reminded him of a previous conversation. "It seems we did indeed survive the battle in Bezenkai," he stated, turning his hand palm up upon his knee. "And I did say we would have things to discuss if that happened."

"You did." Slowly, like a kitten pawing at a leaf, Shizumi's hand inched toward his. Finally it settled there, and the feeling was like fitting a key into a lock. Kagiri closed his hand around hers gently, feeling the pressure of her fingers tighten in return.

It was time, he thought, to start making some memories of his own.

CHAPTER FORTY-FIVE

The next day, Hibikitsu met with the Yatamorans. He did so in his private study, however, not in the throne room, and no one was there to witness the meeting, his Honteno standing guard outside the door to the hall.

"Ambassadors," he began once the trio had been shown into the room. He was seated behind his desk and did not stand to return their bows, nodding instead. "We believe the time has come for you to return home, at least for now."

Hu Yongian started. "Your Majesty," he said, "we have only just begun to establish a bond between our two nations. Surely we may be allowed more time to speak with you, and to educate you in our ways." Even as he spoke his dark eyes were darting about the room, as if searching for something.

Hibikitsu carefully schooled himself not to smile. "That is true," he replied, "and we will look forward to continuing our conversation in future. For now, however, it would be best for you to quit Rimbaku at once." Looking past the man, he fixed his gaze on one of Hu Yongian's ever-present aides instead. "Tell the High Council that Dai Yi sends his regards," he said softly. A quick hand gesture accompanied the statement.

Shen Liang dipped his head slightly, then tapped Hu Yongian on the shoulder. The Chief Ambassador nodded without glancing back. "It shall be done, sire." Without another word, the three men bowed, turned, and departed.

Only once they'd gone did Hibikitsu allow himself to relax. It had worked! He still retained a few of the shadow assassin's memories, including passwords and secret gestures—and the knowledge of which of the visiting trio was truly in charge. He'd worried that they might see through his deception nonetheless. It seemed to have succeeded, however. Yatamoro believed they held control of Rimbaku.

They would be in for a rude surprise when they tried to exert that power.

Rising to his feet, Hibikitsu used his private exit into the gardens beyond, then cut through that to the palace grounds. He was headed for the stables at the far end and was pleased to see that, as he'd hoped, they already had a visitor. She was stroking Shisi's nose and murmuring to the horse, who was shamelessly basking in the attention.

"Your Highness," he said as he approached, bowing. Shisi whinnied a hello.

"Your Majesty." Tsuni's dimples appeared as she smiled and curtsied. "I trust you are recovered from the excitement of the other day?"

"I am. And you?" She nodded. "I wondered if we might talk a moment before we rode."

She ceased petting his horse at once. "Of course." Already she was schooling her features back to the careful politeness she had worn when she'd first arrived, and Hibikitsu struggled to match that, rather than grind his teeth at the thought of playing such games once more.

Offering her his arm, he led her a short way from the stables, to a simple but graceful bench in a small copse. That afforded them some privacy while still being within easy reach of his guards. Hibikitsu gestured for her to sit but paced back and forth instead of joining her immediately.

"I have sent the Yatamorans away," he said at last, his usual diplomacy deserting him. "The Fyushans will depart soon as well. I am sure the Yakami are equally eager to see home once more. But I'd hoped...I'd hoped you might be willing to stay here. With me."

She was watching him closely, those gray eyes ever alert, but he thought he detected just a hint of them crinkling. "You are asking me to extend my visit, but without my chaperones?" she asked.

"How scandalous. What would my brother think?"

"That you have begun to win me over, so much so that I am loath to see you go," he replied, stopping in his tracks and turning to face her fully. "Which you have." He took a deep breath before plunging on. "Our marriage would be an expedient one for both our nations, but I would not even consider it for that alone. I want more, as I'm sure you do. I hope...that is, if you..." Oh, why was he so bad at this? He was the ruler of all Rimbaku!

Tsuni stood and, with a single step, closed the distance between them. One hand rose to rest upon his cheek, light as a feather, soft as silk, and powerful as a tsunami. "I am a dutiful daughter of Higinasi," she told him, her voice soft. "If my brother the king ordered me to marry, I would do so without hesitation. But yes, I desire more than political convenience. I would wish for a man who valued me for myself, and who I valued in return. A man I liked and admired. A man I could love."

Hibikitsu reached up and covered her hand, trapping it against him. He gazed into her eyes. They were so wide, so clear, he could see the sky in them.

He could see his future.

"Tell me I am such a man," he begged, casting aside composure, rank, and dignity alike. "For you are that to me, and so much more."

Her smile lit her face like the sun, and indeed he basked in its warmth. She did not answer in words but leaned in slightly—and when their lips touched, he knew.

He was home.

Futoba had been weighing her decision carefully and had put off replying, but at last felt she must. Thus, the next day when the Rojiri met with Hibikitsu, she cleared her throat. "Your Majesty?"

He had been speaking quietly with Noniki but paused at once to give her his full attention. Despite knowing what had happened, Futoba could not help but feel this was the same man she had served before. Certainly his powerful presence had not changed!

Though today he seemed unusually cheerful.

"Yes, Futoba?" he asked.

"Your Majesty, I have been considering your offer of an estate in Atsani," she said, speaking quickly lest she lose her nerve. "And while I am deeply honored and grateful, I feel I must decline." He quirked an eyebrow but did not stop her as she rushed to explain. "My family's estates are familiar to me, sire. They are comfortable. They are home. But that is not why I wish to remain there." She forced herself to slow down and choose her words carefully, even though she had rehearsed them in her head many times over. "I do not believe you are best served by having all your Rojiri in a single tier, sire. Atsani is lovely, to be sure, and convenient to here, but if all of us live there how are we to know what happens in Motohiri or Sakiriti or below? How are we to be approachable by residents of Bejinuri? My home is in Motohiri. I know my neighbors there. I have a sense of the other residents. And I feel that is an important connection to not only maintain but encourage."

He studied her a second—and then smiled. "You feared to upset me by rejecting my gift," he said, but lightly. "Futoba, never fear. I appreciate your candor and your consideration. And you are right. I had not considered that, but as you are all from different walks of life, so too does it make sense for you to be from— and in—different tiers of the city."

Kagiri, sitting on the emperor's left, smiled. "In that case, sire, this seems an appropriate time to make an announcement. Thanks to your generous stipend, I have just this morning purchased a small home…in Mazihini. It is near the barracks so that I can be closer to my aiashe, and a pleasant little place, easily big enough for two." He held out his hand and Shizumi beside him placed hers in it, a shy smile flitting across her face.

"Besides," Kagiri added, now grinning. "This way Noniki and Seikoku can have the main house at Sorainasei all to themselves. No more sneaking around!" he teased, and his brother and Seikoku both laughed.

Hibikitsu joined in. "That seems a wise move, and I am happy for you both," he assured them. Then he glanced at the pair on his other side. "For all four of you," he amended.

"Thank you, sire," Seikoku replied, only the faintest blush suggesting any trace of embarrassment. "And I had a suggestion for someone to fill our missing seat, who I believe would also work toward Futoba's excellent suggestion."

She explained who she meant, and the emperor nodded—then pushed back his chair and stood. "I would very much like to meet this man, and to see him as he truly is," he stated. "Thus I believe a visit to Sakiriti may be in order—but perhaps in a more modest guise." He winked, and Futoba banished any lingering worries she might have had about the assassin's influence. How could this not be the emperor she had grown to admire so?

Everyone else was rising, though of course they could not all descend upon the merchant at once. So she remained behind, as did Takami, Kagiri, and Shizumi. Seikoku would lead the way, naturally, with Noniki at her side. Master Eijiri had expressed an interest and was the best suited to judge another person of his profession.

As the others filed out, Takami approached her. "I understand and respect your choice," he said with a wry grin. "But I can't help wishing you'd accepted the offer, if only so that I would have another ally in Atsani."

She laughed but then sobered, thinking about what he and Seikoku had said about their neighbors. "Let us discuss it," she suggested, reclaiming her seat. "Perhaps we can find a way to make that situation more agreeable as well."

Seikoku spotted Iwaki Matsu even before she'd entered his showroom, for the front was open once more and he was standing barely in the shade, speaking with a customer. He did glance up and see her, raising a hand to acknowledge her presence, but then resumed his conversation.

That was good, as it gave her time to show the others around the space. All of them considered it carefully. "It is a handsome shop," Master Eijiri stated with the confidence of a master himself. "Clearly your friend has found a space he is comfortable with. Some would say that shows a lack of ambition, but I consider it a mark of wisdom that he does not risk overextending himself."

"I would agree," Hibikitsu said quietly. It was strange to see the emperor in simpler clothes, his kitoro handsome enough but not regal, only minor jewels at his ears and fingers and throat. He looked for all the world like a lesser noble, though there was no disguising his sheer presence. "I like the look of this place very much, and that can only reflect well upon its owner."

The man in question had finished his previous interactions and now approached. "Good day, Madame Buhiyo!" he called as he neared them. "Or, rather, Seikoku." His wide face split into a warm smile. "And you have brought more friends. Welcome, all!" He bowed to each of them in turn. "I am Iwaki Matsu, at your service. If there is anything you require, please let me know, but I prefer to let people peruse at their own pace, without my interference."

"Do you find that works best?" Hibikitsu asked seriously. "I often feel some people do not know what they want, or even what is best for them."

The merchant laughed. "That is certainly true," he agreed. "Yet who am I to say? If someone appears to be foundering, I will step in and offer assistance, certainly. But if they go straight to an item or wander the shop and find something that captures their interest, then I know that was their own choice and not my forcing an opinion upon them."

"You are a wise man," the disguised emperor stated. "Tell me, what are your thoughts on our emperor, and the state of the kingdom as a whole?"

Matsu spread his hands. "I am but a simple merchant, sir. Such matters are far beyond me." Seeing that would not satisfy them, he frowned. "But I must say, since you ask—I like what I have seen and heard of late. I think our young ruler is earnest about wishing to help our people, and I admire the changes he has introduced.

There is a life and an energy to Awaihinshi that has not been here as long as I have been alive, and it is a pleasure to see." He smiled. "I am eager to see what comes next."

Hibikitsu laughed. "Well said, sir. Perhaps you will have the opportunity to do more than see it."

They left soon after, returning to Aihiri, but Seikoku could already tell the emperor had made up his mind. Noniki and Master Eijiri quickly concurred. Provided he was willing, it seemed they had found their final Rojiri.

Upon the others' return, Takami went straight to Seikoku, with Futoba right behind him. "We have been discussing the tensions with our neighbors," he explained to the pretty former thief. "Futoba has helped me see things from a different perspective. I believe I understand better now and perhaps see a way for us to resolve some of those differences."

"Oh?" His friend smiled. "I am all ears." She listened intently as he explained. He admired that about her. When he was done, she nodded. "Well reasoned." Her smile extended to Futoba. "And thank you for helping us with this. It has weighed upon me, I must admit."

"I can prepare the initial list," Takami assured her. "I know at least some of them, and others by reputation. I will have it ready by tonight."

Seikoku considered. "And tomorrow is Dayabei. Well timed." She laughed and turned back toward where Noniki waited. "Why don't we meet around noon tomorrow to discuss it, then proceed from there? You could come to Sorainasei."

He bowed. "I would be delighted."

The following evening, Takami and Seikoku entered Karo Wakiza's office together, just at sundown. As expected, Watane Yatahei and Sunao Iensen were already seated before the governor's desk. All three men turned as they entered. Sunao sneered and Wakiza's nod was stiff, but Watane smiled.

"Good evening, my lords," Takami began, bowing. "We had hoped for a moment to speak with just the three of you, before anyone else arrived." He unfolded one goji, setting it beside Watane and gesturing for Seikoku to take that one, before placing the other next to it.

As he settled himself, Seikoku took up the conversation. "As you all know," she said, "there are still several estates here in Atsani that lay unclaimed. The emperor is eager to find worthy families for them, and we would like your advice on who might be best."

Lord Wakiza looked startled, as he so often did—but not displeased, for once. "You wish *our* advice?" he said after a moment, his bushy eyebrows raised.

"Of course," Takami put in. "The three of you have been stalwart members of the nobility for many years, and your families are among the highest and most noble." He produced from his sleeve the list he had written out last night and proffered it to the governor. "I have put together my own thoughts but would be eager to hear yours."

Wakiza accepted the scroll and scanned it a second before standing and coming around the desk so that the other two nobles could see as well. "Hm, yes," he muttered as he read. "The Ichiro are a fine family, no question. As are the Mori."

"I am acquainted with Ugata Genichi," Lord Watane offered. "A good man, and a noble house."

Lord Suneo harrumphed but eventually added, "Masage Matsu is a decent sort, too."

"Excellent!" Seikoku said brightly, accepting the scroll back from the three men. "As there are four estates, those are the four houses we will recommend to the emperor." She dipped her head. "Thank you, my lords. We value your wisdom and experience."

"Yes. Well." Wakiza was noticeably puffed up as he returned to his seat. "Thank you, Madam Buhiyo, for consulting us." He cleared his throat. "Perhaps, for our next meeting, I will be able to provide more seating. As we will soon have even more neighbors to welcome, it seems."

The others nodded, and Takami repressed a grin. It had worked! Futoba had pointed out that the three nobles—the last of the original great houses—most likely felt threatened by so much change. Appealing to them, asking their opinion, reassured them that they were not being forgotten or dismissed. Change was coming, there was no denying that, but they would all do their best to retain an appreciation of the past as well.

Lady Makino arrived soon after with her nephew, and it was a far more genial group that greeted her. She also showed proper deference to their host, which only made everyone more agreeable.

The next morning, Shizumi rose well before dawn, as always. Splashing water on her face, she donned clean hosode and ponmei, collected her sword from its stand, and exited her room.

Kagiri was waiting for her in the Honjofu's common room, similarly attired and armed. "Good morning," he said with the small, shy smile she liked so much, and she cursed her own face for flushing so easily.

"Morning." For an instant she felt self-conscious, wearing only a thin undershirt and loose drawstring pants. Then thought about what would have happened had she *not* been wearing them and became even more flustered.

If her companion noticed, he was polite enough to ignore her discomfort. "Shall we?" was all he said, and she nodded, not trusting herself to speak yet as she followed him outside.

She stopped just beyond the door, however, at the sight facing her. There were her Honjofu, as usual, ready to drill and spar. But they had been joined by a score of other men and women, all of whom she recognized.

Including the sturdy woman in front, who pounded a fist to her chest in salute.

"Good morning, Taikoro Misataki. Dogenriku Kagiri," Reizei called out, her voice clear and strong. "I had hoped we might join you in your morning practice. If you don't mind."

Shizumi was not slow to recognize the olive branch being offered, or to accept it. "Good morning, Taikoro Atukai," she replied, returning the salute. "We would be delighted."

It was the first time she'd seen Reizei smile since becoming head of the Honteno, and the sight made Shizumi forget her earlier embarrassment as the three of them led the way to the practice grounds.

Together.

Hibikitsu was standing upon the palace's front porch, looking out over the city and the lands beyond, when his Rojiri began to appear. First came Kagiri, Shizumi, and Reizei, all three sweat-sheened from morning practice, and his heart warmed at seeing them walking together, talking and laughing. As they spotted him and moved to join him, Noniki and Seikoku appeared at Aihiri's main gates, waving hello. Takami and Futoba were not far behind, then Master Eijiri. Last came his newest advisor, Iwaki Matsu, who had only accepted the appointment the day before.

All of them gathered around him, and Hibikitsu said nothing at first. He just reveled in the experience. Here he stood, gazing upon his domain, his trusted councilors at his side and his back. As they all watched, the sun rose, its first rays bringing rose and gold and peach to chase away the shadows. Sparkling motes filled the air. Birds began to sing in the trees. The very air stirred, fresh and alive.

"The Relicant Empire," he said at last, his words soft, meant only for the ears of those around him, "is no more." Several of his companions started, and he held up a hand and smiled. "That is done, and good riddance. This is the dawn of a new age for our people. We are bonebound no longer." His smile widened as he considered all that had happened, all they had done—and all they would yet do, in this new land filled once more with magic and wonder and endless potential.

The Empire of Light had begun.

THE END

GLOSSARY

Adai: a kind of soup broth, made from seaweed, dried fish flakes, mushrooms, and water

Ahaiinko: a formal stamp of office used to sign official documents

Aiashe: "foot bone," a foot soldier in Rimbaku's army, typically garbed in maikiro, hanketo, suneoto, and jingaso and armed with yanoi and chokoto

Aikaye: "sea bone," a sailor-warrior in Rimbaku's navy

Aio-akeo: a riverboat that runs the channel between Tabichi and Iwikaru

Aishone: relic bones

Aisho Hasume: Bone Collectors, a group of Buddhist-like traveling priests who wear the skulls and bones of their revered teachers dangling from their belts.

Aitachi: The Relicant Touch, the ability to absorb ancestral memories, skills, and knowledge by touching or consuming objects or people from the past

Akatai: family or household demons; malevolent ancestral spirits

Aragei: chicken that has been chopped into chunks and fried

Atorido: a traditional hanging lantern with four or six sides

Atuma-yio: sweet potato

Awaihinshi: The City of Polished Light, the marble capital of Rimbaku. Divided into six tiers (one for each level of the soul), with a shanty town/slum (Suranmui) at the bottom outside the walls and the emperor's palace at the top. Each tier has an outer wall of a different shade of marble, growing lighter in shade witch each height, from black to white. The tiers are:
   One: Aihiri, the Imperial compound at the very top. Walls of purest white marble.

Two: Atsani, where the Daijin and other important nobles live—and home to Sorainasei, the first "town" in Awaihinshi. Walls of palest yellow.

Three: Motohiri, where the most influential merchants and the minor nobles live. Walls of peach.

Four: Sakiriti, mid- to lesser merchants and the most important artisans. Walls of the hue of cherry blossoms (a pale rose).

Five: Bejinuri. Other artisans and craftsmen. Walls of pale violet (red wisteria).

Six: Mazihini, laborers and other menials. The walls surrounding this level are pale blue like water, and the outer walls of the city as a whole.

Bakiro: a bag, typically a large bag used for carrying one's personal items and equipment

Banezhan: a cylindrical ring worn on the thumb when using a bow, most often made of bone, ivory, horn, or jade.

Bannin: guards, watchmen

Baraken: a wooden practice sword, typically made of either teak or bamboo

Bezenkai: a southern province

Birabiro: a town in Korito, closest to the Fyushan-Rimbakan border

Botetsu: a little village in Yunigiri

Buhiyo: a mayor, responsible for a town or small city

Burahone: the Bone Blind. These women's aitachi is so strong they are constantly overwhelmed by memories and knowledge, drawing it from the very elements around them.

Chahito: the pommel or endcap of a sword

Chasai: symbolic baton, typically of lacquered wood with metal caps at both ends and a tassel at one.

Chayaburi: a small, fast sailboat

Chinbiro: a town in Korito, near Birabiro

Chituju: a house steward

Chohu: a prosperous merchant house specializing in gemstones

Chokoto: a straight-edged sword with a ring pommel

Chonmage: a hair bun, particularly favored by warriors

Chosinichi: A "reservoir," someone who can hold absorbed skills for a long time

Chunsin-inori: a full feast, served in three courses, each on its own tray

Cuioburi: the smallest class of military boat, most often used for patrols and search missions

Darakada: "body thief," a sorcerer whose magic allows him to steal another's face and form

Dayabei: the seventh and final day of a sihu, often a rest day

Deo: a breastplate or cuirass, part of a suit of armor

Dobuichi: "animal-touched," those who use their aitachi on animal bones instead of human ones

Dojo Kuge: artistocratic bureaucrats

Doh Bridge: a wide bridge spanning the Zinyang River and connecting Obanari to Hochiro

Edishu River: a small river running from the Tonawa west to the ocean. Awaihinshi sits beside it.

Essa: a doctor.

Esuge: the Rimbakan cedar, the most commonly used wood in the land

Eioha: a form of dumpling

Eikono: a formal outer robe with a round collar, wide sleeves, a long tail, and sewn sides

Enwara: a small town in Bezenkai, south of Ginzai

Eto-riantzu: a large wheeled cart with sliding front doors

Ferume: an inkbrush, used for writing

Fumisoni: a style of kisoni, the most elaborate and formal, with long, wide sleeves

Furotingawa: "floating tower", a legendary tower, long since in ruins, at the southern edge of Rimbaku, near the mouth of a river

Furukotai: the largest town in Korito, home to the regional governor

Fyushu: a rival nation to Rimbaku's north, constantly testing the borders. Symbol: a black gauntlet clenched in a fist.

Ganabo: a massive two-handed war club, usually spiked or studded

Gensaiba: "Living blades," legendary warriors of mythic ability

Ginzai: the nearest large town to the brothers' home

Goji: a folding stool most often used by men in full armor

Gotaiburi: a large, multi-masted boat designed to carry troops

Guisuke bitte: a chest for holding one's armor

Guisuke kai: a stylized stand for displaying armor, usually set atop a guisuke bitte

Haidoto: thigh guards, part of a suit of armor

Hakami: close-fitting pants, often worn under armor

Hakara Ikibanichi: the Brothers of Many Spirits, a monastic order

Hanketo: armored gauntlets

Hantien: a short, padded winter coat

Happoa Kappua: "The Foamy Cup." A tavern in Ginzai

Hakichuekai: a small, brightly colored bird, known for its trilling and its sociability

Heioki: fried octopus balls

Higeibara: the red spider lily, the official crest of Rimbaku

Higinasi: a nation bordering Rimbaku to the southwest. Symbol: a stylized blue wave

Himsu: a town in Hochiro

Hiromura: a small village in Bezenkai

Honjofu: "Bone warrior," Rimbaku's elite military unit. Clad all in black armor.

Honteno: "Emperor's bones," the Rimbaku Imperial Guard. Clad all in red armor.

Horohaba: a lost city of Ritakhou, known as the "City of Beasts" for its renowned menagerie

Hosode: an undershirt, usually plain and unbleached and typically of silk.

Hozaiburi: a large, heavy warship.

Iematsu: the red pine tree, often used for beams and posts

Ikibanichari: Castle of Many Spirits, the mountain monastery of the Hakara Ikibanichi

Iniro: a small, segmented box worn at the belt to hold small items, often beautifully carved and detailed

Irogaso: a circular bamboo hat

Irohito: a small town strategically located at the intersection of the Tonawa and Edishu rivers, guarding the way to Awaihinshi

Ishtaya: a tailor or seamstress

Itoyako: the lily of the valley, known for its soft, drooping petals that shade from white to pink

Ittei: a blunt iron rod with a wrapped handle and a hooked tine just above that, used by guards when they were not allowed to carry swords

Jagimato: a town in Saruto, between the Wagata and Edishu rivers

Jigekugi: lesser bureaucrats, the lowest rank of nobility

Jingaso: a conical iron helm, worn by the aiashe

Jogoturi: "Lords of the Street," a gang in Ginzai

Jubanichi: The "perfect touch"—someone who absorbs quickly and holds for a long time

Kaemusei: "the Silent Change" or "The Silent," a magical being of limitless hunger

Kanashi: a hair stick

Kaoni: a hip- or mid-thigh-length open coat with long, wide sleeves, worn over a kitoro

Karo: a regional governor, who reports to the Emperor

Karute: a helmet, usually with a menatu attached in front and one or more modato above

Kazure: iron plates hanging from the front and back of the deo to protect the pelvis and upper leg

Kenroichi: A solid touch, someone who can absorb decently and hold it decently

Kibango: small sweet dumplings made from rice flour

Kindichi: bosses or kings

Kisoni: A loose robe, wider and looser than a kitoro, that can be worn as either an undergarment or an outer layer.

Kitoro: a silk outer garment, like a wide-sleeved robe, usually decorated.

Koshitsu: a graverobber

Kosshiki: "the Bone Spirit," sword of the Relicant Emperor

Kogotano: a small utility knife, often found in a small channel carved out of a sword scabbard, or in a writing set

Kotone: baby bird

Kune mato: a merchant's safe, usually made of metal or thick wood and with several locks.

Magojifu: a small town in Bezenkai, between Ginzai and the Rumiri river.

Maikiro: a war vest of lacquered plates on a cotton backing, secured by cotton straps, worn by aiashe. Smaller plates hang from the front and sides to protect the groin and thighs.

Mamusha: a large, deadly snake, very aggressive

Matoyan: a small hunting village up in the mountains between Rimbaku and Yatamoro

Matekai: a wizard or wizards.

Megaita: a green tea made with roasted brown rice

Menatu: a warrior's face mask, made of metal and hooked onto or tied to a karute

Modato: a crest affixed to the top of a karute

Mosi: an inkstick, made of soot and animal glue, ground down and mixed with water to create ink

Mukanichi: An "untouched," someone who can't really absorb at all, the lowest of all people

Muraito: A larger town or small city not far above Ginzai, on the southern edge of a mid-sized lake

Nahiya: a townhouse, usually two or three stories tall, with separate apartments on each floor

Naritaba: a pole weapon, a wooden or metal shaft with a curved single-edge blade at the end. The blades were forged in the same way as nihono. Often used by mounted warriors, and by women warriors.

Nafti: a fruit, round and juicy, with mottled green and gold skin and crisp white flesh.

Nigasi: a dry, pressed sweet made of sugar and rice flour.

Nihono: a long sword with a curved, single-edged blade, carried by nobles and elite warriors in Rimbaku

Nizukai: a mythic water dragon, daughter of the sea god Satumasu, "king of all waters"

Nodaki: a "field sword," a longer, heavier nihono typically used against cavalry

Okube: a traditional sash-style belt worn around the waist, particularly with a kitoro

Onokura: a small village in Miniri, near the south end of the river that separates Nariyari and Bezenkai

Otainui: housekeeper or household manager

Otomi: a small fishing village on the shores of the Wagata

Pokanu: a type of bird, tall and ostentatious, with bright and luxurious tail feathers

Ponmei: loose cotton pants with a drawstring tie and tapered ankles.

Quisuin: a poisonous snake

Raeteru: the common tree frog

Rajo: purple yams

Rakawa: a small village in Bezenkai

Riantzu: a traditional portable storage chest, usually made with no nails, screws, or adhesive

Rimbaku: "land made barren from cursed magic," the land after the Schism

Ritakhou: "land rich with blessed magic," the land before the Schism

Rojiri: counselors to the emperor

Rumiri River: the wide river that runs north-south through Miniri, connecting the Tonawa to Rimbaku's southern coastline. It is the dividing line between Bezenkai and Nariyari.

Saisaihyu: a ten-day period of purification and contemplation. During this time, everyone is expected to not allow any outside influence—including the use of aishone.

Sashiko: a style of patching clothing, often in a pattern

Sehiro: a steaming basket, usually woven out of bamboo

Senkuniki: ancestral spirits—typically akatai are considered the darker, more malevolent ancestral spirits, while senkuniki are those more inclined toward benevolence

Senkousa: a Bone Reader. These women have strong aitachi and can actually "read" aishone, telling what memories and knowledge and skills each bones possesses.

Senoha-a: a plant, whose name means "Mother of Thousands." Often seen in gardens and homes but highly poisonous, particularly the flowers.

Shakomi: a town in Bezenkai, a little north of Ginzai

Shatage: a shirt, generally thicker than a hosode and dyed or lightly embroidered or both.

Shugiri daimyo: grand nobles, closest to the emperor in status and power

Shugodiri: lesser nobles

Sihu: week

Sokuichi: A "crude touch" or "rough touch," someone who doesn't absorb easily and needs a lot of material to absorb anything

Sorhu: a wide scarf or shawl, either silk (for milder weather) or wool (for cooler weather)

Subayaki: a species of flower, also called the common camellia, related to the tea plant and to the tsodami but less vibrant in color. Its seeds are pressed to produce Subayaki oil, which can be used for skin care and hair care.

Suneoto: armored shin guards

Suponichi: A "sponge," someone who absorbs quickly

Suzeri: an inkstone, used like a small mortar to grind mosi so that it could be mixed with water to create ink

Suzeri kabo: "inkstone box" or writing box, which held the implements and utensils needed for writing.

Taikamage: a vertical hair bun, clean and elegant, with the hair piled up on top of the head and secured by a front comb and, if necessary, several kanashi

Takaneburi: a long, narrow, flat-bottomed boat mostly used on rivers to ferry freight.

Takotsu Hakara: Home of Brotherhood, the mountain monastery of the Hakara Ikibanichi

Tanakia: a wild animal, essentially a racoon dog, rumored to be able to shape-change to human form

Tanu: a modular set of trunks and cabinets, usually arranged in a stepped pattern.

Tawasiri: the Tower of Ghosts, an ancient tower at the southeast tip of Rimbaku, long since abandoned and believed to be haunted. Originally the meeting place of the matekai of Ritakhou.

Tayomi: a traditional flooring made from compressed rice straws tightly bound together and covered with woven straw

Tehuya: the guard on a nihono, roughly disc-shaped

Tienbao: a rice paddy, typically one tien in size (approximately 3200 square feet)

Tokimichi: A "flutter touch," someone who can't hold the absorbed skills for long

Tonawa River: a major river that branches off from the Zinyang and runs south along the eastern edge of Saruto before turning southeast and then east and separating Hochiro above from Bezenkai and Nariyari below.

Torito: rough hemp work trousers with a drawstring tie and tapered ankles, often paired with a hantien

Tsao: a boat hook

Tsekuri: rice wine

Tsodami: the red camellia, the royal flower

Tsukifuko: the Moon of Lawlessness, a month during which no rules or laws apply

Tsurogo: a double-edged nihono

Tukaiono: pickled vegetables and tubers, such as radish

Ujiro: A favorite dessert in Awaihinshi, a steamed cake made from rice, water, and sugar, done in a variety of flavors.

Umi: a long bow, made of laminated wood, bamboo, and leather and typically taller than a grown man, with the upper half twice as long as the lower.

Uridon: a thick rice noodle, often used in soup

Urigani: the art of folding paper into shapes, particularly animals

Utume: the art of packaging, particularly by wrapping an object in carefully chosen layers of paper

Uzumoya: A covered pavilion.

Wagata River: a tributary of the Tonawa that splits off to the west as the Tonawa continues north past Awaihinshi. The Wagata forms the southern border of Saruto.

Wara: a sturdy straw bag traditionally used to hold rice. A full wara provides enough rice to feed two people for one year.

Watamato: a small town in northern Bezenkai, not far below the Wagata River.

Yanoi: straight-bladed spear.

Yanokai: Rimbakan cypress, very durable and water-resistant

Yatamoro: the kingdom neighboring Rimbaku to the east, across the mountains. Symbol: a winged serpent reared back, ready to strike. Ruled by a High Council.

Yori-toki: a dagger with a thick blade made for armor-piercing. Often worn in conjunction with a nihono.

Yoto: the small river that runs through Ginzai

Yudishu: a small town in Nariyari, headquarters of the Kindichi

Yue Judei: "Good Times," a zaihaya in Bejinuri, in Awaihinshi

Zaihaya: a tavern or pub, a casual place where people can go to drink together

Zinyang River: the "Central River," the large river that runs east-west across Rimbaku right through the center of Chibiri, separating Hochiro and Saruto to the south from Obanari and Yunigiri to the north.

Rimbaku is divided into four regions: Kitini (north), (Chibiri) central, Miniri (south), and (Shitimi) island

Within each region are two or more provinces. They are:

Kitini:
- Tabichi (northwest region, bordering Fyushu above and the ocean to the west)
- Korito (northeast region, bordering Fyushu above and Yatamaro to the east)

Chibiri:
- Yunigiri (northwest, bordering the ocean)
- Obanari (northeast, bordering Yatamaro to the east)
- Hochiro (southern band, bordering Yatamaro to the east)
- Saruto (the capital region, with the ocean on one side and the southern band on the other)

Miniri:
- Bezenkai (southwest, bordering the ocean)
- Nariyari (southeast, bordering Higinasi to the west)

Shitimi:
- Iwikaru (the northern island)
- Tatsuma (the southern island)

Rimbaku is roughly 1200 miles wide by 2000 miles long, or 2,400,000 square miles (somewhere between China and India in size).

Military groupings, smallest to largest:

Bantao -> Squad (4-10)

Shotao -> Platoon or troop (2-4 squads, 16-40)

Chotao -> Company (2-4 platoons, 60-160)

Dantao -> Battalion (4-6 companies, 300-900)

Reitao -> Regiment (2-4 battalions, 600-2000)

Tyodao -> Brigade (3-6 battalions, 1000-3000)

Sudao -> Division (3 or more brigades or regiments, 3k-6k)

Gaodao -> Corps (2 or more divisions, 25-50k)

Gyunao -> Army (2 or more corps, 100k-150k)

Gyunshadao -> Army Group (2 or more armies)

Chukogao -> Regional Theater (the entire military force in a region)

Sanseidao -> Front (the entire military force in a war)

Military ranks:

Sotaisho: commander-in-chief, usually the Emperor himself

[Karo: military governor]

Dogenriku: Lord General, the field marshal (in charge of tactics, fills in for the Emperor on the battlefield if he is not present)

Taisho: general

Issa: colonel

Chusa: lieutenant colonel

Shosa: major

Taisu: captain

Chuisu: lieutenant

Shosu: junior lieutenant

Gunso: Sergeant

Gocho: Corporal

Naval ranks:
    Dogenkaishu: Lord Admiral
    Kagono: admiral
    Kagusho: vice-admiral
    Daiso: captain
    Kumigashi: commander
    Kogashiri: lieutenant commander
    Chudai: lieutenant

Special units:
    Taikoro: Lord Commander, in charge of an entire elite
        force (like the Honjofu or the Honteno)
    Chuisu: lieutenant, can command a chotao
    Gunso: sergeant, can command a shotao
    Gocho: corporal, can command a bantao

ABOUT THE AUTHOR

AARON ROSENBERG is the best-selling, award-winning author of over 50 novels, including the Twin Cities Cryptids urban fantasy/cozy series, the DuckBob SF comedy series, the Relicant Chronicles epic fantasy series, the Areyat Islands fantasy pirate mystery series, the upcoming BEO Reports urban fantasy series, and, with David Niall Wilson, the O.C.L.T. occult thriller series. His tie-in work contains novels for *Star Trek*, *Warhammer*, *World of WarCraft*, *Stargate: Atlantis*, *Shadowrun*, *Mutants & Masterminds*, and *Eureka* and short stories for *The X-Files*, World of Darkness, *Crusader Kings II*, *Deadlands*, *Master of Orion*, and *Europa Universalis IV*. He has written children's books (including the original series STEM Squad and Pete and Penny's Pizza Puzzles, the award-winning *Bandslam: The Junior Novel* and the #1 best-selling *42: The Jackie Robinson Story*), educational books, and roleplaying games (including the original games *Asylum*, *Spookshow*, and *Chosen*; work for White Wolf, Wizards of the Coast, Fantasy Flight, Pinnacle, and many others; the Origins Award-winning *Gamemastering Secrets*; and the Gold ENnie-winning *Lure of the Lich Lord*). He is a founding member of Crazy 8 Press. Aaron lives in New York with his family. You can follow him online at gryphonrose.com, on Facebook at facebook.com/gryphonrose, on BSky at @gryphonrose.bsky.social, on Instagram at the_gryphonrose, and on X (formerly known as Twitter) @gryphonrose.

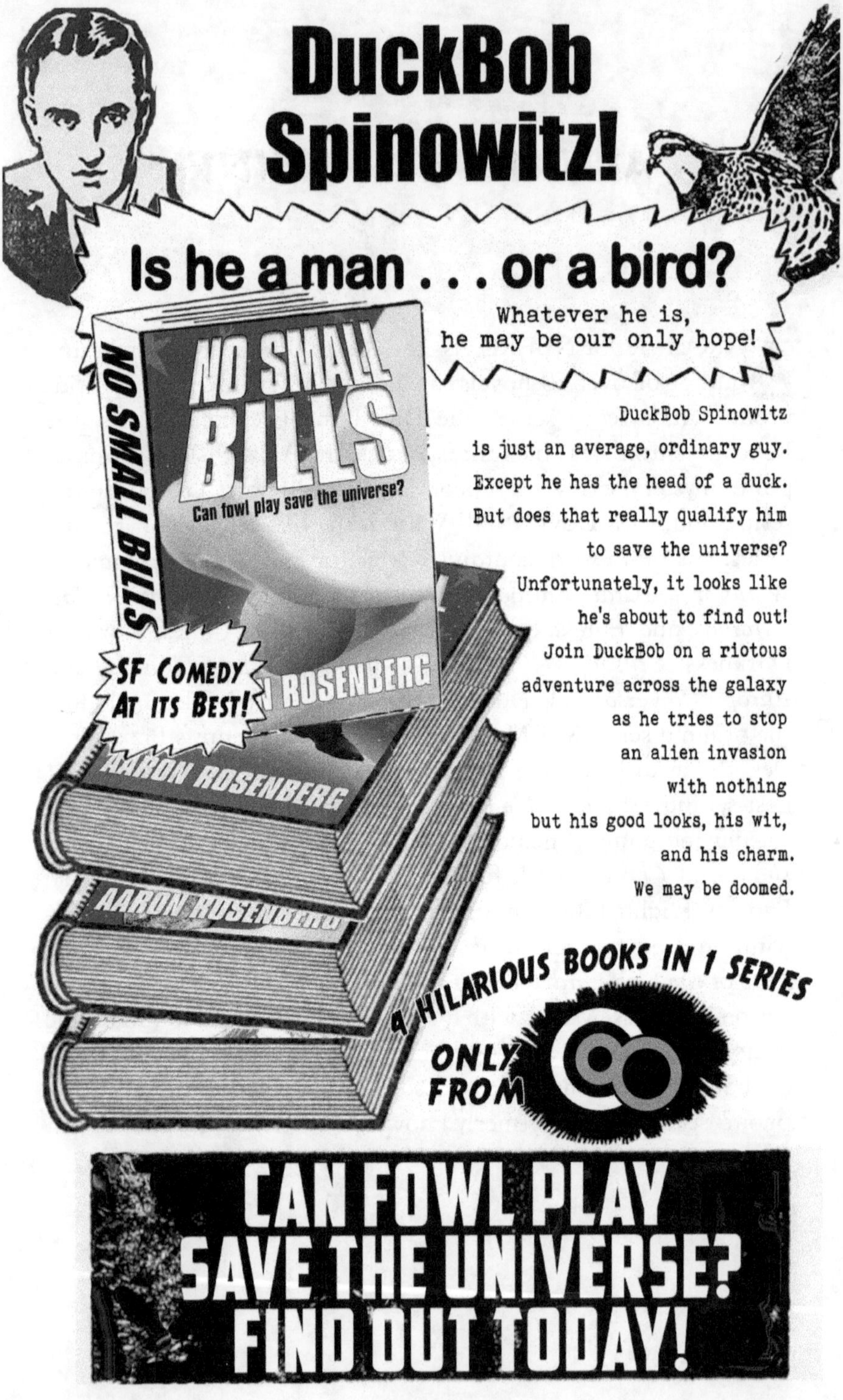

If Jane Austen wrote about pirates, this would be that book!

Isabella Parsons is the well-mannered daughter of a baron in Regency England.

Cannon Belle Pearcy is a feared pirate captain raiding the German Sea.

They are one and the same.

But when a handsome Navy commander arrives on the scene, intent upon quelling the recent pirate threat-and wooing the loveliest lady in the region-Bella's two worlds start to collide!

Other problems quickly ensue, including a second Navy ship, an intriguing other suitor, and a deadly threat from her combined past.

Now Bella faces dangers both on land and at sea, in each of her identities. She finds herself battling to keep either from destroying the other, or the people she holds dear. All while struggling with a threat she never expected: true love.

The Adventures of
CANNON BELLE
Aaron Rosenberg

A thrilling new historic romance, full of adventure and intrigue, from the author of the Areyat Isles pirate-fantasy-mystery series and the Twin Cities Cryptids urban fantasy series!

PIRACY, MYSTERY, & ADVENTURE

awaits a pair of...brothers?

Sundra is a prince running for his life.
Ruhi is a young woman disguised
in order to seek her freedom.
When they are captured by pirates,
they claim to be brothers.
Now the pair has to navigate cruel masters,
mysterious murders, missing mages,
vicious feuds, and violent storms.
But at least they have each other.